D1472210

THE BLOOD THAT BINDS

(Thicker Than Blood #3)

By

USA Today Bestselling Authors
Madeline Sheehan & Claire C. Riley

PRAISE FOR THE BLOOD THAT BINDS

'Passion, Strength and vulnerability, these characters had it all. After witnessing such horrors, they show us that even in the direst of circumstances, it's our humanity that's our greatest weapon. Love is survival, even in the apocalypse.'
International bestselling author Ker Dukey

'The Blood that Binds is a heart-in-your-throat love story, that had me on the edge of my seat at times. Chock full of characters that jump off the page, I didn't want it to end.'
Author Simone Nicole

'This is a love story. A hate story. A story of personal demons and powerful desires set in a world full of heartbreak and hope. Sheehan and Riley's deft portrayal of torn families and torn hearts--and the ways in which we make them whole--will keep you reading to the very last page.'
Sarah Lyons Fleming, Author of the End of the World series.

'This book is a rollercoaster of a ride from start to finish."
Charlie – We Licked that Book Blog

'There is tons of angst, a few twists, and real LOVE. Sweet love. Vulnerable love. I loved it from start to finish!'
Goodreads reviewer

'Gripping, intense and emotional, these two authors put both characters and readers through the wringer but I wouldn't have it any other way.'
Goodreads reviewer

DEDICATION

Madeline here, dedicating this beloved book to two people. First to Claire, for her help in getting me writing during two very difficult times in my life. I'm eternally grateful for the much-needed kicks in the ass.

And also to Simone, for her help in getting me through this thing called life. You deserve the stars on a silver platter, you goddamn gorgeous soul, but all I have for you is this book.

From Claire to Elizabeth — the best friend I could ever hope to have. You're always there for me through the good, the bad, and the downright ugly, and boy, have there been some ugly haha! Your friendship means so much to me, and I don't know how I'd cope without you in my life. You're the Maverick to my Goose, and I'm the butter to your potato. Always and forever, love.

ABOUT THE BOOK

Two brothers. A childhood sweetheart.

Life has never been easy for this trio, and especially not after the end of civilization as they knew it. Having had their formative years ripped from them, they were thrust into a shattered, savage world, a world where they only had each other.

Love and loss.

Weary travelers on the brink, there is a storm brewing, a turbulent tempest that has nothing to do with the weather. When tragedy strikes, everything changes in the blink of an eye— facades come undone, and loyalty is pushed to a breaking point.

A diamond in the rough.

Immersed back into something akin to normal society, a safe haven in the midst of misery, our travelers are forced to finally confront their demons—long-kept secrets that have been haunting them for nearly a decade.

Love is never easy.
And love during the end of the world is a hell of a lot more complicated.

THE BLOOD THAT BINDS

(Thicker Than Blood #3)

By

USA Today Bestselling Authors
Madeline Sheehan & Claire C. Riley

PROLOGUE

We were just kids when it happened, with barely a foothold on life before Mother Nature made up her mind to sucker punch the world.

The Vaal Fever.

An infectious disease born from poverty and strife had crept its way out of the third world and into the hustle and bustle of the privileged, where it slowly but surely began to decimate humankind — first with fear, then with the disease itself.

Whole families were wiped out, entire cities burned to the ground. The government had all but imploded, and free, functioning societies became a thing of the past. The world we knew was gone, our simple lives eviscerated.

Humankind fell in near totality, the dead eventually far outnumbering the living. A new breed of humans, a never-ending army of the dead, stalked the streets, clawing their way into our homes, quickly rising to the top of the food chain.

What remained of our battered species turned feral, desperate to survive, desperate to once again thrive, and willing to do whatever it took to claw their way back to the top. It was every man and woman for themselves, survival of the fittest, a race to the finish line where the only prize that awaited you was even more horrors greater than you could ever imagine.

These were our formative years—we came of age in a broken world, headed toward an unfathomable future. The rules had been obliterated and rewritten.

Living was a thing of the past.

Here and now, we simply survived.

ONE

WILLOW

Approaching a darkened doorway, loose floorboards creaked beneath my feet. At least a quarter of the entranceway was covered in thick spiderwebs, their eight-legged owner paying me little mind as I ducked beneath it, finding myself inside a master bedroom of what had once been a large and impressive home. It was still impressive — how else could you describe the sight of two worlds colliding?

The roof had caved in, causing considerable damage to the entire front of the house, this room especially. A nearby tree had grown in through a broken window, a branch as thick as a man jutting halfway across the room. The skeletal remains of two people lay tucked neatly into a four-poster bed, the large, ornate structure heavily covered in moss. Nature hadn't just taken hold here, it had claimed this space as its own. It was a familiar sight these days — man struggling while the earth flourished.

Passing a partially open closet, I peered inside, finding a nest made up of sticks and bits of fabric, with at least fifteen baby opossums wriggling inside it. All fifteen were happily clinging to the back of their mother, oblivious to my presence. The mother, however, had begun hissing at the sight of me. The longer I stood there, the more aggressive she grew, until her hisses had become growls.

I could kill her quickly, using the trusty piece of pipe dangling from the heavy pack on my back. She'd be the first real meal we'd come across in months. It was only the beginning of summer, but it was gearing up to be the hottest to date — game was scarce, and everything edible was quickly withering and dying under the unrelenting sun. The earth didn't seem to care that those of us still breathing had been existing in crisis mode for years now. She just kept on turning despite us... *or maybe even to spite us.*

Sighing, I backed away from the closet. "Don't mind me," I whispered to the still growling opossum.

Sure, I was hungry — starving actually — but I wasn't knocking on death's door... yet. I'd been managing my daily hunger pains with what roots and vegetation we'd been lucky enough to find. And I'd have to be quite literally dying before I'd consider ripping a mother from her babies. I'd had my mother ripped from me at the age of sixteen; never would I wish that kind of pain on another living thing, let alone be the cause of it.

Ducking beneath the jutting branch, I approached a half-collapsed armoire. A long sundress still hung over the doors, its straps trapped between them. Once white, it was now stained in varying shades of brown and green, the hem tattered and frayed.

Once upon a time, I would have balked at the idea of ever wearing something like this—I'd always been a fishnet stockings and combat boots kind of girl—but now that beautiful dresses had become a thing of the past, serving no purpose in this new, cruel world, I couldn't help but wonder if I might have missed out on something. Touching it gently, lightly rubbing the fragile material between my fingers, I tried to envision what I would look like in something similar.

Catching a glimpse of myself in a nearby mirror—my sweat-stained tank top sagging at the neck and dirty cargo pants blown out at the knees—I nearly laughed out loud. I hadn't had a decent meal in months and here I was romanticizing over a dress. One hard tug and the dress ripped free from the armoire. Tossing it away, I moved to the dresser, prying the top drawer open after several hard pulls on the wet and swollen wood. The entire structure was soggy and rotting, the clothing inside covered in mold, and home to several species of insects that scattered in all directions as I peered inside. With a frustrated sigh, I slammed the drawer shut.

The farmhouse had been the first semi-decent structure we'd come across in a long while, offering us a much-needed chance to rest and regain our bearings from the constant walking in unrelenting heat... I supposed it was too much to ask that it have a few other offerings as well.

"Find anything?"

Lucas brushed the webbing out of his way, sending the spider scurrying to what remained of its silken tapestry. Meandering through the bedroom, Lucas paused at the tree, tucking his dirty-blond waves back behind his ears. Even unkempt and with several weeks' worth of grime caking his clothing, Lucas almost always appeared well rested and refreshed while the rest of the living tended to look more like me—with dark circles ringing their eyes and more than a few leaves stuck in their hair.

"Nope. Just some moldy undies and this lovely tree." Patting the branch as I ducked beneath it once more, I eyed the closet over Lucas's shoulder. I didn't dare tell him about the family of opossums inside, fearing he'd have them roasting over an open fire in five seconds flat.

"And our hosts, of course." Lucas gestured to the skeletons in the bed. "Nice way to go, right? You don't see that anymore."

A vision of my mother tucked in her bed surfaced—*the whites of her eyes turned yellow; the rasping grate of her labored breathing echoing around an otherwise silent room.* My breath hitched and shuddered, and I quickly shoved the memory away.

"True," I replied dryly. "It's hard to stay dead in bed when you're busy trying to eat your neighbors."

Lucas laughed, as I'd known he would, and the happy, soothing sound of him was an instant balm to my somber mood.

"Oh, come on, Willow. Don't tell me you wouldn't have loved the chance to tear Mrs. Pickering's face off?"

Mr. and Mrs. Pickering had been my neighbors once upon a time, an elderly couple from Asheville—our hometown. They'd never liked my family—mostly because we'd been a mixed-race family in a predominantly white town, but also because *we didn't keep up with the Joneses.* Oftentimes my dad would go just a bit too long without mowing the lawn, and my mom's idea of gardening was letting the weeds grow in abundance.

"You've got me there," I said. "Still, the very last place I want to die is *in a bed.*" I stuck out my tongue. "How fucking boring."

"I know, I know—you want to go out in a blaze of glory. How does it go again?" Smiling, Lucas leaned back casually against the tree branch.

"Well, I'm surrounded by Creepers," I started. "And they've got me cornered. There's no way out."

"Mhm, mhm." Lucas nodded exaggeratedly. "But are we talking about Runners or Shamblers?"

None of the dead could actually run, but some were faster than others. Their level of agility and speed depended on how far along they were in their decomposition. Though the Vaal Fever didn't stop decomposition altogether, it certainly slowed it down.

"Runners, duh." I scoffed. "I can't claim glory if I'm taken out by a bunch of half-rotten slowpokes."

"Of course not. Whatever was I thinking? So you're surrounded by Runners and there's no way out. Then what?"

"Hundreds of Runners," I corrected. "Maybe even thousands."

"Oh, so now it's a mega horde?"

"You and Logan have been killed already — early on, actually." I flashed Lucas a saccharine-sweet smile. "I mean, I tried to help, but you know what you guys are like."

"Jeez, Will — why not tell me how you really feel."

"Listen here, this is *my* glorious demise, not yours."

"You're so right. Please, go on." Lucas made a twirling gesture with his hand.

"Thank you, I will. So I'm dodging Runners, shoving one into another, jumping over the bodies of the ones I've already killed. I'm karate chopping, high kicking—"

"Karate chopping? Last time you told this story, you'd jerry-rigged a lawn mower into a chainsaw and there was blood and guts raining everywhere. Now you're karate chopping?"

"Excuse me? Can I finish my story?"

Laughing, Lucas pushed away from the tree branch and slung

his arm across my shoulders. Tugging on a handful of my braids, he planted a soft kiss at the corner of my mouth. "I love you," he said fondly.

Relaxing against him, I ran a fingertip down the full length of his aquiline nose, flicking his nose ring. Kissing each of his prominent cheekbones, my fingers found the straight shape of his mouth, bumping over each of his matching lip rings. "I love you, too," I whispered.

My boyfriend since middle school, my best friend, too—my only friend, actually—Lucas had been my entire world for as long as I could remember.

"You two plan on being useful today?"

We broke apart to find Logan standing in the doorway, the remnants of the spiderweb hanging in tatters around his hulking silhouette, the spider crushed beside his boot. His narrowed gaze was fixed on us, his heavy brows pinched tightly together. Who knew how long he'd been standing there—Logan, despite his size, was as quiet as a cat and as stealthy as one too. He could move in and out of places with no one the wiser. Meanwhile, Lucas and I couldn't seem to take two steps without the whole world taking notice.

That wasn't the only difference between the brothers; almost three years Lucas's senior, Logan outsized Lucas in every way. He was taller, bigger, bulkier, and what was only a smattering of hair across Lucas's cheeks and chin was a full-fledged beard on Logan. Even their shared features were noticeably different—Lucas's blue eyes were light and guileless while Logan's were heavy and hard; Lucas's long locks usually hung free, while Logan kept his pulled back wound into a tight knot. *Tightly wound… just like the man himself.*

Lucas sighed. "We've been looking—we just haven't found anything yet. What about you?"

8

Logan continued to eye us both, his expression as stony as ever. "The garage is barricaded," he growled. "Sounds like there's a couple of Creepers inside. Who's going to help me clear it?"

"Willow is!" Lucas exclaimed.

"Traitor!" I sputtered, stomping my foot.

Lucas shrugged. "You snooze, you lose, Wilbur."

"Don't call me Wilbur, *Lucifer*."

"Don't call me Lucifer, *Willard*."

"Don't call me Willard, *shithead*."

"Oooh, shithead. Real classy, Will, *real classy*."

"You know they say that people who curse are more intelligent than those who don't, right?"

Lucas chuckled loudly. "Who says that? More importantly, where are they now?" His chiseled features went comically slack as he let out a deathly groan—a near-perfect imitation of the dead.

"*Hey*," Logan snapped. "If you two are done fucking around, can one of you get your ass downstairs?"

Lucas and I shared a glance. Logan rarely relaxed; he was *all* business *all* of the time. In his mind, every day was a new battle he had to fight where he was the general and Lucas and I were his unwilling soldiers. And with the current heat index, lack of water, and subsequent food shortage worsening his mood, Logan was only going to grow grumpier.

But truth be told, Logan had always been this way. He had never been able to simply "sit down and take a load off", and the end of the world had only made his compulsions that much worse.

First, the farmhouse would need to be cleared—checked for both threats and supplies. Then it would need to be secured—locked up tight so nothing could sneak up on us. Only after that could camp be set up; a camp that was both *defendable* and *escapable*—Logan's two favorite words. And only after camp was set up could we even begin to think of relaxing. Any sort of deviation from the plan and there was a good chance Logan would lose his shit. Scratch that— any sort of deviation and Logan would definitely lose his shit.

"Coming," I muttered. Flipping off Lucas behind my back, I made a dramatic show of trudging into the hall after Logan.

"Could you walk any slower?" Logan bit out.

"I mean, I could," I quipped. "But since you're like Grumplestiltskin on crack today, this is my quick walk."

Logan shot me a look chock-full of disdain and increased his speed, forcing me to jog just to keep pace with him. "Have you always been this much of an asshole?" I muttered.

It was a rhetorical question, because, yes, Logan had always been this much of an asshole. Especially to me. Back before the world had gone crazy, he'd been the shining star of our small town. And in a town where Friday Night Lights had been the main pastime of nearly every single citizen, Logan had practically been a local celebrity, especially after being awarded a state football scholarship. After that, there'd been no reining in his holier-than-thou ego.

Descending the broken staircase, we wove through a maze of decrepit hallways and crumbling rooms, emerging inside a kitchen—a once striking black and silver room equipped with stainless steel appliances that were now tarnished with rust and coated in filth. My eyes immediately found the eyesore in the center, where furniture had been piled up in front of a door, beyond which I could make out the faint sound of shuffling. The stench of rot tinged the damp air, increasing as we drew closer to the barricade. My nose wrinkled—I might've grown accustomed to sharing my world with the dead, but I would never grow accustomed to the smell of them.

Logan headed for the barricade and began dismantling it. The shuffling from behind the door grew louder and more agitated with every piece of furniture he dragged aside.

"They've been in there a while," I murmured, running my fingertip over the countertop, drawing a line through the thick layer of dust. Pausing in front of the refrigerator, I looked over the faded collection of the things hanging there—school photos, a candid family shot, and a business card for a lawn service. **TAMING NATURE IS AN ART FORM,** it read, causing me to snort. Judging by the current state of things, I thought nature might be inclined to disagree. Continuing my trek through the kitchen, I stopped in front of a wall calendar, opened to the month of April, seven years prior.

"Logan?"

"What?"

"What month is it?"

"May... maybe June. Who the fuck cares?"

I tried to recall the last time I'd known the date. Living the way we did—on the road and in the wild—the only calendar we followed was nature's.

"You should suit up," Logan said.

"I'm good." Tearing my eyes away from the calendar, I joined Logan at the door. Grabbing the length of pipe from my pack, I wrapped both hands around the base and planted my feet.

Logan, having just finished with the barricade, straightened and stared at me. "Suit up, Willow," he growled.

I met his pointed look with one of equal measure. "I said, *I'm good.*"

"I'm not opening that door until you're suited up."

"You're not suited up."

"I'm not the one wearing a tank top, practically begging to get bitten."

"It's nine hundred fucking degrees out—what else would I be wearing?"

"We don't know how many are in there. Even Shamblers can get the drop on you if there are enough of them. So-suit-the-fuck-up." He said the last part slowly, deliberately punctuating each word.

Knowing that fighting with Logan always proved pointless, I dropped my pipe and jerked angrily out of my pack. Digging roughly through my belongings, I pulled out my gear—a worn leather jacket, a battered pair of leather gloves, and a hockey mask. Only once I was fully suited up did Logan pull his crowbar from his belt. Scooping up my pipe with a snarl, I readied to swing.

"Stop being pissed at me and pay attention," he commanded.

Stop being pissed at me and pay attention, I mimicked silently.

Logan twisted the knob; the door groaned loudly in protest. He continued twisting and pulling until it flung open with a POP. A blast of hot, putrid air rushed out to greet us as a snarling Creeper stumbled through the open doorway, tripping over Logan's waiting foot. The Creeper, little more than a bag of bones, broke when it fell, its bones splintering and splitting through its paper-thin skin.

"I wouldn't be pissed if you'd stop treating me like a kid," I countered, swinging my pipe. "I'm twenty-three, for fuck's sake." The steel collided with the back of the Creeper's skull, the brittle bone easily giving way. Thick black sludge oozed from the gaping wound, revealing white-gray brain matter. The Vaal Fever, once you were infected, worked quickly to kill you, only to reanimate your brain, even as the rest of your body eventually turned to dust. Despite the working brain, the dead retained no memories of who they'd been; they were nothing more than simple-minded monsters, driven by a singular need—hunger.

"Would it kill you to act like it?" Logan said, just as a second Creeper lurched into the kitchen, taller and larger than the first. Quickly met with Logan's crowbar in its eye socket, its shrunken, spindly arms reached fruitlessly while Logan shoved the crowbar deeper into its head; the moment the steel punctured its brain, it ceased moving. With a grunt, Logan wrenched the tool from the eye socket and the Creeper's body dropped to the floor. When nothing else appeared in the doorway, I flipped my mask up.

"Two? I suited up for *two* sacks of bones? I bet they didn't even have teeth."

With an agitated sigh, Logan moved inside the garage. Glaring after him, I quickly stripped out of my leather gear, stuffing it haphazardly back into my pack before following him in.

The smell of rot and decay doubled inside the dark, dank room, made worse by the stifling heat. Two vehicles sat side by side, both in various states of disarray; on the back wall hung a vast display of neatly hung tools, and on the far wall were several heavy-duty metal shelving units packed full with plastic tubs. Ignoring Logan — who was busy inspecting the wall of tools — I pulled my neck gaiter over my nose and headed for the shelves.

Countless tubs lined the shelves; large sporting equipment hung nearby — a set of golf clubs, a pair of kayaks and matching oars, and a disassembled soccer net. Perusing the shelves, I dragged down a heavy tub, finding it packed full with camping gear — some of which we could use. Setting it aside, I dragged a second tub from the shelves. Wiping the dust from the top, I lifted the lid, revealing a container stuffed to the brim with Christmas decorations. Staring down at them, I found myself lost in a memory.

Dad dressed in his red and green plaid pajamas, mistletoe clutched in his hand, his eyes twinkling as he stares…

... as he stares straight through me, unseeing. A trail of blood runs across his forehead, dripping onto the floor.

I blinked rapidly, forcing back the tears that threatened, and slammed the lid shut on the holiday decor. Shoving the tub away, I reached for another, this one labeled: HALLOWEEN.

"Now that's more like it," I said, holding up a decorative skeleton with glowing yellow eyes.

"Willow, what the fuck are you doing?" Logan demanded. "You're supposed to be looking for shit we can use, not playing with toys."

I scowled at the skeleton in my hand before tossing it aside. "Yes, Sir Dick-a-Lot—right away," I growled softly.

TWO

LOGAN

Grumbling curses beneath my breath, I looked away from Willow. If the house hadn't already implied wealth, the extensive walls of tools before me, most of them were unused and still in their packaging, would have clued me in. Back when the world had still made sense, I'd known the type—rich people who'd had to have at least one of everything, even if they never used it. I would have wagered good money that this particular house had been a vacation spot—a grand country home that had been a wealthy family's means of escape from their busy city lives… or an escape from the end of the world.

After swapping some of my own tools for much-needed replacements, I moved on to the vehicle closest to me—a large black

SUV with old bloody handprints smeared across its windows. Its tan interior was also liberally covered in blood, long ago dried and flaking off.

The second vehicle—another SUV, silver in color—still had its keys in the ignition. Pocketing them, I began searching through a handbag lying on the driver's seat, most of its contents spilled onto the floor. Finding nothing of use, I reached across the dash and popped open the glove box finding a small silver pistol glinting atop a pile of aging papers.

"Jackpot," I breathed.

With the collapse of society, guns and ammunition had been among the first wave of things to disappear. We'd had a few early on, but without bullets, they had very quickly become deadweight.

Examining the pistol, I found it fully loaded and the safety off, something I rectified before removing the magazine and stuffing both pieces into my pockets. Making a mental note to check the house for more ammo, I continued searching the vehicle.

"Holy shit! Holyshitholyshitholyshit!"

Willow's shouting had me bashing my head on the roof of the car in a race to exit it. Rushing around the front of the vehicle, pulling out my crowbar as I ran, I found her surrounded by open storage bins, their contents littering the floor around her.

"Logan, look!" she squealed. "Look at this!"

She was brandishing a box in each hand, shaking them excitedly. I couldn't tell exactly what they were as I was momentarily distracted by her ridiculous getup—a large feather boa, with feathers in every color of the rainbow, and a pair of green googly eyed antennae. She continued to jump around, the googly eyes on top of her head bouncing in tandem with her breasts.

"There's rice and pasta and *fucking chocolate!*"

Declaration delivered, Willow dropped to her knees, tearing open one box while the others tumbled away. At least a dozen individually wrapped cake rolls spilled onto her lap. Scooping up several packages, she tore one open with her teeth and ate the entire thing in three succinct bites, discarding the wrapper without care.

"Mmmahhaddd," she moaned around a mouthful of chocolate and cream. "It's horrible and stale *and ah-mazing.*"

Putting my crowbar away, I approached the mess Willow had made. Out of the half dozen containers she'd pulled from the shelves, two of them were full of food. Not all of it had survived, as was usually the case in regions that experienced a wide range of weather conditions. Oftentimes when canned food froze, the food inside expanded, causing the can to burst. Thankfully, among the rotten canned goods, there were plenty of bagged and boxed items that remained in visibly good condition. A little water, a little heat, and we'd have ourselves a goddamn feast.

"Hey, what are you guys yelling about—wait, is that chocolate?" Lucas raced through the garage, dropping down beside Willow. Tearing open a cake roll, he shoved the entire thing into his mouth.

"It's disgusting," he mumbled, bits of chocolate spraying from his lips. Grabbing another, he ate it twice as fast.

"Slow down," I said, frowning at them. "You're going to make yourselves sick."

"Logan, shut up and eat something!" Willow tossed a cake roll at me; it hit me in the chest before falling to the floor.

"We need to secure the house first," I ground out through gritted teeth. "Luke, did you finish searching upstairs?"

They both ignored me, content to continue stuffing their faces and making a mess of themselves. Content to continue teasing each other and laughing as if they didn't have a care in the world.

Watching them, every muscle in my body began to tense. *They really didn't have a care in the world*—not when I was the one always taking care of everything. Lucas and Willow would have been dead years ago if it wasn't for me, and yet here they were, acting like spoiled children—impulsive and obnoxious, forever forgetting that there was important shit to do, always oblivious to the infinite number of dangers lurking around every corner. Acting like it was just the two of them.

Acting like I wasn't even here.

"Make sure you finish searching upstairs," I growled, spinning away, the fallen cake roll exploding beneath my boot, forcing me to stop and scrape my heel against the floor. Growing angrier with each swipe, I stormed from the garage, my fists clenched.

Resuming my search of the first floor, I found myself growing angrier still. This farmhouse, as grand as it had seemed at first glance, was little more than a garbage heap, each room looking worse than the last. The collapsed roof had caused an infestation, not just of wildlife, but of mold. And once mold took root, it was only a matter of time before the entire house was compromised.

With only one room left to search, I opened the door, startled to find its contents dry and free of mold. It had once been an office, accommodating an ornate desk and an equally elaborate chair. A bay window stretched across one side of the room, framed by bookshelves filled with hardbound books and expensive-looking knickknacks. Everything was covered in dust.

Dropping my pack by the door, I opened one of the windows. Removing its screen, I stuck my head out into the sweltering heat, happy to find that the window was set low enough to the ground to be utilized as a second entrance or an emergency exit.

Next, I rearranged the furniture, moving the bulk toward the door to serve as a barricade come nightfall. Using the window curtains, I wiped down the dusty contents until I was satisfied with the state of the room. Climbing out the window, I surveyed the vast property, thick with trees and so overgrown we'd nearly missed it.

I had a vague idea of where we were. Having passed through little more than farmland and wooded areas, I figured we had to be approaching a town or possibly even a small city. Usually, we worked to avoid once populated places — places where Creepers tended to congregate — but our current food shortage was starting to concern me; we couldn't live off roots forever. The bigger the town, the bigger the payout would be.

As I made my way through the waist-high lawn, bugs rising from the foliage in dense black clouds, I began noticing bits of broken fencing. Toeing through the vegetation for a closer look, something else snagged my attention. I dug deeper, ripping away fistfuls of greenery, exposing the mouthwatering prize beneath — vines covered in clusters of juicy-looking grapes. Plucking one, I broke it open, examining its innards, ensuring that it was in fact grapes I'd discovered and not a poisonous impostor.

Look at the seeds — if they're round, they're grapes, if they're crescent-shaped, they're Fox Grapes.

It was thanks to my mother's green thumb that I knew what little I did — mainly what was edible and what wasn't. Looking back, I wished I'd listened more intently to her gardening nonsense — things that had seemed so insignificant at the time but had ultimately ended up saving our lives after everything had gone to hell.

Popping the grape in my mouth, I moved on, heading toward a small shed in the distance. Unlike my traveling companions, I actually had self-control. I could, and would, abstain from gorging myself until *after* our safety was ensured.

I circled the shed before entering—it was a typical garden-sized hut, windowless and with a barn door–style entryway. The doorframe was warped and rotting, the door latch rusted over. Prying off the latch, I used my crowbar to wrest the doors open; wood crumbled, breaking off in sharp, jagged chunks as the doors popped free.

Inside the shed, spiders hurried to climb up their silk strands, vanishing into the shed rafters. Standing in the entranceway, I surveyed the meager contents with dismay—a riding mower, a stack of dust-covered planter boxes, and a bag of topsoil.

Closing the doors, I made my way back to the house, loud laughter and a trail of cake roll wrappers greeting me in the hallway. No matter how many times I reminded Lucas and Willow to keep quiet, they rarely listened. *Sloppy, forgetful, idiotic*—I ticked off their less desirable traits in my head as I moved quickly down the hall. About to turn into the room, I stopped dead.

With her back to me, Willow stood in front of the open window, pulling her shirt off over her head. Raven black braids swayed across her back as she stretched, her softly curved form a beacon in the blazing sunset. The side of one breast was visible, the tilt of her chin exposing a sleek expanse of neck, while beads of sweat dripped down the concave center, her bronze skin shimmering in the most mesmerizing way.

My dick twitched and hardened, much to my annoyance. It wasn't as if this were the first time I'd seen her without her clothes on. Hell, at this point, I should be numb to it. Living the way we did, we weren't afforded the luxury of modesty, and we'd long ago grown accustomed.

"Are you two kidding me?" I said, barging into the room.

"What if I was someone else — someone dangerous?" I pointed an accusatory finger at Lucas, who lay on the sofa, his arms propped behind his head. "What if I'd been a Creeper? We haven't even set up camp and the two of you are already fucking off."

They'd both jumped when I'd entered — Lucas shot up off the couch while Willow hurried to finish dressing.

"Well?" I demanded when no one spoke.

"Calm down," Willow muttered. "We were just about to start."

"Yeah right," I bit out. "Did one of you at least finish clearing the upstairs?"

When neither of them replied, I turned away, shaking my head. "Set up camp," I growled over my shoulder. "I'll be upstairs finishing what you two should be doing."

As I retreated down the hall, the house was quiet, the only noise from the frantic thrumming of blood through my veins.

My return to the office was met with gloomy expressions and sulking silence; Lucas sat on the couch with his nose buried in a book, while Willow sat on the windowsill, staring off into the fading sunlight. I ignored their silence, satisfied to find they'd actually listened for a change and set up camp while I'd been gone.

Our three threadbare sleeping bags had been arranged in a circle, our makeshift stove and canteens set in the center. Used mostly for boiling rainwater, the stove was nothing more than a large tin can with a small pot that fit over the top of it.

Closing the door behind me, I placed my findings at my feet and began barricading the door before dismantling what was left of my gear — the tool belt I wore at my waist, the blades I kept strapped all over my body, and my steel-toed boots. Stripping off my sweat-soaked socks, I laid them out on the floor to dry.

"Find anything good?" Lucas asked, his tentative tone and anxious expression reminding me so much of our mother when our father had been in one of his moods. As guilt swelled inside me, I gestured at the moth-eaten pillowcase I'd used to carry what I found. "Go ahead and look. Take whatever you want."

Lucas and Willow glanced at each other, grins spreading across their faces. Like kids on Christmas morning, they raced across the room, both of them diving for the pillowcase, briefly yanking it back and forth before dumping its contents onto the floor.

"Yours." Lucas tossed a box of tampons in Willow's direction. Without uttering a word, she set them aside. While Lucas resumed pawing through the goods, I studied Willow, trying to recall the last time she'd alluded to needing supplies. Was she pregnant? I dismissed the panicked thought instantly—she'd shown zero symptoms. So then what? None of us were the picture of health—we were all overworked and undernourished—but if Willow wasn't getting her period anymore, maybe I'd misjudged just how bad off we really were.

Looking at them long and hard, it suddenly struck me how prominent Willow's collarbone was and how chiseled Lucas's cheekbones had become. Another wave of guilt washed over me. These past few months we'd been teetering on starvation, and not a damn thing I did seemed to make a difference.

"There's toothpaste!" Willow jumped to her feet, clutching the several unopened tubes of toothpaste I'd pillaged from one of the upstairs bathrooms. "No more chewing mint leaves." She danced in clumsy circles around the room before bowing down in front of Lucas, holding out a tube in offering.

"For your awful, stinking breath, *good sir*," she said, attempting a British accent.

"Why yes, I do have awful, stinking breath." Lucas attempted the same accent. "It's almost as wretched as yours, *madam*."

Laughing, Willow continued dancing around the room, coming to a twirling stop in front of me. Again, she dropped down into a dramatic bow, holding out another tube of toothpaste. The deep bow caused her too-big T-shirt to sag open, the stretched-out material offering up a bird's-eye view of her breasts. Perfect breasts. High, tight mounds of soft flesh topped with dark nipples. Staring, my mouth went bone dry.

"Hello? Earth to Logan. Would you like some toothpaste?"

With a growl, I snatched the tube from her and slumped back against the wall. Oblivious to my mood, Willow resumed dancing.

"Hey," Lucas said, inching closer to me, holding a box of protein bars. "I found these in the garage—they're your favorite flavor."

Taking two, I pushed the box back at Lucas. "You need those more than I do."

"Ha!" Willow exclaimed from across the room. "A protein bar is not going to help him with those puny little things he calls arms."

Lucas pushed up his shirtsleeve and flexed, making a big show of giving his slight bicep a kiss. "You love my puny arms, Wilma."

"That's what you think, Luke... warm."

"Lukewarm? That's the best you could come up with—*Lukewarm*?"

While Lucas and Willow howled with laughter and made faces at one another, I was once again left feeling like the odd man out. Leaning my head back against the wall, I closed my eyes, grateful there was nothing left to do—

My eyes flew open.

"Did you guys set up the buckets?" Using plastic buckets that attached easily to our packs, we collected rainwater that we'd later filter and use for drinking.

"It's his turn." Willow jabbed a finger at Lucas.

"It's not!" Lucas protested. "I did it last night."

"*I* did it last night," I growled. "One of you can do it tonight — and the other can go pick the grapes I found out back."

Willow's brown eyes went saucer wide. "I call grapes!" she shouted, scrambling toward the window. Tossing one leg over the windowsill, she launched herself outside. There was an audible thud as she landed on the ground below.

"I'm okay!" she shouted back.

Lucas snorted. "Remember how Mom always said Willow was like a bull in a china shop?"

"Yeah, well, Mom had a bad habit of making excuses for people," I muttered.

Lucas glanced over at me, surprised. "That's not the same thing. You can't compare Willow and —"

"I know," I snapped. "I'm not. I'm just —" I stopped speaking and blew out a breath. "I'm just tired."

Lucas stared at me, his brow creasing, again reminding me of Mom and the concerned look she always wore whenever Dad was around. And I just couldn't deal with it right now — the anger that was always welling inside me and the guilt that never seemed to abate. Needing a distraction, I forced my weary body to move; there was a gun safe somewhere in this house and I aimed to find it before darkness fell.

THREE

WILLOW

I tossed and turned that evening, sleeping only in short, fitful bursts, fraught with unwelcome dreams. It was this house, and those horrible Christmas decorations, reminding me of things I didn't want to be reminded of. And it was this room, too hot and dusty, making my skin itch, and smelling like the stale remnants of a life we'd never live again.

At first, I'd hated sleeping outside. I'd spent countless nights too afraid to close my eyes, terrified of the darkness and all the noises hidden in its inky depths. Nowadays, I enjoyed the open air; I no longer lay awake in fear or had trouble finding comfort on rocky terrain. It was the indoors that had become burdensome—rickety shelters that often smelled as bad as they looked and were filled with far more creepy-crawlies than underneath a tree.

We'd endured the unendurable; we'd become experts of the unfathomable; we knew how to stay warm in the winter and how to stay dry in the rain… staying cool during a heatwave, however, was one of the few things we hadn't quite mastered.

Wiping the sheen of sweat from my face, I rolled over and reached for my canteen. Nearby, Lucas was sleeping soundly, softly snoring. I sent him a narrowed-eyed stare, jealous of his ability to sleep through literally anything, including this hellfire heatwave.

"Make sure you ration that."

Whipping around, I found Logan straddling the windowsill, the backdrop of the full moon illuminating the dark shape of him, though his face remained eclipsed in shadows. Sending a scowl in his direction, I proceeded to guzzle everything in my canteen.

Logan made a noise of disbelief. "Are you fucking kidding me? Don't expect to have any of mine tomorrow."

"Sir, no sir," I said, giving him a mock salute with my middle finger.

"You're so fucking funny," he muttered.

"Thank you—I try."

Neither of us said anything more; an uncomfortable silence settled in the room, the tension between us growing as thick as the humidity. Something had to give—*one of us had to give*—and it definitely wasn't going to be Logan.

I reluctantly rose to my feet and crossed the room. Climbing up onto the window ledge, I mirrored Logan's position—one leg in, one leg out, the warm evening air on my toes. Staring into the blackness, there was very little to see other than the starlit sky, nothing to be heard but the chirping of crickets. In the dead of night, when I couldn't see the death and destruction that always surrounded us, I could almost pretend that the world hadn't gone to hell. That someday I'd get to see all the places I used to dream about. That someday, I'd get to grow up and become somebody.

Glancing at Logan, he remained as he'd been — staring stoically across the yard, undoubtedly considering what sort of fresh hell tomorrow would bring, how it would somehow be all my fault, and how he would single-handedly fix it all. In our story, I was always the villain and Logan was always the hero. Lucas mostly played peacekeeper.

"You know," I said lightly. "You haven't slept in days. Maybe you would feel better if you —"

"In case you hadn't noticed," he growled, cutting me off. "You're not sleeping either."

"I would be if it wasn't so hot," I snapped, working hard not to glare at him. "Anyway, it's not the same. At least I tried to sleep."

"You think I don't want to sleep?" He scoffed. "Did you forget that we don't have enough supplies to set up a perimeter alarm here? We're smack dab in the middle of the wide open, *and* we have a window open. You do the fucking math, Willow. Or is that out of your realm of comprehension?"

My upper lip curled. God, I hated him. And lately, he couldn't even pretend to like me. If that was how he was going to be then I wasn't sure how much longer I could keep pretending either.

"What is your actual problem? I was just going to offer to keep watch so you could get some sleep. You know you don't always have to be a dick, right?"

"You want to keep watch?" Logan mocked. "While I go to sleep? *You? Keep watch?*"

I briefly contemplated choking him, or at the very least, shoving him out the window in hopes that a Creeper lay in wait beneath. Instead, I squeezed my eyes shut, reminding myself that once again I would have to be the bigger person, since Logan was clearly content with being a jackass.

"Yeah," I bit out. "I'm not completely incapable."

"And if something or someone finds this place, are you planning on fighting them off barefoot and in your underwear?" He looked me up and down with a snort.

"I am a person of many talents," I replied tightly. "Look, if you don't trust me to keep watch, fine — *whatever* — but you still need sleep. Maybe we should stay here for a few days and you could sleep during the day?"

"It's not safe here. Too open."

"It's not safe anywhere. But at least here we have shelter — *defendable and escapable.* And we could set up several smaller perimeter alarms — I mean, there's more than enough garbage lying around this place to put an alarm outside of every door if we wanted. And all those grapes… Logan, we could live off those grapes for a month."

His widening gaze careened toward me. "We can't stay here for a month!"

Scowling, I tightly replied, "Yeah, I know that — I only meant *we could*, not that *we should*. And before you even mention water, it's going to rain soon — maybe tomorrow or the next day. I bet your knees are killing you. Your back, too, right?"

Logan always insisted on carrying the most, making his pack the heaviest by far. Despite his young age, the constant extra weight had quickly taken its toll on his back and knees, causing him pain whenever the weather shifted.

He looked off with a sigh, his shoulders slumping forward. Even in the dark, I could see how tired he was. The sort of bone-deep exhaustion that oftentimes made him look old beyond his twenty-six years. Watching him, I felt my own exhaustion flare.

"We need a break," I whispered. "Logan, please."

When he faced me, I held his gaze, hoping he would see the truth in my plea. Though obviously tired, his expression was, as usual, as stony as ever.

"We can stay until it rains," he eventually said. "And after that, we'll reassess."

I blinked. "Wait, what?"

"And if it doesn't rain after a few days, we're moving on."

"Whoa, whoa. Wait a second." I held up my hand. "Are you serious right now? Like, this isn't a joke—we can really stay here for a few days?"

Logan looked at me, deadpan. "Since when do I tell jokes?"

I shot upright, squealing, clapping my hands together and slapping my feet against the side of the house. I couldn't believe it—Logan literally never listened to me. In fact, he usually went out of his way to do the opposite of whatever I would suggest.

Logan's hand crashed down on my bare thigh, squeezing me still. "Stop kicking!" he whispered furiously. "This place won't be safe for long if you keep making so much fucking noise!"

Slapping my hands over my mouth, I whispered, "Sorry." It was taking all of my effort to remain still—the thought of being able to lounge around for a few days had me practically vibrating with excitement.

Logan released my leg and cleared his throat. "I need to do a quick perimeter check; make sure you didn't just lead every Creeper in the area straight to us." Jumping from the windowsill, he jogged away, his form quickly merging with the shadows.

With a roll of my eyes, I swung my body back inside the house and leaped on top of Lucas. "You're never going to believe what just happened!"

Lucas sat up with a shout. "What's going on?"

Grabbing his face, I kissed him squarely on the mouth. "I'm a fucking magician, that's what!"

We ate boiled oats for breakfast, thanks to my garage finds. There was coffee too—coffee beans that we'd ground ourselves and then added to a pot of boiling water. If you covered the water while it cooled, the grounds would eventually settle at the bottom—it was a trick we'd been taught early on, during our first winter without power... back when there had been a lot more people than just the three of us.

As the harsh smell of hot coffee filled my nostrils, a lump formed in my throat. A memory surfaced—all the adults huddled around the fireplace, dressed in heavy layers, each clutching steaming mugs of coffee, quietly discussing what they didn't want us kids to hear. Ironic, really, that they were all dead now... alongside their secrets... and we were still here.

After breakfast, Logan announced he'd be heading out to do another needless perimeter check and tasking Lucas and me with straightening up camp. With his departure, I flopped onto my bedroll. "If he ever sat down for more than five minutes, I would die of a heart attack."

Taking a seat beside me, Lucas chewed thoughtfully on his lip rings. "He probably would, too," he said. "He's always got to be working toward something. I think he feels useless if he isn't."

I scoffed. "But nothing is ever good enough for him, either. I mean, remember that group in Virginia? I still don't understand why we didn't stay with them—they even had a doctor! Literally nothing will ever be good enough for him."

Lucas snorted. "He wasn't a doctor; he said he'd been studying to *become a doctor*. He was probably lying, too. They were all insane, and you know it."

I pointed an accusatory finger at Lucas. "Almost a doctor is better than no doctor. *And you know it.*"

"Oh, please. You didn't like them either. You just love hating on Logan."

The group in Virginia had been sizable—around fifty people who'd set up a makeshift city inside a shipping warehouse—a massive building made of concrete surrounded by a heavy-duty gate topped with razor wire. Inside, there'd been pallets piled high with nonperishable food products, and shipping containers set up like apartments. At first glance, to three homeless teenagers, it had seemed like the perfect place.

We'd stayed with them only three days, though we'd only needed one to realize that something was off. They'd prayed at all hours of the day, and when they weren't praying, they were chanting, and when they weren't chanting, they were singing. At first we'd attempted fitting in but after a giant wooden cross had been revealed to us, with a wriggling Creeper nailed to it, we'd known it was time to leave. As they'd fallen to their knees before the crucified monster, we'd quickly gathered our things and ran.

"Fine," I conceded. "But what about the forest people in Kentucky—they weren't completely insane."

"Forest people? You make them sound like they were fairies or something!" Lucas laughed heartily. "If they're still alive, they are definitely insane by now!"

"You don't know that."

"Pretty sure you can't live off magic mushrooms, *Willy*."

"You know I hate when you side with Logan, *Lucy*."

"Yeah, well, you know I hate it when you say stupid things just 'cause you hate my brother."

"Whatever," I muttered. "But just for the record, he hated me first. I just followed suit."

Lucas shook his head. "You'd think after all this time you two would have learned to tolerate one another."

Horrified at the prospect, I shook my head violently. "Never. We're too different."

Lucas looked at me intently, a wry smile curving his lips. "I think it's because you're too similar."

I gasped, clutching my chest in mock outrage. "How dare you?" I said, swatting at him. "How fucking dare you say that to me? I thought you loved me!"

Laughing, Lucas rolled away, quickly jumping to his feet.

"Get back here and apologize," I said, scrambling to stand.

Running from the room, he glanced over his shoulder and grinned. "Never!" he shouted.

"Where are you going?" I demanded from the doorway as he disappeared down the hall. "I thought we were going to lie around naked and eat grapes?"

Lucas skidded to a stop, his boots squeaking audibly across the hardwood floor. Heavy footsteps echoed through the otherwise empty hall as he quickly retraced his steps back to me. Blue eyes smiled at me. "That sounds... *sticky*."

By early afternoon Lucas and I had exhausted the contents of the farmhouse, amassing a decent pile of odds and ends—nothing we needed or could take with us when we left, but things that would serve as entertainment while we were here.

"So many pictures," Lucas mused, flipping idly through the pages of a family photo album. "We didn't do photo albums in my house. Logan had a baby book, but that was about it."

Digging through the contents of an antique steamer trunk, I grumbled, "No need to brag."

Lucas began to chuckle. "Yeah, your mom was nuts. All your school photos hanging in the stairwell were my personal fav—a step-by-step progression of a happy kid turned emo teen with a homemade septum piercing."

I touched the tip of my finger to the tiny gold hoop in my nose, recalling the day I'd pushed a sewing needle through my septum. "God, that hurt," I murmured. "Also, *how dare you call me emo.*"

"If your hallway was an art piece, it would've been called, *The Decline of the Smile.*"

"If you were an art piece," I retorted. "You would be called, *What Not to Wear.*"

Currently, I was wrapped in the rainbow boa I'd discovered yesterday, while Lucas donned several moth-eaten neckties he'd found; he'd fashioned one around his forehead while the others hung loosely from his neck.

Lucas straightened, squaring his shoulders and studiously tightening one of the ties at his neck. "You wish you had my fashion sense."

"You wish I wished that, *Lucario.*"

"You wished that I wished that you wished that, *Willoughby.*"

"You wished that I wished that you wished that I..." Trailing off, I shoved up from the floor. The humidity had thickened and the wind had picked up, whistling softly through the broken corners of the house. But there was something else, too.

"Rain," I breathed, drinking in the sickly sweet scent that always preceded a summer shower.

I ran from the room with Lucas hot on my heels. Together we raced to the stairs, leaping down the broken steps two and three at a time, just barely managing not to lose a foot in the process. Lightning flashed, briefly lighting the dim halls. A clap of thunder boomed overhead, reverberating through the floor beneath our feet, vibrating the walls around us.

"It's a storm!" Lucas shouted, and we both whooped as loud as we could, the thunder shielding us from any nearby Creeper ears. Thunderstorms were the only time that Logan allowed us the freedom to be as loud as we wanted and we always took full advantage.

We collided with Logan in the downstairs hall, causing him to drop the stack of plastic tubs he was carrying. Recognizing them as the storage containers from the garage, I quickly realized his intentions — if it rained long enough to fill them, we'd have enough water for several weeks' worth of drinking, bathing, and maybe even laundry. The thought of cleaning my clothes with something other than creek water inspired another joyful shout.

Inside the office, we hurried to undress, each of us stripping down to our underwear. Lucas and I made a mad dash for the window, toppling over one another as we fell into the grass below in a heap. Jumping to my feet, I tilted my face to the sky, the first drop of rain hitting me square in the forehead. The second hit my nose, the third, fourth, and fifth hit my cheeks in a chorus of small splashes.

The whole world had turned gray — thick clouds were gathered overhead with bursts of light breaking through their heavy veil in rapid, jagged flashes. Thunder continued to crash—a symphony of clangs and bangs that exploded through the air and vibrated the rapidly forming puddles at our feet. Holding my arms out wide, I spun in drunken circles until I was drenched with rain and dizzy with delirium.

"It hasn't rained like this in forever!" Lucas shouted happily. Stomping and sloshing through the high grass, he was moving farther across the lawn.

"You look like you're in a mosh pit!" I shouted back.

"Mosh with me, *Wilhelmina!*"

"With pleasure, *Luciano!*"

I ran to him, the ground soft and wet at my feet. Clasping hands, we kicked and stomped through the high grass, flattening it beneath the crush of our feet. We played hard, tripping and slipping, pushing and shoving one another until we'd made a good-sized circle of flattened greenery, liberally peppered with muddy puddles. Meanwhile, the wind picked up speed and the rain fell harder.

"Playtime's over!" Logan called. He was gesturing wildly, pointing at a nearby group of trees whose heavy branches had begun to dangerously sway. Above us, the gray skies had considerably darkened. Storms had always had deadly potential, but nowadays, without the safety nets the old world offered, the dangers posed were significantly more.

Clasping hands, Lucas and I started for the house where Logan was attempting to secure the lids onto the overflowing containers. Releasing me, Lucas grabbed hold of the stack and together, he and Logan fought against the wind. They'd managed only two lids on before the wind caught hold of the flimsy plastic, sweeping the remaining covers up and over our heads.

I jumped up, catching the corner of a lid; the lid acted like a sail, sweeping me straight off my feet and then depositing me face down in the tall grass.

"Willow!" Logan's usually captive roar was a mere whisper among nature's lethal noise. "Willow, grab hold of something."

I'm trying, I wanted to scream, even as the wind pushed me farther away, aided by the wet, slickened state of things. But I couldn't find my voice. The violent whip of the wind had turned the warm summer rain into a cold barrage of water pellets, causing me to flinch and shiver between gasping breaths.

Finally, my hand snagged on something hard — a tree root that had erupted through the earth, thick enough to anchor myself against. Gripping it, I blinked rapidly through the wall of water, just barely making out the blurry outline of a fast-approaching form. Soon, gruff hands clamped down around my wrists and hauled me to my feet. "Hold on tight!" he shouted.

Even with our combined weight and our arms wrapped around one another, we struggled with each step, the wind intent on blowing us backward. I cried out as something heavy and sharp slammed into our legs, knocking us over and nearly succeeding in knocking us apart. While pain radiated up and down my left leg, Logan hauled me upright once again and together we attempted another fruitless battle forward.

"Luke!" Logan bellowed. "Luke — get your ass in the house! I'm going to try for the shed!"

Turning from the house, Logan and I ran with the wind, lifted by it at times, toward the small, dilapidated building shaking precariously at the edge of the yard.

FOUR

LOGAN

Struggling to keep the doors open, I thrust Willow inside the shed and then jumped in after her, just in time for the wind to slam the doors shut behind me. Trembling from exertion, I placed my hands on the quaking wood, feeling the strength of the wind battering against it. While I stood there, something large crashed against the doors, hard enough to startle me. Backing slowly away from the doors, I eyed the roof with trepidation, hoping it would hold if a heavy branch dropped onto it.

"That's why they call them widow-makers," I muttered. "'Cause they drop down and kill people."

My dad had been a seasonal worker, a jack-of-all-trades, who'd snow plowed, landscaped, repaired fences, and even trimmed trees. On the rare occasion that he hadn't been berating me, he'd been teaching me his trades.

You're going to need these skills someday, he would slur, a bottle of gin pointed in my direction. *You're gonna blow your knee out or knock up that girl a' yours and then you can kiss that fancy-ass scholarship good-fuckin'-bye.*

He'd been right. I had needed the skills, and I had kissed my state scholarship goodbye… just not for the reasons he'd thought. The end of our world hadn't exactly satisfied my desire to watch dear old Dad eat his words but considering the state of things and the fact that he was long gone, it would have to suffice.

"W-what?"

Willow was huddled against the back wall, quivering from head to toe, her teeth chattering violently, furiously rubbing her upper arms in an attempt to warm herself. Mixed with the rainwater dripping from every inch of her, a trail of bright-red blood ran down her calf.

"Your leg is bleeding," I told her. "Make sure you clean that."

When Willow didn't respond, I said, "Did you hear me? I said, make sure you clean that."

"I'm n-n-not stupid," Willow muttered, rolling her eyes. "And I heard y-y-you the first time."

My nostrils flared; my eyes narrowed. "If you're not stupid, then why the fuck am I always having to repeat myself?"

Willow was instantly on her feet, her eyes flashing. "Are you kidding me? W-what the hell was I doing wrong *this time?* I didn't answer f-f-fast enough—that's what your problem is?"

I didn't want to fight with her, especially not right now, but she had such an incredible talent for working my last nerve, for winding me up so fast and in such a way that I lost my grip on sense and reason.

"Look around!" I shouted. "My problem is, *we're hiding in a fucking garden shed*! If we would have left this morning, like I'd wanted to, this wouldn't have happened! But no, *you* wanted to stay!"

Willow's trembling mouth fell open. "If we would have left this morning, we wouldn't have tubs full of fresh water!"

"Filthy water!" I bellowed. "I couldn't get all the lids on, remember? We'll be drinking sediment!"

She was suddenly nose to nose with me. "I'll filter it all myself! Will that make you fucking happy?"

No, I wanted to scream. *No, it absolutely will not make me happy!* But I found myself at a sudden loss for words. I was so angry, I was vibrating, literally shaking with rage, and yet… I was rock hard. Willow's mouth was so goddamn close to mine, her minty breath hot as it blew across my face, her lips wet with rain. Grabbing her and kissing her was suddenly all I could think about. Kissing her and… touching her. Just like last night, when I'd grabbed her thigh; it had been a knee-jerk reaction that I hadn't remedied right away. I'd knowingly kept my hand there, thinking all sorts of fucked-up thoughts, the very same thoughts I was having now.

"Do I need to speak in football analogies for you to comprehend what I'm saying, Logan?" Willow spat. Her fingers snapped in front of my face, and I blinked, my anger quickly rising back to the surface.

"Why are you such a bitch?" I thundered. "Why can't you ever just listen?"

Her eyes grew wide, flashing with flames. "I'm not the one who needs to listen," she shrieked. "You are! You think you know everything, you think you're always right, but you're not, you know that? You're really not!"

"Name one time you haven't needed me to save the day!" I

demanded. "You can't, can you? You know why? Because you're fucking useless."

Hurt flashed briefly across her face, soon replaced with fury. "Fuck you! *Fuck you!*" she screamed, spittle flying past her lips, spraying across my face. She was borderline hysterical now, and so was I — the desire to kiss her warring violently with the desire to shake her.

"You think we need you, but we don't. I'm an adult, remember? Luke and I are both adults — you just like treating us like babies!"

"Oh, you're an adult?" I sneered, grabbing hold of her arms before I had the sense to stop myself. Gripping her biceps, I shook her roughly. "Then maybe you should fucking act like one!"

Shock flashed in Willow's eyes. Screaming, she slapped my hands away and shoved hard at my chest, knocking me back a step. "And maybe you should stop acting like your father!"

We both froze, staring at one another — Willow barely breathing, and me breathing far too hard.

There were things we rarely spoke of… not out loud, anyway, and my father was at the top of that list. But Willow hadn't just brought him up, *she'd compared me to him.* It was a slap in the face, a sucker punch to the gut; there was nothing worse she could have said to me.

Backing slowly away, I moved to a far corner of the shed, giving Willow my back. While the storm continued to rage around us, we raged silently in our separate corners. I refused to look at her, determined to never forgive her for what she'd said.

I'm not like him, I silently recited. *I'm nothing fucking like him.*

Eventually the wind died down and the rain became little more than a drizzle. I moved quickly, pushing through the doors, and striding through the swampy yard without a backward glance.

Willow was there though, following close enough that I could hear every splash of her footsteps.

"You guys okay?" Lucas was hanging out the office window, his forehead creased with concern.

"Never better," I muttered.

As Willow hurried past me, I changed course. Inspecting the tubs of water, they were as I'd expected — filled with debris. Seeing this, I felt doubly vindicated in my anger — I had been right and Willow had been wrong, as was usually the case. But would she ever admit to it? Not a chance in hell.

"Logan?" Lucas called. "You coming in?"

I waved him off. "Yeah, in a minute."

"You're bleeding, you know?"

Glancing down my body, I found a quarter-sized gash on my shin. I shrugged. "I'll take care of it after I do a perimeter check."

I managed a half-assed property search before giving up and heading back; adrenaline had worn off and fatigue was fast setting in. Hauling myself up through the office window, I found camp calm and quiet — Lucas was bent over the stove fiddling with a small fire, and Willow was snoring softly, buried up to her forehead inside her bedroll.

Slipping out of my wet shorts, I laid them out to dry and grabbed my pack.

"So what exactly happened out there?" Lucas whispered. "Willow was, um, kind of upset."

"What always fucking happens. She acts recklessly and then gets pissed off when I try to talk some sense into her."

There was a pause; Lucas took an audible breath. "Logan, she told me what she said. About Dad. You know she didn't mean it, right?"

I resumed digging through my pack, producing the small first aid kit I always carried. It was mostly empty, barring a small tube of disinfectant and a bottle of expired aspirin. Swabbing my leg with disinfectant, I pulled a semi-clean bandanna from my bag and tied it tightly over the gash.

"Here," I muttered, tossing the kit at Lucas. "Make sure Willow cleans her leg."

"Yeah, thanks." Lucas cleared his throat. "Uh, you know, things seem to be getting really bad between you two. I just don't think we can… you know… afford to have another year like the first."

I glanced up sharply. "What are you saying?" I demanded. "Are you actually suggesting that I would do something like Dad—"

"No!" Lucas shouted, startling us both. "How could you even think that?" he demanded. "I only meant how screwed up everything was after that—how screwed up we all were. You guys were always fighting back then too… and now you're fighting again."

"Luke." I sighed my brother's name, suddenly feeling twice as exhausted. "Everything is still screwed up. Everything is always going to be screwed up. Look around you—look at this shithole we're squatting in. Jesus, *look at us*. We're hungry, filthy and just barely getting by. We're a fucking mess—everything is a goddamn, motherfucking mess."

Lucas was silent for a moment, chewing on his lip rings. "I get what you mean," he said softly. "But I don't think it's that bad. We're alive, right? I know I'm okay as long as I have you guys."

I stared at him, unable to think up a response that wasn't crass or cruel. Lucas only felt that way because he had Willow, someone he loved who he could share this hell on earth with. If our roles were reversed, I knew he'd feel differently.

"I'm going to sleep," I eventually muttered. "Do you think you can keep watch for me?" When Lucas nodded, I turned away.

Stretching out over my bedroll, I prayed for oblivion.

I woke to hushed whispers and muffled giggles. I'd slept for a few hours at least, judging by the darkened state of things. The stove was still going—I could hear the crackle of the fire and see the flicker of the flames dancing along the wall.

"You said that part already," Lucas was saying.

"Oh-ho, I'm so sorry," Willow replied around a yawn. "What are you—the Wonderland police?"

"Yep. Now, are you ready for your sentence?"

"Sentence!" Willow feigned outrage. "But there hasn't even been a verdict!"

"Sentence first," Lucas replied solemnly. "Verdict later."

Reciting the story of *Alice in Wonderland* was something Willow had started doing during our first year on our own. When she'd been scared or had a hard time falling asleep she'd start whispering the lines; Lucas would often join in, adding his own nonsense to the story in an attempt to make her laugh. As the years passed, what had begun as a comfort had since become an obnoxious ritual. They told the stupid story so goddamn often that I now knew it by heart, even their silly versions. Like the one they were currently telling, where Alice was Alastair, the most infamous Drag Queen of Wonderland, and the Queen of Hearts was actually the Queen of Farts, having obtained her power by stealing and eating all the beans in all the land. There was no need for beheading in this adaptation—this queen could kill with a single toot of her most lethal butt-trumpet. Hearing them, it would have been easy to mistake them for children, not the twenty something adults they really were.

I didn't need to turn around to know that Willow was nestled between my brother's legs, and Lucas's arms were wrapped around her, his chin resting on top of her head. They'd been sitting that way for years — on our family room floor while watching television, in the school hallway during their free periods, and at my football games, under the bleachers, completely oblivious to the world around them. The comfort they found in each other, the ease in which they interacted, was completely foreign to me. I'd never been like that with anyone, not with any girlfriend, not even with my own mother.

"Twinkle, twinkle little bat, how I wonder where you're at..." Willow trailed off with another yawn. They continued on, each of them murmuring different lines, no longer following any sort of order. Lucas was the last to speak before the room eclipsed into silence. I waited several minutes and was about to roll over when I heard the distinct smack of a kiss, followed closely by the rustling of a sleeping bag.

I went still, hoping they weren't about to have sex... even as some small, depraved part of me wished they would. Willow couldn't be quiet if her life depended on it, and the way she always panted during sex, those muffled mewling noises she always made... I was getting hard just thinking about it.

I squeezed my eyes shut and ground my teeth together, trying to think of anyone but Willow. Only my lust-addled brain had become a broken record that kept skipping straight back to her.

It doesn't mean anything. I was just pent up in more ways than one. It had been years since I'd been with anyone — Willow had been the only girl in my life for so long now, of course it was her I was focusing on. It didn't actually mean anything — other than I was becoming desperate.

It definitely didn't mean that I *liked her.*

"You know, I used to pray that we'd fallen down a rabbit hole. That none of this was real and someday we'd find our way back home." Willow's voice was thick with sleep and heavy with melancholy. "…which is super funny considering how much I hated it there."

"Aw, come on, Will. Asheville wasn't all bad."

"Maybe not for you — *Lucky Logan*'s little brother."

My jaw locked at the mention of my old nickname, given to me by my high school football coach. I hadn't liked it then, and I definitely didn't like it now.

Lucas chuckled. "Like that mattered. He's always been better at everything. No one even noticed me."

"I noticed you."

"No way. I noticed you first. Everyone noticed you."

Lucas and Willow hadn't always been friends, and I never paid her any attention until she'd started hanging around Lucas — but by then she'd been hard to miss. She'd gone from being virtually invisible to the one and only twelve-year-old in town with a nose ring and dressing in anything that would draw attention to her — typically the most flamboyant, ridiculous getups she could find. Lucas quickly followed suit, first with the attention-seeking clothing and then later with the self-mutilation.

Our father's reaction to Lucas's lip rings still instilled the same amount of fury in me that it had initially. He'd only laughed at Lucas, called him a few colorful names, and went back to his booze. But if it had been me that had come home with lip rings, they would have been ripped straight from my face, and that would have been the least of it. Lucas liked to make it sound like he'd had it rough, when, in reality, no one had ever expected or demanded a single thing from him. He'd been free from all of our father's expectations... and condemnations.

"Not in a good way," Willow replied. "Everyone hated me."

"I didn't hate you."

"You don't count. You like literally everyone."

"No. I just don't *hate* everyone."

"I don't hate everyone. I just don't *like* everyone."

They laughed softly, their laughter eventually fading into comfortable sighs, sounding so goddamn in sync with one another that every muscle in my body tensed with the sudden urge to destroy something. Yet, I remained as I was—stock-still and glaring at the wall and feeling so goddamn empty. Gapingly empty. Like my chest was a cavernous hole. And angry, too—helplessly angry, unsure if I was angry because I felt empty or if I felt empty because all I could seem to feel was angry. Whichever it was, I couldn't get a handle on it.

Was this how my dad had felt—constantly angry and empty? Were those feelings why he'd never had a kind word for anyone, and why he'd drunk himself into a nightly stupor? A brief pang of pity for the man quickly mutated into a hot, roiling wave of disgust. I would not be wasting a single second pitying that piece of shit and I'd be damned before I allowed any part of his poisonous existence to take root inside me.

I took a deep, shaking breath. I needed to clear my head, and the only way that was going to happen was if I could have some real time for myself—more specifically, time away from Willow. My thoughts spun in circles—this farmhouse was safe enough, wasn't it? It was definitely the soundest structure we'd come across in months. Maybe I could leave them here to scout ahead for a few days? The more I thought about it, the more attractive the idea became.

It wasn't as if I hadn't ever left them on their own before.

And they were adults, after all, *right, Willow?*

FIVE

WILLOW

"Go over it one more time," Logan demanded.

It was dawn, the sun just barely cresting on the horizon. Everything was wet and covered in debris from yesterday's storm; mud and leaves and broken branches as far as the eye could see. The three of us stood on the crumbling walkway in front of the farmhouse—Logan strapped in full gear, alert and eager, while Lucas and I were slumped and disheveled, having just rolled out of bed.

Logan had woken us just minutes ago, informing us of his decision to scout ahead on his own. This wasn't entirely unheard of; Logan had, on occasion, left us alone in order to do some solo exploration. Yet, there was something that felt distinctively off about this; it had come out of nowhere and Logan never did anything without careful, calculated consideration.

"We need to stay in the house as much as possible," Lucas replied cheerfully, despite having to repeat himself for a third time at Logan's behest. "And keep our weapons on us at all times."

"And be quiet," Logan added.

"And only sleep inside and make sure the room is barricaded while we're sleeping."

"And be quiet," Logan growled.

"And make sure to boil the water before drinking it."

"And be fucking quiet!" Logan exploded.

"Bro, that's the opposite of quiet," Lucas replied lightly, giving his brother a friendly knock on the shoulder.

There was a beat of silence while Logan glowered at something off in the distance and Lucas tried to nervously smile everything away. I could only stand there with my arms folded over my chest, neither glaring nor smiling, wishing Logan would leave already. I was sick of him, but also sick over what I'd said to him.

And maybe you should stop acting like your father! Replaying the moment over in my head, I inwardly cringed. Their father had been a cold, cruel monster of a man and although Logan wasn't exactly a warm and friendly person, I would never call him cold or cruel. Room temperature, maybe; grumpy as hell, definitely, and with all the personality of a bologna sandwich… but not at all like their father. Not even close.

"We'll be fine," Lucas said. "It's not like you haven't left us on our own before."

"And how many times have I shown up just in time," Logan bit out. "Because I've lost count."

I had to fight against the urge to roll my eyes. In Logan's warped mind, every little thing Lucas and I did constituted as a near-crisis. Like the time Lucas had fallen into a dried-up creek bed and sprained his ankle — nothing else had happened, and we hadn't been in any immediate danger. Three summers later, Logan was still bringing it up.

"We're not kids anymore," I snapped before I could stop myself.

Two sets of ocean blue gazes shot to me, one narrowed in accusation, one wide and imploring, begging me to back off.

"Then fucking act like it," Logan snapped back.

"I would if you'd let me!" I yelled, nearly stamping my foot. Lucas hurried to grab my hand, squeezing it tightly. "We'll be fine," Lucas said to Logan, still squeezing my hand. "Right, Willow?"

"Yes," I bit out. "We'll be fine — just go."

Logan's expression hardened considerably, his cold gaze turning downright icy. "Sleep inside," he said, facing Lucas. "Barricade the damn door. Boil the water. Keep your weapons on you at all times and be fucking quiet."

Ever the peacekeeper, Lucas flashed Logan another placating smile. "Barricade, boil, be quiet — you got it. And you be safe out there, okay?"

Logan gave Lucas a single sharp nod before turning away. As he started down the overgrown walkway, I ripped my hand free from Lucas's and rushed back inside the house. Climbing inside my sleeping bag, I ducked my face beneath the soft, raggedy material and closed my eyes. I was glad to be rid of Logan, happy that Lucas and I could be on our own for a little while — only instead of reveling in those feelings, it was my guilt that was taking center stage. And wasn't that just like Logan — leaving me too upset to even enjoy his absence.

The familiar thud of Lucas's steps preceded him down the hall; entering the office, he sat down on the floor beside me, leaning into me. "He's just going through something," Lucas said. "I know he's worse than usual, but he's just stressed and… and going through something…" Lucas trailed off, sounding helpless.

We were all going through something—the whole goddamn world was going through something. But that didn't give Logan the right to keep treating me as if I were an inconvenience. As if he wished I wasn't here at all.

Pushing the sleeping bag away from my face, I looked up at Lucas. "Do you ever think about going our own way?" It wasn't the first time I'd conjured up the idea of ditching Logan, but it was the first time I'd voiced it.

Lucas blinked. "What—like away from Logan?"

"I'm not saying we just up and leave him in the middle of nowhere," I hurried to amend. "Just that once we find somewhere decent, maybe we could venture out on our own. Luke—we've never been on our own. Remember all our plans—we were going to travel the world!"

The girl I used to be reared her rebellious head—the girl who'd been trapped inside a small stifling town, governed by a set of rules that had never made sense to her. That town and those rules were long gone and yet I was still feeling trapped—trapped by Lucas's stifling big brother and governed by another set of rules that also didn't make sense to me.

"It's not like we can just hop a plane to Europe. It's really dangerous out there." Lucas shook his head, his eyebrows tangling into a deep frown. "And where would we even go? And how would we stay in contact with Logan?"

I opened my mouth only to close it, my chest deflating along with my excitement. "You're right," I replied mutely. "I don't know what I was thinking." Feeling the sudden urge to cry, I ducked my head back beneath the sleeping bag.

"Aw, come on, Will, don't be like that—things will get better soon, I promise."

"I'm fine," I muttered from beneath the sleeping bag. "Just tired."

Lucas fell quiet; several minutes passed in silence, the temperature inside my sleeping bag growing uncomfortably hot. Just when I thought I couldn't take another stifling breath, Lucas suddenly got to his feet. As the door to the room clicked shut behind him, I shoved out of the sleeping bag. Glowering up at the ceiling, I wondered if Lucas was going to want to follow all of Logan's ridiculous rules, leaving us trapped inside this hot, musty hellhole for however long it took for Logan to return.

The office door banged open and I shot upright; Lucas stood in the doorway, wearing only his boxers and untied boots, balancing what looked to be a cupboard door in his hand. He had a dirty dish towel draped over one arm and several hastily pulled wildflowers trapped between his teeth, the dirt-covered roots dangling near his chin.

"No, nmpo, waitmn, noj," Lucas mumbled around the mouthful of flowers.

"What was that?" I laughed, grinning as he placed the cupboard door on my lap. Nestled into the cupboard's decorative indentations, a handful of grapes and two chocolate cake rolls awaited me.

Pulling the flowers from his mouth, he held them out in offering. "*Je m'appelle*, Lucas," he said, mimicking a French accent. "*Tu t'appelle comment!*"

"I have no idea what I just said," Lucas continued. "It's all I could remember from French class. It sounded fancy, though."

Laughing, I raised the flowers to my nose. "I'm pretty sure you just asked me what my name is."

He flashed me a suggestive smile, a single dimple popping in his left cheek. "Well, what is it?"

Tossing a grape in my mouth, I tapped a finger to my cheek. "Hmm—"

"No, don't tell me!" he interrupted. "It's Williemae, isn't it? Yep, it's Williemae—you look like a Williemae."

"I most certainly do not!" I exclaimed, throwing a grape and hitting him square in the forehead. About to throw another, Lucas caught my hand and leaned over me, pressing a kiss to my lips.

"Guess what?" he whispered.

I smiled against his lips. "What?"

"Logan's not here… so we don't have to be quiet."

"But didn't he say, and I'm quoting here, to *be fucking quiet*?"

Lucas chuckled. "Who's gonna make us?"

"You rebel!" I laughed, shoving the tray aside.

We kissed eagerly; Lucas's hands skimmed my sides before gently pushing me onto my back. Climbing over top of me, he hooked his fingers into the straps of my tank top, sliding them down my arms while trailing soft kisses across my neck and breasts. Tangling my fingers into his long waves, I closed my eyes.

This was Lucas in his purest form—gentle and loving and forever thinking of me. I swallowed hard, hoping that this one time he might be a little less gentle with me. That perhaps, instead of softly stroking the curve of my hip like he was, he would grab it, squeeze it even, and hold me still. Or maybe, instead of the way he was tenderly fusing our bodies together, he might roughly spin me around, his body colliding with mine in a heated frenzy.

Opening my eyes, I found Lucas looking down at me, his gaze filled with lustful adoration. "I love you," he whispered, his lips splitting into a smile that was almost shy.

Swallowing back my desires, I cradled his head in my hands and pulled his mouth back to mine.

"How do you think they died?"

Swinging our legs to and fro, Lucas and I sat side by side on the tree branch that had grown through the master bedroom. Empty grapevines and torn cake roll wrappers cluttered the floor beneath our feet.

It had been two days since Logan's departure, and after another lackluster search of the house and an unfortunate run-in with a wasp nest in the attic, we'd run out of things to do. I wasn't complaining, though—I was more than content to bum around for a few days, and damn near ecstatic that Logan wasn't here to bully us about it.

Gazing at the skeletal remains on the bed, Lucas chewed on his lip rings. "I don't know. I'm betting they weren't bitten." He shrugged. "So maybe they were sick with something? Or maybe they stumbled across this place just like we did. Only when they got here they decided that they didn't want to live in a world like this."

"You haven't ever thought about *that*, have you?" I asked slowly.

"No," Lucas replied, making a face. Glancing at me, his expression quickly sobered. "You?"

There had been times when I'd wished for death—but they were tangled times, trapped inside a multitude of trauma and pain. Thinking back, I found I couldn't always differentiate between what had been real and what had been something my overloaded brain had simply conjured up. So I didn't discuss them, not even with Lucas.

"No way!" I replied with a bit too much forced enthusiasm. "Can't die before I get to go to Europe, can I?"

Lucas watched me closely for several seconds, his gaze softening. "Hey," he said, nudging me with his elbow. "Wanna get out of here for a little bit? Go exploring?"

I shot off the branch, tugging Lucas down with me. "Yes, please, let's get out of here!"

"We can't go too far," he warned, as I was pulling him down the stairs. "And we definitely can't tell Logan. Willow—are you listening to me?"

"Nope!" Dragging him across the office, I climbed up onto the windowsill, leaping into the grass below. Lucas landed beside me, both of us scrambling to our feet.

"Tag!" I yelled, punching Lucas in the shoulder as I took off running. "You're it, Lucille!"

My heart thumping wildly in my chest, my legs and arms pumping hard and fast. Yet, despite my best effort, Lucas quickly gained on me, his long legs eating up the distance between us with infuriating ease.

"Tag!" He laughed, his warm breath tickling my ear as he leaned in and tugged on my braids. Passing me, he called over his shoulder, "Gotta be quicker than that, Williemae."

"Don't call me that!" I shouted after him. "Locus-Pocus!"

Lucas passed the garden shed, disappearing behind a grove of thick oaks and bushy pines. I followed after him, the forest canopy making the air refreshingly cooler. Slowing, I sucked in deliberate breaths, breathing in the woodsy scents, much preferable to the stale, musty air inside the farmhouse.

We carried on running, weaving around clusters of blooming magnolia trees, leaping over dried creek beds, our surroundings quickly becoming little more than a blur of browns and greens. It felt so good to run—to be so well rested and well fed that we had the energy to even want to run.

"Up ahead," Lucas panted, pointing. "Do you see that?"

Following his finger up a steep hill, where light was pouring in through a break in the forest, I grinned and nodded. We turned together, where I managed to shift into first place for only a moment; the higher the hill, the slower I ran. Lucas flashed me a smug smile as he loped ahead, once again reclaiming the lead while I only continued to slow, cursing after Lucas as he ran through the opening into the light. I laughed.

And then he was gone.

Just... *gone.*

One second Lucas had been just ahead of me, grinning over his shoulder, and the next he wasn't. I blinked, my steps faltering, only to find myself face to face with a Creeper who'd stumbled out from behind a nearby tree. Staggering backward, just barely missing its grasping hands, the Creeper heaved forward once more. Another near miss.

I danced around it, pulling my blade from my belt holster, and quickly struck the base of its skull. The sharpened steel slid easily into the soft, fleshy rot and the Creeper ceased moving, its prone body dropping to the forest floor.

Turning toward the light, I called out for Lucas, receiving a garbled growl in response. Spinning around, I caught sight of another Creeper; squirming on its stomach, both its legs dragging uselessly behind it, it was clawing its way across the ground through the grass.

Cursing, I ran for the light, breaching the tree line only to come skidding to a stop. Tottering at the edge of a cliff, my arms pinwheeled as I desperately tried to reclaim my balance, causing me to lose my grip on my knife. As I fell backward onto my ass, the ground crumbled and gave way beneath me, revealing a ravine as deep as it was wide… and teeming with Creepers.

While my blade vanished below and I scrambled for safety, bits of dirt and rock flying in every direction, dozens of milky gazes swung upward. Growls and snarls wrought the air as the Creepers clambered forward, trampling one another in a frenzied bid to reach me. My frantic gaze swept up and down the ravine; there were hundreds of them — Creepers as far as the eye could see.

My hands pressed to my heaving chest, I searched the mangled faces of the bulging crowd below. "Luke?" I screamed. "Luke, where are you!"

The ravine had been trapping Creepers for many years now, judging by its occupants' differing stages of decomposition. There'd been a bridge here at some point, too — jagged bits of concrete and rebar jutted out from earth on both sides of the chasm, the actual bridge all but gone.

"Luke!" I wailed his name, fearing the worst.

The Creeper with the broken legs crawled through the forest line, growling in earnest as it continued its desperate bid toward me. Tears and sweat blurring my vision, I jogged away from it, keeping along the edge of the ravine.

"Lucas!" I called. "Luke, tell me where you are!"

The growing mass of bodies only continued to surge upward, reanimated corpses barreling over each other until their bony hands were nearly grappling at the dirt near my feet. Worse, the commotion had alerted two more Creepers who'd stumbled from the woods, both of them headed in my direction. My empty hand flexed, missing my blade.

Always carry a backup weapon, Logan's commanding tone echoed in my thoughts. But I'd been so excited to be free of that musty, rotting house, I'd stupidly forgotten the length of pipe I usually carried.

"Lucas?" I screamed his name, my voice breaking on a sob. My time was up; I couldn't stay here, I was attracting too much attention, and without a weapon, I was as good as dead; and yet... how could I leave?

Swiping the tears from my eyes, I rushed the trio of Creepers, shoving the one closest to me and sending it stumbling straight into the ravine. As the activity below grew louder and more agitated, I spun on the second, barreling my fist into its chest — once, twice — it staggered back with each swing of my fist until it was teetering on the edge. One push and it tumbled over into the hungry hands of the dead.

Not bothering with the Crawler, I rushed back the way we'd come, jumping at every noise, checking over my shoulder every other minute, each time expecting to find that the Creepers from the ravine had caught up with me. Though I wanted to, I didn't dare call out for Lucas, afraid of leading the dead back to camp.

As the garden shed came into view, I glanced behind me once more, turning just in time to clip my arm against a tree. Jagged bark cut into the bare skin on my shoulder and arm. Biting back the cry that threatened, I gripped my arm and picked up my pace.

Pulling myself up through the office window, I tumbled into the room, grasping for the weapons we'd forgotten to bring with us. Once I was fully suited up, I forced myself to stand, fear making me dizzy.

"I'm coming, Lucas," I whispered, climbing back through the window.

Lucas, Lucas, Lucas! As I ran back through the woods, I chanted his name like a mantra, like a prayer, like a fevered wish that this had all been just a bad dream and that he would be there at the ravine when I returned, waiting for me with a smile on his beautiful face.

SIX

LOGAN

*S*tanding on the edge of a street corner, I assessed the desolate scene before me. Hollowed-out shops cast long shadows across a crumbling two-lane road. Ahead, a streetlight lay on its side in the center of the intersection. Nearby, a busted sign swung idly from its chain.

Behind me loomed a familiar-looking barricade—a two-story monstrosity composed of stacked cars and concrete highway dividers with a multilayered soft-fence middle. It was nearly identical to the barricade the National Guard had erected around my hometown back when this nightmare had first begun. And it was the same ugly structure I'd seen erected around almost every other town I'd come across since.

The farmhouse we'd found wasn't as isolated as I'd initially thought—something I'd quickly learned only a few miles into my journey down the highway when I'd come across a second farmhouse. And another half dozen miles later, another one. Eventually the long distances between homes began to lessen, as did the size of the homes, until the houses became virtual carbon copies of one another, with only a driveway and small sliver of lawn between each. I continued on through several neighborhoods, eventually finding my way here—Main Street in the Town of Elkins Point, population 8,216, according to the welcome sign I'd passed on the road in.

My tire iron firmly in hand, I started down the sidewalk, pausing to glance inside each storefront. It was rare to find a town this empty, even small towns like this one. In fact, there'd been a distinct lack of Creepers in these parts, something that should've been cause for celebration... only, I found it concerning. Creepers, unless caught up in a moving horde, tended to congregate in places just like this—once populated areas. I didn't know whether it was muscle memory—some leftover spark of who they'd been—or simply because towns were remnants of people and people were their favorite prey. And yet, I hadn't seen a single Creeper since the two at the house—the ones Willow and I had disposed of.

Willow.

Just leave, she'd said.

It had taken me all of yesterday and the better part of today to find this place and I was still seething. It would serve her right if I did leave—leaving her to fend for herself for the first time in her life. She wasn't without skills but she was for damn sure without sense and I didn't doubt she would make it little more than a week without my direction. Lucas either.

I closed my eyes briefly. Of course, I could never leave my brother behind. It wasn't his fault he was so impressionable, and so goddamn softhearted. And in love with a raging bitch.

Peering into a shattered storefront, CAROLE'S CAFÉ painted boldly overhead, I climbed inside. Snaking around toppled furniture and scattered dishes, I made my way to the back of the store where its display counters had been smashed and cupboard doors ripped from their hinges. The cash register, torn from its wires, lay upside down on the floor, its drawer open and its contents long gone.

Ducking beneath the bar flap, I muscled my way through a door marked EMPLOYEES ONLY — a tight squeeze due to a heavy shelving unit tipped on its side, blocking the door from fully opening. Finding myself inside a kitchen, I gazed at the various pots, pans, and stacks of dishes piled on the work surfaces. Numerous machines and gadgets that I had no name for lay among them, rusted into oblivion. The entire room was dusty, but otherwise undisturbed. Standing there, envisioning steam rising from the pots, hearing the clang of dishes being stacked, the din of the employees rushing around, I felt as if I were standing in the middle of two worlds, toeing the line between before… and after.

And I hated it.

I didn't want to see the before; I didn't want to look at what could have been, at everything this world had taken from me.

"That's what you get," I muttered.

That's what you get! Those four words pounded through my thoughts like a battering ram, wreaking havoc on my emotions, upending a tornado of memories.

I was seven years old again. My father, knees bent, hands on his thighs, shouting in my face, *you hear me, you disrespectful little shit — that's what you fucking get!* And then he wasn't just shouting, he was gripping a handful of my shirt and he was shaking me so hard that my front teeth broke.

Just go...

"Fuck you," I growled with a heavy, panting breath.

You're just like your father...

"*Fuck you.*" Anger surging. I sent the tire iron smashing into a stack of dishes, sending plates flying across the room in different directions.

I was fourteen years old and this time we were eye to eye and toe to toe. I could smell the gin on his breath. And this time he wasn't shouting, he was screaming. And instead of shaking me, he curled his hand into a fist and smashed his knuckles into my nose, breaking it.

A spike of adrenaline and a second surge of anger came crashing together in the center of my chest, swooping upward in a breathless rush.

"Fuck you and this fucking world!" I roared, and swung again, sending the socket end of the tire iron into a nearby coffee maker. Iron collided with metal, the painful reverberations of which I felt echo up and down my arm.

Hell, yes, that felt good!

I swung again at another stack of dishes, sending an explosion of broken shards down the countertop. Another surge of adrenaline shot through me, a heady rush twice as potent as its predecessor.

I swung again and again, in front of me, behind me. I was a human-shaped tornado, nothing but a spinning gust of anger, destroying without rhyme or reason. Somewhere in the back of my mind, I knew that I was making too much noise, that I needed to be fucking quiet like I preached about endlessly, only I couldn't seem to care just then. Maybe I'd finally snapped.

Like father, like son, I thought bitterly.

I continued swinging and smashing my way around the room until not a single surface remained untouched, until the floor was covered in broken bits and I had kicked up so much dust and debris that I was choking on it. Breathing hard, sweat dripping down my face and back, my arms fell limply to my sides. Surveying my ruins, I felt a sense of satisfaction that the room matched the rest of things now — utterly fucking destroyed.

Ceramic shards and slivers of glass crunched beneath my boots as I retreated from the kitchen, my tire iron dragging noisily behind me. Righting a toppled table and chair, I relieved myself of my pack and sat down hard. Droplets of sweat fell from my face, splashing down on the grubby tabletop, out of sync with the slow pitter-patter of blood dripping from my right hand. I had no idea how I'd cut myself, nor did I care. Squeezing my hand into a fist, the blood dripped faster.

I felt strangely detached and oddly drunk. My muscles were tense but also heavy with fatigue; my thoughts were exceptionally blank for the first time in a long time — maybe the first time ever. Energy still thrummed through me, my wild pulse still visible in my veins. Yet, if I were to close my eyes, I wondered if I might fall asleep.

I have no idea how long I sat there like that — unwilling, or maybe even unable, to move. There were moments that felt as if minutes were dragging past at a snail's pace, and moments where it seemed as if entire hours had flown by without notice. Even after the sun had dropped behind the buildings, knowing full well that it would be dark soon, I still didn't move.

Then, as the last vestiges of light streaking dimly across the ravaged shop began to fade, I heard something — a faint scratching noise off in the distance.

I went stock-still, waiting to hear it again. *Scraaaatch-scraaaatch.*

Rising from the chair, I moved to the front of the building, peering outside.

Scraaaaatch-scraaaaatch.

Whatever it was, it was growing louder. Closer.

Scraaaatch-scraaaatch.

Scraaaaatch-scraaaaatch.

I glanced up and down the street, unable to pinpoint its location. The otherwise silence served as an echo-chamber, making the sound seem as if it were coming from every direction.

Scraaaatch-scraaaatch. Scraaaaatch-scraaaaatch.

The stink of it reached me first—the same putrid stench all the dead carried with them—and moments later a figure emerged from behind an abandoned delivery truck. It limped across the street, its left leg and what remained of its left foot—a bony stub being dragged across the concrete—was the source of the scratching noise.

It continued toward me, soon close enough for me to fully appreciate the sheer horror of its face. Its eyes were milky white—a sign of just how old it was—and the skin around its jaw had been shredded and left hanging in rotten, shriveled ribbons.

I glanced back at the table where my tire iron lay and was debating on whether to kill it or let it pass by, when a familiar sounding hum gave me pause. There was a shout, followed by the sound of tires squealing. As the Creeper swung in the direction of the approaching commotion, I dropped down into a crouch, ducking back behind the wall.

A military Jeep was speeding down the street, flanked by two motorcycles. All three vehicles slowed as they passed the Creeper, encircling it.

"Shit," I whispered, counting six—no, seven people. All of

them were armed.

"Y'all, I got this," a gritty, feminine voice drawled. One of the motorcyclists climbed off their bike; helmeted, with a long blonde braid hanging down her back, she wore a tight red leather jacket that showed off her ample curves.

Instead of using the sawed-off shotgun strapped to her back, she pulled a wooden baseball bat from her saddlebag and charged the Creeper, swinging with all the skill and grace of a pro ballplayer. The bat clipped the Creeper under its chin, shattering whatever jawbones were still intact, and sending it staggering backward. Despite its injuries, it quickly regained its purpose and began careening toward her once again.

"That's it, sugar," she taunted, crooking a gloved finger. "Come to mama."

"Britta!" the driver of the Jeep called out. He was a heavily bearded man wearing military-style camouflage; standing in his seat, his elbows were perched on the top of the roll cage—an impressive DIY made from steel tubing and heavy-duty fencing. "We're burnin' diesel and daylight—hurry up and kill that fucker!"

"Patience, Davey—jeez loueez. How many times I gotta tell ya that killin' is an art form?"

"Your art is gonna make me late for dinner."

At that, titters of laughter rose from the group.

"It's beef stew tonight, Brit," another man called out. "You wouldn't make a man miss his favorite meal now, would ya?"

Ignoring her companions, Britta swung again, this time catching the Creeper on the side of its face. It folded to one side, toppling over. Unable to get back up again, it began a pitiful crawl forward. Britta backed away slowly, humming a familiar-sounding tune, and swinging the bat around like a baton twirler in a marching band.

The loud crack of a bullet ejecting from its chamber made us both jump — Britta and me. On the ground, the Creeper lay unmoving, brain matter seeping from the newly smoking hole in its skull. The second motorcyclist had dismounted their bike and was currently tucking their pistol back inside their chest holster. Removing their helmet, a fair-skinned face was revealed, with messy, short brown hair cut into a pixie style.

"Dagnabbit, Lei!" Britta huffed. "You've gone and spoiled my fun again."

"You know I hate when you play with them," Lei replied. Her tone was gentle, yet commanding, and with no trace of the accent that both Britta and Davey possessed.

"Quit your whining, Harley Quinn, and help me load the body." The man who'd expressed worry over missing his dinner sauntered past Britta, smirking. He was a big guy, well built, who looked to be in early to mid-thirties, but what really struck me was his clean-shaven face. In fact, all of them were well groomed and clean; even their vehicles were clean. It all made sense now — why this town was so tidy, and why there weren't any Creepers hanging around anywhere. Whoever these people were, I was positive that they had a pretty nice setup somewhere nearby.

The man stopped suddenly, abruptly glancing in my direction. Reflexes in check, I dropped down. His steps picked up again, growing louder as he headed toward me. Heart pounding, I held my breath, my hand poised to grab the gun tucked into my belt. I'd shoot him if I had to, though I doubted I'd get very far with six armed people on my tail, and with vehicles at their disposal. Still, I'd never go down without a fight.

"What's the holdup, Joe — you see somethin' in there?"

The footsteps halted. "Thought I did," Joe murmured, too close for comfort. He was standing directly on the other side of the wall, mere inches from me. All he would have to do was lean in through the broken storefront and look to his right.

"Probably just a critter. I'm guessin' that's what the Dead Head here was chasin' after."

"Yeah, maybe." Though Joe sounded uncertain, his footsteps resumed, fading in the opposite direction. Sagging against the wall, I blew out a silent breath.

"Alright, you fools, that's that—street's clean! Let's giddyap 'fore Joshua locks us out for the night!"

"Oh, please, Davey-cakes." Britta laughed. "He would never lock his missus out here—would he, Lei?"

"The rules are the rules." Lei's voice still held some of her previous command, but there were traces of humor now, too.

Peeking around the wall, I watched Britta mount her bike, revving her engine. She was the first to pull away, followed closely by Lei, with the Jeep bringing up the rear. Making a U-turn at the barricade, they sped off down the street.

Jumping up, I hurried to grab my things. I wouldn't be spending the night here now, not with armed people patrolling the goddamn streets. First lesson learned at the end of the world was not to trust anyone… not even your own parents.

I ran back the way I'd come, this time keeping off the roads. That evening, I ended up setting up camp inside a semi-remote home just outside of town. It wasn't optimal; camp consisted of a loosely barricaded garage, where I managed only a few broken hours of shut-eye in the back seat of a rusted-out Chevy Cavalier.

Come sunup, I resumed walking, still keeping off the roads, hoping to minimize leading anyone back with me. I stopped to eat only once, and cut my normal respite times in half, hoping to make it back before nightfall.

As the sun was setting on the third day of my journey, I finally breached the property line of the farmhouse. Circling around to the back of the home, I could see that the office window was open, and no one was manning it. Shaking my head, I announced my arrival with a quick two-finger whistle.

Unsurprisingly, no one answered.

Reaching for the windowsill, I hauled myself inside. As I'd suspected, neither Lucas nor Willow were here.

"Jesus Christ," I gritted out. Camp was a disaster — bedrolls and clothing had been haphazardly tossed around. Packages of food lay strewn about, grapes were smashed on the floor, ants trailing over top of them. Worse, the door to the room had been left open.

Dropping my gear, I headed into the hall and whistled once more. Again, no one answered. Knowing that they had to be here somewhere, I began searching the house. Not even Lucas and Willow were so thoughtless as to venture out near nightfall unless absolutely necessary, and definitely not without their gear.

When I'd finished combing through the house, I stood in the foyer, the sinking sensation in my stomach doubling. I was seconds away from freaking out when I heard a loud thump. Relief flooding me, I darted down the hall and burst into the office, ready to tear into them for not listening to me. *Again.*

Willow shrieked when she saw me and staggered back a few steps. "L-Logan," she whispered hoarsely.

I knew right away that something wasn't right — Willow was uncommonly dirty and far more disheveled than was typical. She'd been crying too; tear tracks lined her face, streaks of wet through the grime on her cheeks and chin.

"Where's Luke?" I asked slowly, noting that she was alone.

Willow opened her mouth and then seemed to freeze that way. She stared at me, her expression quickly crumbling. Bending forward, gripping her stomach as if it hurt her, she opened her mouth again, releasing a noise that sounded as if a sob were trying to claw its way out of her throat.

"Willow," I growled, rushing to her. Gripping her arms, I noticed that one of them was bleeding, the skin around the scratch-like wounds on her shoulder was angry and swollen. Nausea rose in my stomach, burning a fast track up my chest and into my throat.

"Willow," I rasped. "Were you bit?"

She raised her trembling chin, her shell-shocked gaze locking with mine. "I... lost him. Luke is—" She took a gasping breath, releasing it with a shudder that seemed to take all the energy from her. As her knees buckled, she whispered hoarsely, "He's gone— Luke is gone."

SEVEN

WILLOW

Rocks loosened and crumbled beneath my feet, skittering down the steep side of the ravine, each of them landing with resonating thuds that seemed to echo from all around. Scrambling for a sturdier ledge, I paused to swipe the gathering perspiration from my eyes. Sweat clung to every inch of me, making my clothes stick uncomfortably. My arms and legs ached terribly, my left leg especially, as I struggled to keep my balance and my muscles strained to keep me still. My leg was infected—courtesy of the injury I'd sustained during the violent rainstorm. For the last several nights I'd done my best to try and clean it, though my ministrations only seemed to make the wound angrier. Today, the painful throbbing had seemed to have taken on a life of its own.

"Not so fast!" Logan shouted from below — the canyon nothing more than a silent, empty abyss. The hundreds of Creepers had disappeared; though how they'd escaped their rocky confines, we hadn't figured out. "You've got to go slow!"

For four days I'd searched for Lucas — three of them with Logan. Four days, three nights, and a handful of hours spent combing the woods around the ravine, searching up and down the highway near the farmhouse, and in and around the house itself, hoping Lucas might return there. We didn't sleep, we hardly ate, and we rarely spoke — we only searched and searched and yet, there was still no sign of him. It was as if he'd vanished into thin air. Eventually, after plenty of begging on my end, Logan finally agreed to attempt crossing the ravine in order to search the other side.

"Whatever," I mumbled, the single word barely audible. I resumed my descent, this time slower; arms and legs quivering with exertion, I ensured my fingers found purchase in the more substantial rocks jutting from the ravine wall. As my feet finally hit the ground, my left leg buckled, forcing me to cling to the wall until I was steady. Breathing through the pain, I briefly considered telling Logan about my leg, dismissing the thought almost immediately. He was angry enough as it was, and there'd be time for that later... after we searched the ravine.

Logan stood in the center of the ravine, his arms folded across his chest, his eyes narrowed, surveying our new surroundings. Remnants of the horde lay all around us; the earth was trampled — small trees lay crushed, not a single flower or blade of grass to be found. Nearby, a small stream slushed lazily along, discolored by gore, and clogged with bones and bits of clothing. My muddy gaze bounced nervously around, terrified I might actually find something of Lucas among them.

"Are you sure this is where he fell?" Logan demanded.

My hands knotted into fists. He'd only asked me that question several thousand times, each time growing more and more agitated by my unchanging answer.

"No," I bit out. "I already told you—I didn't see exactly where he fell."

All I'd seen—and I'd never forget it—was Lucas running, grinning over his shoulder, his blond hair blazing gold in the sunlight, just before he dropped out of sight. It was burned forever into my memories.

"It doesn't make sense," he muttered. "A horde that size doesn't just disappear."

"They were climbing on top of each other—maybe they climbed out?"

Logan shook his head. "They couldn't have all climbed out—there'd still be some down here." He'd begun walking away mid-sentence, disappearing behind a rocky overhang. I stared after him, feeling nauseous and fatigued, fighting the urge to sit down where I stood.

"Willow! Get the fuck over here—I found something!"

A jolt of adrenaline forced me to move; I limped quickly along the edge of the stream, following Logan around the large outcropping of boulders.

There was a car there—a rusty four-door sedan, its entire front end resembled an accordion, as if it had been driven full speed off the ledge and smashed headfirst into the gorge below. It had landed in such a way, mostly hidden by the rocky overhang, that it hadn't been visible from above.

"The driver's still in there." Logan yanked fruitlessly on the vehicle's busted door handle. Muttering curses, he divested himself of his pack and pulled a crowbar from his tool belt.

I limped closer, peering through the grime-coated windows. The skeletal remains of the driver remained pinned to their seat, having been crushed by the mangled dashboard.

"The windows on the other side are busted open," Logan called out from inside the car. Having successfully pried the door open, he was rooting around in the back seat. "And there's blood here, too. Not sure how old it is. You think Luke could have fit through here?"

I tried to envision a scenario where Lucas had fallen from a cliff into a ravine full of Creepers and somehow managed to evade the Creepers by slipping into the small space between the car and the rock wall, finding shelter through a half-open window. It seemed impossible... but a lot of things seemed impossible until you're faced with them. And we'd been defying odds for years now.

"He's skinny enough," I agreed quietly. It was a desperately needed sliver of hope to cling to while the rest of me fell to pieces. Chewing the inside of my cheek, I looked over the numerous dried blood smears on and around the car, feeling caught between hoping that it was Lucas's blood, and yet also not wanting to think about what that might mean for him.

"There's nothing here. Let's move." Sliding out of the car, Logan shoved the crowbar back in his belt and pulled on his pack. He marched off without another word or backward glance, his boots pounding the ground with purpose.

Initially, I tried to keep pace with him, but as the hours passed and the temperature continued to rise, my nausea worsened and my steps began to drag until the distance between us was little more than a blur.

"Logan!" I rasped, my words falling on deaf ears.

I attempted picking up my pace only to catch the tip of my boot on a rock. Tripping, I fell hard on my hands and knees. I stayed that way—my eyes squeezed shut, the pebbled ground cutting painfully into my palms, too tired to move.

"Hey," Lucas said. *"Wanna get out of here for a little bit? Go exploring?"*

"Oh my god, yes!"

Lucas laughed as I dragged him from the room. "We can't go too far, and we definitely can't tell Logan! Willow—are you listening to me?"

Nope, I hadn't been.

I *never* listened.

"I should have said no," I whispered, my fingertips digging down into the rocks and dirt. "Why didn't I say no?"

"Willow, what the fuck are you doing?"

My head snapped up. Logan towered over me, the breadth of him providing a nice respite from the brutal sun. Despite every inch of me screaming in protest, I managed to pull myself up, sitting back on my heels. "I feel sick," I said hoarsely.

Logan leveled me with a scathing glare. "Are you fucking kidding me—you feel sick? Jesus, Willow, we have no idea what happened to that horde—what if it's still down here? Do you want to get trapped down here like—" Logan abruptly stopped speaking. Lips pressed together, nostrils flaring, he looked away.

"Like Luke," I whispered.

Turning back to me, his blue eyes blazed with disdain. "Get up," he said sharply. "Let's go."

Limp and listless, I merely stared up at him.

"Get up, Willow," he seethed. "Get the fuck up!"

"Logan, I feel sick. My leg, I think it's—"

"I don't give a shit how you feel!" he roared. Cursing, he roughly fumbled with the buckles on his pack before heaving it away. "Luke is gone, you selfish bitch! He's fucking gone, and you know what? That's on you! Do you hear me, Willow? You fucking did this!"

Logan ran his fingers through his already messy hair, further disheveling it. "He wouldn't've been out here if it weren't for you! He would have stayed in the house like I'd told him to!" Logan's fist swung at the air. "He would have fucking listened if it weren't for you!"

"And now you're gonna sit here and whine about feeling sick when Luke is... when Luke is... " Voice cracking, he trailed off and spun away.

My chin trembled and my eyes blurred. I'd been waiting for this—Logan's inevitable explosion. I'd expected it days ago when he'd first arrived to find Lucas gone. Of course, I'd known Logan would blame me; he blamed me for everything. What I hadn't expected was just how bad his condemnation would feel.

"He just disappeared," I whispered brokenly. "He just... disappeared."

Logan's gaze swung back to me, red-faced, his bloodshot eyes wide with rage. "People don't just disappear! Something happens to them! *Someone* happens to them!"

Pain lanced my insides. My chest heaved, a dry sob erupting from deep within. Somehow, maybe aided by the torment gnawing away at me, I forced myself to stand. Dizzy and in pain, I waited until the world stopped swimming, and then began limping toward the cliff.

"What are you doing?" Logan demanded.

I said nothing, and I didn't dare glance back. Without Lucas, there was nothing here for me—Logan had just made that abundantly clear. Grabbing hold of a long root jutting out from the rocky wall, I called upon every bit of strength I possessed and hauled myself up.

"Willow, what the fuck are you doing?"

My next step crumbled beneath my foot and I slipped back down to the ground, pain radiating up and down my left leg. Fighting back a whimper, I grabbed the root once more. "I'm fucking leaving!" I cried out.

"Leaving?" Logan taunted. "But I thought you felt sick."

Another step crumbled beneath my weight and again I slid down the wall, slapping it in frustration before collapsing against it.

Behind me, Logan began to laugh—a deep, maniacal rumble that beat at me harder than hands ever could. Still holding tightly to the root, I turned to face him. "Stop it!" I hoarsely demanded. "Stop fucking laughing!"

"Oh, this is too much," he sneered. "Where exactly are you going to go, Willow? Better yet, how will you get there? Your sense of direction is shit, and you can't go more than two days without *fucking everything up*."

I took a trembling step toward him, my body aching from head to toe, the pain in my leg causing my eyes to water. Logan watched my approach; no longer laughing, his biceps bulged, his fingers twitching. He looked as if he might want to break something. Like he might want to break *me*. Good. I'd finally had enough of him, too.

"Do it," I rasped, raising my chin. "Go ahead and hit me."

Logan went noticeably still, the hateful look on his face shifting into one of surprise.

I shook my head tightly. "No, you don't get to play dumb! I know you hate me. I know you've always hated me. So do it—hit me!"

Logan, *damn him*, began to turn away.

"No!" I screamed, my grief and fury rebuilding anew—a tsunami of emotions that crashed over me and sent me hurtling toward him.

My palms slapped into his chest. "You. Hate. Me." I emphasized each word with another slap of my hands. "You've always hated me and now Luke is gone and it's all my fault, so just do it! Hit me! Fucking hit me!"

Logan caught my wrists, gripping them painfully. "Stop it," he snarled.

"Do it!" I screamed again, my traitorous voice breaking. "Do it! Do it! Do it!" I struggled in his grip, twisting and thrashing until he released me.

"I said, stop it!" he roared.

"Fuck you!" I screamed hoarsely, coming at him again, pounding on his chest with everything I had. I wanted him to feel what I felt. I wanted it to build up inside of him like it had built up inside of me. And then I wanted him to hit me. Slap me. Shake me. I didn't care which, just that I needed his violent retribution, like I needed air to breathe.

Instead, he only stood there.

He stood there and let me hit him until every last bit of energy I'd scraped together had leached from my body and I was slumped against him, shaking and sobbing and he was gripping my arms, holding me upright.

Once I'd quieted, I'd expected him to shove me away, only we remained locked together—me gripping his shirt, him holding tight to my arms, each of us pressed close enough together that I could feel the heavy vibrations of his heart against my cheek and the low pulse in his fingertips on my arms. We weren't hugging, not even a little bit; we were merely holding one another upright, our grips fierce.

Only when the ground suddenly exploded did we jump apart,

scrambling away from the body of a Creeper that had fallen from above. There was little time to react before another body came crashing to the ground in another messy explosion.

"Time to go!" Logan dove to reclaim his pack.

Backing away from the bodies, I blinked up at the cliff's edge. There was a noise—something that sounded a lot like a hum. Like the buzz of bees, only harsher. The harder I listened, the louder the sound grew.

As a shadow fell over the ravine, blocking out the sun, suddenly bodies began to pour over the edge—a waterfall of living death. *They* were the noise, the hum—a raw symphony of a hundred toneless groans echoing throughout a no longer empty ravine.

"Run!" Logan shouted.

EIGHT

LOGAN

Peering over my shoulder, I found Willow several yards behind me, struggling to keep any sort of pace. Shoulders slumped, head bent, she was visibly limping. Sick or not, she had definitely done something to her leg, though I wasn't about to ask what. We hadn't spoken since she'd been begging me to hit her.

I'd wanted to hit her—I'd wanted to hit her from the moment she'd told me what happened, and every moment since, right up until the moment she'd squared off with me and demanded I do just that. Suddenly all that rage I'd felt did a tire-squealing U-turn and rushed back my way. Every slap, every shove, I deserved them all. Because I knew, deep down, whose fault this really was.

I'd known they wouldn't listen to me—they never fucking did.

I'd known they'd go on acting like the world was their playground instead of the bloodthirsty cesspool it really was. I'd known and yet I'd left them on their own anyway.

It took me a moment to realize my eyes were burning, not from sweat but from tears, and that my chest was on fire; I couldn't seem to take a full breath. Staggering to a stop, I stood in the center of the deep ravine, the sun blazing on the back of my neck, barely breathing, trying to force dry the tears blurring my vision.

I hadn't cried yet, and sure as fuck wasn't going to cry now — not with an entire town of Creepers on my tail, and definitely not in front of Willow. Only the tears didn't seem to care what I wanted — they were coming with or without my permission.

Lucas was gone.

There was no way he'd survived that fall; and even if he had, he wouldn't have survived the Creepers waiting below. Without any sign of him, dead or alive, I was forced to finally admit the painful truth I'd been ignoring for days now — my little brother had been devoured, or he'd become one of the devourers. Either way, *Lucas was gone.*

I couldn't believe it, but I knew I had to accept it or risk losing my mind entirely. Not that I was claiming any sort of sanity to begin with; I just knew that if I kept going like this — not sleeping, not eating, just desperately searching without even a hint of a trail — that it wouldn't be long before this world swallowed me up too.

With a frustrated growl, I started walking again, forcing myself through a bout of grief so stifling it felt as if I were wading through quicksand. With each step forward, my breaths eventually came easier, my steps quicker. Once I had myself under some semblance of control, I glanced back at Willow, blinking in surprise when I didn't immediately spot her. Shading my eyes, finding her sprawled on the ground, my surprise turned quickly to dread.

Running, I skidded to a sliding stop beside her. Untangling her from her pack, I rolled her onto her back, pushing her braids from her face. "Willow! Willow, wake up!"

I could see now that she was still breathing, but it was ragged and dry, and heat was rolling off her skin in hot, heavy waves. Her color was way off—too dark around her eyes, wan over her cheeks and around her mouth.

"Willow?" I lightly slapped her cheeks, trying to rouse her.

Her eyelids fluttered. Her dry lips parted. "I feel sick," she whispered.

"Yeah, I can see that. Is it your stomach—like the flu or something?"

I could count on one hand the number of times each of us had been sick over the years, every one of those times having occurred very early on. Since, we'd only suffered the occasional headache or stomach upset due to either dehydration or expired food products.

Her eyelids fluttered again. "I... don't... know," she rasped with visible effort. "Everything... hurts... but... my leg... bad... "

I scooted down, tugging up the tattered and torn hem of her cargo pants, just barely touching her when she cried out, jerking her leg. Ripping open her pant leg, I sucked in a hard breath. Her entire calf was dark and swollen, covered with angry-looking blisters.

"You didn't clean your wound, Willow," I ground out, though I doubted she'd heard me—her eyes were closed, her features twisted with pain.

Sitting back on my heels, I scrubbed a sweaty hand down my face. There wasn't time for this. It would have been hard enough getting out of here back when we were two abled bodies. The cliff walls were steep, nearly straight up and down surfaces that even a professional climber would struggle with. With Willow incapacitated, I didn't have a fucking clue what to do.

"We should have never come down here," I bit out. I'd initially told her as much, worried that we might not find a way out, but she'd begged and pleaded and—

"And now here we fucking are," I finished angrily.

I thought about leaving her—about getting up and walking away and never looking back. I didn't know where I'd go or what I would do, because what did any of that matter anymore? The only thing that had ever mattered to me, or to Willow, was gone now.

Lucas was gone.

And yet, even as I entertained the idea of walking away, I was already shrugging out of my pack and dumping my things on the ground. I did the same with Willow's belongings, sorting only the bare necessities from each, repacking them quickly into mine.

"Willow, we can't stay here. Willow, come on, wake up!" I gave her cheeks another slap. Groaning, her eyes fluttered again.

"I'm going to pick you up, okay? Ready?" Hooking my hands under her arms, I hauled her upright. "Put your weight on me… stay off your leg… yeah, just like that."

After some painful maneuvering on Willow's part, I had her firmly tucked into my side, my arm wrapped tightly around her waist, holding her up.

"They're… coming," she whispered. "You hear it… the hum…"

I paused, listening. Foremost, I heard Willow's labored breaths; past that, I could make out the trickle of the stream, the caw of a bird, and… yeah, there it was… the not-so-distant buzzing of an approaching horde.

"Go," she said, her breath crackling with the effort it took for her to speak. "I won't blame you. Just leave me and go." Struggling to keep her eyes open, sweat was streaking down her forehead and cheeks in steady streams.

"Shut up," I gritted, shrugging her up higher.

Try as we might to make significant gains, it wasn't long before the sounds of the dead had amplified, signaling that the horde was nearly upon us. Willow was barely walking now; her feet dragging as I pulled her along, my fingers slipping on her sweat-slickened skin.

"Come on," I grunted, summoning all my strength. But it was no good; Willow was little more than deadweight. Behind us, the hum had become a roar; the horde was close enough to smell, the sick scent of their festering bodies permeating the sweltering air.

Laying Willow on the ground, her features gone slack, I hurried to rid myself of my pack, taking only a long length of bungee cord. Tying the rope around Willow's middle, I secured a tight knot at her waist and hoisted her up onto my shoulder. It took a few stumbling tries to manipulate her listless body into a piggyback position; once she was situated on my back, I tied the rope around my middle, using the last bit of it to bind her hands together around my neck, ensuring that she couldn't fall. Glancing at the discarded pack, at what remained of everything we'd painstakingly accumulated over the years, I cursed Willow for forcing us to leave it all behind.

And then I took off running.

NINE

LOGAN

This would not be how it ended for me—trapped in a gorge with a bunch of motherfucking Creepers. It was too goddamn easy a death—like shooting fish in a barrel. I hadn't fought this hard for this long only to end up as a chew toy.

So I ran.

I ran until the trampled ground beneath my heavy footfalls turned green, lush with tall grass and colorfully dotted with wildflowers. I ran until the spring ran clear—the water on this side of the ravine not tainted with human remains. I ran until my muscles were taut and burning, feeling as if they were tearing in two and the strain on my back became so great that I thought it might be breaking.

I jumped at the first climbable stretch of rock I came across, where the ravine wall had given way. Gripping a thick portion of overhang, I hoisted us up onto the ledge. It was only about four feet off the ground and just wide enough to stand on. Feeling the strain of Willow's unsecure weight on my back, I pressed tightly to the wall, trying to catch my breath. Each intake of air felt as if I were sucking down fire.

As I was struggling to climb onto another rocky outcropping, the first few Creepers tumbled into view. Digging my fingertips behind the jagged edges of a car-sized boulder, I dragged myself slowly up and over, a groan ripping free from my swollen throat. Dragging myself to standing, I looked below, finding three Creepers snarling underfoot — Runners by the looks of them. Beyond them, the front end of the horde had surged into view. They'd reach us in no time, trampling one another, climbing over each other until one of them reached us.

Grimacing, I shifted Willow into a slightly more comfortable position on my back and resumed climbing. I managed the next ten feet without incident, helped along by a ten-foot stretch of cracked bedrock that had broken in such a way that offered the ease of steps. Eventually my good luck ran out along with the steps. Gauging the considerable distance between us and the top of the wall, it was mostly a straight shot of smooth rock, with only the tiniest of footholds scattered throughout.

Here goes nothing, I thought, and started climbing. Willow's weight on my back was brutal in this position — each time she shifted even the slightest, I would nearly lose my balance, forcing me to use up precious seconds steadying myself.

Arms quaking with fatigue, eyes blurry and burning, sweat drenching every inch of me, I reached for the next rocky grip and missed it. I was teetering on my barely there foothold, fighting to keep my balance, when Willow's head flopped suddenly to one side, shifting her weight in the other direction.

We fell instantly, scuttling down the wall, crashing hard onto a boulder below. Groaning in pain, I dragged myself upright and peered over the edge, wishing I hadn't. The dirt and debris I'd kicked up during our free fall had sent the horde into an all-out frenzy; I had only minutes before they reached us.

Gritting my teeth against the strain burning fiery pathways across my back, I resumed climbing. My grunts turned to groans, my groans soon becoming breathless heaves as I fought to remain upright despite the weight on my back, and to keep climbing despite the pain.

Eventually my fingertips skimmed the edge. Only a handful of feet away, it taunted me. There was nothing left to grip but the edge itself and I wasn't Superman—I couldn't do a pull-up with a whole other person tied to my back, let alone an unconscious person. Especially not after the grueling workout I'd already endured.

I stood there, balanced precariously on two separate rocks, wondering if this was how it would end—picked off only a few dozen inches from safety. Hell, maybe I deserved such a stupid death; I'd basically offered myself up on a silver fucking platter by coming down here in the first place.

I flinched, shuddering, as the first Creeper to reach the death summit wrapped its hand around my ankle. A surge of adrenaline shot through me, and I gripped the edge of the cliff, digging my fingertips into rock and dirt. Shoving off the footholds, a groan built low in my chest as I struggled to pull our combined weight up the wall; the groan echoing louder as I continued to lift us until it exploded past my gritted teeth in a roar.

Dragging us those final inches to safety, I collapsed onto my side, my chest heaving from exertion, content to never move again. Even as the first set of spindly hands appeared over the edge, I merely blinked at them.

Get up! I ordered myself. *Get the fuck up! You didn't just scale that cliff to die at the top of it!*

I fought to stand; my body shrieking and screaming in protest. Looping my arms beneath Willow's legs, I took off running once again, much slower this time. Staying close to the edge of the ravine, I let it lead me back the way we'd come, only breaking away once I found the gap in the forest that would lead me back to the farmhouse.

Running on empty, forced to push past pain in ways I'd never had to before, I lost myself out there. It wasn't just the physical demands, it was the emotional ones as well; the combination of both requiring me to exist outside my body, outside my pain.

Knowing I didn't have enough strength to get Willow through our window, I entered the farmhouse through the front door, jogging sluggishly through the halls. Our room remained as we'd left it, messy and with Lucas's things still lying around — our things now. The only things we had left.

Collapsing on the floor, my hands were shaking as I fought to loosen the knots at my neck and waist. Bloodied and burning, my fingers couldn't manage it, forcing me to slice the rope with one of my blades. Willow's body thumped to the floor behind me and for several minutes, I just lay there.

Eventually I forced myself to move, staggering as I tried to stand. My head pounding, my vision doubling, I stumbled in a drunken circle, finding Willow still in the tangled heap she'd fallen in. Dropping back down, I checked her pulse — finding it steady, I rolled her onto Lucas's bedroll. Glancing around, I found Lucas's canteen nearby; taking a deep drink, I tried encouraging Willow to do the same, only managing to get a few sips in her while she coughed and sputtered the rest onto the floor. Recalling the expired aspirin in the first aid kit I'd left for Willow, I started rummaging through the messy room, carelessly tossing things aside until I'd found it. After taking a handful of pills for myself, I crushed another handful, sprinkling the broken bits onto Willow's tongue, and then forcing her to drink until she'd swallowed them all. She continued to cough and gag, fighting me despite her semiconscious state.

Once she'd quieted, I began removing her clothing as carefully as I could manage, so as not to disturb her injured leg. Pausing to look at her wound; the skin was swollen and fiery red around the puncture mark, spreading outward. It was already much worse than it had been only an hour before.

Cursing, I set to work washing away the sweat and grime caked on her skin, cleaned her wound, first with water and then dabbing with the remaining disinfectant. Then I cleaned the rest of her, hoping it might help to cool her fever as well. She slept through most of it—periodically moaning in pain and sometimes shivering. After cleaning her, I wrapped one of Lucas's shirts around her injured leg, knotting it loosely in place, then dressed her in a T-shirt and sweatpants. They were both too large for her tiny frame—her hip bones were jutting out, her ribs were clearly visible; Willow looked quite a bit thinner than she'd appeared only days ago. My stomach flipped anxiously; I'd been so consumed with searching for Lucas, I hadn't realized that she hadn't been eating; nor had I noticed how sick she was. Another giant lapse in judgment that could be laid at my feet.

Trembling head to toe from exertion, I collapsed on the floor beside Willow. Bone tired, my vision swimming, I blinked once, twice, and fell into a dreamless sleep.

I awoke with a jolt and I flipped over, relieved to find Willow as I'd left her. She hadn't moved much since I'd cleaned her; her skin was still pale and sickly looking, though her chest continued to rise steadily with each breath. Pressing the back of my hand to her cheek, finding her skin still hot to the touch, I frowned.

Sitting up, groaning as my sore muscles protested, I scrubbed the sleep from my eyes. It was late morning, I assumed, based on the location of the sun. Incredibly, I'd slept straight through the night without waking. Even more incredible was the door I'd forgotten to close and the window I'd never shut.

Idiot, I thought, reaching for the aspirin. I shook a few pills into my mouth, swallowing them dry. Shaking out a few more, I nudged Willow.

"Luke?" she whispered hoarsely, her eyelids fluttering.

Ignoring the pang of pain my brother's name evoked, I helped her sit up, propping her against the wall. Placing the pills on her tongue, I held my canteen to her lips and she drank eagerly.

"How do you feel?" I asked.

Slumped against the wall, she stared groggily across the room, her lips glistening with spilled water. "Bad," she eventually replied in a rough, hushed tone. "Really... bad."

"Yeah..." Sitting back on my heels, I scratched at my beard. "About that... I'm pretty sure your leg is infected—you probably need antibiotics."

"Great," she murmured.

"There's a town nearby," I said. "There might be something there."

Her bloodshot gaze met mine, surprisingly discerning, considering how sick she was. "Funny," she whispered hoarsely.

I dropped my gaze. Her sarcasm was warranted; there was almost zero chance of finding anything resembling medicine. Right after guns and ammunition, medicine had been next on the list of highly coveted items to rapidly disappear from what remained of the world. We still came across the occasional bottle of expired vitamins or over-the-counter pain pills, however, medical-grade pharmaceuticals were long gone.

When I looked up again, Willow's head had rolled back against the wall, her eyes closed once more. With a frustrated sigh, I rose to my feet and scrubbed my hands over my face. If Lucas were here, he would be beside himself, begging me to do whatever it took to help Willow. And he would hate me for how I'd treated her yesterday—for the horrible things I'd said to her.

I found myself pacing the room, eventually making my way into the hallway. I looked around blankly, my heart stuttering in my chest. I had to do something, but what? Searching for antibiotics would be a fool's errand, but I at least had to try. *How though*, I wondered, knowing I couldn't carry her again; currently my sore muscles could barely carry my own weight. Neither could I leave her here—immobile and unable to defend herself.

I found myself in the middle of the kitchen. Hands on my neck, I stared up at the ceiling, wondering how I was going to get from here to the town; wondering how I was going to fix this mess.

Dropping my hands, I barked out a hollow laugh.

I'd never actually fixed anything, not one single thing—our current circumstances were proof enough of that. I'd simply been slapping band-aids over gaping wounds and ignoring the seepage. I was everything my father had said I was going to be—I was just like him: full of holes and utterly helpless to fill them.

Gunshots echoed in my memories—one, two, three. I recalled the look of madness on my father's face shifting to one of surprise. I recalled his hand gripping his chest, as if he could somehow stop his blood from leaving his body.

I recalled having to use a sled to haul his body from the room, and the thump-thump as the sled descended the stairs. I remembered Willow was crumpled on the floor, her young face frozen in horror, and Lucas, with tears streaming down his cheeks, had run from the scene as fast as he could.

Not me though; I hadn't been afraid or in pain.

I'd been angry.

And I'd been angry ever since.

It was the culmination of a life lived under an iron fist, and the by-product of having your world ripped from beneath your feet. And it was the consequences of an eighteen-year-old who'd been forced to take responsibility, not just for himself, for the lives of two other teenagers.

My hand shot out, gripping the countertop.

We'd never had a chance. All these years, traveling across a dozen different states, working us to the bone, I'd only been prolonging the inevitable. This was always how it would end, because none of us had ever truly left that house—Lucas was still gone, Willow was still crumpled on the floor, and I was still angry.

Angry and still dragging my dead father along behind me.

My head jerked, the smothering deluge of emotions instantly clearing. Taking off across the kitchen, I flung the garage door open and ran inside. My boots ground to a halt in front of two flat-bottom kayaks.

I had a sled. Now all I needed was some rope.

TEN

WILLOW

One minute I was trudging slowly through the ravine, desperately trying to keep up with Logan, and the next…

I was running up the walk to Lucas's house, excitedly knocking on the door. Overhead, the porch light flickered while mosquitoes buzzed around my ears. Waiting, I ran my hands down the front of my dress, smoothing out its wrinkles.

A thick head of blonde curls peeked from behind the curtain, a wide smile appearing. The door popped open and Lucas's mom exclaimed, "Oh, just look at you! Now if you'll just let me fix that heavy eye makeup…" she trailed off as her gaze reached my feet. Her wide eyes raced back to mine. "Willow! You can't wear combat boots to the homecoming dance!"

"Oh my god, Mom, stop it." The door opened fully, revealing Lucas wearing the three-piece suit we'd found at the local thrift store the previous week. It was a dark twill pattern and, according to the saleslady, a European cut. It was also far too short on him, showing a good portion of his striped socks and several inches of his arms.

Kissing his mother quickly on the cheek, Lucas rushed onto the porch, grabbing my hand. "Bye, Mom!" he called over his shoulder, tugging me down the steps.

"Lucas—what on earth are you wearing?" she called after him. "What happened to your Sunday suit? Lucas—you look like Huckleberry Finn in those floods! Lucas? Lucas, get back here!"

Giggling, we raced down the driveway, down the sidewalk, not slowing until we'd turned the corner on our street. Ducking beneath the heavy canopy of an elm tree, I clutched my stomach, laughing.

"Oh my god, did you see her face? Your mom is too precious for this world."

Lucas kicked off his shoes and began shrugging out of his too-small jacket. "I'm just glad your mom didn't follow you over with her camera bag." Lucas paused, placing his hands on his hips and lifting his chin. "How many times do I need to remind you kids that film is better than digital," he scolded me in a comically high-pitched voice. "A phone camera will never capture all the details, and details are the most important part of photography, dontcha know."

Grinning, I fumbled with the side zipper on my dress. "I promised I'd smile for the yearbook photo in exchange for not taking our picture tonight."

Lucas guffawed. "And she believed you?"

"I can be very persuasive." Wearing only my strapless bra and underwear, along with a pair of torn fishnet stockings and my combat boots, I handed my dress to Lucas. "Your gown, milady."

When we'd gone shopping for our homecoming outfits, it had been me who'd picked out the suit, with my size in mind, while Lucas had picked out a dress that he could also comfortably wear.

Taking the length of satin, Lucas paused to look up and down my body with a sly smile. "Too bad you can't go like that."

"Ha," I retorted, preening under his admiring gaze. "They're all going to completely freak out when they see you in a dress – if I showed up in my underwear, too, we'd have a county-wide catastrophe on our hands. I can see tomorrow's byline now – **LOCAL SATAN WORSHIPPERS CRASH GOOD, GOD-FEARING HOMECOMING.***"*

"Satan worshippers," Lucas snorted. "Don't insult me."

Having successfully switched clothing, we ducked back beneath the veil of wispy branches and continued on down the sidewalk, this time arm in arm. It was our first year of high school, our first homecoming dance, and we were determined to make a lasting first impression. Or rather, I was determined to make an impression, while Lucas was always content to do whatever I wanted.

Soon, we could hear the thumping bass and the din of a multitude of voices. Breaching the school property line, the path to the gymnasium had been fitted with an arch of green and gold balloons, our school's colors. Small groups of students milled around outside the entrance, all of them stopping to watch our approach.

"Oh look, the circus freaks are here."

"Logan, isn't that your brother?"

Logan stood, the tallest among his smirking teammates, scowling in our direction. Like the rest of his varsity team, he wore his football jersey over his dress shirt.

"Oh look, it's the homecoming court of assholes," I sneered, pausing to do a dramatic genuflect. Standing straight, I met each of their gazes head-on, ending with Logan. "What's it like to peak at seventeen, Your Majesty?"

As his scowl turned downright murderous, I hurried to retake Lucas's arm and we ran into the gym, howling with laughter.

"You need to drink, Willow. Come on, just drink a little bit — come on, drink something, *damn it.*"

A voice reached me; sunken somewhere in the dark recesses of my mind, I grabbed hold of that voice, tethered myself to it, letting it pull me, coughing and spluttering, back to consciousness. Someone was holding me upright; a bottle was pushed past my lips, warm water was pouring into my mouth. Reflexively, I coughed again, sputtering as I tried to swallow. I felt myself being raised higher.

Muscle aches, the likes of which I'd never felt before, burned agonizing pathways through my body. Making everything worse, one second I was burning hot, feeling as if I might suffocate from the extreme heat, and then just as quickly, I was shivering and shaking once more.

"Lucas?" I rasped.

"Willow, you need to drink something," the voice demanded.

I blinked, focusing on the blurry face before me. I knew that mouth. That nose. That unruly beard. Those hard eyes, which right now, burned with concern. *Logan was concerned for me? I must still be dreaming.*

"Where… are… we?" It took all my strength to say three measly words, leaving me exhausted and drifting off to sleep again. "Tired," I managed to slur.

"I don't care if you're tired," Logan snapped, nudging the bottle against my lips. "I need you to drink something."

No, I thought, reaching up, fumbling with the air before finding his hand. I attempted pushing him away, though he didn't budge.

"Drink something!"

"Sleep," I whispered, closing my eyes. And the world slipped away once again.

Lucas and I were stretched out over freshly cut grass, sharing a pair of earbuds. The overhead sun glistened on our skin; our backpacks and forgotten textbooks spread out around us. Two empty beer bottles and half a pack of cigarettes sat between us.

"That's not ironic, Will!" Laughing, Lucas played with my hair, wrapping one of my braids around his finger. "I mean, maybe there's some situational irony there, but that's about it."

"What? Come on! A 'no smoking' sign on a cigarette break — that's ironic."

"Nope. It's only ironic if they didn't already know the sign was there."

Blinking over at him, I chewed thoughtfully on my lower lip. "Okay, so what about meeting the man of your dreams and then meeting his beautiful wife — that's definitely ironic."

"Meh, kinda. I think that's still situational irony. You wouldn't expect to meet the man of your dreams only to then meet his beautiful wife, right?"

Making a face at the sky, I shook my head and said, "Can you imagine how shitty that would be? To meet the person of your dreams and they're already with someone else."

Lucas rolled toward me, pressing a soft kiss to my temple. "Good thing we found each other, huh?"

"What the fuck, Luke — I thought you said you were going to the library."

Logan stood above us. His short blond hair spiked with sweat. He was fresh from football practice, a duffel bag brimming with gear slung on his shoulder.

Lucas scrambled to sit, hurrying to stuff the empty beer bottles into his backpack, drawing Logan's attention straight to them.

"Are you kidding me — you're back here, drinking?"

"It was only one beer," Lucas mumbled.

"Yeah, and who does that sound like?" Logan demanded. "This is bullshit — you know better."

"Hey, crazy," I snapped. "He only had one beer — calm down!"

Logan's jaw tightened. Ignoring me, he said to Lucas, "You keep fucking off like this, you're never going to get out of here — is that what you want? To be stuck in this shithole forever, with her?" *Not waiting for a response, Logan continued bitingly. "I'll be in the truck — if you're not there in five minutes, I'm leaving without you."*

"Oh no," I called after him. "However will he make it home without you? What with you living three short blocks away and all."

Logan's shoulders stiffened, though he continued stalking away. I glared after him, feeling myself growing angrier. I didn't understand why he hated me so much.

"Great." Lucas flopped backward on the grass with a groan. "My whole family is crazy — can I move in with you?"

"Yep," I said, settling back beside him. "And wouldn't that be ironic."

Lucas began to laugh. "No, Will, it definitely wouldn't be — not even a little bit."

I awoke to grunts and groans, scraping and scuffling noises. I knew those noises, I knew what they meant; only, just as quickly as my panic rose, my thoughts drifted away as my eyes drifted closed.

There was an audible thump to my right; my eyes flew open. A rotten stench filled my nostrils, making my stomach churn anew. The world was blurring in and out of focus, but there was something there, just to my right.

"Lucas?" I whispered, his name sticking in my throat. "Is... that you?"

My vision continued to blur in and out of focus, until I could suddenly see, and what I saw was Lucas, his beautiful face drawing closer, a smile splitting his lips. I lifted a quivering hand, reaching for him. As my vision wavered again, Lucas's features began to morph into the decaying face of a Creeper. Growling, it grabbed at me, gripping a handful of my hair and painfully twisting it. Its jaws snapping like angry traps, its mouth a fetid black hole, it used its grip on me to pull itself closer.

"No," I demanded faintly. Weakly, I tried to move, tried to push its hand away. Breathing hard, my muscles burning from exertion, my fingers closed around its arm, my nails digging into its scummy flesh. As its skin peeled away from its bones, my hand fell away with its skin. Too weak to do anything more, a strangled cry rose in my throat.

There was a blast—an explosion that ricocheted all around me. As the Creeper's hold on me disappeared, Logan took its place beside me.

"Were you bitten?" he demanded. Frantic hands pulled at my clothing, roughly turning me this way and that. I tried to speak—I tried to tell him that I hadn't been bitten—but my mouth refused to cooperate.

"Not bitten," he said, sounding relieved. "Not bitten... not bitten...."

Reaching up, I pressed a limp hand to my chest and tried to speak... only no words came. No words. No tears. Just nothing. I was a silent passenger in my own body.

"We gotta keep going, okay? Willow, can you hear me?"

As Logan melted away, I was left staring up at the sky, the heat of the sun beating down on me. I thought I saw a bird—a black shapeless thing that dipped and dove through the never-ending blue above me. I stared at it, envying its freedom, the ease in which it could rise above this world, utterly untethered.

Turning away, blinking sluggishly, my eyes feeling as if they had glue in them, I glimpsed the passing brickwork of a dilapidated home. Then another house with a faded **FOR SALE** sign hanging crookedly amid an overgrown lawn. Both were gone before I could blink again.

Eventually my eyes closed, the world winking into darkness once more.

Idly, I wondered if I would ever wake up again.

ELEVEN

LOGAN

Cursing, I swung at the block of empty shelves, cursing again as my fist collided with solid wood. Shaking out my injured hand, I bit back a groan. My hands were a mess, my nails cracked, my fingers blistered, the skin on my palms rubbed raw after two long days of pulling Willow behind me in the kayak. Punching that shelf, splitting open the skin over my knuckles, had only succeeded in adding insult to injury.

I'd managed to drag Willow to Elkins Point, where I'd combed through every building, only to come up empty-handed every time. There was nothing here; the entire town had been picked clean of medicine, not even a box of bandages remained. There'd been very little to find along the way as well, with the exception of a small group of Creepers that had nearly gotten the drop on me. Recalling the one that had almost bitten Willow, I continued cursing. I was exhausted, in pain, and without a clue as to what I should do next.

Returning to the front of what had once been the town's apothecary, I dropped down beside Willow, still secured in the kayak, and pressed my palm to her cheek. She was still in the thick of it, sleeping fitfully; the aspirin I'd been giving her only providing brief bouts of relief from her fever and chills. She still called out for Lucas, seeming to be completely unaware of what had happened only days ago. She wouldn't eat; she drank very little, and her leg...

Jesus, her leg was a goddamn mess and getting worse.

As gently as I could, I unwrapped the sweat-soaked shirt from her calf, cringing at the sight of her swollen leg, still bewildered by how quickly it had gone from bad to worse. It only proved what I'd guessed all along—how precarious our situation had always been, and how unbelievably lucky we'd all been... up until recently.

Leaving Willow's leg unbound, I sat back on my heels and dropped my face to my hands, wondering if I should attempt searching out the camp I assumed was nearby. But in what direction would I search first? I hadn't come across a single map—not one single shred of fucking paper that might help me figure out where to look.

This was the end of the line—there was nothing more I could do. Willow would either get better on her own, or... an image of Lucas falling into that goddamn ravine came to mind. God only knew what had happened to him after that.

"No," I growled, jumping up. She was all I had left in this miserable fucking world, and I wasn't going to just sit here and watch her die.

After redressing Willow's leg and slipping back into my gear,

I gathered up the length of rope and dragged Willow inside the kayak out onto the street. The road curved left as we departed the main drag, the town quickly disappearing from view. Approaching a fork in the road, I made a split-second decision to venture right, a direction that took us through small clusters of homes among short stretches of wooded areas. Each neighborhood we traveled through I noted the distinct lack of street signs. It was subtle at first, only a few signs missing from their posts, and then it was on every corner, both post and sign gone.

They were smart, whoever *they* were. Leaving the town virtually untouched while strategically removing any information that might lead wayward travelers to their location. It was what I would do if I were them—if I had the good fortune of finding an entire town's worth of resources and enough people to form a working community. At least, that's what I was hoping they were— decent people with decent intentions and the materials needed to realize those intentions.

I continued down the road, the clusters of homes growing farther apart until there were no more neighborhoods to circle through. Until I'd run out of road and was left standing in front of a crumbling concrete road barrier and rusted sign that read: DEAD END. Beyond that, trees as far as I could see.

Panicking, I dropped the rope and turned in a circle. "I missed something," I muttered. "I must have missed something..." Glancing at the setting sun, I knew there wouldn't be enough time to head back to town before darkness fell. Looking at Willow, still sleeping in the kayak, blissfully unaware of the danger I had just put us in, I knew she didn't have that kind of time either.

"Fuck," I said, shaking my head. "*Fuck.*"

Running my hands through my messy hair, I stared at the

DEAD END sign, my frustration turning quickly to anger.

"Fuck you," I spat, pulling the gun from my tool belt. Aiming for the sign, I unloaded the entire magazine. Once it was empty, I whipped the weapon as hard as I could, slinging it at that goddamn sign. It clanked hard against the metal post before falling out of sight.

Laughing through a sob, I sat down hard on the ground beside Willow. "I'm sorry," I said hoarsely. "I'm so fucking sorry."

"I'm sorry, too. I really liked that sign."

I jumped to my feet—a bit of black leather and a long blonde braid were visible between the trees, as was the double-barreled shotgun aimed at my face. Reflexively, my hand went to my crowbar.

"Now, don't be doin' anything stupid, son." A new voice emerged from behind me, deep and definitely male. Never mind the blonde's shotgun; I was outmanned. Letting the crowbar clatter to the ground, I put my hands in the air.

Meanwhile, the blonde had exited the trees, pausing on the side of the road. Twirling her shotgun like a baton, she said, "Stupider, you mean—'cause he's already been doin' stupid stuff, Davey-cakes. What do you call shootin' up a sign and wastin' valuable ammo? It ain't exactly smart."

The man behind me—Davey—snorted. "You got me there, Britta."

Britta twirled her gun straight up into the air, catching it with one hand and then shoving it into the holster on her thigh. Her heavily lined eyes narrowed in my direction. "You got any more guns on ya, sugar?"

I swallowed. "No, I'm just—"

My words cut off as I was grabbed from behind and a thick arm encircled my neck, tight enough to reduce my air flow but not cut it off. I struggled at first, gripping the arm at my neck, only to freeze the moment I felt the hard press of a gun to my ribs. Releasing the arm, I lowered my hands, holding my palms out.

"Smart," Davey murmured, tightening his hold.

Britta rushed forward and began patting me down. "Good gravy, he's got more blades on him than Edward Scissorhands," she said, pulling out the strap of knives I kept tucked into each of my boots. "And all these tools—you into some kinky construction shit, Eddie?" Laughing, Britta divested me of my tool belt, adding it to the growing pile of weapons she'd already taken off me.

"Listen," I said, gasping between words. "My-my—" I gestured in Willow's direction. "She's sick... she needs... doctor... antibiotics... please."

They both ignored me—Britta remained busy sorting through my tool belt while Davey roughly pulled my pack from my back and tossed it to Britta. Britta dug briefly through the bag before setting it aside and glancing curiously up at me. "Don't exactly have a whole lotta gear on ya, do ya—y'all got a camp nearby?"

"No," I wheezed. "Lost... gear..."

Rising, Britta folded her arms over her chest and cocked her head to one side. Clicking her tongue to the roof of her mouth, she murmured, "Davey, you keep Eddie here in check—I'm gonna search the girl."

"Don't... fucking touch... her," I said, my fight renewed. Davey instantly tightened his hold, cutting off my air and forcibly turning me away from Willow. I kicked out, my legs hitting nothing.

"Calm the fuck down," Davey growled. "Actin' like a fool ain't gonna help your girl."

My blood thundered through my ears as I fought for both air and calm. The moment I stopped struggling, Davey's grip on my neck loosened, leaving me sagging in his hold, gasping for breath.

"Oh, she's real bad, alright—got an infected leg!" Britta called out.

"Bitten?" Davey asked.

"Not that I can see. Looks like a cut of some sort. Blood poisonin', maybe. Eddie here wasn't lyin' — she's gotta see Doc, and fast."

My racing heart stuttered. They had a doctor?

"You think takin' them to camp is wise?" Davey asked. "We don't know jack shit about 'em."

"I know this girl's gonna die if we don't. Fact is, she'll likely still die even if we do."

A moment later, I heard the sound of the kayak being dragged across the concrete.

My elbow found purchase in Davey's gut, my boot in his shin. Grunting in pain, he faltered, losing his grip on me. I grabbed his arm, twisted it as I ducked beneath it, and roughly yanked it behind his back.

"Drop the gun," I demanded, pressing on his arm. Hissing in pain, Davey's firearm clattered to the concrete. "I go where she goes!" I called out to Britta.

Britta paused at the edge of the woods, tossing me a cursory glance over her shoulder. "Then you better stop your flirtin' with Davey and hurry the fuck up." Disappearing behind the trees, her voice echoed throughout the dead end. "Ain't nobody gettin' in after sundown."

"She's tellin' the truth," Davey growled. "You wanna be with your girl, we need to move. Once we're outta sunlight, we're outta luck. House rules. No exceptions."

I considered his words, every passing second taking Willow farther from me. Finally, with no other options, I released Davey with a hard shove. Spinning around, he looked from me to his gun, but made no move toward either. Face to face with him, I recognized him as the paramilitary guy who'd been driving the

Jeep in Elkins Point. Up close, he was a great deal older than I'd initially thought—with salt and pepper hair, a matching beard, and deep lines etched into his suntanned skin.

My gaze shot to the trees Britta had disappeared behind. "Are you going to shoot me?" I asked.

"Remains to be seen," he said. "You gonna do as you're told?"

"Remains to be seen," I retorted.

Snorting, he shook his head at me and gestured toward the woods. "Either way, we best get a move on."

Taking a deep breath, I nodded in agreement. Whatever happened next, whoever these people were, I was out of options and Willow was out of time.

The walk through the woods was more of a trek through a dimly lit maze; the forest here was thick, far denser and darker than it had been by the farmhouse. There were no pathways, no notable landmarks, nothing but a handful of game trails that led nowhere.

We'd been walking only ten minutes or so when I realized that Davey had no intention of allowing me to catch up to Britta and Willow. His pace was deliberately slow as he led me in wide zigzagging patterns, either to throw off my sense of direction, or for some more nefarious reason.

Eventually the forest began to thin, opening into a dirt and gravel parking lot, lined with old streetlights and concrete parking bumpers. There was a definite road here, too—a well-worn dirt roadway newly imprinted with numerous tire tracks. Staring down the empty road, I wondered if it led to the highway.

"You comin' or what?" Davey stood at the far end of the lot, impatiently tapping his fingers on the stock of his gun.

The path descended a steep hill, branching out in several directions at the bottom. Davey directed me to the right, back into the rapidly darkening forest. Eventually the path began to widen, the forest opening into another lot. Beyond the lot, a ten-foot-high wall stood, made from a compilation of various slabs of wood, in a hundred different colors. The mishmash of colors and textures gave it an overall shoddy appearance, like that of an old quilt faded with age. A small guardhouse loomed behind the wall, towering a good six feet above the wall; two people stood inside, each of them holding a long-range rifle.

Both rifles were pointed at me.

Davey whistled and the wall jerked, revealing a rolling gateway. As the gate continued to roll slowly open, a man and woman were unveiled.

The woman I recognized as the short-haired motorcyclist I'd seen during my initial trip to Elkins Point, but the man I hadn't seen before. For all intents and purposes, he seemed like an average man, of average build, with average features; however, his dark eyes told a very different story—a distinctly not-average story.

"Hello," the woman said brusquely, clasping her hands together. "I'm sure you're wondering about your companion, so let me first assure you that she's with our doctor who's been instructed to do whatever she can to help her."

I opened my mouth, only to close it when the woman held up her finger. "You, however, are an entirely different matter," she continued, her tone distinctly hardening. "This is our place. The people here are *our* people, and we take their safety very, very seriously."

Much like the man's, the woman's looks were similarly deceiving. She looked to be in her mid to late thirties and was on the smaller side, with dainty, pert features. At first glance, she appeared diminutive, almost shy even. Her skin was fair, dotted with freckles, her hair short and moderately styled, and she dressed plainly in dark, solid colors. You didn't really see her type anymore, the sort of person you wouldn't ever pick out of a crowd, that you'd never mark as exceptional in any way. Those people hadn't survived very long.

It was ultimately her eyes that gave her away and hinted at who she really was. Golden brown in color, they were, at first glance, sad eyes... maybe even a little angry, too. But the longer I looked at her, the longer she looked at me, the harder her gaze grew until I was looking into the steely-eyed stare of a woman who'd definitely seen some shit. A woman who knew full well what a threat looked like... and I fit her description.

"First things first," she said. "I want to know how many more of you there are and where your camp is."

I shook my head. "There's just us—I mean, there were three of us... but now it's just us."

One of her dark brows peaked. "And why is that?"

Scrubbing my hand over my face, I sighed. "I'd left them at the farmhouse to scout ahead and they were fucking around in the woods and..." I trailed off while I fought for composure. "... and now it's just the two of us," I finished through my teeth.

"So you're telling me that it's just been the three of you surviving out there?" she asked, disbelief tinging her words. "This entire time, just the three of you?"

"Yes."

Glancing at the man beside her, a silent exchange occurred between them. "Suppose we choose to believe you," the woman said slowly. "Would you care to share how you found us?"

"I didn't." I jerked my chin in Davey's direction. "You found me."

"You can't expect me to believe it was just a happy coincidence that you ended up on our dead end."

I struggled for calm. The rational side of me understood their need for safety protocols, but the irrational side of me was desperate to get inside that wall, desperate to get to Willow. The sun had already set, night was upon us and I couldn't let that gate close with me stuck on the wrong side of it.

"I saw you in town," I practically snarled, no longer able to mask my growing anger. "And I figured you had a camp nearby but I didn't have any plans on coming to look for you until Willow got sick. So, yeah, I was looking for you, but I didn't know *where* you were, only that you were here somewhere."

"So it was you who made the mess at Carole's."

My chest tightened, frustration squeezing all the air from my lungs. "Does it fucking matter?"

"Watch your fuckin' mouth, son," Davey growled, stepping toward me.

My glare swung in his direction. "*Fuck you* — I'm not your son."

"It does matter," the woman said evenly. "I need to know where your head is. It's all relevant."

For a moment, I only stared at her. "You want to know where my head is?" I finally said, laughing bitterly. "Lady, my little brother is dead and Willow is... *I don't even know what Willow is because you've got her in there while I'm stuck out here with you asking me where my fucking head is! It's been just the three of us for God only knows how long and... and if she dies too... Jesus Christ, this whole fucking thing is all my fault...* " My words died off in anguish.

Davey was practically on top of me now, his weapon clutched in his hands, ready and willing to use it if given the go-ahead. I barely spared him a glance. He was merely the muscle; it was the other two, the not quite so average man and woman that posed a much greater threat.

"And I get it," I continued through my teeth. "I really do. You don't know if you can trust me, but you've got to believe me—I don't give a shit about this place, and what you have or don't have—all I care about is Willow."

The woman's head tilted; her eyes bored into mine. "And what if we can't help Willow—what happens then?"

Every fiber of my being roared in protest at the mere suggestion. "Then I'll leave." I managed to spit out. My next two words didn't come easily; I felt as if my tongue were wading through quicksand. "... *without her.*"

No one spoke. Not the woman or the man beside her. Not Davey, who was still staring daggers in my peripheral. Not the two guards in the tower with their rifles still trained on me, or the handful of people who'd gathered at the gates.

Then the woman's clasped hands broke apart and her rigid posture relaxed. She was a quiet, unassuming woman once again. Inclining her head, she said, "Follow me."

TWELVE

LOGAN

Antibiotics. I shook my head, still unable to believe it.

Sitting on a cushioned chair, my legs bounced anxiously, my feet tapping against a spotless linoleum floor. Nearby an old box fan was noisily blowing warm air in my direction. At my side, Willow lay asleep in one of two hospital beds—*actual* hospital beds—with a blood pressure cuff wrapped loosely around one arm and an IV line inserted in her other. The IV pole stood between us, a bag of fluid dangling from each hook, one filled with saline, the other with antibiotics, both dripping slowly through the tubing. There was more medical equipment arranged around the small room—several tanks of oxygen, an ultrasound machine, even a small x-ray machine. It even smelled like a hospital—the sharp scent of antiseptic and cleaning products.

And electricity, I thought, still feeling rattled as I blinked up at the overhead light for the hundredth time, watching as it flickered.

And an actual fucking doctor.

She'd introduced herself as Keshia. *But everyone calls me Doc*, she'd said with a warm smile and a shrug. She was an older woman, tall and thin, with long salt and pepper locks that hung halfway down her back. Instead of a white lab coat, she wore cutoff denim shorts and a black tank top, showing off a full sleeve of tattoos on both arms. Fiddling with the stethoscope hanging around her neck, she told me that Willow had a bad case of cellulitis on her leg and what looked to be blood poisoning.

She explained that the bagged antibiotics had expired long ago, but with limited resources available, anything at all was better than nothing at all. Then she'd treated Willow's leg with a topical ointment she'd made from her homegrown penicillin cultures, the same ointment she used to treat the wounds on my hands. Both my hands were bandaged now and throbbing fiercely.

Willow and I were alone now, but the door to the room remained open, allowing me full view of an adjoining room—a waiting area that also doubled as triage. On one end of the room were a handful of mismatched chairs and a cluttered desk; on the other end, a wheeled stretcher sat surrounded by emergency medical bags—the sort that EMTs used to carry with them.

Currently, Doc was seated at the desk, idly flipping through the pages of a large hardback book. In a nearby chair, Davey was staring at me, his rifle cradled in his arms. On the wall behind him hung several health educational posters. Just above the front door hung a wooden sign with the words: CAMP NURSE crudely painted in white and red.

I'd seen similar signs on my way here—REGISTRATION OFFICE, CAMPSTORE, DINING HALL, BATHHOUSE—making it clear that this place had once been a summer camp. Despite its origins, to call this place a mere camp would have been a grave understatement. Roughly the size of a football field, the cordoned space bordered a lake and was protected by a fortified wall. They had children here, families, *even a goddamn doctor*. I still couldn't quite believe it.

Looking at Willow, her skin had taken on an ashy hue and she had deep, dark circles ringing her closed eyes. Staring at her, I was reminded of someone else. Somewhere else.

"Logan."

The door creaked open; Mackenzie stood in my bedroom doorway, holding a candle in her hands, motioning for me to join her.

Beside me, Lucas was sound asleep, shivering as he slept. Tossing my blankets over him, I moved quietly into the hall, closing the door partway behind me.

"We're leaving Asheville," Mackenzie whispered, her breath visible in the freezing cold corridor. "Tomorrow."

I blinked at her. "What do you mean, you're leaving? It's the middle of fucking winter, where the hell are you going?"

She shook her head and the candle flickered, reflecting off the tears in her eyes. "My dad heard another FEMA broadcast on the radio today, and my mom has been begging to leave for weeks, ever since... " she trailed off, her gaze dropping to the floor. "They just told me we're leaving tomorrow."

"Just the three of you?" I asked.

"Mr. and Mrs. Gleason are coming—the Harts too." She began shifting uncomfortably,

My nostrils flared. "So everyone is just picking up and leaving?"

Mackenzie shifted uncomfortably. "I think you and Luke could probably come," she said in a small voice.

I doubted that. Mackenzie's parents might have loved me once, but that had changed once we'd begun living under one roof. They'd gotten to see firsthand how my family operated, and they hadn't liked what they'd seen.

"I can't even get Luke out of bed," I told her, growing angry. Mackenzie already knew this; every day she'd watch me attempt to coax him from beneath his covers, trying desperately to convince him to eat.

"I'm sure he'd get up if he knew you were leaving…"

"What about Willow and her mom?" I bit out. "Are we just going to leave them here?"

"My dad said Willow's mom isn't going to last the week," she whispered. *"… and you know my mom doesn't like Willow."*

"Nobody likes Willow," I snapped. "What the fuck does that have to do with anything? We still can't leave her here alone."

"Logan, my mom is scared of her. She's been coming up with all these insane theories about what happened and she's got it stuck in her head that it was Willow who… you know… "

"Yeah," I scoffed. *"I'd forgotten what a really scary time it's been for* your mom *lately."*

"Don't do that," she whimpered. "That's not fair."

"Don't talk to me about what's not fair. Both of your parents are still breathing."

"Exactly!" she cried out. "So come with us — let's leave this awful place behind!"

I stared at her in the near darkness. Blonde-haired, blue-eyed varsity cheerleader with a cheery disposition, Mackenzie had checked all the right boxes for me. She'd been the cheer to my game and the easygoing smile that had always countered my ever-present scowl. Only now, ever since the world had gone insane, I'd come to realize that all she'd ever really been to me was a means to an end, a helping hand in getting me out of this do-nothing town. In reality, the feelings I had for her had never been more than tepid, at best.

"Luke won't leave Willow," I ground out. "Fuck, Luke won't even leave his bed."

"And you won't leave Luke," she finished in a harsh whisper.

I stared at her, disgusted. "Yeah. He's my little brother, remember?"

Chuffing, she shook her head angrily. "Then I guess that's it."

"Guess so," I bit out.

Her eyes flashed in the candlelight. "We've been together since sophomore year and now I'm leaving and that's all you have to say?"

"What the fuck do you want from me?" I demanded. "Jesus Christ, if you're looking for someone to beg you to stay, look somewhere else. This is bigger than you!"

Mackenzie blinked hard, her tears spilling over just as she spun away with enough force that her candle went out. Leaning back against the wall, I was staring blankly at the empty space Mackenzie had vacated when a coughing fit erupted throughout the hallway.

Moving quickly down the hall, I entered a dimly lit room on the right. A low fire crackled in the fireplace, casting shadows over the figures on the bed.

"Logan," Willow breathed. "Can you hold her still—make sure she doesn't fall? I need to get her some water."

"Go," I told her, taking a seat on the bed as Willow rushed from the room. Her mother offered me a weak smile; shriveled and emaciated, with dark circles ringing her eyes, she looked nothing like the vibrant, bright-eyed woman she'd once been.

"Logan," she whispered. "Logan, once I'm gone… I want you to take Willow and Luke and… and get out of here. You can't stay… here. You need to… go south… where it's warm. Find… food."

She began to cough again, deep, rattling spasms that shook the entire bed. As blood sprayed from her mouth, I grabbed a nearby towel, already stained with her blood, and wiped at her chin.

"And keep Willow… safe," she wheezed once she could speak. "She's a smart girl… but she's stubborn. Too… stubborn for her own good. Promise me… you'll keep my… baby… safe."

My throat tight, I gripped her hand between both of mine. "I promise," I whispered hoarsely. "I'll keep her safe—you don't need to worry."

"You're a good… boy," she rasped. "You're not…like… " she trailed off as she began to cough again. And this time she didn't stop.

A few hours later, she fell into unconsciousness.

By the end of the week, she was dead.

"Come on, Willow," I quietly gritted out. "Where's the girl who never backs down from a fight—who's always up in everybody's face?"

A flood of memories flashed, the thousands of reckless things she'd done throughout the years. Stupid things, selfish things, but also brave things, too. Yeah, she was definitely brave. And stubborn. And overwhelming. And… so… *goddamn all-consuming.*

"I knew a woman like that."

The short-haired woman from earlier, the one who'd claimed this camp as hers, was standing in the doorway, holding my bag and tool belt in her hands.

"She was always primed for a fight." Entering the room, the woman placed my things by the door. "And never afraid to speak her mind, and sometimes she was brave to the point of stupid." She paused at the edge of Willow's bed. "The infection took her," the woman continued wistfully. "I'll never get over it. A spirit like hers deserved so much better than to die in a bed."

I snorted softly. "Willow says that shit all the time—how she wants to go out in a blaze of glory."

The woman smiled. "Your Willow certainly does seem to have a lot in common with my Evelyn... and if Willow is anything like she was then I know she'll fight this with everything she has."

My Willow. Shaking my head, I said, "She's not mine—we're not together." I fumbled to get the right words out. "My brother and her—they were together."

The woman's gaze shot to mine, the faraway look in her eyes fading fast. "I see. I guess I just assumed you two were together—you seemed like a man desperate to save the woman you love."

Shocked silent and blinking rapidly, I spent the next several seconds clearing my throat. "No, it's not like that between us... we, uh, we don't even like each other... " Realizing how ridiculous I sounded, my words dwindled and I quickly changed topics. "Yeah, so about earlier—you guys were right to be cautious. I'm sorry I was being a dick."

She laughed lightly. "Apologies aren't your forte, I'm guessing? Look, I'm not in any position to be holding someone's emotions in a time of crisis against them. As long as you've got yourself under control now, I think we'll be fine... " she trailed off, tilting her head to one side. "You know, I've just realized, I haven't even asked you your name."

"Logan," I offered.

"It's nice to meet you, Logan—my name is Liesel. And now that we've been formally introduced, I'd like to officially welcome you and Willow to Silver Lake, formerly known as Silver Lake Summer Camp for Youths."

"Yeah, thanks," I replied. "… you seem to have a really nice setup here. I haven't seen anything like it in… " I trailed off as I realized I hadn't *ever* seen anything quite like it. Most of the camps we'd come across had been shoddily thrown together with no real sense of order. Fanatics or hopeless cases seemed to be all the world had left to offer.

Leisel flashed me a wry smile. "Exactly. So you can understand our caution when it comes to newcomers, yes?"

"Yeah. I get it."

"Good, and now that that's settled, Davey will be showing you to your cabin." Stepping aside, she waved Davey forward.

"My cabin?" Startled, I looked at Willow. "Can't I just stay with her?"

Leisel pressed her lips together, her gaze hardening. "I'm afraid not. This isn't just our doctor's office, it's her home too."

She said nothing else, though the rest went without saying—I was still a stranger who still posed a threat, and they were going to continue taking every necessary precaution.

"Is this cabin nearby?" I asked. "I'd like to be close to her."

"It's a small camp; everything is close. However, you don't need to worry. If Willow's condition changes in any way during the night, someone will come for you."

Glancing again at Willow, I rubbed anxiously at the back of my neck. They weren't going to hurt her—I felt that in my gut. But I still couldn't fathom leaving her, especially after everything I'd gone through to get her here. Yet, if I wanted these people to trust me, I knew I needed to trust them first.

"Alright," I said reluctantly.

"Good." Liesel clapped her hands together. "Logan, Davey, I'll leave you to it."

Davey stepped forward, eyeing me contemptuously. "You comin' or what?"

As we passed through an area cluttered with cabins, a dozen different smells assaulted me—burning wood, cooking meat, and the fresh damp scent of a nearby body of water.

Counting twelve cabins in total, Davey led me to the last in the row, the seemingly worst of the bunch, with a thin, rickety door and a crumbling front step. While Doc's home merely had the outward aesthetics of a log cabin, the smaller structures on this side of camp were actual cabins, each with a suspended floor and a crawl space underneath.

Upon entering, Davey flicked a switch and two wall-mounted lantern lights flickered on. The cabin consisted of two rooms—the room I was standing in, and what looked to be a small bathroom. Two sets of wooden bunk beds, along with two small dressers, adorned each corner of the room. A lamp sat alone in the center of the room, missing both bulb and shade. Near the entrance, a dust-covered wrought-iron stove had been fitted with piping that crawled up the wall and out through the roof, serving as a chimney. All above me, exposed beams crisscrossed beneath the peaked ceiling, draped with cobwebs.

"Don't be keepin' the lights on all night—we run on solar power here," Davey said. "And don't be leavin' the cabin either until someone comes for ya. We got patrols going round the clock and the guards at the gate can see the whole place at any given time. Ain't nobody does nothin' without someone else seein', ya get me?"

"What if I have to piss?" I asked, deadpan. "Should I just pick a corner?"

"The whole camp runs on well water," Davey retorted. "Got a septic tank, too. You can piss in the toilet—you can even flush it."

I blinked in surprise.

Smiling smugly, Davey turned to leave. "Welcome back to civilization, shithead," he said, slamming the door behind him.

I hurried to fasten the lock—a single hook-and-eye latch, where one good shove would render it useless. Turning, I faced the room with skepticism. Was this place for real? Lights, a doctor, and running water?

Dropping my bag, I rushed inside the small bathroom. It was nothing special—an old toilet with exposed piping and a porcelain sink set atop a small cupboard, its metal fixtures rusted and flaking. A mirror hung above the sink, cloudy and speckled with spots. Twisting the levers on the sink, my breath hitched as clear water sputtered from the rusty faucet.

I might have run my hands beneath it if they hadn't been bandaged; instead, I dropped my head beneath the stream, swallowing mouthful after delicious mouthful. Having drunk my fill, I flushed the toilet merely to see if it would. As water rushed into the bowl, quickly spiraling down the drain, for several seconds, I could only stare.

Making my way back into the other room in a daze, I eventually wandered to the nearest window. Pulling back the torn swathe of fabric hanging there, I pushed open the cracked and cloudy glass-paned window and peered outside.

The lights were on inside the cabin closest to me and I could see figures moving in a way that seemed like they were dancing. Although faint, I could hear music—a familiar song that had me quickly closing the window and staggering back. Backing straight into a bunk bed, I sat down hard, the unexpected feel of the soft mattress beneath me had me shooting back up to my feet.

"Fuck," I whispered, swallowing hard.

This was the kind of place I'd always hoped to find; somewhere safe for Lucas and Willow, where they could carry on being careless and reckless and completely self-absorbed, and I wouldn't have to constantly worry about them. A place where I could finally fulfill my promise to Willow's mother.

Unshed tears burned behind my eyes; what sort of cruel cosmic joke was this—finding the answer to my prayers just days after losing Lucas, and with Willow barely hanging on? I couldn't be here alone. This wasn't right; I didn't deserve this without them— this place with electricity and running water. Without them… none of this meant anything.

I heard a noise—a weak, anguished sound that had me glancing wildly around the room, searching for the source. Realizing it was me, I barked out a laugh that caught in my throat and ended on a sob. Sinking to the floor, I stared miserably across the room.

"I found it, Luke," I whispered hoarsely. "I found that fucking place I'd always promised."

THIRTEEN

WILLOW

The first thing I'm aware of is pain.

So. Much. Fucking. Pain.

Pulsating, throbbing pain that brought tears to my eyes. As I struggled to lift my hand, to move muscles that didn't seem to want to cooperate, a gasp lodged in my throat, burning its way through my next breath. I felt like lead, like dead swollen weight set aflame.

"Hey there, honey," an unfamiliar voice called out. "Everything's okay. Just lay back—lay still. I'll get you something for the pain, alright?"

Jerking in surprise, I fought to open my crust-covered eyes, frantic to understand what was happening—why I was in so much pain, why I couldn't move, and who was speaking to me. As my eyes peeled painfully open, and I blinked through the glaring light above, an unknown face hovered in and out of focus.

"Who..." I croaked. "Where..."

Dark eyes crinkled at the corners. "You're safe, honey, no one's gonna hurt you here." The no-nonsense voice turned soft and soothing. "No need to fret. Now I'm going to get you something for the pain—you just hold tight."

I felt a cold rush up my arm, followed quickly by a hot flush, heat that began in my arm and spread quickly through my entire body. The pain in my leg faded as my thoughts muddled.

"There we go," the voice said. "Now you just rest, alright? I'm going to go get that good-looking young man of yours."

Luke? A wave of relief washed over me even as my stomach flipped.

It came back to me slowly, a trickle of memories that quickly turned into an avalanche. Events flashed out of order: Lucas and I dancing in the rain. Logan yelling at me, demanding that I drink something. Lucas and I running through the woods, laughing. Lucas presenting me with breakfast in bed, flowers caught between his teeth. *Lucas grinning at me just before dropping out of sight.*

Tears formed and fell, streaking hot tracks down my cheeks. Every breath felt like fire in my lungs. All these years together, fighting to stay alive, and for what? It was all for nothing. Lucas was gone and I was...

I was in hell.

"Willow?" A faraway voice tugged at me, deep and gruff and distinct. Prying my heavy eyelids open again, I found Logan looming over me, his eyes bloodshot and ringed with bruising, his skin smudged with dirt. His hair was a mess—stringy and greasy, with large clumps that had been pulled from his bun, left sticking up in all different directions.

"You're awake," Logan rasped. "Jesus Christ, you're actually fucking awake."

The unfamiliar face stood opposite Logan, lifting my arm, wrapping something around it. A blood pressure cuff, I realized, as it tightened uncomfortably. I looked at Logan, still not quite understanding what was happening.

"She's a doctor," he explained, swallowing thickly. "We're in a camp... there's people here..."

"You can call me Doc—everyone else does," the voice said. "Now how's that pain? Has it lessened some?"

Keeping my eyes on Logan, I nodded jerkily.

"Now, you're not out of the woods yet," the voice continued. "You've been pretty out of it for the last few days, but your fever has finally broken and some of the swelling in your leg has gone down. Even your color is looking better. Vitals are good..." the voice trailed off as something cool was placed on my chest. "Take a deep breath for me, honey. Good, good. Yes, I'd say everything is looking as good as can be expected right now."

"Where... are we?" I attempted to ask, the words barely audible.

"You're at Silver Lake, honey," the voice replied, sounding farther away than it had just seconds ago. "Let me be the first to officially welcome you." Footsteps echoed all around and the unfamiliar face reappeared. "Help her drink this, Logan—just a few sips, mind you."

"It's a camp," Logan muttered as he helped to lift my head. "They've got walls and running water and electricity." Cool water dripped into my mouth and my lips parted, feeling suddenly parched. Though as the first drops trickled past my throat, I began to cough, sputtering and heaving, until I could breathe again.

"That's enough for now," the unfamiliar voice chastised. "She can try again later."

"So you've found it," I rasped once I'd stopped coughing. "Your perfect place…"

We stared at one another, Logan's red-rimmed eyes boring into mine, until my eyelids began to droop, and Logan's pained expression slipped away into darkness.

I awoke with a start, pain and panic forcing me upright even as my body resisted the movement. Falling back against the bed with a groan, I gritted my teeth, tears blurring my vision, breathing sharply against the throbbing pain. Once I could see through my tears, I glanced around the dim room, startled to find Logan sleeping upright in a chair beside my bed.

His arms folded over his chest, his head was bent back against the wall, his eyes closed as his chest rhythmically rose and fell. Even in sleep, he scowled, and every so often he would twitch and shift, clearly uncomfortable and sleeping fitfully. Noticeably wet, his blond hair was pulled into a loose ball on top of his head, several strands hanging free and dripping water onto the clean white T-shirt he was wearing. A vague memory niggled my thoughts — the unfamiliar voice demanding that Logan take a shower.

I continued watching him sleep, soon recalling more events with better clarity. Despite me fighting him every step of the way, Logan had managed to do exactly what he'd always promised he'd do — he'd found us a safe haven. And Lucas, the very best of us, the kindest soul I'd ever known, would never get to see it.

Pain sliced through my chest, making breathing difficult once more. Why hadn't Logan left me in that ravine? Lucas was gone, and it was all my fault, and yet... here I was. Logan had saved me... why?

Still staring at Logan, tears filling my eyes, I rasped, "You should have just let me die."

FOURTEEN

LOGAN

"**B**e careful," I warned, grabbing hold of Willow's elbow as she attempted to stand.

Willow scowled, and for a moment I'd thought she might argue. Instead, she merely gripped the walker more tightly, and pulled herself up with a grunt.

Two weeks since our fortunate run-in with Britta and Davey; two weeks of waiting by Willow's side while she healed, slowly but surely. She was able to get out of bed now and use the walker Doc had given her in order to get herself to and from rooms. Yet, despite her physical improvements, she seemed to be on an emotional decline—she spoke very little, some days not at all. Mostly, she slept or read the books that Doc would lend her.

I'd been concerned at first; it wasn't like Willow to be quiet, but Doc had mentioned to me that everyone deals with grief differently. *Some people lash out,* she'd said. *Others tuck themselves away and wallow.* Then she'd looked me in the eyes and said pointedly, *and some people never deal with it at all.*

"Go slow," I said, cringing as Willow began limping forward at a pace that seemed far too fast for someone who was still healing. Though the swelling in her calf had gone down considerably, her leg remained bandaged and Doc was still applying topical antibiotics to her wound a few times a day.

"I *am* going slow," Willow muttered, just before stumbling.

My grip tightened on her arm, halting her fall. "Christ — why don't you ever listen? I told you to let me carry you."

"I'm not a baby; I don't need to be carried." Yanking her arm from my grip, Willow resumed limping through the room while I hovered at her elbow. Crossing the threshold into the waiting room, she stumbled again; I reached for her and she shoved me away.

"Back off," she snapped. "It's not like I don't know how to walk all of a sudden."

Yeah, I wanted to snap back, *but you also almost died from an infection in your leg that left you bedridden and at death's door for three weeks, all because you didn't clean your wound like I'd fucking told you to.* But I stayed silent, mostly due to the look Doc was giving me from her waiting place by the front door — a pointed look that was telling me to *keep my mouth shut.*

"This is a fiercely stubborn woman we've got here, honey," Doc whispered as she came to stand beside me. "You need to let her do her thing, alright?"

"You mean fiercely stupid?" I muttered, holding my hands up in acquiescence. I'd only wanted to help, to prevent Willow from hurting herself; but, as was always the case, Willow was dead set on proving herself, even to the point of stupidity.

Leaving Doc's place, we followed a well-worn path toward the center of camp. Willow remained in the lead, setting the pace. As we moved slowly around the small grove of trees that kept the Nurse's building partially hidden from the rest of camp, Willow began to slow, eventually coming to a stop at the concrete base of an empty flagpole. Approaching her, I found her eyes saucer wide and her jaw hanging slack.

It was midmorning and camp was bustling with activity. People paused to glance curiously at our trio, some even flashing curious smiles in Willow's direction. An older man, walking his dog on a leash, tipped his hat in greeting. A woman carrying a baby in a sling waved hello. Nearby, a small group of children were playing hopscotch in the dirt.

While I'd had weeks to grow somewhat accustomed to our new surroundings, this was Willow's first day outside of Doc's cabin. "Are you okay?" I asked.

She swallowed hard. "Yeah," she whispered. "I guess I just didn't expect it to look so... so..." she trailed off with another hard swallow.

"Normal?"

Her eyes met mine, her throat still bobbing. She merely nodded in answer.

"If we go any slower, we'll be walking backward," Doc said cheerfully as she passed us. "And it'll be a damn shame to have to eat a cold breakfast."

At the mention of food, Willow appeared to shake off her shock and resumed hobbling down the walkway. The dining hall loomed to our left, the single largest building in camp. Constructed in the shape of a rectangle, it boasted a wraparound porch with both steps and a ramp, and potted wildflowers lining the balustrade. Inside, there were sky-high ceilings, wall-to-wall windows and massive stone fireplaces built into either end. Sunlight poured in through the windows, illuminating the numerous tables and chairs filling the vast space. Up above, timber framework crisscrossed smartly along the ceiling. If it weren't for the wire mesh reinforcing each window, or the several armed guards waiting in line for their breakfasts, it might have looked like we were walking into a casual reception.

"Now, Willow," Doc said, holding the double doors open. "The dining hall is open all day, every day; however, there are only two sit-downs for food—breakfast and dinner—two hours each. We don't have a formal lunch and there're no snacks given out, just two carefully rationed meals, nutritionally balanced to give you everything you need. Of course, if we have a good crop or a great hunt, there'll be more to go around."

Meanwhile, the din of noise inside the hall had noticeably lowered; people had paused their morning conversations in favor of staring at us. They'd all seen me many times already, though only briefly. I ate all my meals with Willow and usually only left Doc's to wash or sleep. However, very few of them had actually seen Willow, and it was obvious that the mystery surrounding her had become a source of excitement for them; new faces certainly weren't a regular occurrence at Silver Lake.

"Hello!" a tiny voice exclaimed. A little boy, no more than four or five years old, jumped in front of Willow, enthusiastically waving his arms around. "My name is Béla! I was named after my grandpa who's dead! He was from Hungary—but not the hungry kind of hungry—the country kind of hungry!"

While the dining hall tittered with laughter, Willow's head

had whipped around, her frantic gaze finding mine. "L-logan," she stammered.

I glanced blankly between Willow and the boy, unsure what she wanted me to do—I couldn't exactly kick a kid out of her pathway. I'd already had my introductory meeting with Béla, whose dead grandfather was from Hungary—which he seemed to enjoy conveying to each new person he encountered. I hadn't known what to say to him either and had ended up only staring at him for several moments before turning around and walking off.

Luckily, a smiling young woman soon came rushing up beside the boy, slipping her hand into his. "We should let our new friends eat," she whispered, tugging him away. "We'll talk to them later, okay?"

"Okay, bye!" Béla called out, waving. "Bye!"

"Logan," Doc said softly, watching Willow with concern. "Why don't you two find us a table while I go make up some plates?" With a quick pat on my shoulder, Doc hurried off.

"I'm leaving," Willow hissed through her teeth, as soon as Doc was out of earshot. Jerking her walker around, she limped noisily across the floor, banging through the double doors. The dining hall had fallen silent; all eyes were on me. Cursing beneath my breath, I took off after her.

"Willow?" I called, jogging down the steps. "Willow, where the fuck are you going?"

She slammed to a stop and spun around, her walker thumping loudly against the ground. She was pale, her eyes wet with tears and trembling from head to toe.

"I'm leaving!" she cried.

"Yeah, you said that already. But *where* are you going? Doc's is that way," I said, pointing.

"I'm not going to Doc's—I'm leaving this... this... this fucking mirage!" She swung her walker around, on the move once again. I stared after her, unsure of what to do. On a good day, Willow was irrational at best, and today was definitely not a good day.

"Open the gate!" she began to scream, waving frantically at the guard tower as she hobbled in the direction of the wall. "Open the gate and let me out of here!"

"Willow!" I shouted, breaking into a run. "*Willow!*"

"Open the gate!" She screamed again, while the pair of people inside the tower stared down at her with bewildered expressions.

"Willow, stop this shit right fucking now!" I demanded, coming up quickly behind her.

Willow whipped around, chucking her walker in my direction. The flimsy piece of equipment went wide, missing me entirely. "Don't come near me, Logan—don't you dare come any closer!"

"Where the hell are you going to go? You can barely walk, you have no gear, no supplies, no weapons..." Glaring at her, I held my hands up in question.

"I can't be here!" she cried. "This place—the people! There's kids here, Logan! There's little kids here—I can't even remember the last time we saw a kid!"

I shook my head, confused. "That's a good thing, isn't it? It means it's safe."

Willow's teary-eyed gaze turned instantly hard. "Why does everyone keep saying that? It's not safe here—it's not safe anywhere!"

Above us, from inside the guard tower, I heard the crackle of a walkie-talkie. "We have a little bit of a situation at the gate—might want to send Leisel and Joshua down."

"There's a fucking wall, *Willow*," I gritted out, gesturing. "The wall makes it safe."

"It's not a magic wall, *Logan!*" she screamed. "We both know how quickly things can change! Just because you can't see the problem doesn't mean it's not still out there!" Her chest was heaving, her eyes and hair wild. I could see that she was spiraling into a full-blown panic attack, but I was suddenly too mad at her to care.

"Are you fucking serious right now?" I exploded. "You don't need to tell me what's out there—it's me who's been leading the two of you all over the goddamn country trying to find a place just like this, remember?"

"How could I possibly forget when you never shut up about it! Saint fucking Logan, who risked it all for Luke and Willow."

Jaw locked and nostrils flaring, I stepped closer. "You're goddamn right, I risked it all! Did you forget that it was me who carried your ass out of that Creeper-infested ravine? And it was *me* who dragged you around in that fucking kayak until my hands busted open! And it was me who found this place, trying to find *you* help—*remember?*"

"No!" she screamed. "I actually don't fucking remember! But now that I know, how does it feel knowing it was all for nothing— that everything you did was stupid and pointless? Because Luke is still gone, and I wish I was too!"

We were standing only about a foot apart—Willow somewhat lopsided, leaning most of her weight onto her uninjured side. Her eyes were wet and wide, tears streaking down her face; her expression was feral, her chest shuddering with every panicked, angry breath. Meanwhile, I stood in shock, shaking with fury. I'd dealt with her shit for years—*too many goddamn years!* I didn't deserve this; I especially didn't deserve this after risking everything to save her life.

"You know what?" I bit out, pain and anger punctuating each of my words. "Fuck it. You're an ungrateful fucking bitch, and I'm done with you. You wanna walk out of here, you go right ahead. It wouldn't be the first idiotic thing you've done, but it might be the last!"

Something ugly flashed in Willow's eyes, her expression twisting with rage. "Fuck you, Logan!" she shrieked. "Fuck you straight to hell!"

"Thanks to you, I'm already fucking there!" I thundered in reply, spinning away.

As I stormed off, Willow continued to shriek; I could still hear her screaming as I rounded a corner, the intensity of her cries causing a pressure-like sensation in the center of my chest that made it difficult to take a full breath.

I headed to my cabin first, only to find that I couldn't breathe any better inside the small, stifling space. I couldn't breathe, I couldn't think, the room was pulsing, the walls were closing in, inching closer and closer until I couldn't take it anymore—*I had to get the fuck out.*

Bursting through the cabin door, I sprinted toward the south side of camp. This early, there wouldn't be anyone around, but once breakfast had ended and work began, the entire camp would become a hub of activity.

There was no shortage of work to do in Silver Lake—there was daily food preparation and cleanup, maintenance chores, along with alternating fishing and hunting excursions. On top of the daily duties, Silver Lake was in the midst of a mass expansion—east side cabins had already had their additions built, providing the occupants more living space, though construction had only recently begun on the west side of camp, where my cabin was located.

Having reached the lake's edge, I scooped up a handful of small rocks and tossed them, one by one, into the shimmering water. The air smelled good here, fresh and even a bit sweet. Throwing the last of my rocks, I shoved my hands into my pockets and gazed out over the lake, noting the fencing sticking far above the water's surface. Looking in either direction, the fencing appeared to span the entire length of camp, attaching to the edge of both walls. They'd really thought of everything here—even the possibility of Creepers, or other undesirables, entering via the lakeside.

As the sun continued to rise and its reflection in the lake turned the water to liquid silver, I found my thoughts straying back to Willow. "Nope," I muttered, shaking free. I wouldn't be thinking about Willow; I was absolutely one hundred percent not at all going to think about Willow. And I definitely wouldn't be going after her. She was on her own this time. Good fucking riddance.

"Shit," I muttered, rubbing the heel of my palm over my chest. Of course I had to go after her. She was going to get herself killed if I didn't. Sighing, I turned to leave.

"Logan!" On the beach, Leisel was fast approaching. "I need a word!"

"Jesus Christ." I scrubbed my hands over my face; there was certainly no shortage of mothers in Silver Lake.

"I heard you and Willow had a fight."

"Yeah, I'm guessing everyone heard," I muttered. "Hope they enjoyed the fucking show."

"Logan, fighting is normal; it's human nature," she continued. "It's not the fighting that worries me. It's the level of anger… Logan, I've been watching you these past weeks, the way you interact with others, the way you talk to Willow, especially. You've got a lot of pent-up anger inside of you."

I shook my head. "No, it's not like that. Willow and I, we've just always been like this."

"You've always been like what?" she asked.

I kept shaking my head, growing angrier with each passing second. I didn't want to talk to anyone, let alone Leisel, and I definitely didn't want to have to explain myself or the complexities of Willow's and my... relationship, for lack of a better word.

"Like what, Logan?" Leisel pressed. "Explain it to me."

"Jesus Christ, okay. We're just like... like... *this!*" I made an all-encompassing gesture. "We fight all the time and can't fucking stand each other. We only put up with each other because of Luke."

"And Luke is... your brother," Leisel said slowly, "who's gone."

Gone—I fucking hated that goddamn word. It felt too final and yet inexplicably incomplete at the same time. "Yes," I replied tightly.

Leisel sighed. "You and Willow have obviously been through a lot together, and from where I'm standing, it looks like you care a great deal about her. I don't think very many people would go through what you did to save someone they didn't care about.

"But look, you don't need to like Willow. Like her, don't like her, that doesn't really matter. Certainly not to me. How you treat her though, now that speaks volumes about the sort of man you are."

"What is this?" I demanded. "What exactly is happening here? Are you psychoanalyzing me or are you trying to tell me it's time for me to go?"

"I might tell you it's time to go," she replied. "If I ever feel like you pose a threat to Silver Lake."

"And what about Willow?" I snarled, "Will she be getting the same speech or was this just for me?"

"There it is again," Leisel calmly replied. "Logan, why are you so angry? Do you even know?"

"I've got a better question—why aren't *you* angry?"

Leisel smiled, looking genuinely amused. "Oh, I was," she said, laughing a little. "I was more than angry even. I'd lost everyone I'd ever cared about, one by one, until I'd ended up completely alone, not knowing how I was going to survive. Not knowing *if* I wanted to survive."

"Join the fucking club. There isn't anyone alive today that hasn't lost everything."

"True," she said. "But it's how we deal with our losses that set us apart. And from what I can tell, and from what Doc has mentioned to me, you aren't dealing with yours. And that makes you dangerous. I've told you before, that this place and these people are everything to me. If I'm to let you continue on here, then I need to know you're not a UXO."

I blinked at her. "I don't know what the fuck that is."

"It's a bomb," she said, still so infuriatingly calm. "It's a bomb that hasn't detonated yet, making it dangerous to everyone around it."

"You think *I'm* a bomb?" I might have laughed if it wasn't for her serious expression.

I wasn't a bomb. I was the cautious one, the one who didn't take risks and who kept everyone safe. Who always did the perimeter checks; who rationed our food and water, and who always remembered to set the water buckets out. Who reminded everyone to sharpen their blades and keep their socks dry and keep their voices down. I was always the careful one; it was Willow who was foolish, who was reckless and wild, careless and carefree, and selfish to a fault.

"Maybe," Leisel replied. "You tell me."

"Jesus Christ!" I spat. "I don't know what you want from me right now. To admit that I'm *maybe* a bomb?" I threw my arms wide. "Sure, maybe I'm a fucking bomb—happy now? But as far as I can see, Willow is the one always holding the fuse, while I'm left to clean up her messes!"

Studying me, Leisel's head canted to one side. "Is that really how you see yourself? Because the person you project to the world is very different from the man you just described."

Running my hands through my hair, I fought for calm. I was really out of practice when it came to social etiquette, that much I'd realized right off the bat. But my problems in camp weren't simply faulty social skills. I wasn't used to not being in charge; neither was I accustomed to dealing with anyone other than Lucas or Willow. And I definitely wasn't used to being scolded and treated as if I were a misbehaving child.

"I get it," I ground out. "I'm angry. But I don't know what you expect me to do about it. I can't just not be angry anymore; it's not a faucet I can just turn off."

"You don't need to turn it off. Being angry isn't the enemy — it's where that anger goes when it's of no more use to you. Or in your case, where it doesn't go."

"So what then? What the fuck am I supposed to do?"

Leisel shrugged. "Talk to someone. Tell someone how you're feeling and why. It's okay to be vulnerable sometimes, you know? It's at least better than the alternative."

"Which would be detonating," I replied flatly.

"Precisely," she replied, clasping her hands together. Turning to go, she paused. "Oh, and one more thing.

"There are no free rides here, Logan — everyone in camp has to contribute. It's the only way this place works. If you and Willow are going to continue on with us, then you're both going to have to start pulling your weight. I know Willow is still on the mend, but I think you're more than capable of working, wouldn't you agree?"

"Yeah, definitely." My hands were mostly healed; I was well fed and well rested and feeling healthier and stronger than I had in years. If staying here meant I'd have to work then I damn sure would be getting to work.

"Great—I'll talk with Joshua and see where he wants you. Are you any good with tools?"

"I'm a fast learner," I said. "Did some electrical and plumbing work growing up, some roofing too."

"A jack-of-all-trades."

"Not me," I told her, shaking my head. "My dad—only he was usually too drunk to finish the job."

Again, Leisel tilted her head to one side, studying me in a way that was starting to become very unnerving. And very fucking annoying.

"How old are you?" she finally asked.

The question caught me off guard. I opened my mouth to answer, only to close it when I realized I didn't know the answer. "Do you know what year it is?"

Leisel told me the date and I quickly counted. "Twenty-five," I replied slowly. "No, wait—I'm twenty-six. I turned twenty-six in... April."

It felt strange to think about my age, and even stranger to think about the birthday that had passed by without any recognition, not even my own. Birthdays were among the long list of frivolous things I'd stopped concerning myself with many years ago.

"The beard makes you look older," Leisel mused. "And what about Willow—how old is she?"

I sighed, "Twenty-three, almost twenty-four."

"So you were just kids then."

"When the world ended?" I snorted. "I guess so."

She smiled faintly. "The world didn't end."

Cocking an eyebrow, I muttered, "You sure about that?"

Leisel turned to leave again, still smiling over her shoulder. "We're still here, aren't we?"

FIFTEEN

WILLOW

Morning reached me much like it always had—with the rise of the sun and the sounds of the world waking up around me. *Waking up without me.*

Eyes squeezed shut, my heart pounding in my chest, I relived my last moment with Lucas—watching him drop out of sight, never to be seen again. My eyes flew open as I was forced to face the daily realization that Lucas was gone. *That Lucas was forever gone.* And just as it did every morning for the last month, that realization would set the tone for the entire day; I felt too heavy to move. The world outside this bed, outside Doc's cabin, seemed too big and bright.

"Rise and shine, sleepyhead." My curtains were thrown open,

bright sunlight spilled into the room. "It's beautiful outside—be a damn shame for you to miss it."

Doc stood over me, holding a steaming mug of coffee. She was still in her pajamas—a pair of loose-fitting cotton shorts and a T-shirt, with a silken wrap wound around her head, hiding her long locks.

Wincing against the sunlight, I pulled my covers over my head. "No thank you," I mumbled.

"Today is the day." Doc's no-nonsense tone followed her determined footsteps around the room. Another set of curtains were pulled open; more sunlight spilled inside. "You have to get out of that damn bed and rejoin the land of living."

The blankets were yanked away from my face; Doc loomed over me, her expression kind yet stern. "Honey, you and I both know that the only thing stopping you from leaving this cabin is *you*. Now, I'd much rather watch you walk out of here on your own two feet, but if you're going to make me carry you, then so be it…"

"Okay," I snapped softly, quickly shifting upright and scooting away.

Doc eyed me over the rim of her coffee. "Mmhm, now we're gettin' somewhere. You'd do well with a shower today, too. And to take out those braids and give that hair a good brushing."

Twisting my sheet in my hands, I eyed the soft material with contempt. Obviously, Doc was right—there was no good reason for me to not get up and out. My leg was more or less healed; what remained of my wound was a small red line that rarely caused me pain anymore. And maybe that was the problem—the better I was feeling physically, the worse I felt mentally. I'd even begun wishing the infection would return, if only to divert my unending thoughts of Lucas. Without the fever to confuse me, without the pain to distract me, and without the drugs to numb me, I was feeling everything—all the grief and guilt and sorrow—tenfold.

"Britta dropped off a few more things for you last night," Doc continued, "another pair of pants and some clean underthings. I put them with the rest of your stuff."

Aside from Doc and Leisel, Britta was the only other person I saw on a regular basis. She seemed to constantly need medical treatment; every other day, she would show up requiring a bandage or the occasional stitch. Loud and always laughing, she was nosy too, oftentimes poking her head in my room, even going as far as to pull up a chair beside my bed and having entire conversations with me, despite the fact that I rarely replied.

"I have some free time this morning," Doc said over her shoulder as she moved toward the door. "Once you're dressed, I'll show you where the bathhouse is."

My gaze jerked back to Doc, my scowl deepening. I hadn't ventured outside since the day Logan and I had fought by the gate; the mere thought of everything and everyone beyond Doc's cabin left me feeling nauseous. There were so many people out there; after so long with only the three of us, the idea of living among such a large group felt way too daunting. Furthering my anxiety was the noticeable lack of Logan in my life. After years of him constantly berating me, and always breathing down my neck, judging my every move, two weeks without even as much as a glimpse of him felt... wrong.

"I've been cleaning myself," I muttered.

Pausing, Doc glanced back at me, her lips pursed with impatience. "Willow, a sponge bath in that itty-bitty bathroom isn't the same as an actual shower. Is this what you think that boy, Lucas, would have wanted for you? To waste away in a hospital bed?"

At the mention of Lucas, my eyes went wide. "That's not fair," I bit out.

Despite my melancholy, Doc had become something of a friendly face; at the very least, a regular face, and I'd grown comfortable with her to the point of confiding in her. Something I was absolutely regretting at this moment.

"Nothing in the world is fair, honey, but that doesn't mean we stop living. Now get up and let's go."

As she disappeared around the corner, I stared after her, my stomach fluttering. A shuddering breath fled my lips and, before I could talk myself out of it, I'd slid out of bed and was limping across the room, shuffling through the collection of clothing I'd been slowly accumulating. Grabbing several items, I pulled my socks and boots on and, with another trembling breath, left my room.

Perched on the edge of her desk, freshly dressed in jeans and a tank top, Doc glanced at me with a smile. "Ready?" she said, moving to the door without waiting for an answer.

As the front door swung open; the sun hit me first, followed by a warm breeze of fresh air. Doc descended the porch steps, gesturing for me to follow. "We'll go this way," she said, directing me off the beaten path. "Fewer people."

Following a short ways behind her, I kept my head down, until a moderate-sized cabin came into view, a large wooden sign hanging above the doorless entrance that read: **BATHHOUSE**. "Here we are," Doc announced. "Jordy takes care of cleaning and whatnot. Come on, I'll introduce you."

Jordy must have heard us coming; a tall, slim figure appeared around the side of the brick partition that led inside the bathhouse. With short dark hair and eyes to match, he wore only a pair of green khaki shorts that hung low on his hips, highlighting the sharp

V-shape chiseled into his lower abdomen. Despite his lean frame, tight muscles corded his arms and legs, and for a brief moment, he reminded me of Lucas.

"What's up, Doc?" he asked, smiling broadly, his deep voice thickly accented.

"The sky, honey, that's what," Doc said, chuckling. "But down here is Willow, and Willow is in desperate need of a shower."

Jordy's gaze slid to me, his dark eyes appraising me from head to foot. "That bad, huh?"

"Worse," Doc replied, and they both laughed.

Feeling the heat of embarrassment fan my cheeks, I glared at the ground. "Okay," I muttered. "I get it—I stink. Did you forget that I almost died recently?"

"Almost died?" Jordy continued to laugh. "Mate, that's an everyday occurrence in this world—stop acting like you're special or something."

My head jerked up, my glare clashing with Jordy's easygoing grin. But before I could think up a response, Doc was shoving a wide-tooth comb in my hand. "For your hair," she said, giving me a gentle shove forward. "I'll see you back at my place, alright?"

"Doc?" I asked, turning as she walked off. Was she really leaving me here with a complete stranger?

"Honey, I've got to get to the dining hall before they stop serving breakfast," she said. "You want to eat, don't you?"

"No worries," Jordy said. "I'll show you what's what. We've got shampoo and soap, and even rubber duckies if that's what you're into."

"Go on, Willow," Doc called out. "Jordy is good people. I promise!"

Swallowing back the countless number of irrational fears swirling inside me, I turned back to Jordy.

"Is it because I'm an Aussie? That why you don't trust me?" he asked, laughing. "We ain't all criminals and convicts, I promise." Still laughing, Jordy signaled for me to follow him, leading me inside the bathhouse, pointing out two wooden benches that sat on either side of the entranceway—one bench piled high with stacks of neatly folded towels and the other laden with toiletries. At least a dozen ceramic sinks adorned the entrance room, each sink with its own mirror and small shelf. Everything had been cleaned to a shine.

"Crappers are thataway," he said, pointing to a room on the left. "And showers are thataway." He waved toward a second adjoining room separated by a thick vinyl curtain. The curtain was pulled to one side, providing me a glimpse of at least a half dozen shower stalls.

"The water isn't hot," Jordy warned. "It gets pumped from the well, so unless it sits in the sun for a while, it's usually pretty cold."

Shaking my head, I mumbled, "I'm used to creek baths and showers in the rain. I'm still in awe that you guys even have running water."

"Ahhh, yes," he replied with a laugh. "I remember those days. Don't worry—soon you'll be whining about cold water like everyone else around here." Flashing me another lackadaisical grin, he continued, "Anyway, I'll get out of your way. Holler if you need something."

Standing in front of one of the many sinks, wrapped in a faded-blue towel, still wet from my shower, I stared at my reflection in the mirror, not really recognizing myself. Lifting a finger to my face, I slowly traced the shape of my mouth. I looked different than I remembered—my cheeks were rounder and my lips fuller than the last time I'd taken more than a brief look at myself. And my breasts were fuller, I realized, glancing down at my chest.

Turning slightly, I ran a hand through my unbound and freshly washed hair. My hair had never been something I'd concerned myself with before. Never knowing when I'd be able to wash it next, I'd always kept it in braids in an attempt to keep myself as neat as possible. I was thinking about it now, though, as I gazed over the long length of curls, the tips of which were brushing my waistline.

I looked... surprisingly good, even with the bags under my eyes. A little older, too. In fact, the more I stared at myself, the more I thought I might resemble my mother. Brushing my fingers through my hair, recalling the feel of her gentle hands doing the same, I swallowed hard, shuddering through a sudden torrent of emotion.

As my expression crumbled, I turned away from the mirror, sucking in deep breaths in an attempt to not cry. I dressed quickly in clean jeans and a T-shirt, knotting the oversized top at my waist. Finished cleaning up after myself, I took a steadying breath, and headed out into the heat of the day.

Jordy was lounging in a beach chair just outside the bathhouse; noticing me, his eyes went wide as he scrambled to stand. "Feel better?" he asked.

My gaze switched to my feet. "Yeah."

"Cool, cool." His appraising gaze turned downright appreciative and I flushed under the intensity. Barring Lucas, I couldn't remember anyone ever looking at me in such a way. "Hey, I really like your hair like that — you scrub up alright"

"Um, thanks..." Reaching to touch my hair, I quickly folded my arms over my chest. "I, um — I guess I should probably be getting back to Doc's now."

"I'll walk you back," he offered with a shrug.

"No, that's okay. I'm sure you're really busy — "

Jordy laughed. "You kidding, mate? I'm only busy working on my tan right now. Towels are washed, shelves restocked... " He shrugged again. "Come on, let me walk you back. It's no trouble;

I'm happy to do it. I need to stretch my legs anyway."

I glanced back the way I'd come—the shortcut through the trees—and then, with a reluctant sigh, agreed to follow Jordy down the path that soon led us into the heart of camp. At the first sight of people—a pair of women who only spared us a brief greeting—my unease doubled.

"Are you always this tense?" Jordy asked.

Surprised, my gaze shot to his. Out of all the colorful words that had been used to describe me throughout the course of my life, tense had never been among them. It was Logan who'd always been the tense one, who was always keyed up and on edge. Yet, even as I thought it, I was suddenly aware of the rigid way I was holding myself, of the downward turn of my mouth, and the nervous way I kept glancing around. Was this who I was now?

Unsure of what to say, I merely shrugged miserably in response.

As we looped around the center of camp, Jordy began pointing out different buildings, telling me about each. I attempted listening at first, but like everything else lately, it ended up being too much for me. While Jordy continued his tour, I gazed up at the clouds overhead, finding a formation that looked a little like a rabbit. And several others that had a definite resemblance to teacups.

It's always teatime, I heard Lucas say.

"And we've no time to wash the things between whiles," I whispered.

"What's that?" Jordy asked.

I shook my head and looked away, surprised to find that we'd walked into an area of camp full of cabins, several of which were in various states of repair. A construction crew bustled to and fro between buildings, shouting to be heard over the sound of tools. As I scanned the numerous faces, my gaze halted on the only one

I recognized.

Logan was seated astride a long beam at the top of a newly built structure, his blond hair glowing gold in the sun, his tool belt strapped around his waist, a hammer in hand. Plucking a nail from the several pressed between his lips, he held it in place as he nailed it in; he repeated this until he'd run out of nails, he paused to pull his shirt up, using the hem of it to wipe the sweat from his face.

"I'm gonna hit up a mate real quick," Jordy said. "You don't mind, do ya?"

"No," I replied, waving him off. "Go ahead."

While Jordy walked away, I looked back to Logan, startled to find his narrowed gaze clashing with mine. If Logan was surprised to see me, his stern features gave nothing away. Staring at one another, I found myself thinking about my hair again—how pretty it had looked in the mirror—and the unmistakable feeling of guilt began to stir in my belly. The longer we stared at one another, the guiltier I felt—guilt for thinking about something as frivolous as hair. Guilt for taking a shower, and having enjoyed it, too. And the worst guilt of all—the guilt that had left me unable to get out of bed, unable to face my new reality, the reality where I was alive and Lucas was not.

"Ready?" As Jordy returned to my side and Logan's eyes flicked to the slim, shirtless man beside me, I dropped my gaze, feeling suddenly embarrassed for reasons I couldn't quite explain. Wrapping my arms around my middle, I limped quickly down the path, feeling Logan's hard stare burning holes into my back.

SIXTEEN

LOGAN

What the fuck.

Jaw locked, nostrils flared, I watched Willow walk off with Jordy—the idiot who manned the bathhouse. He was young, in his early twenties, and seemed to suffer from an aversion to shirts and shoes, as I'd yet to see him wearing either. He was always grinning and telling jokes—mostly to the women in camp—and giving the impression of being an easygoing, carefree kind of guy, which was, word for word, my very least favorite type of person.

Willow didn't appear altogether comfortable with his attention either; the sole reason I hadn't yet chucked my hammer at Jordy's perfectly coiffed head of hair. That, and the fact that I hadn't even recognized Willow at first.

Her hair was down, hanging to her waist in tight, unruly curls, glistening wet in the bright sunlight. I couldn't remember having ever seen her hair loose like this before, even back before the world had gone to shit. Her clothes were ones I'd never seen before too; form-fitting jeans and a knotted T-shirt showing several inches of smooth skin at her waist. She'd gained some weight since I'd last seen her; her curves had reappeared, and her cheeks were as plump as I remembered them. Even her limp had improved considerably; it was hardly noticeable unless you were looking for it. In time, it would probably disappear entirely.

Willow had healed.

She'd also, at some point over the last two weeks, grown into *a seriously fucking beautiful woman.*

I'd never really understood what Lucas had seen in her, and maybe that was because, for me, her obnoxious personality and over-the-top outfits had always overshadowed her looks. But looking at her now…

Staring after her, I was still reeling.

"Hey, Logan! You done over there? Wanna grab a water break?"

Seated astride the beam beside mine, Elijah — EJ for short — was eagerly waving a hammer around. Fresh out of high school when the world called it quits, EJ had just enlisted in the army — a decision he claimed had saved his life. Though he hadn't been a soldier very long, he still wore his dog tags all these years later, and kept his head and face freshly shaved. Like me, he was a regular on the construction crew, usually serving as foreman when Joshua was busy elsewhere.

While I was thinking up an excuse, another voice chimed in. "I think a water break sounds great, don't you, Logan?" Peering up at me, Leisel mouthed *UXO*, before walking off.

Glaring after her, fighting back my rising anger, I gritted out, "Sure, EJ. A water break sounds great."

"Sweet!" EJ's enthusiasm was palpable as he swung his leg over the beam, jumping to the ground below. Sighing, I slipped my hammer into my tool belt and followed suit. I was genuinely thirsty, and I really didn't want Liesel following me around every day, treating me like some sort of pariah — thinking that at any moment I was going to explode.

"Did you see that twelve-point Buck the hunting crew brought in yesterday? We're gonna be feastin' tonight." Grinning, EJ fell in step beside me. "Man, we're never that lucky; rabbits and turkey, that's all we ever seem to get."

As per usual, EJ would talk enough for both of us, while I merely grunted and nodded in reply. Every day it felt like someone was always wanting to talk to me about something utterly irrelevant — I didn't give a single shit about weather patterns, personal grudges, or the absolute worst of all, *who was hooking up with who*. And maybe this was typical when your community consisted of only fifty-odd people — but for me, the constant chatting was quickly becoming hellish. Admittedly, I'd even begun to miss the solitude I'd once claimed to hate.

"Hey there, slowpokes." Britta was headed our way, twirling a hammer in her hand as if it were a baton. "What's the holdup on your cabin? Mine's nearly done."

"Thought you liked a man who could last a while?" EJ retorted.

"Nah, boy — what I like is a man who can keep up." With a wink, she sauntered off.

"*Fuck me*," EJ groaned, turning in a circle to watch her leave. "The things I would do to her if only she'd let me..." Shaking his head, he flashed me a grin. "How about you, Logan — you into older women?"

"Sure," I muttered. In truth, I didn't have a clue what I liked — something I'd only just realized. I liked women — that much I knew, but as far as a particular type of woman, I'd never given it much thought. Back before everything had gone to shit, I'd ogled my fair share and I'd certainly enjoyed sex, it just hadn't been a priority. My main focus had always been getting through school and then getting the hell out of town.

My thoughts strayed back to the countless nights I'd been forced to listen to Lucas and Willow having sex. A minor annoyance that, as more and more time passed, had become torturous. Back then, I'd chalked up my attraction to Willow as a fluke, only brought about by our close living quarters and the distinct lack of females in my life. Now, I no longer had the luxury of ignorance to hide behind; now, I was surrounded by other people, some of them good-looking women, and not a single one inspired the same sort of reaction in me that Willow did.

The realization made me scowl.

I was still scowling as I reached the water cooler, hard enough that I felt a headache coming on. Snatching a cup from the stack, I quickly filled it, dumping the water over my face and neck. Only once I'd cooled down and could trust myself to speak without screaming did I turn to EJ.

"So what's up with that Jordy guy?" I heard myself ask. Briefly closing my eyes, I cursed myself silently.

EJ glanced at me, brows raised. "What do you mean?"

Striving for nonchalance, I bent down, busying myself with refilling my cup. "Just saw him with Willow and wanted to know what kind of guy he was."

"Oh man, Willow was walking around camp today?" EJ smiled.

"How'd I miss that? She must be feeling better."

Having not spoken to Willow in several weeks, I merely shrugged and continued drinking my water. Word spread quickly around camp; case and point, everyone had known about mine and Willow's fight at the gate only minutes after it had happened. Which meant everyone also knew that I was no longer visiting Willow at Doc's anymore. They could make all the assumptions they wanted, but I wasn't about to add any fuel to their gossip fires.

"Jordy's alright, I guess," EJ continued. "And the girls seem to like him." At that, EJ rolled his eyes.

As my turbulent thoughts turned downright tumultuous, I suddenly felt like smashing to pieces all those brand-new beams I'd just installed. Which... why? What the fuck was my problem? Willow could do whatever the hell she wanted. She wasn't my business anymore. I'd fulfilled my promise and gotten her to safety and in doing so, there was no known reason to concern myself with her ever again.

Only the more I tried to convince myself of just that, the more I found myself feeling the opposite.

Jesus Christ, my headache was quickly becoming a migraine.

"Hey, man, you okay?" EJ asked.

I gave a sharp nod. "Fan-fucking-tastic," I replied through gritted teeth.

It was the wrong response, I realized, as EJ's curious gaze turned downright speculative. "Was Willow your girl?" he asked. "'Cause I thought Britta had said something about her being with your brother."

I found my fists clenching, disliking his implication that I shouldn't be concerned with who Willow spent her time with. I'd spent the last decade concerned about her; why would that suddenly change? But before I could think of a reply that didn't include me knocking EJ flat on his ass, there was a sudden commotion.

"Someone get Doc! Hank fell off the roof!"

Our cups clattering to the ground, EJ and I broke into a run, slowing at the edge of a small crowd forming around a cabin. A woman turned away in a hurry, her hand covering her mouth. Taking her place in the growing circle of people, I saw Hank. He lay on the ground, his face covered in blood. His left arm was bent backward, looking as if it had two elbows; someone had already torn his pant leg away, revealing an ugly wound on his thigh—a jagged shard of bone jutting through his mottled skin. The older man looked dazed—the whites of his eyes showing. He was panting and shaking, clearly in shock.

"Where's Doc? Someone get Doc!"

"We need the stretcher!"

"Everyone back up, back up—give 'em some space!"

The crowd hurried to part as Doc and two others came running through, pulling a stretcher along with them—the rolling sort you used to see in ambulances. Hank startled back to consciousness as he was lifted and shifted onto the gurney. His eyes bulging, a cross between a moan and wail burst from his lips in a spray of blood.

As they rushed Hank away, others followed. Those that remained formed small horror-stricken groups, speaking among themselves in hushed tones. I stood alone, wondering what I should be doing.

As the minutes ticked by and no one returned to work, I eventually collected my things and headed home. I'd only just arrived at my cabin when I noticed a familiar figure limping down the path, looking around as if she didn't know where she was.

"Willow?" I called out.

Willow faltered before freezing on me, her eyes widening in surprise. Standing yards apart, we stared at one another, her expression tight with strain, me unable to think of a single thing to say to her.

I cleared my throat. "Is everything… okay?"

Willow shook free from her freeze. Moving cautiously closer, she stammered, "Did you… did you see what happened?"

"The guy who fell off the roof? Yeah."

Rubbing her hands up and down her arms as if she were cold, she whispered, "I couldn't be in there—he was screaming, and there were… *people everywhere, and blood…* so much blood."

"I… uh, I was just going home," I said, jerking my chin at the cabin. "You could come in… if you wanted to?"

Willow glanced at the cabin, her tight expression relaxing fractionally. "I mean… if you don't… mind?"

It wasn't that I necessarily minded her company, only that I still didn't know what to say to her. Which was ridiculous. This was Willow; annoying, obnoxious, never-listens-worth-a-damn Willow. So why did everything feel twice as stiff all of a sudden?

With a silent growl of frustration, I pulled the door open. Willow followed me in, passing me as I paused at the entrance, the sweet smell of her flooding my senses. She had always smelled vaguely like flowers, but her scent, coupled with that of the soap she'd recently used, was downright intoxicating.

Fidgeting with the knot on her T-shirt, Willow's eyes bounced around the room before freezing on the sleeping bag on the floor. Her throat visibly bobbed.

"That's Luke's," she said thickly.

Idly, I rubbed at my neck. "Yeah."

"Do you, um, have anything else of his?" she asked hesitantly.

"Just his bag." I gestured to where it was propped against the wall.

"I thought we'd lost everything..." Her words died away as she stepped farther into the room, her eyes sweeping the full length of it. "So, um, how come you're not sleeping in a bed?"

Still rubbing my neck, my gaze dropped to the floor. It felt hypocritical to admit that after years of trying to find a place just like this one, and all the creature comforts it offered, I couldn't even enjoy something as basic as a mattress; that after all this time sleeping on the ground, I'd found that's where I was more comfortable.

"The door's got one of those stupid little clasp locks," I muttered. "It's not exactly safe, you know?"

"So you're sleeping on the floor in front of the door?"

"Yeah."

"Huh. Sounds like you."

Looking up, I found her mouth quirked into almost a smile and I felt myself relax a fraction. Unbuckling my tool belt, I slung it onto the dresser and took a seat on a bottom bunk.

"I can't believe you're really not sleeping in a bed," Willow continued. "I mean, when was the last time we even had clean beds to sleep in?" Pushing tentatively on the mattress, she stretched out on her back, causing her cropped shirt to pull up farther, exposing a great deal of her skin and I found myself visually roaming all the dips and valleys of her ribcage, the barely there hill of her stomach, and the mouthwatering space between the waist of her jeans and rise of her hip bones.

"It's pretty comfy," Willow said, turning toward me. "Not as comfy as Doc's, but still, you should maybe try it."

I quickly refocused on her face. "Uh, yeah. Maybe. Speaking of

Doc—how's your leg?"

Willow shifted to sitting, kicking her legs out one at a time. "Okay, I guess. It still aches. Mostly right here." She leaned down to rub her calf, a move that caused her heavy mane of curls to fall forward. The sudden urge to run my hands through it was unmistakable.

I shot up off the bed, turning to the window. "Yeah, so, I'm guessing you'll have to move out of Doc's now. At least until Hank heals up?" Recalling the blood spraying from Hank's mouth, I grimaced. *If he healed up.*

"I hadn't even thought of that."

Still staring out the window, I gave a sharp shake of my head. Of course she hadn't. When had Willow ever put any thought into anything?

"You'll probably have to stay here," I practically growled, growing more agitated by the second, though I wasn't entirely sure why. Willow had always been clueless; this wasn't anything new. "There's limited cabins, you know? Friends and families are paired up."

"Oh," she replied quietly. "I mean, yeah, that makes sense..." she trailed off and I turned around to find her gaze on the hands in her lap, her brow deeply furrowed. "Are you sure you'd be okay with that? I mean, because of our fight..."

Sighing, I dragged my hands up and down my face. "We always fight. Not sure why that fight is any different than all the others. Let's just blame this place, okay? It's a shock to your system—I'm still... *adjusting.*" I spat the word as if it tasted bad.

Willow's entire expression shifted. Her eyes lightened and the line between her brows disappeared. Admitting I wasn't good at something was not an easy task for me, and she knew it.

"I thought it was just me," she breathed. "It's so noisy here and everyone always wants to talk, you know? It's so weird."

I snorted. Weird was putting it mildly. "Yeah."

"And they're always up in your space." Willow faked a shudder.

I nodded gravely. "Telling you about their day and shit."

"*Yes.*" Willow's eyes grew wide. "And walking right into your room and acting like you're best friends."

"And thinking you're a UXO."

"A what?"

"Nothing—never mind. You know, they actually complain about what's for dinner?"

"Apparently they complain about their showers, too. It's insane, right?"

"I think they forgot what it's like to be out there. They've been safe behind these walls…" I let my words die off with a shake of my head.

"And they all seem so happy, too," Willow added, scoffing. "Like nothing ever happened."

"You always seemed happy," I bit out before I could stop myself. "You and Luke were always running around, singing and dancing, without a care in the fucking world."

Willow's mouth fell open just as mine snapped shut, our tentative camaraderie gone in the blink of an eye. Looking away, Willow's bottom lip disappeared beneath the top, her expression crumbling.

"We *were* happy," she whispered. "At least, we tried to be."

The pain in her voice straight up slayed me; it ate at me from the inside out, leaving me feeling hollow and empty. Cursing beneath my breath, I ran my hands hastily through my hair.

"I'm sorry," I ground out. "I don't know why I said that. It's been a long fucking…" I paused and swallowed, wondering if

Liesel's impression of me might actually be true.

"Life?" Willow offered hesitantly.

"Yeah," I muttered. "That works."

"Logan, listen, about what I said —"

"It's fine," I said quickly, waving away whatever she was going to say. I didn't want to talk about it anymore. I didn't even want to think about it. "Like I said, it's this fucking place."

"It's not fine. I was acting completely crazy. I shouldn't have yelled at you. And you were right — I *was* being selfish. You pulled me out of the ravine and you brought me here and you saved me and I-I-I'm sorry, Logan. I'm just really *fucking* sorry for everything."

For a moment, I could only stare. Willow didn't apologize, at least, never quite so easily. And she definitely didn't agree with me, especially when it came to my less than gracious depictions of her. Shaking off my shock, I fumbled to find a fast reply. "I was just angry — I didn't mean what I said either."

"But you were right," she bit out, her crestfallen expression beginning to tremble, her hands fisting in her lap. "About everything."

While Willow's unexpected declaration hung trapped in the growing quiet between us, I was left struggling to get my thoughts in order. An admission like this from Willow would have left me feeling smug once; now, though, I found myself lacking the assurance I once had, and wondering if I'd ever been right. About anything.

"Let's just forget it happened, alright?" My head was pounding, my temples throbbing, the tendons in my neck feeling as if they might snap from strain.

"But —"

"Willow, stop. It's over and done with. We can... Fuck, I don't know — we can start fresh or something."

"Are you serious?" Willow looked bewildered. "Start fresh? Even after... everything?"

"We've both got to live here, right? We don't need to make it harder than it already is."

We stared at one another, Willow worrying her bottom lip, me wondering if I wasn't just talking nonsense. There was so much shit between us — the history that suffocated our every move. We'd known each other forever and disliked one another for twice as long. We were comfortable in those roles, and yet... for whatever reason... those roles didn't seem to quite fit anymore.

"Okay," she eventually murmured, sounding every bit as unsure as I was feeling. "Let's start... fresh."

SEVENTEEN

WILLOW

Limping past the animal paddocks, I followed the signs that would lead me to the garden—little wooden placards nailed to trees with small red flowers painted on each. I'd slept very little the night before, kept awake for a variety of reasons, the most pressing being the job I was beginning this morning—my very first job.

It was a week of firsts for me, actually. After an extensive discussion with Leisel, she'd agreed that it was time for me to move out of Doc's cabin and begin pulling my weight around camp. Regarding living arrangements, I'd been given two options—living with Ella or living with Logan, the only two people in camp who lived alone. Having never met Ella, I'd chosen Logan—figuring the devil you knew was infinitely preferable to the devil you didn't, and that maybe Logan was right—maybe we could start fresh. Next, we'd discussed my skills, or lack thereof, eventually concluding that I'd try my hand in the garden, tending to the crops grown in camp and I'd agreed. Working outside, doing a job that didn't require a lot of human interaction, definitely felt like the best option for me.

The sound of bleating sheep and whinnying horses intensified my headache, the sharp smell of manure making me feel downright nauseous. Placing my hand on my stomach, I picked up my pace, hurrying past the barns.

"Hey, Willow—wait up!" Turning, I found Jordy jogging toward me, dressed in swim trunks and a faded Hawaiian print shirt, the open ends flapping as he ran.

"Hey," I said, forcing a smile. "Wow, look at you—you're actually wearing a shirt."

Popping his collar, he flashed me a comically brazen look— wagging his brows while twisting his lips. "Sure am," he replied. "You like?"

Taking a closer look at the faded pattern, I found the flowery print also contained turtles on surfboards. "It's very you, Jordy." I smiled again, a little less forced. "The turtles are cute."

Jordy brushed a speck of invisible lint from his shoulder. "Just like the bloke wearing it, right?"

I burst into laughter, quickly followed by a pang of longing so sharp, my breath hitched. Jordy was silly in a way that reminded me of Lucas. It didn't help that his height and build, and chiseled good looks were also so unnervingly similar.

"So," Jordy continued with a sly smile. "Where're ya' headed this morning?"

"I'm supposed to meet Cassie."

"Ahhh, so you're on spud duty, huh? Did ya' pull the short straw?"

Shrugging, I said, "I don't think they knew what to do with me. I can't build anything. I don't know how to cook. I refuse to hunt, and —"

"You refuse to hunt? How come? Can't imagine anyone surviving outside the wall without having to hunt once in a while."

"Logan and Luke did that," I said. "I did a lot of foraging. I don't really like... killing."

As I said it, I could hear the echo of distant screaming, the thud of angry fists, and then a series of gunshots — one tiny explosion after another, sending small clumps of lead tearing through the fabric of the atmosphere. Small, and yet capable of so many monumental alterations.

I blew out a slow breath, allowing the warm breeze to carry my nightmare away.

"Yeah, I feel ya." Jordy flashed another grin. "Well, so, what're you doing after work — you wanna hang out or something?"

Frozen in place, I blinked at Jordy. Was he asking me to hang out or was he asking me out on a date? The possibility that he could be interested in me *in that way* made my stomach flip, and not in a good way.

"I, um, I told Doc I would eat dinner with her today, so, you know." I gave an apologetic shrug.

"Great," he said. "So I'll see you and Doc for tea, then. Oh, and, you know where to find me if you want to cool off later." Flashing another grin, he jogged off.

I stared after him for a moment, wondering if I was just out of practice interacting with people who weren't Lucas, the only person who'd ever known me well enough to read between the lines. Or was Jordy just that pushy? One thing was for certain, I definitely wasn't interested in anything more than friendship. With a short shake of my head, I continued on.

Four women and a teenage boy stood near the garden entrance, loading tools from a nearby shed into several large wheelbarrows. Cassie, who I'd been introduced to only yesterday, glanced up from her work. "Hello, Willow — right on time!" she called out.

Cassie was a curvy woman with dark, close-cropped hair. She wore large hoop earrings and rings on each finger; a floppy-brimmed hat hung around her neck, and a pair of dirty gloves had been stuffed in her pants pocket. Her pale skin was heavily freckled, and she had an intricate tangle of laugh lines around each of her mismatched eyes — one brown, one blue. She could have been anywhere between thirty-five and fifty-five, there was just something timeless about her.

"Hey," I replied quietly, feeling inexplicably shy as I took in the curious gazes of the others.

"Willow, meet Avery, Ruth, and Ella." Cassie pointed to each of the women as she named them. Smiles and waves were exchanged from everyone but Ella, whose crossed arms and cocked hip suggested I'd made the right decision to move in with Logan.

"And this is Ruth's boy, Stuart." Stuart, who had a vintage cassette player clipped to his jeans and a pair of headphones over his ears, didn't even look up.

"Not many working batteries to be found anymore, so Xavi built Stuart a solar-paneled Walkman. That man's a genius and a godsend, if you ask me." Shaking her head, Cassie continued, "Anyway, you'll be working with me today, Willow, so I can show you what's what. Go on and grab that wheelbarrow for me."

Pulling a long chain from inside her tunic, Cassie produced a key that opened the padlock on the garden gate. It was nothing like the impressive wall surrounding camp, just a stretch of chain-link fencing offering light protection to the crops inside. Holding the gate open, Cassie gestured for the others to enter, each of them pushing their own wheelbarrow.

"Compost is over there," Cassie said, pointing. "And the good stuff is this way." She gestured me inside; grabbing the wheelbarrow, I pushed forward.

The garden was lush with color and overflowing with crops. Rows of raised beds greeted me, each teeming with growth; bright-yellow squash, dark-green bell peppers, red and purple heads of cabbage. Cucumber vines hung from climbing trellises; tomato plants grew inside cylindrical cages, their green and red fruit visible from within. Elevated planters sat covered in greenery, each one labeled with a sign detailing its contents: CHARD. ROSEMARY. PARSLEY. DILL WEED. It was nothing short of a rainbow — a well-organized, properly constructed rainbow.

"Are you any good at growing?" Cassie asked.

"I don't know," I admitted. "I like plants. I mean, I like nature and stuff, but I've never tried growing anything before... "

"My mom loved plants," I continued. "She had a lot of houseplants but they never lasted very long. My dad used to tease her and tell her she loved her plants to death."

Cassie threw her head back, laughing. "So I'll be working with a black thumb, then?"

"A black thumb?" I asked.

Glancing back at me, she smiled warmly. "It's the opposite of a green thumb."

A nervous laugh escaped me. "Oh. Yeah, maybe."

"Well, we'll see what we can do with you. Leisel mentioned you're good at identifying plants?"

"Yeah, sort of. My, um, my boyfriend's mom used to garden. She taught him a few things and he taught me. Mainly what's edible and what's not." I swallowed past the lump forming in my throat and shrugged.

"Invaluable information to have in these unprecedented times," Cassie replied. "I'm guessing bugs and dirt don't bother you?"

"No, not at all. I actually kinda like bugs. They're just trying to survive, same as us… " I trailed off as we approached several small trees, their spindly branches hanging heavy with bright-red apples. They were young trees, stabilized by thick wire wrapped around their trunks, affixed to wooden posts on either side. I slowed as we passed, staring at the juicy-looking fruit.

"Red Delicious," Cassie said, laughing again. "Just about ready for picking, too. How do you like your apple pie, Willow? Hot or cold?"

I stuttered and stammered through my answer, much to Cassie's amusement. "We'll start with hot and go from there," she said. "You don't mind honey in your pie, do you?"

"Honey?" I repeated dumbly.

"Sugar is a hot commodity these days, and we haven't come across any in a long time. So I use honey in all my baked goods. We have our own apiary, behind the horse stable, though no one dares go near it but me."

Apple pie. Honey. Baked goods. An apiary. I comprehended what Cassie was saying, and yet, I couldn't fathom it. Apple trees were one thing, but warm apple pie with fresh honey was on a whole other level.

"We'll be working just up there." Cassie gestured ahead. "Potatoes and squash are ready for harvest."

To the left were several farmed rows covered in bright-yellow squash growing along leafy vines. To the right were dozens of raised beds containing sprawling bushy plants, some of them sprouting tiny blue flowers.

"You too, Ella!" Cassie called out. "Over here, please — squash and potatoes today."

Glancing back, I found Ella trudging up behind me, violently shoving her wheelbarrow along. Her long blonde hair was tied to one side in a thick braid and, although her expression was partially hidden behind large sunglasses, the flat line of her mouth gave the distinct impression that she was unhappy. Dropping her wheelbarrow with a thud, she said, "Newbs always get the shit jobs."

Cassie remained smiling. "Very true, Ella. I like to start everyone off with the hardest tasks; makes you more grateful for the easy ones." Looking at me, she said, "Don't mind Ella, she's always grumpy in the morning."

"Whatever," Ella snapped. Reclaiming her wheelbarrow, she marched off in the direction of the raised beds.

"See those first twelve beds?" Cassie continued on jovially as if Ella's temper tantrum was an everyday occurrence. "Those are my early bloomers — they all need to be harvested today. The main crop will be ready by the end of summer and everything after that will be ready around Christmastime."

Signaling me to follow, Cassie continued, "Now, the best way to dig up potatoes is to use your hand and very gently pull up the whole plant. Go slow and be careful — you don't want to break the stem."

Cassie bent down beside a bed, pulling a trowel from her back pocket. Using the tool, she loosened the soil around the plant; setting the trowel aside, she dug her hands into the soil, and slowly pulled up the entire plant. Once free, I counted eight potatoes hanging from their mother, all varying in size. One by one, Cassie carefully plucked six of them, placing them in the wheelbarrow.

"Then we put it back and let the little ones grow some more," she said, repotting the plant with quick, sure hands. "And we say a little prayer of thanks."

Straightening, Cassie held out the trowel and nodded at the next plant. "Now you try."

Reluctantly, I took the tool and bent down beside the bed. Knees planted firmly in the dirt, I began digging carefully around the plant. Once the soil was loose, I dug my fingertips around the base, feeling my way down until I couldn't feel any more plant. Taking a breath, I tugged slowly upward, mindful of the roots, revealing a bounty of fresh, fat potatoes.

"Just pull them off?" Feeling uncertain, I glanced up at Cassie.

"Just pull them off," she repeated warmly.

Plucking off the biggest potatoes, I placed them into the wheelbarrow, then pushed the nearly empty plant back into the earth. Finished, I stood, wiping off my dirty hands on my jeans.

"You're a natural!" Cassie exclaimed, clapping her hands together. "Well done, Willow."

I found myself smiling in the face of her praise; I couldn't ever remember being good at anything before. Other than causing trouble. I'd never had any lofty career goals; all I'd ever wanted was to be free of my suffocatingly small hometown and see the world. Then later, living wild, I'd never felt any real sense of purpose. Forced to live day to day, most of my time had been eaten up with chores necessary for survival. But this—digging my hands in the dirt, contributing to something bigger than me—felt *damn good.*

Cassie remained by my side while I continued on; each successful harvest leaving me feeling more secure in my newfound ability. Soon, she left me on my own, happily stating that she wasn't needed anymore.

In time, Ella—who'd stormed off to the opposite end of the potato beds—had worked her way back to me. Digging side by side, I tossed surreptitious glances in her direction, wondering what her deal was, curiosity eventually getting the better of me.

"Hey, so, did you say you were new here?"

"No," Ella said woodenly, keeping her eyes on her work. "I've been here a while—Cassie just likes to torture me." Letting out an angry sigh, she continued. "I left, and now I'm back, and that's all you need to know, *new girl*."

"Willow," I said sharply, feeling a surge of indignation. *Yeah, Ella and I definitely wouldn't have worked as roommates.*

"Excuse me?" Ella peered over the top of her sunglasses.

"My name is Willow." I purposefully punctuated each syllable. "Not *new girl*."

With a roll of her eyes, Ella pushed her sunglasses back up the bridge of her nose. "Okay? And what? Do you want a medal for having a name?" Scoffing, she stood, brushing the dirt from her pants.

My temper flared and I jumped to my feet. "No, I don't want a fucking medal, but some respect would be great. *Thanks*." Before she could respond, I'd grabbed hold of my wheelbarrow and jerked it away. Dropping down beside an untouched bed of potatoes, I resumed working.

I worked diligently until meeting Ella in the middle once more. Pulling her sunglasses from her face, revealing delicate ivory features and cheeks smattered with freckles, she presented me with a canteen from her hip. "Thirsty, *Willow*?"

I stared at her. Back in school, when someone would speak to me the way Ella was, I usually ended up with a week's worth of detention for fighting. Only the more I stared at Ella, noting the tight lines around her eyes and mouth, I felt a sense of familiarity.

Pain recognized pain.

"You're sweating like a pig," Ella continued, shaking the canteen at me. "I can't have you dying of dehydration and leaving me to pick all the potatoes, can I?"

My lips curled in a silent snarl. Of course I was sweating—I'd been working my goddamn ass off. I was hot and sweaty, and covered in dirt, my back and knees aching as if I'd been curled up inside a wooden box for hours... but it felt good. *I* felt good. And I wasn't going to let Ella ruin my first good mood in months. Snatching the canteen from her, I drank deeply, not even pausing for breath until I heard Logan's angry voice echoing in my thoughts, demanding that I *ration it*. Reluctantly, I handed it back.

"Finish it," she said, pushing it back at me. "It's not like we don't have more."

Feeling instantly foolish, I muttered my thanks and drank what was left.

"Hungry, girls?" Cassie headed toward us, a burlap bag brimming with shiny red apples slung over her shoulder. Tossing two apples our way, Ella bit into hers right away, crunching loudly as she chewed, while I stared at the flawless fruit, turning it over in my hand.

It wasn't as if it was the first time I'd seen an apple since the beginning of this nightmare, but it was the first time that eating one felt like a perfectly normal thing to do. I didn't have to save it for later or share it; I didn't have to figure out how to ration a single apple for the next week. All those years we'd spent searching for our next meal, living in a constant state of hunger, were really and truly behind us now.

Cassie bent down in front of me. "Everything okay, Willow?"

I swallowed. "Yeah," I whispered, bringing the apple to my

lips. Biting down, juices exploded in my mouth, trickling down my chin.

Smiling, Cassie patted me on the shoulder and stood. "Good to hear. Well, girls, I'm headed over to Doc's — figured with everything poor Hank's going through, he could use an apple or two himself."

"She likes you," Ella stated matter-of-factly, frowning at Cassie's rapidly retreating form. "You won't be picking potatoes very long."

A burst of laughter landed me with a piece of apple caught in my throat. As I choked through my next several breaths, Ella snapped, "What the hell is so funny?"

"Nothing really…" I continued to cough until I'd cleared my throat. "I mean, it's just funny because no one ever used to like me… except for Luke," I quickly amended. "My um… my… " my words trailed off. I didn't know what to call Lucas anymore. I couldn't keep calling him my boyfriend, could I? And *my dead boyfriend* didn't exactly have the nicest ring to it.

"I get it," Ella said with a bitter sigh. Looking out across camp, she chucked her apple core away. "I have one of those, too."

"Oh, I, um, didn't realize," I stammered.

"How would you? You're not psychic. You asked where I went. Well, I went with him, and then… " She paused and sighed again. "And then I came back."

I shook my head. "Where'd you guys go?"

"Everdeen — his camp. We used to hook up occasionally, you know? Like when we'd see each other at trades and stuff, and then one day he asked me to stay with him." She shrugged again. "So I did."

I blinked at her, the apple in my hand forgotten. "Wait, what? There's another camp? A camp like this one?"

"It's not as big as Silver Lake, but they do okay." Ella tilted her head to one side. "You seem surprised."

"I *am* surprised," I breathed. "I didn't think places like this existed anymore; we hadn't come across a camp in years until this one, and now you're telling me there's two?" Stunned, I continued to shake my head. "Everdeen — how close is it?"

"About a three day drive — a week if we take the horses. We trade with them a few times a year; the next trip will be right after the fall harvest. If you want to go, you'll have to tell Leisel now — the convoys fill up quickly."

Remembering the apple in my hand, I took another bite. Chewing, I wondered how many communities we'd missed over the years, questioning what might have gone differently if we'd found one years ago. Wondering if Lucas might still be alive. At that last thought, my mood soured.

"Anyway," Ella said. "We've got more fucking potatoes to pick." Rising, she stalked off down the row muttering to herself. "More fucking potatoes. More fucking squash. More fucking apples. More fucking herbs. More fucking bullshit. More, more, more."

Lounging in bed after work, nursing the aggravated ache in my leg, I was leafing through an old magazine I'd found tucked inside the bathroom cupboard when Logan arrived home. Fresh from work, he was shirtless, with his tool belt slung over one shoulder. Pausing in the entranceway, he glanced at me as if he were surprised to find me here — the same look he'd given me each day since I'd moved in. Tossing the magazine aside, I sat up and gave a small wave, feeling instantly stupid for doing so. Dropping my hands in my lap, I muttered hello.

Logan looked up from toeing his boots off. "Hey. How was your first day?"

"Good, I guess. I like Cassie. I don't know about Ella, though."

"Ella?" he asked. "Blonde girl? Always wearing sunglasses?"

"That's her," I replied.

"Yeah, she seems like a bitch."

"Maybe." I shrugged. "I think she's just in a lot of pain."

Logan puttered through the cabin quickly before heading inside the bathroom, closing the door behind him. I stared after him, wondering when modesty had crept back into our lives. Instead of changing without reservation, Logan and I now took turns dressing inside the bathroom behind a closed door. The closed doors at every turn, was perhaps the strangest thing of all.

He reemerged moments later with a wet face and beard and wearing clean jeans and T-shirt. "You headed to dinner?"

"I'm not really hungry," I admitted. Shrugging, I turned my attention to a fraying thread on the knee of my jeans. "I think I'll probably stay in tonight." While it was true that working in the blistering heat all day hadn't done my appetite any favors, it was the thought of having to see everyone again, after having just seen them all at breakfast, along with Jordy's insistence that he sit with me this evening. Just the thought of having to try and make conversation felt... overwhelming.

Logan frowned deeply. "Is it your leg? Do you need to see Doc?"

I waved my hand at him. "No, it's fine — *I'm fine*. I'm really not hungry. I'm exhausted and, I mean, I've had enough of people for one day."

Logan took a seat on his bed, sighing. "Tell me about it," he muttered. "EJ... he never shuts the fuck up."

As we lapsed into silence, I tried to think up something more to say. Try as we might to make small talk with one another, to *start fresh*, things remained impossibly awkward and tense, as if our history couldn't help but stifle a fresh start that might be possible otherwise. If Lucas were still here, I knew what he would do, what he'd always done when it came to Logan. No matter how stubborn, no matter how hardheaded or surly Logan would become, Lucas had always tried to reach him.

I cleared my throat. "Hey, so, do you know about Everdeen? I guess it's another camp that Silver Lake trades with sometimes."

Logan glanced up, blinking through his bleary-eyed stare. "Yeah, I've heard it mentioned—I think it's some sort of gated trailer park."

"Don't you think it's crazy that there are two camps like this?" I continued. "And that they're close enough to trade? I mean, how many camps do you think we've missed over the years?"

"Camps like *this one*? Not many, is my guess. Yeah, there's other people out there, but are they as well organized and as vigilant as this place? Not a chance in hell. "

"You never know," I mused. "There could be others."

"Yeah, and you remember what some of those other places were like, right? Everyone was fucking nuts. And that was early on. Shit tends to roll downhill."

"Or maybe," I replied smartly, with a finger in the air. "Some of those places got their shit together and rolled it right back up the hill. Maybe they're all doing great right now. Maybe they've elected a president and a Congress and they're getting ready to send monkeys to the moon."

Logan blinked back his surprise, a smile tugging at his eyes and mouth, before falling back on his bed with a short, "Fuck that. If the monkeys get to leave this shithole planet, *then we're going with them."*

Chuckling, I fell back on my own bed. And this time, when the cabin eclipsed into silence, it felt substantially less awkward and infinitely more companionable. I nearly laugh out loud as I shook my head.

Logan and I, companionable?

Ha. There was no freaking way.

EIGHTEEN

LOGAN

"Move over, Eddie." Britta dropped her tray onto the table with a clatter, sending bits of food flying in my direction. Covered in gore from her head to hands, she took the seat directly beside mine, tucked a napkin into the collar of her blood-soaked top and began to eat. Frowning, I shifted my chair quickly away from Britta's, and closer to Willow's.

"What is all over you?" Ella asked. "Is that... *blood*?" Ella, seated at the table across from Willow, wrinkled her nose in Britta's direction.

"Sure is, sugar. Blood an' guts an' who knows what else. I was outside the wall pullin' rabbits outta traps and this Dead Head shows up outta nowhere, grabbin' my rabbit, playin' fuckin' tug-a-war with me." Britta paused to scoop a spoonful of mashed potatoes into her mouth. "Dang thing didn't want *me* at all—just wanted my rabbit. Tore it right in half and got to eatin'."

"Gross," Ella muttered. "Couldn't you have cleaned up before you came here?"

"An' chance missin' dinner?" Britta looked momentarily aghast before she resumed eating with vigor.

"I ever tell you guys the joke about the vulture who boarded an airplane with two dead rabbits?" Jordy asked, sending a wink in Willow's direction. "And the flight attendant says, 'sorry, mate, only one carry-on per passenger.'"

"What do you call a hundred rabbits eating backward?" EJ added. "*A receding hare line.*"

Ella scoffed. "Not funny, Elijah."

EJ grinned at the scowling blonde. "Not funny to *you* maybe, GabriElla."

Glancing at Willow, I found her watching the banter around the table with a small, amused smile. Meanwhile, I was contemplating gouging out my eardrums with the fork I was white-knuckling.

"I'm headed home," I gritted out softly. With barely a glance in my direction, Willow only nodded in reply.

As I stalked my way toward the doors, laughter rang out loudly. Glancing back at the table I'd just departed, everyone was doubled over—even Ella was laughing—while Jordy rose from his seat and bowed dramatically.

Scowling, I pushed through the double doors, happy to leave the noise behind. *So much for Willow wanting to avoid people.* Beginning with Britta, each day over the past two weeks had brought about new dining companions. Jordy had appeared next, armed with jokes that weren't funny, and flirting with Willow like his life depended on it. And Willow did nothing to dispel his attention. In fact, lately she seemed to be lapping it up. The tables had turned since high school; it was Willow who had a penchant for making friends now, whereas I'd become the outsider.

Inside the cabin, I reclaimed my tool belt and headed to my makeshift workbench—an old metal desk that fit nicely at the end of my bed. Rummaging through my tools, I began sanding a set of hanging shelves we'd been given. I wasn't sure what I was going to do with them, other than sand them down and slap some finish on them. Regardless, it felt good to keep my hands busy and mind occupied on things that didn't involve Willow.

The workbench wasn't the only new addition to the cabin— new-to-us curtains had replaced the tattered, torn ones, and a hand-me-down table and chairs graced a corner of the cabin. A small hand-braided rug sat in the center of the room and both bunk beds were fitted with clean sheets and covered in mismatched pillows and blankets. The clothing we'd both been slowly accumulating was neatly folded and put away inside our separate dressers… at least, my clothing was put away. Willow's things were half shoved into open drawers and strewn over her unmade bed.

Yet, however homey the cabin was beginning to look, and however like a home it was starting to feel, I'd made sure to keep Lucas's bag packed full of supplies, and stored directly under my bunk, ready to grab and go in the case of an emergency.

"We have… mail."

Willow stood in the entranceway, staring down at a letter in her hand, as if she'd never seen one before.

Tossing my sandpaper aside, I turned to her. "What do you mean, *we have mail*?"

"*I mean*, we have literal mail. Look, it's even addressed to us." Moving closer, Willow waved the envelope around. "Willow and

Logan, Silver Lakes Community, Cabin Twelve." She chuckled. "They even made it sound official."

I snatched the envelope from her. Sure enough, someone had written our names together — *Willow and Logan* — as if we were a pair, a couple even. Before I could think too long or hard on that particular notion, I flung the envelope toward the table and turned back to my workbench, quickly reclaiming my sandpaper.

"Who brought it?" I asked, as I resumed sanding.

"Davey, I think."

Choking on a laugh, I cleared my throat. "Davey's the fucking mailman?"

"Davey is whatever Leisel and Joshua want him to be... oh my god, Logan, *it's a wedding invitation.*"

Willow had torn open the envelope, letting it flutter to the floor. Holding a small yellow index card, she scanned the card, her eyes widening. "Maria and James invite you to join in the celebration of their wedding on Saturday, August fifteenth. The ceremony and reception will take place in the dining hall. Five p.m." Willow glanced up at me, perplexed. "A wedding? People still do that?"

Bending down, I scooped up the shredded envelope and shoved it in my pocket. "Who are Maria and James?"

"They're Maria and James — I mean, Jim. You know, they have that weird little kid who never stops talking about his dead grandpa?"

"Great," I muttered. "My favorite person."

Snorting, Willow tossed the card onto the table and kicked her boots off, leaving them where they'd landed — in the middle of the room. As she disappeared inside the bathroom, the door clicking shut behind her, I picked up her boots, setting them neatly on her side of the room. I'd only just resumed working on the shelves when Willow emerged from the bathroom, her hair down, and wearing only an oversized T-shirt with a pair of pink underwear, clearly discernible as she took a seat at the table, with one long, smooth leg folded beneath her and the other propped beside her.

Jesus... I inwardly groaned at the sweet sight of her half undressed.

Living with Willow was rapidly becoming unbearable. Without Lucas around to dissuade me from staring, I was left free to drink my fill of her. Which, in turn, left me in a constant state of agitation, arousal, or both. Willow, at least, seemed oblivious.

"Have you ever been to a wedding?" she asked idly, her focus on the mason jar full of homemade skin cream — a recent gift from Cassie. Twisting open the tin top, she scooped some of the mixture into her hands and began smoothing it up and down her arms. Moving onto her legs, she lifted each one high into the air, slowly massaging the lotion into her skin. I would have thought she was doing it purely to torment me, if it weren't for the fact that we'd regularly seen one another in various stages of undress over the years.

"Logan?"

I blinked back to her face. "Huh?"

"I said — have you ever been to a wedding?"

Turning back to the bench, I resumed sanding with vigor. "Once when I was little. One of my mom's friends, I think."

"Which friend?"

"Mrs. Vernon — you know, the woman who worked at the library."

"Mrs. Vernon," she repeated slowly, her voice softening. "Yeah, I remember her."

Picking up on the melancholy in her tone, I turned to find Willow with her lotion set aside, sitting slumped over the table, her chin cradled in her hands. "She used to let me and Luke hang out in the reading loft after hours," she said, gazing out across the room. I tried to think of something to say, some way to comfort her, when she suddenly sat up with a burst of laughter.

"Oh my god, do you remember the night Luke and I came home absolutely annihilated? Like, we couldn't even walk?"

How could I forget the absolute fuss my mom had made over it—the lengths she'd gone to hide the entire infuriating episode from our father. After rushing Luke off to bed, she'd appointed me in charge of getting Willow safely home.

"Yeah," I replied, my tone as dry as the scowl on my face. "You threw up in my truck."

Willow laughed harder. "We'd been at the library that night—we found a bottle of tequila in Mrs. Vernon's desk and I totally pressured Luke into drinking it with me."

"And then you threw up in your driveway," I continued.

"And Luke was singing the ABC's the whole walk home…"

"And then you threw up on your porch."

"And then he just collapsed in the front yard—I couldn't get him up." Willow was breathless with laughter, clutching her stomach.

"And then you threw up all over your dad…"

As Willow continued to laugh, tears flooded her cheeks, her laughter growing louder and shriller, until she was no longer laughing, but crying, I stepped toward her. "Willow—" I began.

"No, no—I'm fine," she rushed to say, even as tears continued rolling down her cheeks. "I'm sorry—I don't know what just happened. I just… I just miss him." Looking up at me, she attempted to smile, waving her hand in the air as if to wave her words away.

I remained standing there—I wanted to tell her that I missed him, too, that every time I thought of Lucas I felt a crushing sensation in my chest so intense it would freeze me in place and leave me struggling to breathe. I wanted to commiserate with her—the only other person on this planet who'd loved my brother as much as I did, but something was stopping me. The very same hesitation that had been stopping me from connecting with anyone my whole goddamn life.

"Hey, um, so, tell me what the wedding was like—the one you went to." Wet and rimmed in red, Willow's brown eyes implored me.

"Uh, well, it was boring, I guess. Everyone was drunk and doing stupid dances, and you know how I feel about that shit."

"What kind of dances?"

"I don't know—the chicken dance. The Macarena. Stupid stuff."

Willow's eyes shot to mine, a familiar spark burning within. A smile played across her lips. "I think we should go," she said, tapping the invitation lying on the table. "I want to see what it's like."

My eyes crossed. Just the thought of being at an event like that—where the whole camp would undoubtedly be in attendance—was enough to make my skin crawl. "No way."

"Oh, come on, Logan. It might be fun."

"No way, I'm not going."

"Why not?"

"Why would I?"

"To see what it's like—*obviously*. The same reason people used to go to zoos—to see things they haven't seen before."

"First," I told her. "I've already been to a wedding—I don't need to see what it's like. And second, did you just compare Silver Lake to a *fucking zoo*?"

Willow pursed her lips. "I hadn't meant to, but now that you mention it—it's kind of like we're in a cage, right?" She shrugged. "Maybe we should start charging the Creepers admission?"

Despite myself, I barked out a laugh. Willow's gaze shot to

mine, her eyes growing wide.

"Logan, did you just… *laugh*?"

My mouth flattened. "No."

"Yes, you did!" Grinning, Willow was bouncing in her seat, pointing at me. "I saw it. I heard you. That's twice in two weeks!"

"I wasn't laughing," I growled, even as my lips twitched. The sight of her — happy in a way I hadn't seen her since losing Lucas — was making me feel all sorts of things I wasn't used to feeling. Things I *shouldn't* be feeling.

"*Yes, you were,*" she mocked. "I saw it — you can't deny it. *I made Logan laugh, again.*" She said the last part in a singsong voice that reminded me of the way she and Lucas would tease one another.

Closing my eyes, I sucked in a hard breath. In all the years Willow and I had known one another, it was only during these last two weeks of living together without Lucas that we'd fallen into a comfortable rhythm together. And I liked it. *I really fucking liked it.* Was it wrong, I wondered, to enjoy something that had only come about at the expense of my brother? Not wanting to think about the answer, I turned away and resumed sanding the bench. This time twice as hard.

"Alright," Willow said around a yawn. "I guess I'm gonna go to bed."

I remained as I was, with my back to Willow, bent over the bench, still furiously sanding. Not until I'd finished one entire shelf and swept the dust into a pile did I finally rise. Turning, I found Willow propped up in bed, a book in hand, fast asleep. One bare leg was slung over her blankets and her T-shirt was pushed up to her waist. I took my time looking at her — the length of her leg, the dip of her waist, the soft upward curve of her mouth — as if she'd fallen asleep smiling.

Silently crossing the room, I slid the book gently from her hand, turning it over. Missing its cover, its pages stained and torn, the title page read: ALICE'S ADVENTURES IN WONDERLAND. Setting it aside, I pulled the blankets out from beneath her, tucking them at her waist. Staring down at her, I found my hand drawn to her face, to a loose curl hanging over one eye. As I was gently pushing it aside, Willow shifted and I quickly snatched my hand back. With a soft sigh, she rolled onto her side, tugging the blankets up to her chin.

I backed away, my heart hammering in my chest, still attempting to convince myself that what I felt for Willow was only the inevitable result of a long stretch of unrequited lust and loneliness. Those excuses had barely worked while living on the road; here in Silver Lake, they didn't hold up at all.

With a frustrated growl, I wrenched my shirt over my head, tossing it onto the top bunk where I'd begun keeping all my dirty laundry. Stripping down to my boxers, I switched the lights off and climbed into bed. Glaring at the bunk above me, I knew it was time to own up to my feelings—at least, to myself.

Turning toward Willow, the silhouette of her sleeping form just barely visible in the meager moonlight, I listened to her rhythmic breaths. In and out and in and out, until my own breaths slowed and my eyelids began to droop.

NINETEEN

WILLOW

"So y'all are comin', right?" Britta raised one sharply curved brow.

It was early morning, the sun a glowing sliver on the horizon, the scents of cooking food rushing up to greet us alongside the warm morning breeze. Britta and I had crossed paths on our way to the dining hall, both of us headed to breakfast before work. Joining me, Britta was eager to share the news that EJ had asked her to attend Maria and Jim's wedding with him, an offer that Britta had found downright hysterical. He was too young for her, and too straitlaced and clean-cut for her to even consider. She preferred her men more rugged, more like Logan, she'd said, winking.

"I'm coming," I replied slowly. Britta liked… Logan? Moody,

miserable Logan? Something about that made me feel… strange.

"Not Eddie, though, huh?" Laughing, she mimed a scissor motion with her fingers.

"Nope. He's being, you know… himself." I flicked my eyes skyward. "He hates all forms of fun. Always has, always will."

I'd hounded Logan for the past few days, attempting to convince him to come along, but in true Logan fashion, my persistence had only resulted in him digging his heels in further, remaining absolutely adamant about not attending.

"That man is backed up worse than Talladega on race day," Britta said with a sly grin. "I could set him straight. Whip us up some of my daddy's hooch and get me a few hours alone with him—he'd be right as rain. Not like it'd be a hardship. That man is hotter'n Georgia asphalt."

I stopped walking, staring after her. The imagery she'd just provided me with—her and Logan alone together—made my stomach flip, and not in a good way.

"Speak of the devil," Britta drawled, as Logan pushed through the dining hall doors. "We were just talkin' 'bout you, Eddie, weren't we, Will?"

Logan descended the stairs without as much as a glance in Britta's direction, his long blond hair hanging wild and free around his face and shoulders. He'd so rarely worn it down since letting it grow out, not even to sleep, and so I was shocked to see it. Even more surprised to find that he looked considerably younger because of it, too.

"Uh, hey," I said, blinking up at him. "Your hair is… down."

Logan sent a hand through his unruly waves, shoving it back from his face. "Yeah," he replied. Silence followed while we stared at each other. "I've got to go to work," he eventually said. "Got to finish Joe's roof before it rains today."

Britta made a noise of disbelief. "The sky's as blue as an old country song—how you figure it's gonna rain?"

"His knees," I said.

"My knees," Logan replied, both of us speaking at once.

"Every damn time," he said with a roll of his eyes and a small, surprising smile. "See you later?"

"Yep," I replied, smiling after him as he turned to leave.

"Well, well, well," Britta murmured, coming to stand beside me. Together, we watched as Logan disappeared down the path. "That was mighty interestin'."

Glancing sideways, I asked, "What was interesting?"

"That."

"*What?*"

"Oh hey there, Eddie." Britta batted her eyelashes and furiously fanned herself with her hand. "My, oh, my, look at your hair hangin' down all gorgeous and shit."

My eyes flared wide and my face flushed hot. "That's not what happened."

Britta leered at me. "Ain't it though?"

"That's not what I said to him. And that's disgusting." I marched loudly up the stairs and wrenched open the double doors.

Britta was still laughing when she joined me in the food line. "What's wrong, sugar? Was it somethin' I said?"

"'Morning, Willow, Britta. You want cinnamon or honey on your oatmeal?" Behind the counter, Xavier held up two steaming bowls of oats.

Along with Betsey, Xavier was in charge of food distribution. Unlike Betsey, a stern-faced former librarian with a headful of snow-white curls, Xavier was an easygoing guy, with short black hair, sun-kissed skin, and a friendly smile for everyone. A former biological engineer, it had been Xavier who'd designed most of the economically friendly resources in Silver Lake—everything from the solar-powered buildings to the biodiesel-run vehicles. Food service, however, he did for fun.

"Cinnamon, please," I replied.

"Honey for me, *honey*," Britta said, pursing her lips into a silky smile.

Shaking the spice over the oats, Xavier flashed Britta a white, toothy grin. "Anything for you, Brit. Speaking of, you should have gotten here earlier; we had eggs again."

"Dammit, Xavi!" Britta growled. "Shouldn't a' told me—can't miss what ya don't know."

There'd been fresh eggs for breakfast every morning up until three days ago, when a fox had dug its way under the wall in the dead of night and murdered half the chickens. The hens that had survived had been so traumatized by the attack, they'd only just started producing eggs again. I wished there was some way to let those poor chickens know that Joshua had caught and killed that fox—providing us with fox stew that very evening. Maybe then they'd sleep a little easier and resume laying eggs on a daily basis again.

"Grab your fruit and move along, ladies," Betsey ordered us with a frown, her many lip lines deepening. "Line's getting backed up."

Britta saluted her. "Yes, ma'am—right away, ma'am."

While Betsey tsked our departure, we hurried to our usual table, where Ella was sitting alone. Sliding onto the bench opposite Britta, I stuck my spoon in my oatmeal and left it there. Britta's comments about Logan were a twister in my gut, having swept away my appetite.

"'Mornin', Willow; 'mornin', Brit." Dropping his tray of food on the table, Jordy slid onto the bench beside me. "I heard we missed the eggs," he said, nudging my arm with his elbow. "Got stuck with the slop again."

"Food is food," EJ said, taking the seat beside Britta.

"Yes," Cassie agreed, dropping down beside Ella. "Be thankful you have some."

"Oh, I'm thankful, alright," Jordy replied. "I'm thankful Betsey's always sneaking me an extra helping." He patted his bare stomach. "I'm a growin' boy, you know?"

Britta snorted. "You grow any taller and you'll be a skyscraper."

"All the better to climb, though, amirite?" Jordy flashed a sly smile around the table.

"Yeah, that's gross," Ella snapped, making a face. "Super fucking gross, Jordy."

Jordy smirked, unconcerned, and gave Ella a long, lingering look. Snarling, Ella flipped him off with both hands that resulted in Jordy throwing his head back with hearty laughter.

Britta banged her spoon on the table. "Did y'all hear—Willow's comin' to Jimmy and Maria's shindig."

"Yeah?" Jordy nudged me again—something he'd been doing with increased frequency lately. A nudge here. A hand there. A grin every time he saw me. "That's awesome—you'll have to save me a dance."

I flushed again, this time due to the intense way Jordy was looking at me—directly into my eyes, as if he were trying to silently convey something. Something I absolutely did not want to know. Unable to hold his gaze for another uncomfortable second, I resumed poking my oatmeal.

"I don't really know any dances," I muttered. It wasn't entirely a lie. Lucas and I had danced all the time, but never the sort of structured dancing that went on at formal events. Rebels without a cause, we'd always danced to the beat of our own drum.

"Hell, Willow—it ain't like it's hard," Britta spoke around a mouthful of food. "You just throw your arms around and shake ya ass. The real issue is what we're gonna wear. I got nothin' but ratty jeans and leather."

"Does it matter?" I asked. "I mean, given the circumstances, are we expected to dress up?"

I hadn't given any thought about what I might wear to the wedding, figuring it didn't matter. Everyone in camp dressed mostly the same, usually in work-appropriate clothing that was sweat-stained, full of holes and half patched together.

"I'm sure some will dress up," Cassie said. "But nobody will make a fuss if you don't."

"Literally nobody," Ella added. "Maria doesn't even have a wedding dress to wear."

"Hell nah. Nu-uh, no way, no how!" Britta thumped her fist on the table. "We are dressin' up for sure. Willow, when was the last time you dressed up?"

I chewed on my bottom lip, thinking back through the years. "Homecoming dance my freshman year, I think?"

Britta shot Cassie a pointed look. "We can't let that stand, Cass. You gotta give her the day off and lemme take her shoppin'. You wanna go shoppin', dontcha, Will?"

Excitement stirred inside me, and I nodded enthusiastically. An adventure was exactly what I suddenly wanted—new clothing would just be the icing on the cake.

"I'm happy to give you the day off," Cassie replied, smiling warmly at me. "We're way ahead of schedule, thanks to you. But I don't know what you think you're going to find out there, Britta—

pickings have been slim for a while. And you'll need to run it by Leisel before you do anything."

"Seems kinda risky to head out only for clothes." Jordy frowned at me. "Is it just the two of you going?"

Britta guffawed. "Oh, bless your heart, Jordy. I'm the best shot in this whole dang camp. I can kill those fuckers with my eyes closed. And you know it."

Jordy put his hands up. "Can't argue that, Brit. All I'm saying is Willow is gonna look good in whatever she wears." He nudged my arm again. "I gotta head out. You be careful out there, alright? I'll see you later?"

"Sure," I mumbled, studiously avoiding eye contact with him.

"That boy has it so dang bad for you," Britta said, eyeing Jordy's departure. "You could tell him to jump and he'd ask how high."

"Jordy has it bad for everyone," Ella said pointedly. "No need to single Willow out."

"Thank you," I said firmly, looking at Britta. "We're just friends — I don't like him like that."

Britta's lips twisted into another sly smile. "Is that 'cause you like someone else *like that*?"

"What? Who?" Realizing her meaning, I flushed hot once more. Slamming my spoon down, I growled, "Could you stop? I already told you, *that's disgusting*."

"Fine, *fiiiine*," Britta drawled, making a face. "I'm just messin' with you, is all." Straightening, she slapped her hands down on the table. "So about our shoppin' trip — you ready to ride?"

"Don't forget to run it by Leisel first," Cassie warned. "Especially if you plan on taking a vehicle. And make sure you're back before dark or — "

Britta groaned loudly. "Jesus Christ on a goddang cracker,

Cassie, I know the rules."

"You ever wonder why they didn't name more schools after women?" Britta pointed a freshly sharpened machete at what remained of the building's overhead lettering. RONALD HOPKINS HIGH SCHOOL, it read, give or take a few missing letters.

We'd been driving for most of the day, stopping at places that looked promising, only to pull away empty-handed. Now we were thirty miles or so from camp, and about to call it quits when we'd happened upon a school. Recalling my high school drama club, and the vast number of costumes they'd kept in storage, I'd suggested checking it out.

"Or why hurricanes and storms were only named after women?" I replied, swinging Britta's beloved baseball bat from hand to hand.

Britta grinned. "Nuh-uh, I'm keepin' that one—that's a dang compliment. We're the hurricanes, sugar, and all them storm chasers better take cover."

Returning her grin, I gestured to the graying sky. "Speaking of storms. Logan's knees never lie."

Britta glanced up just as the first droplets of rain began to fall. "Best make this quick then," she replied, gesturing me toward the school. "Ladies first."

The glass entrance doors had been shattered, and we ducked easily through their gaping holes, stepping onto a floor littered with broken glass and debris. Like most man-made structures, nature was in the process of reclaiming this building as her own— bursting through the cracks in the walls, in the floor, and through the rotted ceiling tiles above.

The main office loomed just ahead, its interior window streaked with dried blood. A Creeper stood just inside, its mangled face staring blankly through the Plexiglas, its head and arms twitching.

Britta pointed and snorted. "I'm hopin' that's what my high school principal is doin' right about now — twitchin' like a dyin' fish. Mr. O'Shea — that fuckin' dirtbag — he used to wear these dang tap shoes, clickin' his way down the hall so that the whole school would know he was comin'. Click-click-click — Lord, did I hate that man."

Laughing, we moved down the hall, passing classrooms filled with toppled-over desks and ransacked shelves. Faded posters wallpapered the once colorfully decorated rooms while graying skeletons sat like Halloween decorations in various states of decay.

"What's up with Eddie's knees, anyway?" Britta asked. "He looks too young for his bones to be hollerin' so loud."

"He played football growing up, so that didn't do him any favors," I murmured, peering inside the damp and decaying remains of the school library. "But I think it's mainly because he always carried the heaviest bag out on the road. And you've seen how many weapons he carries."

Laughing, Britta shook her head. "Boy's got more blades than a butcher."

"More scalpels than a surgeon," I added with a grin.

"More swords than a sea-roving pirate!"

"More knives than a ninja!"

"… do ninjas have knives?"

We staggered down the hall, howling with laughter. And, god, it felt good to laugh so freely, so deep from the belly, and without reservation. I hadn't laughed this hard since… since Lucas.

"Well now, I've seen some crazy shit, but this might take the cake." Britta bent down in front of an open locker, gently fingering the flower-covered vine growing within. The vine, peppered in pink and white blooms, had somehow found its way into the locker from the wall behind it, growing through a busted seam in the metal.

"It's honeysuckle," I told her, smiling wistfully at the flowers that Logan's mother had allowed to grow freely around her garden gate. "It can grow anywhere."

"Sure can," Britta replied, shaking her head. "Times like this, I wish I had a workin' camera."

"Hey, over here," I called out, pushing through a nearby door. Joining me, Britta pulled an industrial-sized flashlight from her belt, bouncing the beam of light around the dark auditorium. The large room was fitted with sloped theater seats, each aisle slanting downward toward the band pit below. Above the pit sat a grand stage, its red velvet curtains hanging in tatters.

"You're thinkin' we should check backstage?" Britta's voice echoed eerily throughout the empty room.

Suddenly conscious of how our voices carried, I glanced nervously around the dark. "Yeah, but keep checking the floor — watch out for crawlers."

"Sugar, who ya think you're talkin' to?" Flashing her teeth, Britta sliced her machete through the air. "Ain't no Dead Head got the drop on me yet."

Gripping my bat with both hands, I followed Britta down the aisle, eyes peeled for the slightest movement.

"You ever play any instruments?" Britta asked.

"No," I laughed softly. "I was usually sitting in detention... you?"

"Girl, same. I was a wild child — hardly ever showed up to class. And when I did, I was always gettin' sent to Mr. O'Shea's office.

That man would be yellin' at me, tappin' that dang tap shoe and tellin' me I'd never amount to nothin'.'"

Chuckling, Britta climbed up onto the stage. Holding her arms wide, she spun in circles. "Look at me now, Mr. O'Shea, I'm a goddang star!"

Laughing, I pulled her across the stage and through the tattered mess of curtains. The backstage area was twice as dark and twice as eerie, with stage props and backdrops looming from every direction, their towering forms casting creepy shadows across the tomb-like room.

"Shine the light over here," I whispered. The beam bounced around me, landing on a row of garment racks, each rack fitted with a clear vinyl covering.

"Well, shit," Britta breathed. "Gotta hand it to you, Will—I woulda never thought to check a dang school for clothes."

Britta propped the flashlight on the floor, shining its light on the clothing racks and we set to work. While I was busy searching for zippers, Britta was slicing through vinyl coverings with her machete.

"Looky here." Britta held out the long billowing skirts of an opulent white wedding dress. "Now, I don't know what Maria's plannin' on wearin', but a woman needs options. Aw, hell, is that a dead mouse in there? Well, we don't need to be tellin' her about that part."

Laughing, I plucked a plum-colored blouse with a pussy-bow collar from the rack, hung alongside a pair of wide-leg black slacks, the bottoms of which had been chewed through with holes. The tag on the hanger read, DONNA—MAMMA MIA!

"I like this," I murmured. It wasn't something I would have ever picked out for myself previously. It was simpler, and far more understated than the bold, attention-getting clothing I'd once worn.

Fingering the soft fabrics, I wondered what Logan's reaction might be to seeing me wearing something so out of character. Would he laugh?

"I woulda knocked 'em dead in the twenties," Britta said, touching the sequin headpiece she was wearing.

"You're going to knock 'em dead now," I told her, nodding earnestly. Though Britta claimed to be in her early forties, she didn't look a day over thirty. Her long blonde hair shone; her sun-kissed skin glowed gold, and she was confident in a way that defied age.

Eventually we amassed two piles of clothing—items we wanted to keep for ourselves and those we'd be gifting to Silver Lake. Among the piles were pinstriped suit coats with matching pants, frilly blouses, and flapper dresses that, with a bit of sewing, could be easily turned into something more modern. Britta had even found herself a little black number, beaded and fringed from bust to hem.

"You find any anything weddin' worthy yet?"

"Not yet…" I trailed off as I pulled another garment bag free from the rack; unzipping the bag, a length of emerald green satin spilled into my hands. Holding the dress up to my chest, I swished the mid-calf-length skirt back and forth around my legs. Two skinny spaghetti straps held up the fitted bodice, which dipped low. At the waist, three small white pearls trailed down the center. The tag read, PARTY EXTRA—THE SOUND OF MUSIC.

"Maybe this one?" I asked, stepping around the rack.

Hands on her hips, Britta let out a low wolf whistle. "Sugar, that is definitely your dress. I don't know about EJ, but you'll have every other red-blooded man pantin' after you."

I turned away, still holding the dress against my body, a small smile tugging at my lips. Britta was right—this was definitely my dress.

TWENTY

WILLOW

Leaping through the shattered doorways, Britta and I skidded to a waterlogged stop, shaking rain from our hair and clothes. We'd just finished loading up the last of the clothing when the sky had opened up.

Squinting at the wall of rain beyond the doorway, water gushed from above, flooding the school's walkway, splashing sharply inside the debris-covered entranceway. A bolt of lightning flashed in the distance, followed by a loud clap of thunder.

"Might as well find someplace to cozy up," Britta said with a sigh. "We ain't goin' nowhere 'til this lets up—can't see a dang thing out there."

"Maybe we could hang out in the cafeteria?" I suggested.

"Now you're talkin'. You remember those little puddin' cups they used to serve in school?" Britta smacked her lips. "I'm thinkin' that was the one thing I liked about school. Wonder if they have an expiration date?"

Following the signs for the cafeteria, we found the double doors barricaded with upended chairs and tables, with two lacrosse sticks crisscrossed through the handles. Thin slats of reinforced windows were coated with dried blood and grime, keeping us from viewing inside. The doors rattled against their confines; telltale growls and snarls rumbling from within.

"Maybe not the cafeteria," I muttered.

"Aw, come on, Willow — I haven't gotten to kill anything all dang day." Britta began maneuvering furniture away from the doors. Without the heavy obstructions, the rattling increased; the doors pushed open a fraction and skeletal fingers tipped in long, yellowed nails slithered through the openings.

"Don't look like too many to me," Britta said, trying to peer inside. "I reckon there's maybe a dozen or so. You good with that?"

Gripping tightly to the bat, I nodded, even as Logan's voice pounded through me. *Absolutely not, Willow — you're not even suited up!*

"Shut up, Logan," I muttered. I could absolutely handle a half dozen Creepers.

"Time to dance with the dead." Britta whipped her machete from its holster and pulled the lacrosse sticks from the handles, tossing them aside. Three Creepers stumbled into the hallway and Britta started swinging, nimbly slicing through all three necks.

Stepping over the fallen carcasses, we moved inside the room. The cafeteria was a disaster — the gruesome remnants of a decade old bloodbath. Tables and chairs lay overturned, bones and backpacks strewn among them; clusters of Creepers, half petrified, turned in unison, their sunken expressions perking up at the sight of us.

"Take the ones on the right." Britta gestured with her machete. "I got left."

Britta sang as she swung her blade, hitting high notes each time she made a killing strike. The noise she made called to every Creeper in the room, turning their attention away from me. Taking advantage of their distraction, I rushed up behind them, swinging. My first hit struck gold; the Creeper crumbled at my feet. The next stumbled sideways and I swung again, sending it hurtling across the floor in a tangle of motionless limbs. A third and fourth Creeper staggered toward me—two teenagers, one distinctly male, one unmistakably female. The boy's neck was broken, his head lolling to the left, while the girl's shriveled legs were wrapped in torn fishnet stockings, her gore-coated combat boots bumping noisily over the rubble-covered linoleum.

My breath hitched; the bat sat heavy in my grip as I watched their approach. It had been a long time since I'd assigned a Creeper any sort of identity; they'd been only mindless monsters among millions of nameless, faceless enemies that needed to be disposed of. But these were different. These reminded me of… me. And of Lucas, and what might have been.

Perhaps even… what should have been.

Both Creepers were nearly upon me now, snarling as they reached for me. I'd waited too long to swing, forcing me to take several steps back in order to find my momentum. I hit the girl first, the barrel of the bat cracking alongside her face, and then the boy, sending the end cap into his rotten middle and shoving him away.

The girl stumbled, growling pitifully, an old gash in her neck having likely damaged her vocal cords. I instantly hated her for that—for being so useless she couldn't even growl properly.

Hating her for not being able to save the boy beside her, hating her for being so incapable she hadn't even been able to save herself.

I continued to swing and shove, only hitting hard enough to maim, unwilling to end their miserable existence just yet. I hit her again, her skin sloughing off as my bat merely grazed her arm. And then again, the crunch of bone shattering in her leg forcing her to fall to her knees.

Facing the boy, I shoved him back again, a scream building deep within my gut. With each shove, the scream only grew, ballooning in my throat until I had no choice but to release it.

Swinging the bat as hard as I could, a wail burst past my lips as the bat collided with his head. Crushing through skull and brain matter, his snarl slipped away as he collapsed to the floor, silent. Meanwhile, the girl continued toward me, dragging herself across the floor, one bleak, miserable eye staring at me from within her dented, deformed skull.

"You're fucking useless," I bit out. "You can't do anything right. *Nothing*. You couldn't even save *him*."

One last swing, wood collided with bone, shattering what was left of her skull, and killing her on impact. She fell forward, half slumping over the boy.

The bat dripping with gore, my brow drenched in sweat, I glanced around the room, finding Britta propped against a wall, a large tin can in one hand, a spoon in the other.

"Feel better?" she asked, one blonde brow cocked high.

Glancing down at the battered Creepers, I shrugged. "A little. What the hell are you eating?"

Grinning, Britta pointed her spoon at me. "Well, now, while you were busy makin' Dead Head smoothies, I found myself some motherfuckin' puddin'." Shoveling a spoonful of pudding into her mouth, she flashed me a toothy, pudding-covered grin. "*And* I found us a nice little place to wait out the storm. Come see."

"So much for waiting out the storm," I said dryly.

Inside the school's kitchen—a direct offshoot from the cafeteria, Britta and I were seated on a steel countertop, a flashlight and an emptied tin of chocolate pudding between us. Britta was humming with her eyes closed, while I stared off across the dark room, listening to the rapid drumming of raindrops hitting the roof and the violent whip of wind whistling all around us. A crack of thunder erupted from above, lighting up the sky with bright white light.

"It's a whopper alright," Britta absentmindedly replied, soon humming again.

"What song is that?" I asked.

Cracking an eye open, Britta sang the first few lines.

I shook my head. "Never heard of it."

"Wait, what? Sugar, are you tryin' to tell me you ain't never heard of Rick Astley?" Britta's eyes were wide and glowing white in the otherwise dark. "You ain't never been Rickrolled back when the internet was still a thing?"

"Rickrolled?"

"Christ, Willow, I don't know if we can be friends now."

"All over some Rick guy—who's probably dead?"

"You don't know Rick. He don't give up, ya know? He never lets anyone down. And he don't run around an' desert you—"

"Okay, okay." I laughed, hands up. "I get it. I'll have to brush up on my Rick Astley."

"Damn straight, you will." Chuckling, Britta's hand went to her stomach, her smile soon fading into a grimace. "Dang, I think this puddin's goin' right through me... Oh, yeah, I need to go... right fuckin' now."

Sliding off the counter, Britta ran across the kitchen, noisily dislodging the chairs we'd stacked in front of the door. The door slammed open and Britta's heavy steps pounded the cafeteria floor, echoing throughout the large space.

Smiling, I leaned my head back against the wall, wondering what Logan was doing right now, my smile quickly fading into a scowl. Was he freaking out? Was he cursing my very existence? I'd never told him about our shopping excursion; I hadn't even thought about telling him because I hadn't planned on being gone long enough for him to need to know.

He would know by now, of course. And in typical Logan fashion, he'd be livid.

I eyed the small pile of food we'd collected. My hope was that if I returned to Silver Lake with enough goods, Logan's anger might be somewhat mollified. Even better, maybe he would finally see me as a capable person—an equal even. At the very least, someone he didn't need to constantly fret over as if I were a child.

Across the room, the door creaked loudly; glancing over my shoulder, I called out, "That was quick—did you even make it to the bathroom?"

Silence followed my words, permeating the surrounding darkness. Gripping the flashlight, I swung the beam toward the door. "Britta?" I whispered, suddenly abundantly aware that when she'd run from the room, she'd removed the barrier of chairs.

Cursing myself for not securing the door after her departure, I slipped quietly off the counter, fumbling for the bat at my feet. Flashlight in one hand, bat in the other, I started slowly across the room, careful not to step on any of the broken dishes and dented cans that cluttered the floor.

Approaching the door, I pressed my ear to the metal, listening for the telltale shuffle of a Creeper. Hearing nothing, I gripped the handle and was slowly pulling it open when it was suddenly ripped from my grip and it smashed into my face. Crying out, I stumbled backward, my hands flying to my nose, the flashlight and bat clattering to the floor.

"We've got a live one here," a nasally, unfamiliar voice rang out. Shrieking, I scrambled backward, tripping in my haste to get away. I was reaching for my boot—for the blade I had tucked inside—when a beam of light blinded me, freezing me in place on the floor; heavy footsteps echoed all around.

"Hey there, pretty little thing." A second unknown voice— deep and grating—punctured the silence. "My, my, what a fuckin' treat you are."

More lights joined the fray, bouncing wildly across the dark room. Looming shadows surrounded me; one shadow drawing close and leaning down. The man was soaked through, rainwater dripping from his crudely cut hair and short, scruffy beard and on to me, while he stared down at me with a slow-growing smile, as if I were a prize he couldn't quite believe he'd won.

"Room's clear," the nasally voice announced. "Just her."

"You'll have to forgive us," the scruffy man rumbled, roughly taking my face in his hand. "It's been so goddamn long since we've seen a woman worth lookin' at." His hand slid into my hair, gripping a handful of it and using it to painfully force me to my feet. My back hit a wall, an involuntary whimper escaping me as the man pinned me in place with his body. The bitter stink of him engulfed me, making me gag.

"I call shotgun." The deep voice laughed, the sound like gravel thrown against glass.

"The fuck you do," the man grinding against me growled. "You'll be waitin' your turn with this one."

My shirt tore beneath his greedy grip, cool air and clammy hands colliding with my bare breasts. I tried to shrink away from his touch, only there was nowhere to go. My pants were yanked open and his hand shoved crudely inside. As his fingers fumbled for purchase, my heart kicked into overdrive, echoing loudly in my ears, beating in tandem with the rain coming down on the roof. This was happening, I realized with darkening dread. This was happening and there was nothing I could do to stop it.

"No," I gasped, turning my face from his eager mouth. "*Please, no.*"

Laughter rang out all around me. "I sure do love it when they beg," the nasally voice proclaimed. "Hell, I'm already hard thinkin' —"

The nasally voice abruptly cut off, his halted words followed closely by a clatter and a thud, and a spiral of light as his flashlight rolled away.

A second flashlight beam began pitching violently around the room. "Dean? Dean, what the fuck? Oh shit—oh shit! Jesus, Mitchell, we ain't alone in —" The second voice cut off with a clatter and a second flashlight rolled away.

Cursing, the man holding me swung me around; gripping my neck in a choking hold, he held me in front of him like a shield. "Who's there?" he shouted, panicked. "Who the fuck is there?"

"I'm your Huckleberry." Britta's boots gently tapped the floor, only the barest shape of her visible in the glow from the flashlights gone askew. The click-click of a gun cocking echoed throughout the room.

"I'll kill her." The man tightened his grip on my throat, leaving me struggling to breathe. "Take another step and I'll fuckin' kill her."

"Nah," Britta replied. "That ain't at all how this is gonna go. You see, I'm the one holdin' the gun, so unless you wanna lose your head like these two fool friends a'yours, you'll be doin' as I say."

A third beam of light clicked on, swinging across the mess on the floor, where two headless bodies lay in a growing pool of blood.

"You'll shoot me the second I let her go," the man protested, a hitch in his voice at the sight of his dead companions.

"Maybe I will, maybe I won't," Britta replied. "But that's the chance you chose to take when you put your hands on my friend here."

The man hesitated for only a moment before releasing me with a frustrated growl, shoving me hard as he turned to run. I'd only just found my balance when a gunshot cracked across the room with a deafening boom. The man collapsed to the floor, breathing hard.

"Please," he cried, holding one hand in the air while the other clutched his bleeding stomach. "Don't. *Please.*"

"Man, oh, man," Britta drawled, stepping closer. "I sure do love it when they beg. Hell, I'm already hard thinkin' 'bout it."

With a wink in my direction, Britta pulled the trigger twice more.

As the concrete road turned to dirt, eventually ending at the edge of an empty gravel lot, Britta veered off into the surrounding woods, skillfully weaving us through the trees until the imposing wall surrounding Silver Lake became visible in the distance. It was late morning; the residents of Silver Lake would be finishing breakfast and heading off to work. After the attack last night, Britta and I had waited out the rest of the storm on the side of the road, sleeping in shifts until daylight. Not that I'd actually slept; I was too worked up over my near miss, and even more worried over what Logan's reaction was going to be.

"You ready for the third degree from Leisel?" Britta glanced over at me, concern creasing her features as she took in the state of my face. I'd been able to change my torn shirt; however, thanks to the would-be rapists, I had a swollen nose and a fat lip, along with a visibly bruised neck, none of which were easily hidden.

"It's only Logan I'm worried about," I muttered. "He's going to kill me."

"You gonna tell 'im the truth?"

"God no!" I exclaimed, shaking my head. "He's already going to freak out because I left without telling him — if he finds out what happened, *he will lose his fucking mind*. Please don't say anything," I implored her.

"Sugar, my lips are sealed. I would never hear the end of it from Lei if she found out; worrywart, that one." Snorting, Britta shook her head. "As if I need worryin' over."

As we approached the wall, shouts rang out from the guard tower; the gate opened, revealing Davey waving us forward. "Where ya been, Brit?" Davey banged on the driver's side door as we passed him. "You get lost out there?"

"When pigs fly," she cracked back, flipping him off through the half-open window.

"How 'bout when the dead walk?" he shouted after us, laughing heartily.

Instead of returning the truck to the garage — a canopy-covered area where all the camp vehicles were kept — Britta pulled to a stop just past the guard tower. "Here come Mom and Pop," she said, gesturing with her chin. "And they look mighty pissed." Following her line of sight, I found Leisel and Joshua walking briskly toward us, their expressions severe.

Pulling the keys from the ignition, Britta jumped out of the truck. "Mornin'," she said cheerfully. "Is that eggs I smell? Did ya' save me some—y'all better have saved me some."

"What happened out there?" Leisel asked Britta, her voice tight.

"Got caught in the storm, is all," Britta replied, "Knew we weren't gonna make it back in time so we parked for the night—no need to be frettin', Lei, we was safe as houses."

"That's it? Just the storm? You didn't run into anyone out there? No issues with the infected?" Leisel's attention turned to me as I came to stand beside Britta. "My god, Willow," she exclaimed. "What happened to your face?"

"She's fine, Lei." Britta waved her hand dismissively. "Tripped down a flight of stairs in the damn dark and fell flat on her face."

Clutching my pack to my chest, I let out a nervous laugh. "It was stupid. We found this school and it was dark inside and I tripped over a bunch of garbage—"

"It wasn't stupid," Britta interjected. "Smarty-pants here came up with the idea of checkin' a school for their drama stuff, and sure enough..." Ducking back in the truck, Britta pulled forth a pile of garment bags. "We got shit here for everyone—even found an honest-to-God weddin' dress for Maria. And we got some food too, so don't you be naggin' me for stayin' out past curfew."

In a rare display of warmth, Joshua smiled at me. "Well done," he said softly, inclining his head.

"Very well done," Leisel added stiffly. "However, I'm not sure everyone will be as easily appeased." Holding my gaze, Leisel jerked her eyes toward the path; following her gaze, my lips parted in silent surprise. Logan, his stance rigid, his hair a mess, as if he'd been running his hands through it all night long, glared across the grass at me. Swallowing, I lifted a tentative hand—a greeting that only caused his expression to darken further. Shaking his head, he turned away, stalking off.

Great. Mumbling my goodbyes, I hurried after Logan, calling his name. Ignoring me, he picked up his pace.

"Logan, wait!" Growling in frustration, I matched his speed, reaching him. As I grabbed hold of his arm, he spun around, roughly shaking me off. His blazing gaze took in the full length of me, his fury flaming brighter at the sight of my swollen face.

"What the fuck," he growled, his chest heaving, "happened to you?"

"I fell," I hurried to explain, tentatively touching my nose. "I tripped down the stairs at this school and—"

Logan grabbed my chin, turning my head to one side and exposing my neck before I could flinch away.

"Who did this?" he demanded, clearly not buying my lie for one second.

Shoving away from him, I moved my hair to cover the bruising. "No one. Like I said, I fell—"

"Bullshit," Logan spat, advancing on me. "You tell me who, you tell me where, *and you tell me right the fuck now, Willow.*"

I released a hard breath, letting my hands fall helpless to my sides. I'd been foolish to think I'd be able to hide anything from Logan; he'd always been able to see straight through me.

"They're all dead," I whispered. "Britta killed them."

Jaw locked and ticcing, Logan appeared even angrier by my admission. "Did they... did they *hurt you?*"

"No!" Frustrated, I brought my hand to my mouth and then

flinched when my lip began to throb. "I'm fine—*everything's fine.*"

"Everything's fine?" Incredulity briefly drowned out the fury marring his features. "Am I hearing you right? You leave camp without me, without even telling me, and then you end up getting attacked and somehow everything is fine? What the fuck, Willow—what fucking planet do you live on where you think anything is fine about this? You could have been killed or... *worse.*"

"But I wasn't!" I protested loudly. "And everything *is* fine. More than fine, actually. Britta and I found some clothes for everyone, some food too."

"Clothes and food?" Logan barked out a humorless laugh. "Jesus, Willow, what good are clothes if you're fucking dead?"

"I knew you were going to do this!" I yelled, flinging my backpack at him. "I knew you wouldn't let me go—that's why I didn't tell you."

Logan grabbed my pack and with it my arm. "You're damn right I wouldn't let you go," he seethed. "Because look what happened—*look at your fucking face!*" He'd graduated to yelling, his body strung tightly and bowing toward mine. "Jesus Christ, you *never* think, do you? How many times have we had this conversation and you're still doing whatever the fuck you want, whenever you want to do it, completely disregarding everyone else's feelings?"

Where his hand clasped my wrist, I could feel the thrum of his pulse pick up a notch and my own fluttered in response. Yanking my arm free with more force than was necessary, I stumbled back a step.

"What do your feelings have to do with this?" I shouted. "And why are you so obsessed with everything I do—why can't you ever just *leave me the fuck alone*?" My shouts had become screams, ending on a shrill, venomous note.

Logan blinked. Staring down at me, the rage that had only

moments ago burned so brightly, began to fade, replaced with something else entirely, something startlingly soft and vulnerable. He opened his mouth and then closed it, only to open it again.

"Is that what you really want?" he finally rasped. "Me to leave you alone?"

"I..." My heart rammed against my ribs, my lips trembling as I struggled to find the words. Hell, my whole body trembled. I'd seen Logan angry before and I'd seen him indifferent twice as much. But I'd never seen him like this—I didn't even have a word to describe what *this* was. Anguish, resentment, and longing all warred for center stage on his twisting expression, while his tone held a horrible hint of... finality.

"Yes," I managed to eke out, regretting my answer the moment it was free. That wasn't at all what I wanted—not that I knew what I wanted, only that this wasn't it.

With a hard inhale, Logan's twisted expression fell away, his infuriating, iron-faced grimace taking its place. Blowing out an equally hard breath, he spat a solitary word—*fine*—and walked away.

Frozen, I could only stare dumbly after him, staring even after I could no longer see him, wondering what the hell had just happened, and feeling like I'd made a horrible mistake.

TWENTY ONE

LOGAN

The ground was a blur beneath my feet. Air rushed in and out of my lungs; sweat beaded on my forehead, dripping down into my eyes, burning them.

I'd recently taken up running again, ever since Willow had returned to camp covered in bruises and demanding that I *leave her the fuck alone.* I hadn't willingly run since before the end of the world; in these unprecedented times you wanted to be conserving energy, not needlessly expending it.

Now, though, doing my damnedest to avoid Willow, I'd found myself needing something to keep me occupied, especially during the meandering hours between work and sleep. Back in high school, back when I'd been an athlete headed for bigger and better things, early morning track time had been my favorite time of the day—just me and my thoughts. Each pump of my legs had been a step closer to freedom. Each thrust of my arms meant I'd been that much closer to getting the hell out of our shitty little town.

Today I also ran with purpose; today I ran to rid myself of the tension coiled tightly inside of me, tension that had been striking and snapping at everyone who'd dared approach me during the last week and a half.

She'd left without me.

But it was more than that. Out of all the people who could have told me, it had been Jordy to deliver the news that Willow had willingly walked outside these walls and into all sorts of possible danger. For clothing that she didn't even need, of all things. All the rules I'd carefully constructed, everything I'd attempted to teach her over the years, had apparently fallen on deaf ears.

I'd paced all day waiting for her return—in the cabin and then later, by the guard tower, walking the length of the gate until I'd worn a path into the ground. When night had fallen, and Willow still hadn't returned, I'd demanded to be let outside the wall in order to search for her. Leisel had refused me, reminding me of their rules—the first and foremost being that no one gets in or out until the sun comes up. She'd attempted to reason with me, assuring me that nothing would happen to Willow, that Britta was the most capable person to be outside the wall with. But Leisel's reassurance meant nothing to me; not when I knew firsthand that being the best didn't always equate to the best outcome. None of us were infallible, including Britta—who was always at Docs for one thing or another. Worse than her tendency to injure herself, were her daredevil antics during a time where just walking down the street should be considered a feat of bravery.

And then she'd waltzed back into camp with her face a mess, acting like nothing had even happened. Like she hadn't walked out of these walls utterly unprepared and ended up ambushed and assaulted by God only knew what sort of sick scumbags she'd encountered, or that I hadn't spent every hour she'd been gone sick to my stomach, unable to shake the feeling that this time I'd lost her for good. I was still sick over it; the idea of her out there without me, and worse, knowing that someone had put their hands on her.

Fists clenched, arms swinging, I ran faster, increasing my speed until my lungs were screaming and my side was throbbing. Ignoring my body's protests, I continued on, flying around a bend in the path and nearly crashing into a handful of oncoming people. As they scattered, I slipped, catching my sneaker on loose gravel, skidding my knees over the wet, uneven terrain. Growling, I shoved off the ground and I took off running again.

When the stab in my side grew unbearable, and the throb in my calves unignorable, when I could barely suck in a breath, only then did I begin to slow.

"Fuck," I gasped, bending forward, hands gripping my knees. It hurt to breathe, the stitch in my side flaring with each intake of air. Saliva pooled in my mouth, forcing me to spit; beads of sweat mixed with rainwater dripped from my hair and face, splashing down around my feet. Staring at the ground below, my mind was still racing, though my body no longer could.

"Yo, Logan, heads-up, man, we're coming through."

I struggled to stand, scrambling out of the way as EJ and Davey came barreling down the path, hauling a massive wooden arch between them. Stuart wasn't far behind, wearing his headphones around his neck, and juggling an unwieldy stack of boxes.

"You think you could give us a hand with this stuff?" EJ panted as they passed me. "There's a ton of crap at Cassie's that needs to be brought to the dining hall — it'll go a lot faster with you helping."

"Here, take these," Stuart said, shoving his stack of boxes at me. "I'll go back for more!" the teenager called out, already jogging away.

Davey shook his head. "And that's the last we'll be seein' of that lazy little shit."

With my arms full, I had little choice but to follow them to the dining hall, where half a dozen people were milling in and out of the building, while others balanced on ladders, stringing lights along the edge of the roof.

Betsey gestured to us from the porch. "Davey, you bring that inside. Put it down in front of the fireplace, please and thank you."

After peeking inside the boxes I was carrying, Betsey directed me to Cassie with a dismissive sweep of her hand. I found Cassie and Ella inside the dining hall, hanging old fishing nets along the walls while others followed behind them, slipping bunches of wildflowers into the mesh. One half of the building had been turned into a chapel, with bench seating on either side of the makeshift aisle, at the head of which EJ and Davey had placed the wooden arch. The other half of the hall had been set up for dining; instead of the usual bare tables and mismatched dinnerware, there were colorful cloths draped over each table, set with matching plates and bowls, and even wineglasses.

I turned in a half circle, taking it all in, angry, ugly thoughts flashing behind my eyes.

A fucking wedding?

What was the point?

Willow had been right about this place, it was a mirage. Everyone here was living a charade, playing pretend, faking it until they made it — only there was nothing left to make. No point to any of it—and definitely no point to flowers and fairy lights and matching fucking dinnerware!

Slamming the boxes down onto a nearby table, I turned to leave, nearly crashing into Joshua. Startled, I stumbled back, muttering apologies.

"Logan," Joshua said. "Just who I was looking for. Are you busy?"

"Uh, no? What's up?"

He drew in close, an unusual move for a man who almost never spoke and almost always kept to himself. "Hank died this morning," he said softly. "And Leisel doesn't want to put a damper on the wedding by announcing it just yet. I know you didn't really know him; figured it wouldn't ruin your night if I asked for your help burying him."

Well, fuck. I didn't know what I'd been expecting him to say, only that it hadn't been *that*. Shaking away my surprise, I replied, "Yeah, I can help—lead the way."

"What about your night?" I wondered aloud as we exited the dining hall.

Joshua cast a questioning glance in my direction. "What about it?"

"You knew Hank pretty well, didn't you—won't this ruin your night?"

Joshua didn't reply right away, eventually breaking the stillness with a heavy sigh. "That's the price you pay for leading, isn't it? You have to shoulder the hard stuff."

As his words settled profoundly between us, I sent a scowl off in the distance. "Seems like an unfair balance if you ask me," I muttered.

Joshua shrugged. "Maybe it is for some. But I've already lived the very worst day of my life, and I know Leisel feels the same. So we make the tough decisions around here, and we shoulder some of the pain for others, and hopefully make their lives a little better, you know? And sometimes doing those things makes me feel like maybe life is worth living again."

On Doc's stoop, Joshua rapped his knuckles lightly on the door and after a moment, the door flung open, revealing a teary-eyed Doc.

"I've cleaned him up the best I could," she said, gesturing us inside. "I wrapped him in what I had, but he's been gone since sunup and I hate to say it but he's really starting to smell."

Placing his hand on Doc's shoulder, Joshua said, "You're going to put this out of your mind for tonight. Tonight is for Jim and Maria. Tomorrow we'll say our goodbyes to Hank."

Sniffling, Doc nodded. "I did everything I could," she said sadly. "But he was just too broken, and I'm no surgeon."

"This isn't your fault, Doc. If it's anyone's fault, it's mine—I shouldn't have had a man his age up on a roof. Now you go ahead and go on over to my place. I'm sure Leisel would love your company. Logan and I have it from here."

That evening, Silver Lake glowed gold beneath the setting sun. The entire community had been decorated with thousands of tiny lights. They adorned nearly every building, and most of the trees, too. What hadn't been strung with lights had been decorated with an abundance of wildflowers.

Glancing down at my hands, I flexed my blistered fingers, the calloused skin on my palms cracking and caked with dirt and blood. Shaking my head, I made a mental note to bring gloves the next time I needed to dig a grave.

Joshua and I had loaded Hank into the back of a pickup truck and driven him outside the wall. Deep in the woods, at least a mile or so from camp, Joshua stopped at a makeshift cemetery among the trees, consisting of five other graves, marked only by small wooden stakes. It had been nearly dinnertime by the time we'd finished and had returned to camp, the early evening air thick with humidity, the sky filled with low-hanging clouds, their vivid hues highlighting the path toward home.

Reaching the cabin, I paused just inside the door, listening to the subtle puttering coming from within the bathroom. Scrubbing a hand across my face, I was contemplating turning around when the bathroom door crashed open, revealing Willow, a small, secret smile playing on her lips.

Then I blinked. This time, *really seeing Willow*.

And shit... I was done for.

Silky green satin, held up with the barest of straps, hugged her curves tightly, emphasizing the small cinch of her waist and the flare of her hips. It fell mid-calf, highlighting the length of her legs. Over and over again, my gaze strayed to the sharp dip in the neckline, where the delectable curve of her breasts were visible, and the barest hint of nipples present beneath the thin, slinky material.

Her long hair had been twisted upward and pinned into a faux-hawk of curls piled high on her head. She was wearing makeup, too — her eyes had been highlighted dark and bold, her lips painted a deep red.

Brushing a loose curl from her eyes, she glanced up at me in surprise, "Oh, hey — I didn't hear you come in."

I didn't know what to say to her; I didn't know what to do with myself. For over a week, it had been taking all my willpower to simply keep away from her. Now, though, face to face with her, I was frozen, trapped inside, wanting to bask in every goddamn gorgeous inch of her.

"It's stupid, you know," she stammered, laughing nervously, her hands gliding over her hips, further outlining her curves. "I'm all dressed up in this thing, only I have no shoes to go with it. I have to wear my boots."

I glanced down at her feet, not having noticed her boots until she'd mentioned them. Seeing them—scuffed and stained and looking nearly identical to the pair she'd worn as a teenager—I nearly smiled.

"I, um, left you some stuff to wear, too. You know, in case you changed your mind about going to the wedding. They're on your bed." Shifting uncomfortably, she ran her hands down her dress again, accentuating her curves once more.

I was watching her mouth move. I heard the words she was saying, but nothing was sticking. It went in one ear and out the other, all while attempting to convince myself that grabbing Willow *and kissing the shit out of Willow* was not something I should be doing.

"Logan?" Willow stepped closer, looking up at me through her long lashes. "Please say something. This not talking thing we've been doing… I don't like it. I didn't mean what I said, I don't want you to stay away from me. I was just mad and being stupid and…" she sighed and shrugged. "I'm sorry, okay?"

I knew what I wanted to say. Or rather, I knew what I felt, even if I couldn't seem to bring myself to find the words that matched the feelings—*long*-harbored feelings, cornered and captured and then left unattended for years. Festering feelings that reeked of even more emotions I was still refusing to name. Which was fucking ridiculous. I was a man now, wasn't I? I should be able to at least own up to my own goddamn feelings.

"Willow..." I moved toward her, reaching for her, her name a mere rumble in my chest. As I cupped her cheek, Willow's eyes shot to mine, widening, yet she didn't turn away. Swallowing hard, my thumb stroked a soft path, pausing dangerously close to her bottom lip. Staring at her mouth, watching as her lower lip began to tremble, I fought for the right words, fought to grab hold of any one of the great many things I was feeling and hold it still long enough to finally name it.

Loud laughing ripped us from our trance, both of us jumping apart and scrambling away as the cabin door flung open and Britta all but fell inside, Ella, EJ and Jordy behind her, all four of them dressed in clothing that looked more like elaborate Halloween costumes than wedding attire. Britta's black dress was heavily decked out in sequins and fringe, matching the feather and sequin headpiece she wore in her hair. Ella's dress was a similar style, only red, and both women wore bright lipstick and heavy eyeliner.

EJ, who couldn't stop staring at Britta, was dressed in a pinstriped suit, complete with a bow tie and pocket handkerchief. Jordy, who'd swapped out his Hawaiian-style shirts for a white button-down and black slacks, wore a fedora on his head, a large feather tucked into the brim. Not one of them was wearing dress shoes — Britta wore snakeskin boots, Ella had on a pair of worn-out ballet flats, while EJ donned a pair of muddy sneakers. Jordy, as usual, was barefoot.

"Dang, Willow!" Britta let out a wolf whistle. "That dress looks even better on." Everyone murmured in agreement. Even EJ, who'd managed to tear his puppy-dog gaze away from Britta long enough to give Willow a cursory glance.

"Seriously beautiful," Jordy added, eyeing Willow in a way that made me want to gouge out his eyeballs with a spoon. And

Willow, who'd never given a single shit about dressing up before, turned practically bashful under Jordy's heated gaze.

Looping her arm through Willow's, Britta turned her attention to me. "Still not comin', huh, Eddie?"

I kept my gaze on Willow, who'd dropped her gaze to the floor. "I'm tired," I managed to grit out.

Britta shrugged. "Suit yourself. Everybody *who isn't a moody asshole* ready to go?"

Ella trilled her lips in exasperation. "One sec," she said, pulling a flask from inside the neckline of her dress. Unscrewing the cap, she took a long swig.

"What is that?" Jordy asked, sniffing the air. "Is that... whiskey?"

"It's scotch," I said, grimacing. It's hard to forget the stench of your father's favorite drink when he'd spent the majority of your childhood screaming in your face.

Willow's gaze snapped to mine, biting down on her lower lip, undoubtedly also remembering things that were better left forgotten. I cursed myself silently, angry for having said anything.

"He's right," Ella muttered, holding up her flask in cheers. "It's scotch. If I'm going to be forced to sit through some ridiculous lovefest then I definitely need to be drunk for it."

"How in the heck did you get your grubby lil' hands on some honest-to-God booze?" Britta demanded. "And why the fuck ain't you sharin' it?"

"Seriously, Ella," EJ added, gesturing. "Pass that over here."

"Hell no," Ella said, clutching the flask to her chest. "Cassie made wine for the wedding — drink that."

"Cassie's wine is weak as hell!"

Shrugging, Ella pushed past the group, pulling open the door. "Not my problem," she said over her shoulder.

"You get your ass back here!" Britta threw the door open, disappearing. With a helpless grin, EJ hurried after her.

"I, um, I'm gonna go, I guess," Willow muttered in my general direction. As Jordy raced to open the door for her, and she moved toward it, her eyes finally lifted, just barely meeting mine. A heartbeat later, she was gone.

TWENTY TWO

WILLOW

Jim and Maria stood beneath the wedding arbor; hand carved by Joshua, intricate designs had been etched into the light oak—flowers and mandalas that ascended its thick base, reaching all the way to the top. Ivy had been wrapped loosely around the entire structure, hanging in delicate strands, the tips of which were brushing the heads of the couple beneath it. Jim held Maria's hands in his, a small smile playing at the corner of his mouth. His suit was one of the ones from the drama club haul; Maria's dress was the cream-colored wedding gown Britta had found.

Betsey stood before them, reading from a small book in her weathered hands. Despite her no-nonsense demeanor, Betsey smiled at the bride. "Maria, do you take James to be your wedded husband? James, do you take Maria to be your wedded wife?"

Keeping their eyes fixed on one another, each responded, "I do."

"Do you promise to love and cherish each other, in sickness and in health, for better or worse, for as long as you both shall live?"

"We do," they replied in unison.

Five rows from the altar, I sat mid-bench between Britta and Jordy. On my left, in a rare show of emotion, Britta was wholly absorbed in the ceremony, sniffling softly. To my right, Jordy seemed to be inching closer until our legs were practically touching.

"You really look incredible," Jordy whispered, nudging my arm.

"Thanks," I whispered distractedly, unable to concentrate on anything other than the feel of Logan's calloused hand still lingering on my cheek. And the absolutely piercing look in his eyes as his thumb slid slowly toward my mouth. Of its own accord, my hand touched my mouth, my fingertips feathering over the swell of my bottom lip, the feeling causing a spike of sensation straight through my core.

I dropped my hand as if it burned me, shooting up out of my seat. As I hurried toward the doors, a cheer rose up across the room while Jim dipped Maria backward and bent to kiss her. More cheers arose as I pushed through the doors, bursting onto the porch, sucking in lungful after lungful of hot, humid air that did nothing to ease the heat already building inside me.

"Willow?" Britta and Ella pushed through the doors, coming to stand on either side of me. "What happened, sugar? You alright?"

"I don't know," I said, breathless. "I really don't know."

"Ella, hand me that flask," Britta demanded.

"No," Ella snapped back. "I told you, it's mine."

Wrapping my arms around myself, I glanced between my two friends. "I loved him," I said, nodding vigorously even as my expression crumpled. "I did. I really, really did."

Britta pressed the back of her hand to my forehead. "Sugar, what, or who, are we talkin' about? You feelin' okay?"

"Luke," I whimpered. "I loved him."

"Of course you did." Britta's brow furrowed. "What's got into you?"

"I don't know," I cried softly. "Everything was fine—" I gestured frantically at the dining hall. "And then I..." I trailed off, shaking my head again. I couldn't bear to speak what I felt out loud; to do so felt as if I were doubly betraying Lucas.

Logan's face flashed in my thoughts—intrusive and unwelcome. His ocean-blue eyes burning into mine, looking at me in ways Lucas never had; like I was the most beautiful person he'd ever laid eyes on, like he couldn't take his eyes off me. Like looking at me would never be enough. Like *having* me would never be enough.

Flashes of images assaulted me. *A fist through a wall. An anguished cry. Desperate mouths fused together while frantic hands fought for—*

"Oh my god," I exclaimed. "What's wrong with me? What the fuck is wrong with me?"

Britta shot Ella a pointed look. "Fine," Ella muttered, reluctantly pulling the flask from her dress. Plucking the flask from Ella's hand, Britta unscrewed the cap and took a swig. Stifling a cough, she pushed it into my hand. "Drink up," she urged, "you'll feel better."

I took a tentative sip, grimacing. "Oh god, it's gross," I rasped.

"Yeah, but not nearly as gross as cryin' at someone else's weddin'."

Ella choked on a laugh and I snorted despite myself. "Cheers to that, I guess," I mumbled, lifting the flask to my lips, chugging what was left. My mouth aflame, I hacked through my next several breaths.

"There ya go," Britta said, slapping me on the back. "Now it's a party."

"Tears and beers," Ella agreed. Taking her flask, she tucked it back inside her dress. "Now, if you'll excuse me, I need a refill."

"Bring back the whole bottle this time, you greedy heifer!" Britta yelled after her. Turning back to me, she asked, "Now what's all this about Lucas?"

Dragging my hands down the side of my face, I could only shake my head. "Oh god, I don't even know, I just—"

Whatever I'd been about to say vanished the second I saw *him*.

Hands shoved deep into his pants pockets, shoulders slightly hunched, Logan was following the path headed toward the dining hall. Wearing the clothing I'd picked out especially for him; black suit pants and a crisp white shirt he'd left untucked. The top two buttons had been left open and his hair hung loose around his shoulders, while his beard and cheeks had been trimmed neat. Seeing him, my heart skipped a beat. A literal fucking beat, like it had tripped over its own feet.

"Hey," Logan said, jogging up the stairs.

"Hey there, yourself," Britta greeted Logan with an appraising look and sly smile. "Thought you weren't comin'?"

Logan looked at me, right at me. Straight through to my damn soul, it felt like. Clearing his throat, he gruffly replied, "I thought Willow might need someone to show her how to do the funky chicken."

His words, *his stupid words*. His stupid face. His stupid eyes. His stupid hand on my stupid cheek and my stupid overblown reaction to it. I exploded into giggles, entirely unintentional, that were rapidly becoming hysterical.

Logan stared at me. "Are you okay?" he asked. When I only continued to laugh, he looked at Britta. "What's going on? Did something happen?"

Britta hooked her arm through mine, tugging me close. "She's good," she said, giving me a squeeze. "Weddin' just got us a little choked up is all."

More nervous laughter erupted from me. I slapped my hand over my mouth to try and stem it, my eyes watering with effort. Just then the dining hall doors flung open and several people stepped onto the porch, Jordy among them.

"Mate, I've been looking for you. They brought the food out—we're eating good tonight." Jordy jerked his thumb over his shoulder. "EJ's grabbing us a table if everyone's ready?"

"Perfect," Britta replied, tugging me toward the doors. "I don't know 'bout y'all, but I'm starvin'."

We filed back inside the hall, currently abuzz with activity. Jugs brimming with plum-colored liquid along with various food dishes had been set out along the tables—baked potatoes covered in chives, deviled eggs, homemade coleslaw, and rabbit stew— the smell alone enough to make your mouth water. There didn't appear to be any sort of assigned seating; guests were either seated or milling around with plates of food in their hands, talking with one another. Loud music played from a small stereo system and a few people were already dancing.

"Over here." EJ waved us over with both arms. "Over here, Brit."

"Lawd," Britta murmured in my ear. "I don't know what I'm gonna do about that silly boy—ignorin' him hasn't been workin'. An' if I take him to bed, you know he's only gonna get twice as riled up—probably try to get me down an aisle or some crazy shit."

I glanced sideways at her. "And that's a bad thing?"

Britta snorted. "Yes and no. EJ's sweet alright, but he don't make me feel that crazy feelin' real low in your belly, like. You know, where you just want 'em so bad that your whole body lights up an' lets ya know it?"

I sucked in a heady breath. Unfortunately, I'd become well acquainted with that very feeling recently. "Have you had that before?" I asked tentatively.

Britta paused before answering; she'd yet to answer me when we'd reached the table. Sliding onto the bench beside her, I asked, "Britta? Are *you* okay?"

She took an audible breath. "Yeah, I had that once, with ma' husband." Another pause and a shake of her head and then she was snatching the jug of wine from the center of the table and pouring us both heaping glassfuls. "Cheers to love, sugar," she said, holding up her glass. "And all the crazy and painful shit that follows."

"Have you been drinking?" Logan dropped down onto the bench beside me before I could respond to Britta, sitting close enough that I could smell the soap in his hair, and the downright provocative scent that was pure *him*. Jordy had joined us as well, taking the seat directly across from me.

"Barely." Thanks to Ella, I was very nicely buzzed, but not even half as buzzed as I suddenly wished I was.

Logan's frown deepened. "Maybe you should eat something."

"I'm good, thanks," I muttered, lifting my glass and drinking deeply.

The sound of clinking glass drew everyone's attention to the head table where Leisel had risen from her seat, tapping her wineglass with a spoon. All over the dining hall, others began doing the same until the entire room was filled with the discordant clanking of metal against glass. Seated at the same table as Leisel, Jim and Maria were grinning at each other and laughing as they pressed their lips together. In response to their kiss, cheers and jeers rose up among the crowd.

"What's happening?" I asked.

"It's an idiotic thing you do at weddings," Ella replied, dramatically flouncing down on the bench between Jordy and EJ. "When you want the bride and groom to kiss."

"Weird," I murmured. Lifting my glass to my lips and finding it empty, I reached for the jug, only to have Logan snatch it away and set it out of reach.

"Hey!" I exclaimed. "What are you doing?"

He gave me a hard look. "*What are you doing?*"

"I'm having a good time," I said through my teeth. "You should try it."

Logan's features pulled taut; a muscle began to tic in his jaw. "You're being irresponsible. And after what happened last week—"

"That's not fair," I whispered angrily. "It's two totally different situations. Now give it back."

"No," he growled, nostrils flaring. "You've had enough."

"Cassie's wine is usually pretty weak, mate," Jordy addressed Logan. "It's only aged a few weeks so—"

"*Fuck off,*" Logan bit out, his angry gaze snapping to Jordy. "*No one* fucking asked you, *mate.*"

I blinked, startled by the malice in Logan's tone and the horrible way he was looking at Jordy. I realized, with a note of surprise, that this wasn't the first time he'd looked at Jordy like this. I'd always attributed it to Logan's dislike for anyone that wasn't like him—an uptight stickler with an endless list of rules—but looking at Logan now, I knew his dislike for Jordy went much deeper.

Jordy's gaze flicked rapidly between me and Logan, as if it couldn't decide where to land. "Okay," he said slowly. "My bad."

"*Well, well, well.*" Ella's smile was downright snakelike. "What an interesting development."

A palpable silence followed. A quick look around the quiet table showed all eyes on Logan and me, expressions ranging from curious to outright amused. Mortification flooded my neck and chest, flashing hotly in my cheeks.

"Well, shit—is it dancin' time already?" Britta made a big show of checking her naked wrist as if she were wearing a watch. "I think it is!" Slapping her hands down on the tabletop, she shoved up out of her seat. "You hear that, Willow? The DJ is playin' our song!" Grabbing my arm, Britta hauled me off the bench and hurried me from the table.

"Lord knows I like gossip as much as the next," she whispered. "But you and Eddie just gave everyone within earshot enough fodder to last 'em the whole dang winter."

Panic thudded through me, my throat painfully bobbing. "It's not what it looks like, I swear it isn't."

"Oh, it most definitely *is* what it looks like," she retorted. "That whole nutty scene you made out there on the porch makes a heck of a lot more sense now—but I'll spare ya the embarrassment of tellin' ya whatcha already know."

Britta paused to scoop a pitcher of wine off a nearby table, along with two empty wineglasses. "Mighty kind of you to share," she said, nodding at the table's startled occupants. Filling our glasses, she tapped her glass to mine, causing purple liquid to slosh over the rims and spill on the floor. "Time to dance!"

Chugging half her glass, Britta sashayed onto the dance floor where the overhead lights had been dimmed, and the fairy lights strung over the rafters caused a reflective glimmer similar to a disco ball. Though the stereo still played, a band was in the process of setting up—a handful of Silver Lake residents with an eclectic collection of instruments—a brown and battered upright piano, two colorfully hand-painted ukuleles, and a drum set consisting of a snare, a floor tom, and a cymbal. While Xavier fiddled with a ukulele, Cassie stood beside him, tapping a tambourine in her hand. She waved when she saw me, pulling her long, flowing dress into a curtsy. *Love it,* she mouthed, pointing at the embroidered skirt—another drama club find.

"Come on, Willow, dance with me." Britta beckoned, shimmying to the beat of the song.

Sipping on my wine, I slid a surreptitious glance back the way we'd come. Only Logan and Ella remained at our table—Ella drinking from her flask while Logan stared daggers at me, his gaze full of all the irritation and displeasure of a disapproving parent.

Mortification clashed with anger, anger clashed with obstinance and obstinance clashed with… longing. Again, the ghost of Logan's touch whispered across my cheek. Feeling sick, I spun around and hastily threw back my drink. With wine dribbling down my chin, I hurried to join Britta on the dance floor.

TWENTY THREE

LOGAN

I *was* a bomb.

I was a *goddamn bomb,* who *goddamn Leisel* had been *goddamn right* about all this *goddamn time.*

And I was seconds away from detonating.

Almost everyone was dancing now, and those who weren't had gravitated to the dance floor to spectate. Only three of us remained on this side of the dining hall—Ella, who'd left to fill her flask but had since returned, Davey, who'd fallen asleep in his chair, and me.

For the last hour I'd been a statue on a bench, my eyes trained on Willow, my entire body attuned to Willow—the way the lights shone on her skin, the way the material of her dress rippled around her body, and the wild way she was dancing—barefoot, laughing as she twisted and twirled and kicked up her feet in all directions. I hardly blinked, I barely breathed. I merely stared and vibrated with a vast assortment of feelings that I could no longer contain.

The strings strung their concluding chords as Cassie ended a fast-paced folk song on a long, drawn-out high note. Applause rippled through the dancers, whoops and whistles, too. Laughing, Willow and Britta collapsed against one another.

I was jealous of Britta.

I was jealous of Jordy.

Hell, I was jealous of everyone that Willow had ever paid any real attention to, anyone she'd ever graced with a smile, anyone she'd spoken to or cared about — I was even jealous of my own brother. And even as sick as *that* made me feel, I was twice as sick of pretending it wasn't true.

Cassie began to sing again, a deep, crooning tune, shimmying her tambourine by her side, while Xavier strummed his ukulele. The crowd thinned out as people began pairing off. I watched as EJ finally drummed up the courage to approach Britta, bowing down before her, making a big show of asking her to dance. Britta, who was noticeably drunk, had thrown her head back laughing. Draping her arms around EJ's neck, she allowed him to spin her away.

Willow stood alone now, her silly smile slipping. She swiped the sweat from her forehead while casting awkward glances around the dance floor. The urge to go to her, to finally be the one to dance with her, was unmistakable. It beat through me, causing my heart to race and my stomach to churn and my legs to bounce… and yet, I still couldn't stand.

"You're a fucking idiot if you ask me," Ella slurred as she staggered around the table. "A really, *really*, good-looking idiot… but still an idiot."

I sent a grimace in her direction. "No one asked you," I bit out. Turning my attention back to the dance floor, everything suddenly stopped—my legs stopped bouncing, my lungs stopped inflating, even my heart stalled out. My vision tunneled, sucking me into a silent world, with Willow standing in the spotlight.

No longer dancing, she stood at the edge of the small crowd, holding her boots in her hand. Jordy stood beside her, his head bent to hers, whispering something in her ear that was causing a small smile to creep up the corners of her mouth. Jordy's hand moved to her waist, her silky dress crinkling beneath his fingers.

Like a flame doused in gasoline, I roared back to life, jumping up and storming across the dining hall. Those who saw me approaching paused, some even going as far as to move out of my way. Willow noticed me at the last second, her eyes going wide.

Up until she'd spotted me, I hadn't any idea of what I'd been planning on doing once I reached them—I'd only known that I'd wanted to tear Jordy to pieces for daring to touch her. For wanting her in the first place. I was angry at Willow, too, for continuing to allow his attention. For having ever smiled at him, and for having the audacity to laugh at his ridiculous jokes. But most of all, for not recognizing what he wanted from her. Or worse, for recognizing it and maybe even wanting it, too.

And then everything ground to a screeching halt once more. I was inches from Willow, close enough to reach out and touch her, when it struck me. This was all wrong. *I* was all wrong. And I could see just how wrong I was reflected in the fear shining in Willow's eyes.

Shoving my hands into my hair, I changed course, racing toward the doors and slamming through them. Coming here had been a mistake—I'd known that much from the moment I'd seen

Willow standing outside the dining hall, the fairy lights glinting off her golden-brown shoulders, her big brown eyes darkening as they collided with mine. But I was a goddamn masochist, and Willow was the poison I couldn't seem to quit.

And yes, I was a goddamn motherfucking bomb, too. But no, I wouldn't be detonating tonight. Or any night. I wasn't going to become my father—I wouldn't be burning down the people I cared about just to smother the fires that raged inside of me. Not now, not fucking ever.

But, oh, how the flames raged.

I arrived at our cabin within minutes, flicking the lights on and immediately tearing off the ridiculous shirt Willow had left for me. Buttons popped free, pinging around the room. Hastily dressing in my own clothes—a pair of jeans and a long-sleeved shirt—I pulled Lucas's pack from beneath the bed and began wrenching open dresser drawers, yanking items from within and stuffing them inside the pack.

"What are you doing?"

I whipped around; Willow stood in the doorway, still holding her boots in her hand. She looked stricken, much like she'd looked when I'd been charging toward her in the dining hall. Turning away, I started packing again, twice as fast.

The soft slap of her feet on the floor echoed around me; I felt the warmth of her behind me. "Logan, what are you doing?" she demanded.

Facing her again, I found our bodies nearly touching. And if she touched me, *if I touched her*, it was all fucking over. I couldn't do a repeat of earlier—I wouldn't let her walk away a second time.

Backing into the dresser, I gritted out, "I'm leaving."

"What?" Eyes narrowed, Willow shook her head. "Where are

you going? *Why are you going?*"

"Why the fuck do you care?" I said. "You wanted me to leave you the fuck alone, remember, so now I'm leaving you the fuck alone."

"Logan, no—I already said *I didn't mean that.*"

"And you definitely don't need me here—you've got friends, your job, this cabin. You've got *fucking Jordy and his shitty jokes.*"

"Jordy... what?" She blinked rapidly, her expression full of confusion. "Logan, you can't just leave—nobody gets in or out until the sun comes up."

"I'll climb it," I said, grabbing the pack and slinging it on my back. "I climbed out of that fucking ravine with you dying on my back and a hundred Creepers clawing for me, I'm pretty sure I can manage a damn wall."

As I moved to leave, Willow stepped in front of me. "Stop it!" she demanded. "Whatever's going on, we can fix it. *You don't need to leave.*"

Tearing my eyes from hers, I growled. "Yeah, I do. I can't be here with you. Not like this."

There it was. My confession—part of it, at least—laid bare between us like a sacrificial lamb. Chancing a look, I found Willow's face a riotous symphony of emotions—her eyes flared wide, her mouth floundering, her trembling hands twisting in the skirt of her dress. Panic rose and fell from her expression like a series of tidal waves plunging toward shore.

"You know what?" she said in a quivering whisper that grew louder and angrier with every word. "You're right, *you should leave.*" Still trembling, she turned slowly away only to spin right back around, an accusatory finger pointed at my chest. "You should definitely leave!" she shrieked.

Swiping an article of clothing from the open drawer behind

me, she slapped it to my chest. "Here, take your shit and fucking leave." The clothing fell to the floor as her hands slapped my chest a second time. "Go, Logan—leave! What are you waiting for? Get the fuck out of here—get away from *me*!"

"Stop it!" I yelled, dodging her onslaught.

"Go on then, fucking go!" she continued, tears and fury flowing.

As she slapped her hands to my chest for a third time, I grabbed her wrists, hauling her up against me. Her softness crashed against my hardness. My heaving chest to her heaving breasts. My desperation breathing in perfect synchrony with hers. She lifted her chin and stared at me, the glint in her eyes holding both a challenge and a dare.

"Just go," she whimpered feebly.

"Fuck you," I growled, giving myself one last second to change my mind...

And then I kissed her.

My hands went to her face, into her hair, to the back of her head, my tongue delving deep inside her mouth the very instant her lips parted. Willow's arms went to my neck, squeezing me to her, pulling herself up against me and matching each plunge of my tongue with a frantic parry of her own.

Roughly skimming the sides of her, I squeezed and kneaded her from hips to ass, grabbing each taut cheek in my hands. Her nails scoured my neck before dragging down the front of my shirt and dipping beneath it. One hand went to my back, while the other grabbed for my belt, jerking it open.

We tumbled backward, tripping over the fallen pack on the floor, my back crashing into the same dresser I'd been tearing apart only moments ago. Grunting in pain, I swung Willow around, lifting her up onto the rickety structure, our mouths and bodies never breaking contact.

Her fingers were in my hair, her legs wound around me. My hands were up the skirt of her dress, ripping her underwear down her legs. We broke apart only for a moment; Willow's eyes were hooded, her lips wet and swollen, parting farther with each panting breath. Yanking my shirt off over my head, I seized her face, my fingertips digging into her cheeks, taking her mouth with mine once again. We kissed faster, harder, our mouths crashing together in sharp, hungry bursts.

"Logan!" Impatient, she rocked herself against me in a desperate, erratic rhythm. Hard to the point of pain, I cursed as I grappled with the zipper on my jeans, shoving them down my legs and shaking them away. My hands returned to her thighs, bunching the liquid material of her dress up around her waist. Gripping her hips, I yanked her to the edge of the dresser.

We locked eyes.

Everything… slowed… down.

Poised at her entrance, wet and ready for me, I pushed slowly inside of her, groaning as her body squeezed mine. Gasping, Willow pitched her hips forward, taking me the rest of the way in. Her fingertips found purchase beneath my shoulder blades; mine dug deep into the fleshy part of her thighs. Her heels bore down into the back of my ass while my feet fought to keep from slipping across the floor.

Everything sped back up again.

The dresser slammed into the wall with each furious thrust, only to teeter forward as Willow swung her hips toward mine. Tearing my mouth from hers, I dropped my face to her neck, biting down. She moaned even as she cried out; her hands found my hair again, clutching fistfuls, and twisting painfully.

I increased my speed, Willow's frenzied whimpers spurring me on. Fabric tore, something crashed to the floor, the dresser continued to brutally strike the wall. My muscles tensed, my orgasm building too soon, leaving me struggling to keep pace. Heaving growls erupted from low in my throat. Once... twice more, I thrust inside her and then I was shoving her away and pulling free from her body. Gripping the edge of the dresser, I groaned through my release.

Breathing hard, I looked up to find Willow with her cheek pressed to the wall and her mouth hanging open, red lipstick smeared across her face. A light sheen of sweat glistened on her forehead and chest. Her dress straps were broken and hanging, the top half of her dress sagging below one perfect teardrop breast. With every ragged intake of air, her chest noticeably rose, forcing the slinky material to slip even lower. Her skirt remained gathered at her waist, her legs were still splayed apart, quivering ever so slightly.

Fucking hell—if I hadn't just finished fucking her, one look at her like this would have had me ready to go.

"Are you... okay?" I asked, hoarsely.

Willow rolled her head along the wall toward me, her eyes glassy.

"Hey," I said, placing my hand on her thigh. "You okay?"

She blinked, the clouds in her gaze clearing. She sat up suddenly, pushing my hand away and wrenching her dress up over her breasts. "I'm fine," she whispered, sliding down from the dresser. Her knees buckled as her feet hit the floor and I hurried to grab her. Again, she pushed me away.

"I said, I'm fine," she bit out.

"Willow," I growled. "What the fuck—"

"No, don't. *Please don't*," she rushed to say, her voice cracking. "I'm fine." Throat bobbing, her eyes filled with tears. Her hand moved to her mouth, crushing a cross between a gasp and sob, and then she was racing across the room and slamming the bathroom door shut behind her.

"Fuck," I muttered, pulling my jeans up. Kicking a pathway through the mess we'd made, I twisted the bathroom doorknob, surprised to find it unlocked. Willow, who'd been sitting on the toilet with her face buried in her hands, jumped up in surprise. "What are you doing—get out!"

I flinched at her tone, my back stiffening. "Not until you tell me what's wrong."

"Nothing. I just need a minute. Can I have a fucking minute, please?"

"Bullshit. You think I don't know you well enough to know when something's wrong?"

"Know me?" Willow let out a hollow laugh. "Most days you can barely look at me, and now you think you *know me*?"

She was dead wrong. I knew her—I knew everything there was to know about her. I knew that when she was staring up at the clouds, she was picking out the ones that most resembled her beloved Alice in Wonderland characters. I knew that whenever she was mad, she almost always swung first and asked questions later. That she was klutzy and accident prone and that her attitude was infuriating, and yet, despite everything, I'd wanted her for longer than I would ever admit to. But instead of saying any of those things, my thick-witted mouth chose to blurt, "I know you well enough to know that you've never hid in a bathroom after fucking my brother."

Willow's mouth fell open and she staggered back as if I'd struck her. Freezing as I realized the extent of my own stupidity, I squeezed my eyes shut, wishing I could eat my words.

Willow recovered first, charging at me. "Move!" she screamed, shoving me. "Let me out of here!"

"I didn't mean that," I gritted out, ducking as her hand came flying at my face. "Willow—do you fucking hear me—I didn't mean that!"

Dodging her hands, I caught her around her middle, pinning her arms to her sides. Pushing her up against the wall, I caged her body with mine. "Stop," I rasped. "Willow, I didn't mean it—*please stop*."

It was minutes before she calmed, though it felt infinitely longer as she continued twisting and thrashing and calling me a colorful variety of names before eventually slumping in my arms. I folded with her, bringing us both to the floor, keeping her close.

"Oh my fucking god…" Her voice was strangled. "Logan, how could we do that to him… again?"

Again.

Again.

She finally admitted it.

She finally admitted it.

After all these years, without Willow ever having acknowledged what had happened between us, without her even alluding to it happening, I'd begun to doubt my own mind, wondering if it had been only a dream, or a hallucination brought on by stress or hunger, or both. Or that maybe, out of sheer fucking loneliness, I'd simply imagined it.

But, no, I hadn't imagined it.

It had happened.

We had happened.

TWENTY FOUR

LOGAN

One, two, three, four… I counted the snow-covered bodies from my upstairs vantage point inside the Bed & Breakfast, clearly discerning each neatly wrapped form. One body, however, was quite a ways away from the rest, unwrapped, and not so neatly placed. As if he'd just been dumped there… like the heap of garbage he was.

It was snowing again; it had snowed every day for countless days. I'd lost all sense of time; day and night had become one and the same. Both were a prison I couldn't escape from… much like this fucking house.

Pushing away from the windowsill, I wandered into the hallway, taking great care not to look to my left, not to look at the room where it had happened. Not that I could forget it, not when I laid awake each night replaying every horrible moment over and over again.

Willow stepped into the hall, her eyes bloodshot, her expression haunted.

"How is he?" I asked, glancing behind her into mine and Lucas's room.

"He won't talk to me. He won't even look at me — he keeps… he just keeps rolling away from me." Her mouth wobbled, tears filling her eyes. "He blames me, I know he does."

"Has he eaten anything?" I couldn't deal with her tears right now — I already had enough garbage to contend with without having to deal with everyone's personal bullshit as well.

Willow shook her head.

"Have you eaten anything?"

Again, she shook her head. "I'm not hungry."

Dragging a hand roughly down my face, I pointed to the stairs. "Go fucking eat something before you get sick," I said, shoving past her into the room.

Lucas remained in the same state he'd been since it happened — he lay in his bed, the covers pulled up over his head, the entire space stinking of unwashed bodies and piss. Tossing the last of the log pile onto the dwindling fire, I bent down beside him.

"Luke." I tugged the blankets down and shook his shoulder. "Luke, you need to eat something."

He snatched the covers back from me, pulling them tightly to his neck. "I'm not hungry," he rasped, his voice dry and grating. "Leave me alone."

"Fine," I sighed.

Pulling the door shut behind me, I resumed wandering aimlessly throughout the house, in search of something I couldn't name.

Passing the kitchen window, I glimpsed a splash of red in the white world beyond. Spinning back, I pressed my fist to the glass, rubbing the frozen condensation away.

Willow was sitting in the snow beside her mother's body, her arms wrapped around her knees, her breath leaving her in visible wisps of white. She was barefoot, wearing nothing but sweatpants and a torn red T-shirt. Cursing, I raced to the back door, flinging it open and shouting her name. She didn't acknowledge me as I reached for her, didn't even flinch when I grabbed her arms and yanked her up onto her feet.

"Are you trying to die?" I demanded, dragging her inside the house and dropping her into a lounge chair. Rushing to the fireplace, I looked over our nearly depleted wood supply in dismay. We'd have to start burning the furniture soon.

Returning to Willow, I wrapped my arm around her waist and walked her to the fireplace, depositing her on a nearby sofa. Realizing her clothes were wet, I ran back upstairs, grabbing several warm articles of clothing, along with the blankets from the bed.

Downstairs again, I dumped everything on the floor beside the sofa. "Willow? Can you change your clothes? You need to get out of the wet stuff." Running my hands through my hair, I continued, "Jesus, it's twenty fucking degrees out – what were you thinking?"

Her eyes found mine, bloodshot and framed in clumps of frozen eyelashes. Her body was listless, as if every bit of energy had been leached from her. "I w-w-wanted my mom," she slurred, as she continued to shiver and shake. "I just wanted my mo-m-m."

I swallowed back the pain that swelled inside me, the heartbreak I felt for her, for Lucas, and even for myself. It was just the three of us now, and if I didn't keep us going, no one else would.

"Alright." I sighed angrily. "Alright, I'll help you – can I help you?" Slowly, sluggishly, she nodded.

After wrangling her wet shirt off her frozen body and replacing it with a long-sleeved flannel, I dragged her sweatpants down her legs, exchanging them for a pair of fleece pajama pants. Tugging thick woolen socks onto each of her feet, I wrapped her tightly in blankets and tossed the last of the wood into the fire.

Leaving Willow to get warm, I took the stairs two at a time back to Lucas. Finding his fire dwindling again, I scanned the room for something to burn. An antique desk sat against one wall, heavy and nearly immobile, but large enough to keep both fires burning until tomorrow. Another trip downstairs and I'd returned with an ax. The first collision of steel against wood and Lucas jolted awake — he blinked sluggishly across the dimly lit room, before eventually rolling away.

Gritting my teeth, I resumed chopping, stopping only once the desk lay in pieces. Tossing some wood onto Lucas's fire, I gathered up as much as I could carry and hurried back to Willow.

She remained as I'd left her — wrapped in blankets in front of the dying fire, still shivering. Dropping the wood, I shoved the sofa closer, then headed to the kitchen to scour the cupboards. Mackenzie's family, along with the Gleasons, had taken almost everything of value with them, leaving the three of us with only a kitchen full of perishables, most of which were already rotten and beginning to stink. Scanning the putrid contents of the pantry, I found half a box of crackers that appeared edible — taking them, I snagged a ceramic mug from the countertop and a pot from the stove. Holding the box of crackers between my teeth, I pushed the sliding doors open, scooping a pot of snow off the porch. That's when I noticed it — the silhouette of a fast-approaching person. Not a person, I realized, taking note of its stiff, jerky movements. An infected.

"Fuck," I muttered, slamming the door closed and quickly locking it. My heart hammering in my chest, I dropped everything I was carrying and ran back up the stairs, reclaiming the ax from my room. I was halfway down the stairs when an angry thud echoed through the building, followed closely by several more. I closed my eyes as my heart rate continued to climb; the infected had found its way onto the porch and was throwing *itself against the sliding doors. I had no idea how long those doors would hold, but I couldn't imagine it being very long.*

Shrugging into my coat, knowing what I would have to do, my stomach roiled with nerves.

Ax in hand, I left the house via the front door, circling quickly around the side. The snow crunched loudly beneath my boots, alerting the infected to my presence. Swinging around, it jolted forward, stumbling down the steps. Jaw snapping, eyes milky yet focused, it lifted up its arms, reaching for me.

My mouth fell open, my hand fell limply to my side, almost losing my grip on the ax.

Mackenzie's long blonde hair was streaked with black, large clumps of it having been ripped straight from her scalp. There were more wounds; she appeared to have been partially eaten before turning herself. Her mouth opened and closed, low, guttural groans erupting from within.

"No," I whispered, backing away. "No, no, no... "

Mackenzie continued to gain on me until she was close enough that I could smell the rot — a musty, heavy smell that surrounded her. I pushed her back with the end of the ax, suddenly unable to wield it. She wasn't the first infected I'd seen — we'd all seen them on the news, on YouTube, and eventually in our own town, too. But our town was small and had cleared out pretty quickly once supplies had begun to dwindle. Occasionally, whenever an infected had been spotted nearby, the adults had always taken care of it.

You're the adult now, *I reminded myself.* Protecting Lucas and Willow is your job now.

Several minutes passed before I'd convinced myself to do it — to kill my girlfriend. I readied myself, and held my breath as I swung, flinching at the last second and sending the sharpened edge of the ax into her neck instead of her skull. Her head canted to one side, the wound exposing the rotten tendons and muscle there, and still she continued coming for me, utterly unfazed.

This time, I swung the ax like a bat, hitting her hard enough that she toppled over, and then I swung again, lodging the blade in the top of her skull. It stuck there, forcing me to step on her face in order to pull it free.

She still wasn't dead – her mouth continued to open and close, her eyes still blinked.

I wanted to run and hide. I wanted to scream and rail against the unfairness of it all. But most of all I wanted someone else to do what needed to be done.

Instead, I swung. I swung until she was no longer moving, no longer recognizable. Just a pile of death at my feet. And then I ran back inside the house, just barely managing to shut and lock the door before I crumbled to the floor and remained there, staring in horror at the gore covering my boots.

"W-what happened?" Willow stood off to the side of the entryway, a blanket wrapped tightly around her.

I blinked up at her, feeling dizzy and disorientated. "This is so fucked," I whispered, banging my head back against the wall. "This is all so fucked – I feel like I'm going insane. How is this real?"

Still banging my head against the wall, I continued speaking frantically, verging on hysteria. "How is any of this real? I feel like – I feel like – "

With a silent roar, I burst up onto my feet and swung my fist into the wall, over and over again. Plaster cracked and caved in, wallpaper ripped, and yet I continued to strike, hoping that with each blow some of the tension, some of the frustration, some of the aching, some of the completely fucked-up feelings building inside of me would start to ease. It wasn't the case; the shitty feelings only continued to grow, growing until I was rapidly pummeling the wall with both hands. We were going to die here – the world was picking us off handfuls at a time – and I was helpless to stop it.

"Logan." Willow was grabbing at my arms, trying to pull me away. "Stop, you're bleeding – stop it!" She slipped between me and the wall, shoving me away with what little strength she had. I grabbed her in surprise, gripping her arms and blinking down at her through blurry, waterlogged eyes.

I was crying, I realized angrily. I was fucking crying, and in front of Willow, no less. I didn't want to cry; I wanted to hit something. I wanted to hurt something. I wanted to feel something other than all this fucking madness swelling inside me.

But I couldn't hit Willow. The lone sliver of sanity that I still possessed realized that much.

So I kissed her instead – I pushed her back against the ruined wall, covered her mouth with mine and kissed her like my life depended on it – which, in that one weak moment, it did.

And when she kissed me back, fisting her hands in my shirt, matching my desperation with equal measure, I kept going, not thinking, just needing.

Just needing to feel something – anything at all – that didn't hurt.

Still sitting on the bathroom floor, I was propped against the wall with Willow draped across my lap, having since cried herself to sleep. Looking down at her, I ran my knuckles lightly against the side of her face. We'd only been kids back then – terrified teenagers consumed with grief who'd had a horrible lapse in judgment. I'd never tried to justify it, not even to myself – there was no justifying a mistake of that caliber. I'd assumed Willow felt the same, and that was why we never spoke of it, and why we'd carried on like nothing had ever happened between us.

But what had occurred tonight *wasn't* the same.

Tonight had been the culmination of feelings that had been building inside me for a hell of a long time, maybe even since the first time. There was no more denying what I felt for Willow. It was what Willow felt for me, or what she didn't feel… that remained to be seen.

With that in mind, I shifted to my feet, lifting Willow in my arms, and carried her to bed. As I slid in beside her, she turned toward me, curling her body around mine with a sigh. Staring down at her, I wished we could stay just like this — safely ensconced in the dead of night where I could touch her without her pushing me away, and where I could sleep beside her without worrying about what might change once the sun came up.

Because, come morning would come reality — the reality was that I was in love with Willow, and Willow was still in love with my brother.

TWENTY FIVE

WILLOW

I awoke slowly, languidly stretching limbs still stiff with sleep. Skin brushed skin as I rolled into the wall of warm muscle nestled tightly beside me, nuzzling my face against it and sliding my fingers over it.

I froze suddenly, my eyes flying open, my breath catching and evaporating. Staring at Logan's chest, recalling every single sordid detail of the night before, I wondered frantically how I was going to avoid having to deal with what we'd done, but more pressing was how to avoid having to deal with Logan.

While my thoughts spiraled into full-on panic mode and I contemplated making a screaming run for it, Logan sighed in his sleep, releasing me as he rolled away. I remained frozen for several seconds, wildly for the clothing strewn all over my bed, and making a run for the bathroom, my footfalls softer and stealthier than ever before.

Closing the door softly behind me, I collapsed against it, staring at my wild-eyed reflection in the mirror. I looked...

Hand to my cheek, I pushed my heavy veil of hair away from my face and swallowed hard. My lids were heavy, my lips were swollen, and there was a small mark on my neck... and another one on my shoulder. Between my legs throbbed with the memory of the man who lay asleep just outside the door.

A man who'd left me looking... *and feeling*... very well fucked.

"Shit," I spat softly, dropping my hand. Cursing, I dug through the clothing I'd gathered, relieved to find I'd grabbed everything I needed. Dressing quickly, I splashed some water over my face and turned to the door, my hand hovering over the knob as a fresh wave of panic gripped me. What if he was awake? What would I say? What *could* I say? I was fairly certain I was one thousand percent tongue-tied at the moment.

Making up my mind to grab my boots and make a run for it, I twisted the knob slowly, careful that it didn't as much as creak. Heart in my throat, I pushed the door open, nearly crumpling in relief to find Logan still facing away from me, still sleeping soundly. Snatching my boots off the floor, I fumbled briefly with the lock on the door and then I was pushing into the early morning, flying barefoot across grass still wet with dew. Forgoing the dining hall—I absolutely couldn't face a single soul in my current state—I ran straight to work.

Stab. Stab. Stab. Stabbing my trowel deep into the dirt, I worked furiously, breaking up a tightly compacted mound of mud and soil.

Thrust. Thrust. Thrust. My hand slowed, my eyes closing, each stab deeper and harder than the last.

I wanted to hate what had happened—at the very least, I wanted to forget it. But… there was no denying the growing throb between my legs, and the way my body kept flushing with heat. I hadn't hated it—not even a little bit—and I definitely wouldn't be forgetting it.

"Willow? You okay, hun?"

My eyes flew open. Cassie was working beside me, tending to the same mound of dirt. In the face of her scrutiny, I felt my flush deepen, wondering if she knew what I'd done last night—if she could tell just by looking at me.

"I'm fine," I muttered as I resumed stabbing the earth. "Hungover, I think."

It wasn't too far from the truth—I'd definitely drank enough to still be feeling it this morning. At least, that's what I was attempting to convince myself—that what had occurred between Logan and I had been the unfortunate result of too much whiskey and wine.

Cassie placed a gloved hand on my arm. "Why don't you clock out early and go get washed up? You've been working your tail off all morning, and I'm sure you want to be refreshed for Hank's celebration."

During the breakfast I'd skipped, it had been announced that Hank had died yesterday morning, succumbing to injuries that had been too extensive for Doc to treat. He'd already been buried, taken to a small cemetery outside of camp, and a small celebration of his life would be held in the dining hall that evening for anyone who wished to attend.

I hadn't planned on attending; I hadn't known Hank. Not that

I could tell Cassie that while she was wiping a tear from her cheek.

Sitting back on my heels, I swiped the sweat from my brow. "Yeah, okay, I could use a shower." Maybe a shower would wash away the scent of Logan that still clung to my skin, and the memory of his hands on me.

His hands cupping my face, squeezing my ass, gripping my thighs tight. I swallowed hard, nearly choking as a wave of need rolled hotly through me. The distant drumming of the dresser against the wall echoed in my thoughts, my mouth both drying and watering at the memory.

Jumping up, I stormed from the garden, with every intention of heading to the Bath House, only… as I neared the heart of camp, I found myself walking in the opposite direction. Nervous anticipation shuddered through me as I approached the construction site. I spotted him immediately, fitting floorboards onto the base of a new addition. He was shirtless, his broad, tan back glistening beneath the hot sun.

EJ noticed me first, nudging Logan. Glancing over his shoulder, Logan rose from kneeling, his low-slung jeans falling even lower on his hips. I sucked in a breath at the full sun-kissed length of him, another potent burst of desire shooting through me. I'd *never* felt like this before. I'd never felt such intense need before — it was as if a tap had burst inside of me.

My heart pounding in my throat, I spun around and hurried down the path. Bursting inside the cabin, I pressed my back against the door and surveyed the room — surprised to find it clean. All that remained from the mess we'd made the night before was the lopsided dresser, one of its legs broken clean off.

Breath after heady breath filled my lungs. Warmth pooled low in my belly, my every nerve lighting up in response to my thoughts.

Slipping my hand between my thighs, I squeezed my legs together, whimpering as my desire intensified.

There was a bang on the door; the wood pushed against my back. I jumped sideways, scrambling backward as Logan pushed inside, pausing in the threshold. Still shirtless, sweat shining from every rock-hard inch of him, intensity rolled off him in hot, heavy waves.

We came together in a frenzy of reckless lips. Tongues tangling, teeth clashing, I jumped up into his arms, wrapping my legs around his waist. While I roughly pawed at him and he fought to hold me, he stumbled sideways, crashing into the wall. Pinning me there, his hands explored my body, kneading my ass and groping my breasts. "Fuck," he groaned against my mouth. "*Fuck.*"

"Willow, darlin'," Britta called out as the cabin door flung open. "You comin' to Hank's — oh shit, my bad." The door slammed shut with her hurried departure.

Like a burning branch plunged into ice water, my feet hit the floor with a gasp. "Stop," I demanded, pushing at Logan. "Logan, *stop!*"

Cursing, he backed quickly away, his hands going to his hair, his chest heaving with heavy breaths. I stared at him, breathing hard, guilt and desire fighting for supremacy.

"We can't," I breathed. "We *can't* do this."

"Too fucking late," he ground out angrily. "We already did."

My eyes went wide. "Fuck you," I spat, fumbling blindly for the door. Flinging it open, I dashed outside. "Britta, wait!"

Racing down the path after Britta, my eyes were burning, my heart was pounding out of my chest. *Oh god.* What was I doing? And with Logan, of all people. Our relationship had always been shaky, volatile at best, held together only by our mutual love of Lucas — a love we'd both betrayed in the worst possible way. *Again.*

Up ahead, Britta glanced over her shoulder. "Done already?"

she asked as I fell in step beside her. "Didn't take Eddie for the *wham-bam, thank you, ma'am* type."

"Don't," I whispered, grabbing her arm, pulling her to a stop. "Please don't make jokes right now."

Britta's expression pulled into a frown. "Oh, sugar, what's the matter? Ain't this what you wanted?"

"No." I shook my head vehemently. "Not with him. Never with *him*."

"Somethin' wrong with Eddie... other than that stick up his ass?"

"*He's Luke's brother*," I said hoarsely. "And I love Luke."

"Sugar, Luke is gone," she said with a sympathetic shrug. "He's dead, and you and Eddie are still alive. We don't stop livin' when someone dies, do we?"

My mouth worked soundlessly while I fumbled for a reply I couldn't find.

"What would Luke want?" she pressed. "Would he want y'all happy?"

I didn't reply. I couldn't. Not because I didn't know the answer, but because I did.

Throwing her arm over my shoulders, Britta tugged me forward. "Look at it this way," she said. "Life has gotten mighty short these days, and it sure ain't sweet. Take Hank, for example." She shrugged again. "If you're lucky enough to find somethin' or someone that makes you feel good, then I say take it."

I stayed silent while we walked, wishing it were that simple. Of course, Luke would want me to be happy. He'd want Logan to be happy, too. But would he want us to be happy together? And what if it went wrong between Logan and me, which it undoubtedly would. What then?

"Stop overthinkin' it," Britta said. "There ain't much good left in the world so you gotta take what you can, when you can, and damn the consequences. And speakin' of Hank, we got a celebration to be gettin' to."

For the second time in two days, the occupants of Silver Lake gathered together at the dining hall in celebration. This time without fairy lights strung from the rafters, without music playing, or jugs of wine and elaborate platters of food passed around. This was a different sort of gathering; the somber celebration of a man's life cut short.

Attendees sat in a makeshift circle at one end of the hall while, one by one, Hank's friends took to the center of the circle to share funny stories involving Hank, and to express how much he would be missed.

"He's with his wife and kids now," Davey said, concluding his speech. "His grandkids, too. He's home."

As Davey stepped away, EJ took his place in the circle. "You remember that time the chickens escaped?" he said wistfully. "And Hank was chasing them through camp with his pants falling down?" As the group began to laugh, EJ started sniffling, quickly growing too choked up to continue.

"Lord, that man is softer than warm butter." Britta shook her head. "Lemme go rescue him" Sliding off the bench we were sharing, she hurried to lead EJ from the circle, taking his place.

"Y'all recall when little Béla asked for a swing and Hank decided to take it upon himself to build one?"

"That's my swing!" From his seat on his mother's lap, Béla clapped happily.

"Yeah, darlin', it's your swing I'm talkin' 'bout," Britta said. "But it weren't always so great, ya know. Ol' Hank had never built a swing before; he didn't have a dang clue what he was doin'. Spent a full week puttin' together some rickety lookin' thing, actin' all proud like he'd built himself a whole ass playground."

"Then he went and broke it," someone called out, as laughter tittered through the group.

"He sure did," Britta agreed with a chuckle. "Hank thought he'd try it out, makin' sure it was safe for Béla; only once he sat himself down the whole thing collapsed on him.

"And what did Hank do? Well, you know he got up off the ground, pulled the splinters from his ass, and started buildin' that swing all over again. That's what I liked about Hank—whatever happened, no matter how big or small, he always held steady. And I'm thinkin' that's just what he'd want us to do now—hold steady."

While the crowd murmured in agreement, Jordy slid into the chair beside me. "Hey," he whispered. "I missed you this morning. And last night. Everything okay?"

"Everything's fine," I muttered.

"Are you sure?" he continued. "Logan seemed hella pissed. And then you ran out... "

"I wasn't feeling well," I replied quickly.

"Feeling better now?"

I kept my eyes facing front. "Not really, no."

"Anything I can do?"

More laughter rippled through the gathering while I shut my eyes with a sigh. "I think... I think I need to get some air." Standing, I rubbed my clammy hands down the front of my jeans and turned to leave.

Jordy stood with me. "Do you want company?"

"No, thanks," I whispered, my gaze freezing on the window. Logan stood just outside, his narrowed eyes meeting mine through the glass, his expression thunderous. Turning abruptly, he disappeared from sight.

"Shit," I breathed, hurrying across the hall, pushing through the double doors and jogging down the stairs. I didn't bother calling out to Logan, his long legs had already carried him halfway across camp.

By the time I'd reached the cabin, I found Logan seated at the table inside, his arms folded tightly over his chest, his thunderous expression unchanged.

"I think—I think we need to talk," I stammered. "I-I think—"

Logan exploded up out of his seat and I jerked in surprise. "You think we should just pretend it never happened—just forget it entirely, right?"

"God, why are you like this?" I shouted. "Why does literally everything have to be a fight?"

"Why am *I* like this? Do you hear yourself? Why are *you* like this?" he demanded, glaring at me from behind the table. "I don't understand you—I don't fucking understand anything you do. You're the most frustrating person I've ever met!"

"And you're not?" I scoffed. "Logan, you've spent your entire life angry at everyone and everything. Don't you ever get sick of being pissed off? I know I'm sick of it."

Logan stepped around the table. "Yeah," he said bitterly. "I should have been more like you and Luke, right? And then maybe *we'd all be dead right now.*"

My nostrils flared. "Fuck you," I gritted out, reaching for the door. "That's always going to be your signature move, isn't it— *everything's Willow's fault.*"

The door slammed shut just as I'd yanked it open. Towering

over me, Logan backed me into a wall. "This isn't going to be like last time," he growled. "You don't get to walk away and pretend it never happened."

"I'm not pretending anything," I spat. "But I'm not going to act like it was okay, either." Frustrated, I clenched my hands into fists. "Because it wasn't okay." Despite my anger, my chin quivered. "Don't you care about that? Don't you care that we hurt him again?"

"It's not the same," he ground out haltingly. "It's not the fucking same."

"Whatever you need to tell yourself," I muttered.

Logan barked out a humorless laugh. "Me? Because your way of dealing with things is so much better? I forgot how well adjusted you are. Must have missed that between all the stupid shit you're always doing."

I unwittingly stepped forward, my hands still balled into angry fists. Logan matched my step, leaving only inches between us

"What?" he growled. "Do you need to hit me again, or fuck me? Tell me, Willow, what do you need from me this time?" He spread his arms out wide and shouted, "Because that's what I'm here for, right? Whatever the fuck you need!"

I stared at him for one long, horrible moment before dragging in a ragged breath. My chest felt cracked open, dissected even. "I hate you," I breathed.

"Do you?" he challenged. "Or does telling yourself that make it easier?"

"No—I really do hate you right now!"

Closing the last remaining inch between us, he said mockingly, "Yeah, sure you do. You know what I think? I don't think you hate me at all. I think this is *you* hating *yourself.*"

"I don't remember anyone asking you what you thought."

"What's worse, Willow?" he continued, ignoring my snub. "That it happened again... *or that you wanted it?*"

I stared up at him, into his burning blue gaze, breathing in the intoxicating scent of him, feeling as equally disgusted by myself as I was turned on by his words. I shook my head, my chest heaving with dozens of vicious sentiments, yet all that came out was, "Both," I hissed. "Happy now?"

"Not even close," he snarled.

We remained that way, frozen in place, staring at one another, until his breathing grew noticeably deeper, his pupils dilating even as I watched. I was not unaffected; my own breaths grew shallow, tinged with a desperate tremble.

His head dropped with a heavy sigh, pressing our foreheads together, taking my face in his hands. "I want you," he said simply, if not a little helplessly. "I can't make it stop—I've tried to make it stop, but I fucking can't."

All the air rushed from my lungs; all the fight fled from my body. It wasn't what he'd said, but the way he'd said it—utterly vulnerable, and so unlike any version of Logan I'd ever seen before.

"I want you, too," I murmured, my painful truth spilling from my lips like a whispered curse.

He pulled back a fraction, surprise lifting his stormy expression, the corner of his mouth tugging into the barest of smiles. And even as I thought I might cry, I found myself drawn to his smile, lifting a finger to trace it, and then pushing up on my toes to kiss it.

Our kiss started out slowly, building until I was gasping into his mouth and pulling at his belt. Holding me close, still kissing me furiously, Logan maneuvered us across the room. As he fell backward onto his bed, I fell with him, sprawling over him.

He hurried to take my shirt off, tossing it away. I dragged his shirt up his chest, yanking it roughly over his head and sending it in the same direction. We kissed frantically while we undressed, until not a single stitch of clothing remained, and I grappled between our bodies, gripping him and guiding him inside me.

His hips pitched upward, mine canted forward, both of us groaning. Gripping his shoulders, I began rocking over him with rapidly growing urgency, clenching around him and crying out each time my body reached another pinnacle of sensation.

And when I could no longer keep pace, when my muscles had seized in the midst of an orgasm so intense there were tears in my eyes, Logan took over. Fingertips biting into the flesh at my hips, thrusting up into me, he began rocking my body over his at a breakneck pace, the dueling rhythms sending me spiraling into an abyss of *pure... fucking... pleasure.*

I collapsed on his chest, quivering from head to toe, crying softly through the aftershocks of my climax. Sex with Lucas had never felt like this. In fact, nothing with Lucas had felt like this.

And God help me, I wanted more.

TWENTY SIX

LOGAN

The sun had long since set, its rising streaks of light filtering inside our small cabin through the cracks in the curtains. Outside, Silver Lake was just waking up, the distant sounds of people walking and talking drifting in through the open windows. I hadn't slept a wink; I'd only lain here, holding tight to the woman snoring softly in my arms.

Fuck.

I was just... *fuck*.

When you've wanted something for so long—so goddamn, motherfucking long—that you'd convinced yourself that you no longer wanted it, that you hated it even, if only to make the days, the months, the years, go by a little easier. And then you finally have it—it's sprawled over top of you—you can touch it, taste it, *love it...*

I felt wrecked. Thoroughly ruined and wrung out... but in the best possible way.

And for the first time in my entire life, I didn't feel the pull to keep moving, to keep searching for something better. The ball of dread and unease that had long ago formed in the pit of my stomach that had been slowly unraveling during our time at Silver Lake had dissipated entirely at some point during the night.

Sleepy brown eyes framed in thick black lashes blinked up at me, eyes that shuttered the moment they'd connected with mine. As Willow attempted to untangle herself from me, I tightened my hold and rolled on top of her. I'd been waiting for her to wake up, knowing the second she saw me, she'd be flooded with guilt again. All night I'd been thinking of ways to redirect those feelings, only to come to the conclusion that I should simply let her deal with them. Only now, faced with the situation, my body had a very different reaction.

"Don't," I growled, taking her chin in hand and forcing her to look at me. "We're not going to fuck and then pretend we didn't. Not anymore."

Her bottom lip disappeared between her teeth as her eyes searched mine. "It's not that," she said, sighing. "It's... I guess I just don't know how to be with anyone but Luke. It's always been me and him... he's all I've known."

It wasn't as if I needed a reminder that she and my brother had been inseparable for over a decade; I'd lived that. But there was something particularly horrible about her invoking his name while she lay naked beneath me, after having spent half the night inside of her. Rolling off her, I swung my legs out of bed and scrubbed a hand down my face, leaving it clasped over my mouth, hoping it might stifle all the angry, immature things I suddenly wanted to say. It felt ridiculous to be jealous of my dead brother—but old habits die hard, I supposed.

The bed shifted as Willow joined me at the edge of the bed, clutching a pillow to her chest. "Logan, I'm sorry, but this is kinda weird for me—isn't it weird for you?"

"Maybe," I replied tightly. "But I'm not really thinking about it." Which was a bald-faced lie. I'd been thinking about it all night long, among a million other things. I just didn't want her to be thinking about it. About *him*. I wanted her to stay in the present with me.

"I don't know how to *not* think about it," she replied. "I feel like everything changed really, really fast and I'm still trying to catch up."

It felt strange hearing her say how quickly everything had happened, because for me it felt as if I'd been living with my imprisoned feelings for years.

"Are you mad?" she continued, her voice rising. "Because if you are, I think that's really unfair. Are we just not going to talk about Luke now that… this happened?"

I flicked my gaze in her direction. "This?"

"Yes, this."

"What's *this*?"

"Oh my god," she ground out, making a face. "You know what this is—*this is us*. Us on the dresser. Us in the bed. Us on the floor after we fell out of bed. *Us, Logan—us!*"

I nearly smiled beneath my hand. *Us.* She really had no idea what that one word did to me, the absolute power it had over me.

Frowning at me, she asked, "Are you going to say anything?" A look of irritation crossed her features. "God, Logan, what is that stupid look on your face? What are you thinking about right now?"

This time it was laughter I was holding back. If she had even an inkling of anything I was thinking, or how I really felt about her, she would run for the hills… instead of just the bathroom.

With a noise of frustration, Willow moved to stand. Grabbing her wrist, I pulled her back into bed, trapping her under me.

"What am I thinking?" I said. "I'm thinking you look really fucking beautiful right now." Ripping the pillow from her clutches, I gazed down the naked length of her body while she laughed and squirmed and cursed. Beautiful was the understatement of the century. Willow was a knockout from head to toe — her face, her body, the way she smiled, the way she moved…

Replacing my gaze with my hand, I felt my way down her body, satisfaction curling through me as her eyes grew hooded and her laughter turned to gasps. "Logan," she breathed, lifting her hips, pushing against my hand. "*Logan.*"

"What?" I growled softly, slipping a finger inside her.

Her eyes widened. Her tongue darted out, wetting her lips. "We're going to be late," she whispered, her hands twisting in the sheets.

"I don't give a shit," I said, adding another finger and working her faster.

"Oh, goddamn you," she groaned, eyelids fluttering. "Logan… *fuck… please!*"

Watching her, I went absolutely crazy inside. Taking her mouth in a brutal kiss, I continued with my hand until she was writhing beneath me and crying out between curses. Unable to hold out any longer, I swapped my hand with my hips, giving us both what we wanted.

We were late. We missed breakfast and ended up being over

an hour late for work—not that anyone at the construction site appeared to notice my untimely, disheveled arrival. Stopping at the water cooler first, I poured myself a cup, drinking it down as if I were out of breath and already sweating from an hour's worth of manual labor, and not all because I'd just had sex with Willow, *again*.

"'Morning," I called out, nodding at Joshua as I passed. "'Morning, Logan," he replied, giving me a curious glance.

"Hey," I greeted EJ, joining him inside the cabin we were working on. Pulling my shirt off, I tucked it into my tool belt and turned toward the ladder.

"Where the hell have you been—" EJ broke off with a laugh. "Hey, man, no need to rub it in."

Shooting EJ a questioning glance, the man only laughed harder. "Your back," he said between chuckles. "Either you got into a knife fight from behind or you had a way better morning than I did."

I attempted looking at my back, glimpsing a streak of blood on my shoulder. Fighting a grin, I pulled my shirt from my tool belt.

"No, no—don't cover up on my account. Those are badges of honor, my friend." EJ was still laughing. "So, you and Willow, huh?"

"Uh, yeah," I muttered. "But maybe just keep that between us, okay."

"Bro." EJ laughed heartily. "You realize everyone already knows, right? Sure, Jordy was a little late to the party—wishful thinkin' probably—but after that whole scene at the wedding, everyone's pretty much up to speed now."

"Yeah, brother, we all know." Joe sauntered inside the cabin with an armful of precut two-by-fours. "In fact, some of us been takin' bets, trying to guess when the two of you were gonna get your shit together." Dropping the wood, he turned to leave but not before tossing a salacious grin in my direction. "And now that you've sealed that deal, maybe you can get Willow to put in a good word for me with Britta?"

"Ignore that asshole," EJ said through clenched teeth once Joe was out of earshot.

I stared at EJ, brows raised. "Okay?"

"I'm just saying, Britta doesn't need that guy in her life."

I shook my head. "Whatever—I'm going to work now."

"No really," he pressed. "He's gone through half the women here already—he only wants Brit because he hasn't had her yet."

As I ascended the ladder, I said, "Not my business."

"She deserves better than him," EJ called after me. "He's not good for her."

"I don't care," I called back.

The tone was set for the rest of the day—EJ continued to talk incessantly about Britta while I ignored him. Which wasn't hard, as all I could think about was Willow—when I would see her next, when I could kiss her next, when I could be inside of her again.

The way she'd torn up my back this morning.

So distracted by my thoughts of her, my work soon grew sloppy. Three times I mis-measured stud length, and twice I brought the hammer down on my hand instead of a nail. By the time dinnertime rolled around, I felt bruised and battered and in desperate need of a change of clothes. But more so, I was desperate to see Willow.

Parting ways with EJ, who was still blathering about Britta, I headed for home, wondering if Willow would be there or if she'd left for the dining hall without me. We hadn't discussed going to dinner together, it was merely wishful thinking on my part.

The cabin door opened as I was reaching for it—Willow stood before me, her face freshly washed, her long curls wound into a thick bun on the top of her head, wearing a blouse I'd never seen before—a black button-down top with a bow at the neck that she'd partially tucked it into a pair of faded flare jeans.

"Hey," she murmured, smiling shyly—a new expression that was completely out of character for her, but one I found myself liking.

"Hey yourself," I said, shifting past her. "Where'd that shirt come from?" I'd waited all day to be with her again—only now that the moment was here, I wasn't sure what I should be doing. Did I kiss her? Hug her? Willow and I had so much history, but this was uncharted territory for us.

"I found it at that school."

The school. Hiding my scowl, determined to keep my pissy thoughts to myself, I headed in the direction of my dresser, pulling my shirt off and tossing it away.

"*Your back,*" Willow suddenly gasped. "Holy shit."

Turning, I found her with her hand pressed to her mouth. "I'm so sorry," she said, between muffled laughter. "Actually, I'm not sorry—like, at all."

Grinning, I grabbed for her, pulling her to me, and tugging at the bow at her neck. The tie popped open, exposing a great deal of her breasts. "You should be sorry," I said, tracing the swell of each. Yeah, I did like her shirt, and not just because of its easy access. The whole outfit made her look put together in a way I'd never seen her before—less like a girl and more like a woman. Less like Lucas's girlfriend... and more like *my* woman.

"The guys at work were giving me shit about it." I bent to kiss her just as she pushed me away.

"Wait, what?" Willow peered up at me, all traces of humor gone. "What were they saying?"

"Nothing really—just stupid jokes and stuff."

"Jokes about us?"

Her sudden switch in demeanor caused a swell of irritation within me. Running my hands through my hair, I said, "Yeah, Willow, *us*. It's not exactly a secret—the whole fucking camp knows."

"And they don't think we're... bad people?"

Folding my arms over my chest, I stared hard at her. "Are you trying to tell me that *you* think we're bad people?"

"No... yes... I don't know. I just mean..." Sighing, she rubbed at her temples. "It feels like it should feel wrong, you know? But then... it doesn't, especially..."

"When?" I'd already guessed what she meant—during sex, of course—but I still wanted to hear her say it. No, I *needed* to hear her say it—for me, for her, and for the ghost of my brother wedged between us.

"I loved him, Logan," she snapped, not rising to my bait. "*I still love him.*"

As if I could have suddenly forgotten. "What does that have to do with anything?" I demanded. "I've never questioned how you felt about him—that's always been pretty fucking obvious."

"But I've questioned it!" Willow shouted. "I questioned it back then and I'm questioning it now, because... *because if we really loved him then I don't know why we keep doing this to him.*"

"Jesus, Willow. We're not doing anything *to him*. He's gone, remember?" I stepped closer, fighting the urge to grab her by her shoulders and shake some sense into her. "And we both know that if Luke were still here, *none of this ever would have happened.*" I spat my last few words, hating the harsh truth of them.

She pinned me with a hard look. "That doesn't make me feel any less guilty. And I keep thinking about how hurt he would be if he knew." Her hard gaze turned tortured. "How the hell am I supposed to live with that?"

I waited a moment before responding, trying desperately to temper my anger. The last thing I wanted to do was start yelling or saying things I didn't really mean.

"We screwed up back in Asheville," I eventually gritted out. "That's never been up for debate. But this is different, everything is fucking different this time, and I don't know how to make you see that.

"Would Luke be hurt if he knew? Probably. And yeah, it fucks me up to think about that. But the fact remains that he's gone. He's never going to know about any of it. It's just me and you in the here and now, Willow, and I'm not going to waste my time or energy feeling guilty over shit I can't change.

"And to be perfectly fucking honest, I wouldn't change it even if I could. And if that makes me a bad brother—" I shrugged angrily. "Then so be it."

Willow went still, her eyes wide and mouth ajar. Whether she was surprised by my honesty or shocked by the brutality of my admission, I wasn't sure, and I didn't care. It was well past time for some honesty, no matter how brutal, to be injected into our fucked-up relationship.

TWENTY SEVEN

WILLOW

Logan and I walked to dinner in stony silence, the short journey rife with tension by the time we'd reached the dining hall. Passing Jordy on the porch, who'd ducked his head at the sight of us, Logan's silent stewing grew increasingly louder. Collecting our dinners without a word, we took our seats at our usual table, where Logan began immediately plowing through his dinner, as if he couldn't eat it fast enough.

This was typical Logan behavior—shutting down instead of dealing with things head-on. And maybe I wasn't any better, but I was attempting to be honest about my feelings, at least. With a hard sigh, I stabbed a potato wedge with my fork and shoved it in my mouth, chewing angrily. All men, I decided, were completely and utterly ridiculous.

"Hey there, lovebirds," Britta dropped her tray noisily onto the table, taking the seat beside me. "Why the long faces—y'all tuckered out from all that horizontal refreshment?"

While Logan only continued shoveling food in his mouth, I dropped my fork on my plate, sending Britta a scathing look. "*Can you not?*" I mouthed silently.

"*Party pooper,*" she mouthed in reply.

"You ever have one of those days where you're like, what's the fucking point?" Ella dropped down beside Logan and plucked a potato wedge from her tray, eyeing it with disgust. "Fucking potatoes again," she said, flicking it away. Pulling her flask from inside her shirt, she took a long swig.

"Somethin' ugly in the air today?" Britta glanced around the table. "Ella, you picked those taters with your own hands—that ain't no small thing. Wasn't so long ago that you were starvin' somewhere—you'd be wise to remember that."

"Because picking potatoes was always my lifelong dream?" Ella snarled in reply. "You might fool everyone else with your happy-hillbilly act, Britta, but you don't fool me. You're all talk, all the time—always flirting with guys half your age and talking yourself up like you're something special, like you know something the rest of us don't, when in reality, you're just a sad old hag *who lost her husband and baby.*" Ella had shoved up from the table mid-speech. Spinning away, she charged across the room, slamming through the double doors.

Britta had a baby? *Oh my god, Britta lost her baby?* I stared openmouthed after Ella, before quickly turning to Britta.

"Don't listen to her," I said in a rush. "She says stupid shit all the time that she doesn't really mean—"

"Oh, she meant it all right," Britta replied evenly. "She's meaner than a wet sittin' hen, that one. It ain't her fault, though—it's this whole goddang world." Shaking her head, Britta pushed her tray away and stood from her seat. "Seems I've lost my appetite."

"Britta, wait." I hurried to place my hand on her wrist. "I'll come with you. We can go for a walk."

"Now don't you worry about me, sugar," Britta said, patting my hand and setting it aside. "It's times like this I like bein' alone. Think I might just take a stroll—maybe find somethin' that needs some killin'." At the mention of bloodshed, the corners of her lips curled up.

As Britta departed the dining hall and I stared sadly after her, Logan finally looked up from his dinner. "What the hell just happened?"

I shook my head, shoulders shrugging. "No idea," I muttered, slumping in my seat.

"Jesus Christ," Logan said, tossing his fork away. "All day I couldn't wait to see you and this is what we're doing—sitting here listening to everyone else's depressing bullshit? Do you wanna get the fuck out of here—go for a drive maybe?"

I jerked in surprise. "A drive? Like, outside the wall?"

Logan was already on his feet, grabbing my hand. "Outside the goddamn wall," he said, pulling me from my seat.

"Did you see the look on Leisel's face?" Laughing, I leaned my head back in the seat, the Jeep's caged top blowing warm wind through my unbound hair. "Oh my god, it was *fucking* epic!"

Leisel had been adamantly opposed to Logan taking one of the vehicles;

she'd begun shaking her head before Logan had finished his request.

"First off," Leisel said. "No one goes out this late in the day unless they're on patrol – what if you don't make it back before sunset? Second, you haven't even been here six months – how can I trust you with something as valuable as a vehicle?"

Before Logan could argue, Joshua had placed his hand over Leisel's. "Logan recently helped us with something important," he said quietly. "I think we can trust him. And if they're not back before sunset, I'm sure they'll be back first thing tomorrow – right guys?"

While Logan and I stammered through our assurances, Leisel, with her mouth set in a straight line, pulled a set of keys from her pocket. "You can take the Jeep," she said woodenly, while side-eyeing Joshua as she continued. "If anything happens, this is on you."

As we flew over the forest floor, onto a barely there dirt road, Logan flashed a smile in my direction, bigger and brighter than any I'd ever seen grace his handsome face and I found myself watching him in a way I'd never done before – freely and without reservation. Had he always been so good-looking? Of course he had, but something felt distinctly different about looking at him now, like I was looking at him without a lens for once, without anything obstructing my view.

I was still staring at him when he pulled the Jeep to the side of a road – a residential neighborhood, the surrounding homes in various stages of decay.

"So we're scavenging?" I asked, unbuckling my seat belt.

"We can if you want," Logan replied. "But I thought you might want to learn how to drive?"

My eyes shot to his, my face splitting into a grin. "Are you serious?" I exclaimed, clapping my hands together. "Are you fucking serious?"

I'd only just started driver's education classes when the world had closed its doors for business. To date, my time behind the wheel amounted to a few quick practices in parking lots, each instance so long ago I barely remembered them.

Climbing into the driver's seat, into Logan's lap, I opened his door, practically pushing him out of it. "Goodbye," I said. "Good day, sir, this is my seat now."

"This is a stick shift," Logan warned as he switched to the passenger seat. "It's not going to be as easy as driving your dad's Suburban."

"I'm ready," I said, gripping the wheel with one hand and the shifter with the other. "My body is ready."

"Great," Logan replied dryly. "Can your body shift into first then?"

"My body can definitely shift into—" My words were cut off by the sharp scream of grinding gears.

"One foot on the brake," Logan instructed. "One on the gas— give it a little gas while you ease up off the clutch."

As it turned out, my body was not, in fact, ready for driving a stick. As I jerked the Jeep up and down the street, I stalled out more than not, grinding gears left and right, and flooding the gas each time I had to start from stopping.

"I just don't get it!" I shouted, throwing the Jeep into neutral and slamming on the brakes. "I can't do four things at once—*I'm not a fucking octopus, Logan.*" As if to further my point, I began angrily flailing my arms around in the air.

Logan burst out laughing—intense, vivid, messy laughter that had him bending over in his seat and clutching his stomach, his guffaws echoing up and down the otherwise silent street. Again, I merely stared at him, somewhat dumbstruck by the unfamiliar sight, but more so startled by my own remarkable reaction to him.

A reaction that began as a warm ball in my belly slowly unfurling, that gradually spread to each and every limb, releasing into the ether with a smile on my face.

Reaching across the seats, I placed my hand on his arm. "This is when it feels right," I heard myself say.

Logan's laughter tapered off quickly; breathing hard, he stared into my eyes. "This feels right?"

Nodding my head, I blew out a slow, shaky breath. "Yes."

His eyes darkened, his features tightened. "I want you," he said.

His declaration was an instant aphrodisiac to a body that was already willing and waiting. "Right here?" I asked, laughing a little.

"Right here," he growled, reaching for me. "*Right fucking now.*"

We never made it back to Silver Lake. After a hot and heavy session in the Jeep, we'd stumbled inside the nearest house, quickly securing it and setting up camp for the night before falling back into bed… or in our case, falling onto the kitchen counter, the dining room table, and finally the living room floor.

With our sleeping bags twisted beneath us, I was half sprawled over Logan's naked body, running my fingers through the trail of hair that spanned the space between his belly button and hips. It was the middle of the night, we'd been sleeping on and off in between being tangled up in one another, and my body was spent, deliciously sore in ways it had never been before. And yet, I still wanted more.

"Logan?"

"Hmm?"

Propping my chin on my hand, I gazed up at him. "Who was

the last person you were with?"

Logan placed his arms behind his head and peered down at me. "What do you mean?"

"Sex, Logan—I'm asking who's the last person you had sex with. Was it that girl in Kentucky? What was her name?" I snapped my fingers. "Krista or Crystal?"

"Crystal," he said slowly. "And yeah, I had sex with her… but she wasn't the last."

I sat up suddenly, folding my legs beneath me. "Wait, what? Who else was there?"

Logan followed my lead, shifting to sitting. "Really? This is what you want to talk about? Right now?"

When I nodded, maybe a bit too enthusiastically considering the subject matter, Logan shot me a dubious glance and shook his head. "Alright, fine," he said, sighing. "Do you remember that couple we ran into in the middle of West Virginia? At the gas station?"

It wasn't often that I had to put actual thought into recalling someone we'd met on the road; they'd been so few and far between. "The married couple?" I asked, my eyes widening. "No way—*her*?"

We'd crossed paths with the young, seemingly happy couple from Vermont at a small country store in the middle of the West Virginia hills, parting ways after only two nights together—they'd headed south, while we'd ventured west. I'd never had even the slightest inkling that something had occurred between Logan and the pretty blonde woman.

"Did Luke know?" I mused, shaking my head. "I mean, he never told me."

"I didn't tell him," Logan muttered, dragging his hands through his unbound hair.

"When did you do it?" I asked abruptly, still stunned. "*Where did you do it?* Did you come on to her or did she come on to you?" I scowled at the idea of either.

"I couldn't sleep and neither could she and, I don't know, it just fucking happened, okay?" Again, he ran his hands through his hair, scratching angrily at his scalp. "Why are we even talking about this?"

"I don't know," I snapped, irritated for reasons I couldn't quite explain. "I guess I just didn't expect that... *her!*"

"You didn't expect what exactly—that after Mackenzie and *you*, I didn't become a monk? Sorry to disappoint you."

"I hardly thought you were a monk," I shot back with a snort. "Since I very clearly remember crazy Krista from Kentucky."

"Crystal," he growled. "And why the fuck does any of this matter?"

It didn't matter. Or at least, it shouldn't have, and yet something was inexplicably bothering me about it. "Sorry—*Crystal*," I scoffed. "Are there any others you've been keeping secret?"

"Willow, what the hell—what's with the inquisition?"

I gaped at him. "So there *are* others?"

"Again, why the fuck does it matter?" Logan's tone took on a razor-sharp edge. "Does it change something between us? Was I supposed to keep my hands to myself while you and Luke humped like rabbits?"

"What? Excuse you—*we didn't hump like rabbits.* And *no*, that's not what I meant." Cursing, my hands rose and fell in my lap. "I guess I'm just surprised. I thought I knew everything about you, and now..." I trailed off with a sigh, before muttering, "This isn't even what I wanted to talk about."

"Hey." Leaning forward, Logan captured my chin, locking eyes with me. "Can you clue me in with what's happening right now?

Because I'm fucking lost."

"Nothing. Never mind." I attempted turning from his touch only to have his hand slip into my hair, holding me still.

"Talk to me," he demanded. "Tell me what you wanted to say. Tell me why you're pissed at me. I want it all, alright? The good and the bad. Don't shut me out."

I had so many feelings in that moment, the most prominent being how I felt each time Logan showed some tenderness or a bit of vulnerability, acts I hadn't been entirely sure he was capable of until recently.

A little bit speechless and a whole hell of a lot turned on, I swallowed past the myriad of feelings lodged in my throat and fumbled for the right words. "I just... I wanted to know if sex had ever been like this for you before. If it had ever been this crazy kind of intense with anyone else."

With his hand still entangled in my hair, he brought his face close to mine. "Willow, nothing has ever felt like this... *no one has ever felt like you do.*" His voice deepened in the most skin-shivering, toe-curling way.

I sucked in a potent breath, my stomach doing a dip dive straight to my core. I couldn't respond right away; I was momentarily lost. Lost inside his heated gaze. Lost in the feel of his warm breath mingling with my own. Lost among the very same intensity I'd been trying to convey.

"Now, tell me why you're mad."

"I'm not," I breathed. Though, part of me wondered if I was, in fact, mad. Mad as in, the Mad Hatter sort of mad. Entirely bonkers and whatnot. This was me and Logan, after all—a man I'd once professed to hate forever, but lately was feeling anything but. Feelings and sensations that seemed to have crept up on me out of nowhere, exploding from the calm like a lightning storm in the dead of night.

And strangely enough, I didn't want to soothe the storm inside me. Instead, I found myself wanting to feed it.

No, *I wanted to be it.*

Like Britta had said, *we're the hurricanes, sugar, and all them storm chasers better take cover.*

Sliding onto Logan's lap, I gripped his face and slanted my mouth over his.

TWENTY EIGHT

LOGAN

The remaining weeks of summer came and went with little fanfare, the blistering weather eventually relenting, giving way to more bearable days and even cooler evenings. With the completion of the additions on the first round of cabins, another round was gearing up to begin. Meanwhile, Willow was readying for the upcoming fall harvest, after which the winter crops would need to be seeded.

While the seasons shifted, summer tumbling into fall, Willow and I were falling into a somewhat comfortable rhythm navigating the unfamiliar terrain of our new relationship. Comfortable for us, at least, not so much for the people around us. When we weren't arguing, we were usually kissing, still unable to keep our hands off each other for any real length of time.

And as we fell into place with one another, so did everything else.

Willow and I began spending more time outside the wall; I'd teach her to drive in between scavenging through the nearby neighborhoods and, in time, she'd become quite good at both, amassing enough odds and ends to open a store of sorts—where people could trade for Willow's scavenged goods. In true Willow fashion, none of what she scavenged and sold were necessities. They were always frivolous finds—entertainment items, along with decorations and knickknacks. While Willow remained the store's gatekeeper, Leisel appointed Stuart in charge of daily management—a job that suited him better than working in the gardens. Headphones hanging around his neck, he was engaging with others for the first time; I'd even seen him smile once or twice.

And he wasn't the only one.

With the completion of my bench turned shelf, currently housing Willow's growing collection of books, I'd been busying myself with a variety of woodworking projects. Not only did it keep my hands busy and my mind occupied, but I'd also turned out to be damn good at it, too. Even better was the genuine pleasure on Willow's face each time I completed something new.

We'd finally found some peace among the chaos. A real home in a godforsaken world. Some happiness to replace the hopelessness.

… or so I'd thought.

"Logan, Willow! Everybody up!"

A heavy fist beat against the cabin door, echoing throughout the small building, rattling the windows. Willow shot upright as I jumped out of bed, the blade I kept beneath the bed already in hand. While Willow scrambled for her clothes, I rushed to the quaking door, throwing it open.

Davey stood just outside, his hard features pinched twice as tight. He glanced from my blade to my naked body, his scowl quickly swerving back to my face. "Put some fuckin' clothes on and get up by the gate," he growled, turning to leave.

"What's going on?" I called after him.

"Just get your ass to the gate!" he flung back. Jogging to the next cabin, he pounded on the door. "Wake up! Everybody up!"

"What's happening?" Willow asked, shoving an armful of clothing at me. She'd already finished dressing and was in the process of winding her hair into a bun.

"No idea," I muttered, shoving my legs into my jeans. "But you stay with me, alright? Don't leave my side."

After tucking several blades into my boots, and a few inside Willow's boots as well, we hurried from the cabin, joining the growing drove of panicked faces moving quickly along the path.

Once everyone had congregated around the guard tower, Leisel and Joshua ascended the tower ladder, peering out at us from high above.

"Everyone!" Leisel called out. "Everyone, please quiet down. I'm going to get straight to the point — yesterday's patrol ran into some car trouble and decided to spend the night in town, and it's a good thing they did, because first thing this morning they spotted a sizable horde heading east on Main."

As the crowd around us sucked in a collective breath, Willow and I looked at each other — her expression stricken. I knew what she was thinking — the same damn thing running through my mind. That maybe this was *our* horde — the same one that had stolen Lucas from us.

"How close are they?" a panicked voice called out.

Leisel held up a finger. "Now, we're all aware that we don't have enough resources or manpower to destroy a horde — certainly not one of this magnitude. Our strategy has always been to redirect them away from Silver Lake so that's what we're going to do, but we don't have a lot of time. Yesterday's patrol has already begun the process of luring them in a different direction, but it's going to take a lot more people." She paused, looking out over the crowd. "So, as much as I hate to ask this of you, I need volunteers."

Several hands shot up, though not nearly enough. Unwilling to chance losing the first home we'd had in years, I grudgingly raised my hand. I didn't particularly want to be involved, but neither did I like the idea of not being a part of the solution, and worse, not knowing what was happening. Beside me, Willow's arm shot up.

"Logan and Willow!" Leisel called out, before I'd had the chance to snatch Willow's arm from view. "Thank you. Please head to the garage with the others."

"You two can ride with me." Joe gestured for us to follow him. "Was talkin' with Davey — we're gonna try an' herd 'em north using the fortified vehicles. Got a couple of trucks scoutin' ahead already."

"She's not going," I growled, pulling Willow to a stop as she turned to follow Joe. "You're not going — no fucking way."

Shaking me off her, she gave me a withering look. "You know you can't actually tell me what to do anymore, right? If you're going, so am I."

"Like hell you are," I growled. "You're going to stay here and —"

"And what? Pick potatoes while you're out there fighting a horde of Creepers? *Fuck that.*"

Meanwhile, Joe had pulled up beside us, seated behind the

wheel of a double-cab pickup truck, an industrial-sized V-shaped plow affixed to the front end. Double rows of solar-powered floodlights sat atop the cab; a metal cage had been erected over the truck bed, and most of the windows had been reinforced with metal grating. The tires had been capped and equipped with metal plates; even the windshield had been fitted with protective wiring.

"She'll be fine," Joe called from inside the truck. "Look at this beast—nothin' is gettin' inside that doesn't belong."

"See," Willow retorted. *"I'll be fine."* Storming past me, she wrenched the passenger door open and climbed inside the truck. Slamming the door shut, she folded her arms across her chest and stared straight ahead.

Joe leaned forward, peering around Willow's resolute form. "You comin', brother?"

Jaw locked and ticcing, I jumped in the back seat. Joe stepped on the gas and as we all lurched forward, my arm shot out, wrapping around the seat in front, pinning Willow in place while the truck barreled and bounced out of camp and into the woods beyond.

Willow's hand covered mine, surprising me by threading her fingers through mine instead of pushing me away. I squeezed her, feeling an overwhelming surge of protectiveness. "You shouldn't be here," I gritted out softly. "If I'm worried about you, I won't be able to concentrate."

"Logan," she replied, her quiet tone matching mine in grit. "Maybe I don't listen very well sometimes, and maybe I occasionally do some reckless things, but when it comes to fighting, I can absolutely do what needs to be done. *And you know it.*"

"I do," I conceded angrily. "But it's different now."

"How? I'm still the same girl, and I'm more than capable of killing Creepers."

"You're not the same girl—you're *my girl* now. And what if something happens to you?" Left unsaid was what would undoubtedly become of me if something did in fact happen to her—a fate so bleak I couldn't even bear to fathom it.

Twisting farther in her seat, she stared hard at me. "And what if something happens to you?" she shot back. "Why is my life more valuable than yours?"

And just like that, I went from wanting to shake some sense into her to wanting to kiss the shit out of her.

Joe blew out an exasperated breath. "Hate to break up some damn good entertainment, but we've got a job to do. Now, on the off chance we get swarmed, it'll be your jobs to get 'em off us. You see the window behind you, just push it open and climb into the bed. Shoot 'em, stab 'em, do whatever you can to get 'em off us.

"And there're some kill bags under your seat, Logan," Joe continued. "We might be takin' out the stragglers by hand, so get yourselves ready."

I reluctantly released Willow to dig beneath me. Dragging forth two canvas bags, one was filled with tactical gear and the other with weapons. Pulling on a plated vest and loading myself up with handguns, I handed a second vest to Willow, along with a serrated blade and a metal billy club, holding tightly to the club as I held her stare with mine. "Do you promise you'll listen to me if shit gets out of control?" I watched a war play out across her features until eventually she gave a sharp nod. Only then did I relinquish both the club and her gaze.

Joe pulled us onto an empty street, save for one truck idling at the curb. Rolling up alongside the vehicle, we found Davey scowling behind the wheel and Britta bounced restlessly in the passenger seat beside him.

"Well, hey there, lovebirds," she sang, waving animatedly. "So glad you could join us on this glorious Monday mornin'."

"It's Monday?" Willow asked. "I thought it was Wednesday."

"Not a clue, sugar. Not a dang clue. It's all relative though, ain't it? 'Sides, Monday feels like a better day to be dealin' with the dead, don't it?"

"It's fuckin' Thursday, ya goddamn idiots," Davey interjected. "Now, listen the fuck up—horde's 'bout half a mile that way." Davey gestured ahead. "We're fixin' a barricade to turn 'em 'round, and we'll be usin' the trucks to keep 'em turnin' the way we want 'em. But shit could get real messy out there—"

"Don't it always?" Joe replied dryly.

Britta grinned. "That it does, Joey. That it does."

Another vehicle was noisily approaching—a rusted-out school bus whose sides had been built up with metal cladding, with sharp spikes welded around each of the windows. Much like the trucks, each window was dressed in metal grating.

"We're doing it just like the last time," Davey continued loudly over the noise. "We'll keep 'em going for a mile or two and then cut the engines and get out of sight. Xavi's team is already up ahead laying the explosives to keep 'em moving north."

"How many times have you guys done this?" I asked.

Over the years we'd run into enough hordes to know that they were impossible to cut through and impractical to fight against. Up until now, stumbling onto the path of a horde meant you turned tail and ran like hell in the opposite direction, hoping they didn't follow. Either that, or you found somewhere to hide and prayed they didn't find you.

"Why? Ya' scared, Eddie?" Britta mocked. When I only stared at her, she laughed harder. "Alright, alright—I'll stop pulling your dick."

"Woman, you could pull mine," Joe said. "Anytime you want, *anywhere you want.*"

"How about, only *in your dreams*?" Britta blew him a kiss.

Davey cleared his throat loudly. "If y'all are 'bout done actin' like hornball teens — we got a job to do. Everybody ready?"

"I'm ready," Britta said, flashing a brow-waggling grin. "Y'all know me — I'm always ready to be killin' somethin'.."

"Ready as I'll ever be," Joe said.

Willow glanced back at me, her determined expression unwavering. "Ready."

I said nothing. Redirecting an entire horde was a foreign concept to me, and I wasn't entirely sure it would work. Especially not once the Creepers got wind of our scent. Neither could I willingly agree to ever be ready to send Willow headfirst into danger.

Together, both trucks pulled onto the road, Davey taking the lead. As the stench of the dead grew more pungent, I began spotting stragglers dragging themselves along the crumbling road. Each Creeper we passed fixed us with its milky gaze and I found myself checking each rotten face, searching for familiar features, and thankfully finding none. Soon, a noise, much like the distant roar of a rock concert, began to vibrate through the air around us, just the tail end of the horde came into view.

Ahead, Davey swerved his truck left and Joe followed suit, bringing us smack dab against the wall of walking dead. The Creepers immediately turned their attention to us, growling and snarling as they clawed, some even throwing their bodies against the side of the truck. I squinted into the distance, trying to locate the other end of the traveling mob, only there appeared to be no end in sight. Bodies remained tightly compacted as far as the eye could see, shoulder to shoulder as they shuffled slowly along the road.

We continued inching along beside the horde, the sounds of the dead growing immense and unnerving. Dead eyes watched us through the windows, decaying hands pawed at the truck, the Creepers close enough that we could see each torn fingernail, each shattered tooth and every shard of broken bone protruding from their rotting flesh.

The sound of screeching tires had me tearing my gaze away from my window. Up ahead, Davey's truck was crawling in Creepers and weaving dangerously in and out of the horde. Flooring the gas, Davey plowed into the center of the road, slamming on the brakes and dislodging the dead. Following closely behind him, Creepers were flung onto our truck, some managing to grip hold.

Willow released a shaky breath and I reached for her, squeezing her arm, while my other hand clenched tighter to the pistol in my grip.

"When I stop, we'll need to get out of sight," Joe said. "Xavi's team is gonna be makin' all sorts of noise to keep the horde moving in the right direction. After that, it'll be our job to get rid of the stragglers.

"Like that one," he continued, pointing to one of the Creepers holding fast to the plow. Bald, with sunken, hollowed features, its eyes were little more than shriveled grapes inside concave sockets. "That motherfucker is staring at me like my number is up and he's the grim reaper come to collect. He's the first to go, ya' hear me? And that bastard is mine."

We continued on in silence until the clear sky ahead exploded in color—a cloud of orange smoke shooting straight into the atmosphere. "That's our cue," Joe said, slowly bringing the truck to a stop and cutting the engine. "Mountain pass is up ahead; Xavi's team should be threading them through it like a needle. Hopefully the ugly fuckers'll just keep on goin'."

"And if they don't?" Willow asked.

"Like I said before, then we'll be killin' whatever's left by hand."

As soon as we'd stopped, the Creepers began to crawl over one another in an attempt to get to us until they covered us completely, their wriggling bodies pressed tightly to the truck, darkening the interior. Engulfed entirely in living death, the truck rocked to and fro, as the growling and groaning intensified outside, echoing around us until it was all I could hear.

As the tension thickened to unbearable levels inside the cab, Joe began to mutter what might have been a prayer. Willow, though she tried to appear unaffected, was trembling slightly. Leaving the pistol on the seat beside me, I wrapped both my arms around her, holding her tightly to me.

A loud boom in the distance caused everyone to jump; the Creepers crowding the truck appeared to pause and turn toward the noise. "Trigger one," Joe whispered. "Everyone in the back — out of sight, out of mind, and all that."

"Willow," I whispered, shaking her arm. "Willow, come on, get back here."

Still trembling, Willow climbed into the back and Joe followed, the three of us sinking to the floor, crouched on our knees.

Bodies continued to slam against the truck, groans and growls renewing with vigor. We sat there, uncomfortably crouched, barely breathing for what felt like forever, until another explosion rang out in the distance.

Joe's wide eyes clashed with mine. *Trigger two,* he mouthed.

Slowly — excruciatingly slowly — the bodies covering the truck began to thin. Light filtered inside the cab once again.

"It's working," Willow whispered. "It's fucking working."

We remained crouched, merely listening to the horde as they

moved around us. The truck still rocked as bodies continued to bang against us. Another thirty minutes passed by in agonizing silence when a third explosion shook the earth.

"Time to finish this shit," Joe said, maneuvering himself back into the driver's seat. Pulling a shotgun from the overhead gun rack, he reached for the door. "Hardly any out there now—should be easy pickings."

As Willow moved to follow suit, I grabbed her arm, holding her still. "Logan, I'm going to be okay," she said, taking my face in her hands. "I promise."

My nostrils flared. My breath sped up. I grabbed her face and kissed her hard on the mouth, brutally stroking her tongue with mine. She kissed me back with equal measure, breaking away far too soon. Breathing hard, and with a look of sheer determination on her face, she pushed open the door and jumped headfirst into the fray.

Climbing out of the truck behind her, I found myself momentarily frozen, blinking against the harsh morning light. The sounds of death sang loudly from every corner of the highway—the whistles of sharpened blades slicing through the air, the grunts and groans of exertion, the inhuman growls of the dead, while sweat and rot made the otherwise cool air feel hot and heavy and stinking of smells far worse than the mind was capable of conjuring.

All around me small battles were being waged—Britta stood on the hood of her truck taunting Creepers, distracting them while Davey, wielding a gleaming machete, beheaded them from behind. Headless bodies littered the ground surrounding their truck, and a short ways away, a pile of heads was quickly amassing. Joe was even farther out, closer to the tree line, swinging his ax in large rolling sweeps each time a Creeper dared get too close, leaving each of his would-be attackers in literal pieces. Willow—only a few yards from me—had gotten straight to work, gripping the closest Creeper by its stained and tattered jacket and rapidly striking its temple with her blade. It slumped upon impact and Willow promptly released it.

Two Creepers had taken notice of my descent from the truck, their heads swiveling around, their bodies following as they began stumbling toward me with raised arms and snapping jaws. A blade in each hand, I lunged for the first, piercing its neck with one blade while sending the other into the side of its sunken skull. Pulling my weapons free, I ducked and spun away from the grasping hands of the second Creeper, reemerging behind it, giving it the same treatment as the first—one blade to the neck, and one to the skull.

Looking for Willow, I found her fighting farther down the road, furiously slashing and stabbing. I fought my way toward her, taking out another three Creepers before reaching her. She acknowledged my arrival with only a brief nod and then we were back-to-back, both of us fighting in tandem, fighting until my muscles burned and every breath felt like a flame-filled gasp; until sweat flung like rain from my sopping skin.

Breathless, chests heaving, Willow and I collapsed shoulder to shoulder, her hand fumbling for mine, and for long several moments we merely surveyed the scene around us—body parts strewn over the concrete and surrounding grassy areas, everything covered in varying colors of muck and gore.

"You good?" I wheezed.

"Uh-huh," she replied tightly, equally out of breath. "You?"

"Me? I'm fucking great. It's a beautiful day—I've got a beautiful girl." Squeezing her hand, I smirked at her. "What could possibly be wrong?"

Despite the hellish landscape and her clear exhaustion, Willow began to laugh. "Logan, did you just make a joke in the middle of a life-or-death crisis?"

"Nope. At the end of a life-or-death crisis."

Still smiling, she gave me a long, heavy-lidded look that made my entire body jerk to attention. "You should *not joke* more often. It's kinda hot."

Brows raised, I grinned at her. "Yeah? How hot? On a scale of one to you need me naked?"

"You need a minute off in them trees, lovebirds?" Britta sauntered toward us, holding a long-handled sword in each hand, both blades dripping with innards. Grinning, she tilted her face to the sky and inhaled. "Lawd, I sure do love the smell of death in the mornin'!"

"Woman, you're straight fuckin' nuts." Davey staggered up a steep incline, his jacket torn and covered in dark spots. At the sight of him, Willow gasped.

"Davey, you bit?" Britta's swords clattered to the ground as she rushed Davey, fumbling with his jacket. "Where ya hurt?"

"Nah, nah, everything's fine." Davey waved her off. "Fell down the embankment and fought with a tree stump at the bottom, is all."

Britta sent her fist into Davey's shoulder. "Goddang it, Davey-cakes, you fuckin' scared me." In response, Davey shoved her sideways, forcing her to hop over several bodies. "Y'all, it's Dead Head hopscotch!" Laughing, she continued hopping over fallen Creepers.

"Hold up now…" Davey glanced at each of us before turning in a slow circle. "Where's Joey?"

"I seen him down the road a bit." Britta pointed a sword in the direction of the horde. "But that was back when we was still fightin' by the trucks."

"Last I saw, he'd been over there," I said, pointing to the tree line.

We were all turning in circles now, looking up and down the long stretch of gory road, taking turns calling out Joe's name.

Britta cocked her head to one side. "Hush now. Y'all hear that...?"

Everyone quieted, our gazes on the tree line where the sounds of twigs snapping and leaves crushing underfoot could be heard.

"What is that?" Willow asked quietly, glancing at me. Ears straining, I merely shook my head in reply.

"Whatever it is, it's about to meet the end of my sword!" Brita grinned. "Come out, come out, whatever you are—"

A figure suddenly broke through the tree line. "Shut up and run!" Joe shouted, waving frantically. "Run, get to the trucks! There's another horde! They're right behind me!"

The trees had already begun to move—swaying as if they too wanted to get as far away from the approaching doom. Then the eerie, inharmonious moans of the dead came rushing up through the undulating trees, echoing up and down the otherwise quiet highway.

"Holy shit," Willow breathed, her hand tightening around mine. "Logan, look. They're everywhere."

Up and down either side of the highway, Creepers were spilling out of the woods, stumbling out from behind trees at a rapid rate, one after another after another.

"I think they doubled back from up ahead," Joe gasped, as the five of us banded together in the center of the road. "Either that or they were lagging way behind the first group. And all that noise we were making—we called 'em straight to us."

"We gotta get back to the trucks," Davey ground out. "We can't let 'em head toward camp. We gotta lead 'em north."

"We'll be fightin' our way back to them trucks." Britta, both swords in hand, leaped from our small circle to neatly cleave the heads off the first approaching Creepers.

"You got another idea?" Davey asked, as Britta reclaimed her place in our group.

"Nope," Britta said. "Fightin' it is — y'all ready for round two?"

No one replied; we simply took off running down the road, eventually splitting into two groups — Joe, Willow and I ran in the direction of our truck, while Davey and Britta headed toward theirs.

"Logan!" Willow was slashing wildly at three converging Creepers, panic causing her to miss her marks. With a heaving grunt, I shoved away the one I'd just killed and grabbed one of her attackers, sending a blade into the base of its skull. Grabbing another around its neck, I dragged it away from Willow while she kicked the third in the knees, sending it sprawling to the ground. Finishing them off, we took off running again, soon closing in on the truck. Joe was already there, shoving Creepers out of his way as he wrestled to open the tailgate.

"Keep 'em off me!" he shouted, crawling inside the cage, kicking frantically at the mottled hands grasping for him. Willow and I dragged his attackers off him, killing them quickly, and then attempting to keep the rest at bay. It was a futile effort — there were just too many of them.

"Willow, get in the truck!" I shouted, shoving her behind me as I took a shot at an approaching Creeper. Shouts arose; somewhere someone was screaming. Distracted, my aim was off; the bullet clipped the Creeper's shoulder, sending it stumbling back. I aimed again, this time the shot found purchase between its eyes.

"Get down!" Joe bellowed from inside the cage. "Get the fuck down!"

I dropped down just as gunfire exploded above me, a steady stream of bullets flying overhead into the approaching mass of bodies. I rolled beneath the truck, shouting Willow's name. If she answered me, I didn't hear her. All I could hear was the sound of the rapid-fire machine gun above me, loud enough to hurt my ears. From my hiding place beneath the truck, I watched as Creepers dropped in mass numbers, only to be replaced by new ones.

I heard the snarl too late; having crawled beneath the truck, the Creeper was already upon me by the time I noticed it. I grabbed its fast-approaching face, digging my fingers into the rotted skin around its mouth, forcing its snapping maw away from me. I released it with just enough time to shoot it straight through its open mouth; the back of its head exploding, blood and brain matter spraying like confetti. Rolling out from beneath the truck, I found myself face to face with another Creeper. *Bang*—I sent it flying backward with a bullet to its face.

Someone was shouting—it was Britta, I realized. She was standing on the top of her truck, a shotgun in hand, shouting as she fired. Meanwhile, Davey's bloodied form was half slumped over the truck's windshield, slowly sinking down to the hood.

"Come and get it, motherfuckers!" Britta stomped her feet on the roof of the truck. "I'll kill every last one of you, ya hear me! I'll kill all y'all!"

The world was madness. Nothing but noise and death and more death.

"Logan!"

I whirled around at the sound of Willow's voice, relieved to find her inside the truck, beckoning me through the partially open door. "I've got Joe's keys!"

"Move over," I demanded, climbing into the driver's seat as she scrambled to get out of my way. "And tell Joe to hang on to something."

Jamming the key into the ignition, I stepped on the gas, making a sharp U-turn in the center of the road and plowing down Creepers as I pulled up alongside Britta's truck. "Get on!" I shouted. Only Britta was oblivious—she was still screaming, still brandishing her weapon despite having run out of ammunition. Creepers were quickly converging on both vehicles, grasping at Davey's prone body. Sprawled on the hood of the truck, Davey's eyes were wide and unseeing, a mouth-sized gash in his neck, blood still spurting from the wound.

"Britta—get on the fucking truck!" I barked. "Get on the goddamn truck right now!"

Britta's bloodshot eyes dropped in my direction, a grin on her dirt-streaked face. "I'm not goin' anywhere, Eddie! Those motherfuckers killed Davey—then they went and bit me!" She pointed to her ankle, where the cuff of her jeans were ripped and dotted with blood.

Even over the gunfire in the back, I heard Willow's sharp intake of air. "Britta!" she screamed, leaning over me. "Get on the truck—get on the fucking truck right now!"

The shooting abruptly stopped; the groans and growls of the dead rose in earnest. "I'm out!" Joe shouted. "It's time to get the hell outta dodge, folks."

"You heard Joey," Britta proclaimed to the sky. "Time for y'all to get a move on."

"Britta!" Willow was verging on hysterical—it was all I could do to keep her from climbing over me and out the window. "Please get on the truck! *Logan, make her get on the truck!*"

"Britta," I spat through clenched teeth. "If you don't get your ass on this truck, we're going to get mobbed and we're all going to die. Is that what you want—you want all our deaths on your hands?"

Britta's wild-eyed gaze landed on me, still bizarrely smiling. "Well, dang, Eddie, you sure know how to hit a girl where it hurts, dontcha?"

With a resigned sigh, she tossed her shotgun in the air, catching it and twirling it around. Holding it like a golf club, she sent the grip of the gun slamming into the head of a Creeper crawling up the windshield. "That's for Davey," she snarled. Another toss of her weapon, another twirl, too, and then Britta sent the battered tip of her boot straight into the face of a Creeper dangling from the side of the truck. "And that one's for me, you goddamn, stupid, ugly fuckers!"

"Britta!" Willow continued to scream. "Get on the fucking truck!"

"Christ on a goddang cracker, Willow," Britta said. "I'm fuckin' comin'." Leaping across vehicles, she landed with an audible thud on the roof above me.

"Hang on to something!" I shouted, stomping on the gas once more. The tires spun, kicking up gore as the truck blasted forward, the plow swiping oncoming Creepers off their feet and out of the way.

"We've got to stop!" Willow cried. "We've got to stop and help her!"

Swerving sharply right, clipping the corner of a cluster of Creepers, I ground out, "I can't stop here—they'll be on us again in minutes."

Flying at top speed down the interstate, I took the first exit, pulling into an abandoned strip mall. Willow had thrown open the door before the truck was fully stopped, clambering out onto the pavement with a yelp. Cursing, I threw the truck into PARK and rushed outside to help her. Joe, too, had flown from the back of the truck, climbing up the cage toward the roof. Meanwhile, Britta was seated between the two racks of floodlights on the roof, her legs dangling over the windshield, looking substantially less stricken than the rest of us.

"Where's the bite, Brit?" Joe was frantic, hauling Britta off the truck. Depositing her onto the pavement, he quickly sliced open the leg of her jeans, revealing a very red and angry imprint of teeth just above her ankle. There wasn't much blood; it was mostly a surface wound. But in the end that wouldn't matter. The bite had pierced the skin and once the infection spread to the bloodstream, no one lasted very long.

"Oh, Jesus, Brit, what the fuck did you do?" Joe jumped to his feet, palms pressed to his forehead, turning away.

"Oh shit," Willow whispered, dropping to her knees beside her friend. "Oh shit, oh shit, Britta..."

"Told y'all to leave me there," Britta said plainly. "I fuckin' told y'all—" Britta's words abruptly cut off. Wet sprayed across my face. I blinked, temporarily stunned as I took in the blood spatter across Britta and Willow's equally owl-eyed expressions, both of them gaping at Britta's partially severed limb.

With a panicked shout, Joe brought his ax down again, severing Britta's leg only a few inches above her bite.

And then Britta began to scream. "My foot! Joey, my goddang motherfuckin' foot!"

"Hold her still!" Joe shouted. Tossing the ax away, he began fumbling with his belt buckle, pulling the thick strip of leather free. I dropped down beside Britta, attempting to help Willow hold her still as blood pumped from the stump, coating my hands in seconds. Britta continued to scream and thrash in my grip, all the while cursing Joe.

Whipping off his shirt, Joe sat on Britta's middle, working frantically to wrap it around her bleeding stump. Securing the belt over the makeshift bandage, he pulled and tied it tight.

Britta was still screaming and thrashing, though her movements had begun to slow and her screams had become nonsensical. Willow continued sobbing at her side, hugging Britta more than she was holding her.

"Help me get her in the truck," Joe said, breathless. Jumping up, he swiped a blood-soaked hand across his face. "We gotta get back to camp — we gotta get her to Doc."

At some point between lifting her off the pavement and laying her across the back seat, Britta stopped fighting. Willow scrambled inside, cradling Britta's lolling head in her lap, while Joe began pulling various things from beneath the seats, shoving whatever he found beneath Britta's ruined leg, in order to keep it elevated.

Shirtless, face and chest painted in Britta's blood, he turned to me, the whites of his eyes stark against his bloodied skin. "Drive, brother," he growled. "As fast as you fuckin' can."

TWENTY NINE

WILLOW

"You're going to be fine," I murmured, clutching tightly to Britta's head, stroking her sweat-slicked hair. "You're going to be fine—everything's going to be fine." I shuddered, my stomach roiling with each intake of air. Along with varying degrees of body odor, the tinny, thick smell of blood filled the cab. Joe and I were covered in it; the seats were swimming in it. Despite Joe's attempt at a tourniquet, Britta was still bleeding profusely.

I continued to whisper while Logan drove faster, almost carelessly, barreling over broken roads with single-minded focus—to get Britta home as fast as humanly possible. The pickup crested a small rise in the road before slamming down again as Logan took a hard left, sending us flying through the forest that bordered Silver Lake.

All thoughts of the second horde had been temporarily forgotten; we could only deal with one catastrophe at a time and right now everyone's sole focus was on Britta.

"Open the gates!" Logan shouted, laying on the horn as the truck skidded to a stop outside the main gate. "Open up—Britta's hurt—open the fuck up!"

Shouts arose from the guard tower above and the camp beyond. As the gate began to slide open, Logan stomped on the gas, forcing Joe and I to redouble our hold on Britta and brace ourselves against the seats. We lurched to another sudden stop; doors flew open, sunlight streaming inside the cab, highlighting the macabre scene.

"We need Doc—Britta's hurt!"

There was more shouting; familiar faces swimming in and out of sight; hands pulling at me from every direction. I scrambled out of the way, allowing more capable people to take my place. Standing there in the dirt, I watched as Joe, helped by several others, carried Britta off in the direction of Doc's cabin. Her head hung limply over Joe's arm, her arms and legs swinging lifelessly. I slapped my hand over my mouth, stifling a sob as, suddenly, strong arms were wrapping around me, pulling me close. I slumped against Logan, gripping handfuls of his shirt, burying my face in his neck.

"It's okay," he muttered, soothing his hands up and down my back. "She's gonna be okay."

"You didn't see her," I whispered hoarsely. "There was so much blood—she was so pale." My knees shook along with my words; the adrenaline that had been coursing through me only seconds ago had begun to wane.

"What the hell happened?"

Logan and I broke apart to find Leisel, accompanied by Maria and Betsey, hurrying toward us. Taking in the state of us—the blood and gore coating our clothing — their eyes widened.

"There was a second horde," Logan hurried to explain. "Or maybe it was the original one that backtracked... or... I don't fucking know." He paused, dragging his bloodied hands over his bound hair. "We were just about done clearing the last of them, and then all of a sudden they were coming out of the trees — hundreds more, from every direction."

"Britta was bitten," I whispered hoarsely. As three sets of shocked gazes shot to me, I swallowed and tried to speak. "And... and Joe cut off her foot. She's at Doc's."

Leisel's eyes closed; she took a deep breath before opening them. "And Davey? Please tell me —"

"He's gone," Logan interjected, his gruff tone faltering slightly. "I don't know how it happened, just that it happened after the second horde showed up. We were all running to the trucks and... " he trailed off, shaking his head.

Leisel's features flared as she fought to keep herself composed. Behind her, Maria and Betsey were staring mutely at us, their expressions stricken.

"And what about the others?" Leisel asked. "Did you see anyone from Xavi's team? Jim? Anyone?"

Logan shook his head. "I haven't seen anyone else since this morning."

Maria covered her mouth with her hands, just barely suppressing a sob. With a shushing sound, Betsey turned to her, gathering the young woman into her arms.

"Okay, I need to think," Leisel muttered, her brows drawing in tight, pressing her lips together as she looked to the sky. "First, I need to brief the rest of the camp on what's happened — you two come with me."

"Wait," I hurried to say. "Can I go check on Britta?"

Leisel gave a sharp nod. "That's fine—I only need one of you. Logan, I'm going to collect everyone and then I'm headed to the dining hall—see you in five?"

As the three women headed back the way they'd come, Logan turned to me. "Hey," he said, taking my face in his hands. "Are you okay?"

Despite feeling the very furthest thing from okay, I nodded. I'd been through worse than this—I already knew it wouldn't break me.

"Okay, look," he said, glancing in the direction of the dining hall. "I've got to go, but I'll come find you once I know what's going on."

As Logan disappeared down the path, I dashed to Doc's. The usual smells of cleaning agents and antiseptic greeted me upon entering the cabin, though stronger than usual, along with the same sickening scent of blood and sweat that had permeated the truck.

Approaching the room I'd once occupied, I found Britta. She lay in the same bed I'd nearly died in, her lips blue, her skin pale and shining with sweat, her hands and leg tied to the bed railings. Joe stood at her bedside, dressed in ill-fitting scrubs and looking considerably cleaner than he had just minutes ago. The room itself looked pristine. Every surface was damp and glistening, the smell of disinfectant nearly unbearable.

Brushing past me into the room, her arms filled with bags of fluid, Doc cast a glance in my direction. "Perfect timing, Willow—I'm going to need another set of hands."

"There's ma' girl," Britta slurred, attempting to lift her head. Blinking sluggishly, she tried to smile, only managing a slight grimace. "Now, Willow, what tha' fuck did y'all do with ma' foot? Joey won't tell me where's run off to."

Flinching, Joe dropped his gaze to the floor.

"I… um…" I stammered.

"She's drugged," Doc said. "She doesn't have a clue what's going on and she'll be sleeping soon. You remember where the scrubs are? Go get yourself cleaned up."

"I remember," I called over my shoulder, already hurrying toward the bathroom. I undressed in a hurry, leaving my bloodied clothing in a small pile under the sink. Scrubbing myself clean, I donned a set of purple scrubs before hurrying back to Britta.

"They got Davey and they got my goddang foot." Chuckling softly, Britta's eyes were rolling back in her head, showing white. She attempted lifting her hands, frowning when she found she couldn't move them. "Hey… y'all… I'm stuck…" She pulled weakly at her binds.

"That's okay, honey," Doc replied. "There's nowhere you need to be right now. Why don't you start counting back from ten—can you do that for me?"

Britta's fingers twitched. A deep frown furrowed her face. "I can't move… my god… dang… hands…"

Covering one of Britta's hands with both of mine, I held her still. "Hey," I whispered. "You don't need to move. You just need to sleep, okay? Let's count together. Ten, nine…"

Britta's fingers loosely squeezed mine. "Eight," she joined in. "Seven…"

It occurred to me then that this might potentially be the last time I would ever speak to my friend. That, despite Joe's split-second decision to take off her foot, she could still be infected. And even if she didn't turn, there was still the possibility of her dying from blood loss or various other infections.

"Britta," I rasped, bending my face to her ear as she continued to count. "I just want you to know… I just wanted to say…" I shook my head as tears filled my eyes and emotion clogged my throat. "… thank you for being my friend." Britta didn't respond—her eyes had closed, her hand limp in mine. Releasing her hand, my shaking fingers slid a clump of sweat-soaked hair from her face.

"That's not going to keep her out for long," Doc said briskly, rushing around to the other side of the bed where a rolling tray of silver instruments had been laid out. "And I'll need to cauterize her leg before she wakes up—the pain alone could give her a heart attack."

"Joe, get your butt over here. Put this between her teeth, alright?" Doc shook a strip of leather at him; distinct teeth-marks already punctured the bit of material, telling me it had been similarly used before.

"Willow, you put some gloves on." Doc nodded sharply toward a box on the counter. "While Joe holds her hands, I'll need you to hold her leg still."

Firing up a small metal blow torch, Doc used it to heat the flat end of a large silver scalpel. It dawned on me then, the full horror of what was going to happen. My eyes went wide, feeling the burning rise of vomit in my throat.

"Everyone ready?" Doc asked. Tools aside, Doc began removing the impromptu dressing from Britta's leg. Blood continued gushing from the wound, mangled flesh and exposed bone where Britta's foot should be. "There's extra skin to work with," Doc muttered. "Figured as much. Willow, hold her leg—hold it as tightly as you can."

Picking up the blowtorch, Doc resumed heating the scalpel. "Here we go," she said firmly, sparing me and Joe a brief look, just before pressing the heated scalpel to the end of Britta's leg.

The smell of burning flesh, not unlike the smell of burning hair, filled my nostrils. Britta's body jerked—her eyes fluttered behind closed lids and her fingers twitched, yet she didn't wake. Holding tightly to her leg, I locked eyes with Joe and for a moment we only stared at one another, as if neither of us could bear to watch as Doc pressed the scalpel to Britta's stump for a second time. This time Britta's mouth opened around a moan and the leg I was clinging to jerked violently.

"Hold her still," Doc snapped. "We're nearly there!"

I tightened my grip, my fingertips digging into Britta's bloody flesh. With the third press of the heated scalpel, Britta's eyes flew open with a bloodcurdling scream, partially muffled behind the bit of leather stuffed between her teeth. Her back arched upward even as we all fought to hold her to the bed. She went still just as suddenly as she'd woken, her eyes rolling back and her body going limp.

Silence engulfed the room. Joe sat down hard in his chair, his throat working furiously. Doc turned away, placing her instruments onto the cart and wiping the sweat from her brow with the crook of her arm. Releasing Britta's leg from my shaky grip, I retook her hand in mine.

"She needs antibiotics and more fluids," Doc muttered as she began moving around the room, gathering up various items. "I need to clean and dress her leg. She needs blood, too, which means I need to find those damn blood type tests from that last hospital raid. Then I'll need to find out if anyone in camp is compatible…" Trailing off, Doc pressed the back of her shaking hand to her forehead and went still. Taking several breaths, she turned to me. "I'll be back shortly — don't let anyone in this room, do you hear me? If either of you leave, make sure to scrub back in before returning. We need to keep as sterile an environment as possible."

As Doc pulled the door closed behind her, I turned back to Britta, tightening my hold on her hand, sending prayers up to a god I didn't believe in—begging him to save my friend.

A knock at the door had Joe and I jerking upright—me from my slouched position beside Britta's bed and Joe from his chair, holding his head in his hands.

"Who the fuck is it?" Joe snapped.

"Logan," an equally irritated baritone clapped back. "I'm looking for Willow."

"Coming," I called, scrambling for the door. "Don't come in—the room is sterile."

Opening the door just enough to enable me to slide through, I quickly pulled it closed behind me. Hurriedly pulling off my gloves, I tossed them into a nearby trash bin and threw my arms around Logan.

"Britta?" he asked, his face buried in my hair. He'd cleaned up some—his clothes were clean, his hands and face washed, his hair wet and wound into a tight ball atop his head.

"Doc cauterized her leg," I whispered against his chest. "But she still needs blood and antibiotics and…" My words fell away as my eyes began to burn. I felt suddenly exhausted and weak and a whole host of other disconcerting and overwrought feelings that I couldn't even find the strength to name. Fisting my hands in the back of his shirt, I began to cry in earnest.

"Willow," he said, once my tears had quieted. "Jesus Christ, I hate doing this to you right now, but I have to go."

I glanced up sharply. "What? Go *where*?"

Logan sighed heavily. "I have to go back out there. Leisel is putting a team together to help find the others—she needs someone to show them where everything happened."

Backing away from his arms, I blinked furiously. "No, no fucking way," I said, swiping angrily at my tear-stained cheeks. "You were just out there—tell her to find someone else!"

He shook his head. "It has to be me. She wants to recover Davey's body—if we can—and then see if we can locate Xavi's team."

I glared at him, jaw clenched, my sore muscles straining to the point of pain. We'd barely survived the first two rounds with the horde and he wanted to go for a third? Did he have a death wish?

"*Please don't do this.*" I said those four words with so much force that they shook as they left me.

"I don't have a choice," he said. "It's either me, you or Joe, and Joe just hacked off Britta's foot, and you're barely standing as it is."

"You're never going to stop, are you?" I bit out. "You're always going to be like this, aren't you?"

"What the fuck, Willow—be like *what*?"

"Like this!" I shouted, desperation mixed with fury and fear unfurling in my belly. "Always having to save the day. Always having to take charge of everything. Never thinking about how anyone else feels. *Not caring how anyone else feels!*"

Logan went momentarily slack-jawed before his mouth snapped shut and his eyes flashed with fire. "What the fuck is wrong with you? They need my help—I'm going to help them."

"I need you, too!" I shouted. "I need you here and alive but that doesn't matter to you, does it? You're just going to go back out there, not giving a shit about how I feel!"

"How can you be so selfish?" he demanded.

My eyes widened with renewed rage. "I'm selfish because I don't want you to *die?* I'm selfish because we just lost Davey and we might lose Britta, and if I lose you too, then I don't know what the fuck I'll do!"

"No," Logan growled. "You're selfish because you don't want me to help—because you want me to stay here like a goddamn coward when I should be out there trying to stop more people from dying!"

"Why do you always have to be the fucking hero? *Why can't you be selfish for a change?*" Furious tears fell from my eyes and I angrily swiped them away.

"I'm not trying to be a hero! But I'm not going to be a coward either. Not for you, not for anyone." Logan squeezed his eyes shut, regaining control of his temper with a growl and a quick shake of his head. "Look," he gritted out. "Please understand… I'm just trying to do the right thing—for us, and for Silver Lake, too.

"I'll be back," he continued, drawing closer. "I promise you." He reached for me and I flinched away, my eyes and nostrils flaring as I fought against another wave of tears.

"Willow—Jesus Christ—I've got to go." Scrubbing a hand over his face, Logan began moving toward the door. "Stay with Britta—I'll be back before you know it." He paused with one hand on the handle, looking as if he wanted to say something more… do something more.

Glaring at him through narrowed, tear-filled eyes, I resisted the urge to run to him—to continue begging him to stay. With one last, lingering look, Logan let the door shut behind him. I remained where I stood, my feet rooted to the floor, still staring after him long after he'd left. Hoping that, at any moment, he would burst through the door, having changed his mind.

But also, silently adding his name to my growing list of prayers.

Later that evening, I found myself standing outside Doc's cabin, my gaze on the darkening sky above, visually tracing the dim outline of the moon in the distance. Night was fast approaching and yet no one from either team had returned—Xavi's or Leisel's.

The realization that they could all be dead right now, that they could have been killed or worse, while I waited for news that might never come, had settled in my gut like an iron fist. Every breath felt like fire, every beat of my heart felt like the crush of an anvil.

Why hadn't I hugged Logan goodbye? Why had I yelled at him instead of telling him to be careful? Why did I do any of the things I did? Logan was right—I was selfish. Selfish, stupid, and mean.

"Willow!" Cassie hurried along the path. "Can you believe all this?" she said tearfully. "No one has come back yet and Davey... *Davey's gone.* First Hank and now Davey" Wringing her hands together, she shook her head. "And Britta... my god, how is Britta?"

Floundering for a response, I mumbled, "I don't really know. I think she'll be okay. I mean, Joe took off her foot really fast, and Doc thinks the blood loss may have helped keep the virus out of her system." I shrugged helplessly. "And she said her newest batch of antibiotics are even better than the previous ones—stronger, or something..." I trailed off as Cassie's eyes filled with fresh tears.

"Oh god, poor Britta," Cassie cried out softly, covering her mouth with her hand. "Oh that poor, poor woman."

I said nothing more—what else was there to say? In truth, I didn't know if Joe had taken off her foot in time, nor did I know if Doc's antibiotics would be powerful enough to stop a secondary infection from taking root.

"Did you know that Britta was the one to bring me to Silver Lake?" Cassie gazed across camp, wiping tears from her cheeks. "She found me hiding in my old RV. The engine had blown and I'd been sitting there on the side of a road in the middle of nowhere for nearly two weeks, out of food and wondering what the heck I was going to do. My wife... well, I'd lost her recently... and then after the RV died, I was just about ready to throw in the towel, you know what I mean?

"The evening I was going to do it—I was sitting in bed and holding the gun and trying to convince myself there was nothing left for me here. I'm not a quitter—I'd never quit anything before, but the thought of carrying on without Stephanie felt pointless. So there I was with a gun pressed to my temple, when there was suddenly a knock on the RV. Scared me so bad, I nearly shot myself anyway." Cassie, who was still crying, chuckled through her tears. "It was as if she'd been sent to save me. My god, I really don't know what I'll do if she doesn't make it...

"And Leisel," Cassie continued. "She's the heart and soul of this place—none of us would be here without her. I can't believe she went willingly into... God only knows what."

My anger, which had somewhat faded since Logan's departure, suddenly returned with a vengeance—not at Logan, but at Leisel. Anger that she'd dragged Logan out there with her. Not that he'd needed to be dragged; he'd gone willingly, too... *damn him.*

"I need to go," I said tightly—everything felt tight, my throat especially—and without another word, headed for home.

Inside the cabin, I crawled into Logan's bed, burying my face into his pillow and swallowing back the tears that threatened to fall as the scent of him filled me completely. I didn't want to cry anymore. After all, if I cried now, it would mean that I believed the worst. I had to stay positive—I at least had to try to stay positive. But as day turned to night and night turned back into day, and Logan had yet to return, it became increasingly harder to feel anything but terror.

At some point, I drifted off into a dreamless sleep only to wake with a jolt, greeted by darkness and silence, and the empty echo of a cabin that contained only me and an ever-worsening sense of dread in my gut. I forced myself out of bed, feeling sweaty and sick—what few hours of sleep I'd gotten, having done nothing for me other than while away the remainder of the day.

Inside the bathroom, I splashed some water on my face and stared miserably at my reflection, trying to will myself into action. I needed to shower, to eat something. I needed to check on Britta. I needed to go to work. There were so many things that needed to be done that I found myself too exhausted to know where to begin. Climbing back into bed, I clutched Logan's pillow to my chest once more. "Logan," I whispered raggedly. "Come home—please, please come home."

I could no longer imagine my world without him. Logan was my rock, my safety net… and had been for far longer than I'd ever been willing to admit to before.

I found myself crying—a flash flood of desperation and unease, sobs racking my body so hard and for so long that I eventually cried myself to sleep.

This time I didn't wake again until dawn.

THIRTY

WILLOW

T wo days passed without any word from Logan and the others. Two horrible days during which my anxiety worsened to the point where sleep had become impossible and eating had become a chore. I attempted going to work only to be repeatedly sent home by Cassie; unfit to work, unable to function, I merely wandered with a stomach full of unease, the dark circles under my eyes soon returning with a vengeance, and my clothes fitting looser.

On the third day, after yet another agonizingly long night, fraught with unease and unwelcome dreams, I found myself walking aimlessly through camp, shivers rippling through me despite the mild day. The sun was hidden behind heavy clouds, as it had been for the last couple of days, as if it too were having trouble finding the strength to do what needed to be done.

Eventually, I reached the outskirts of the bathhouse, mindlessly joining the slow trickle of people headed inside, mumbling the requisite hellos while grabbing what I needed from the various bins. Headed for the showers, I stood mutely beneath the cold flow, uncaring when my skin goose pebbled and my teeth began to chatter.

Logan.

My hands fisted against the tile, my chin touching my chest, a silent scream building within me. With every fiber of my being, with every thought in my head, with every beat of my heart, I willed him to return to me.

As a sob slipped free and my head jerked up, I clasped my hand over my mouth and slammed the water off. Toweling off, I dressed quickly, and hastily braided my hair down one side.

Exiting the bathhouse, I headed to the dining hall, hoping that eating something might calm the ever-present roiling in my quickly shrinking stomach. Keeping my head down, I hurried through the cavernous hall, feeling exponentially worse by the distinct lack of people inside. I wasn't the only one feeling the loss of those who'd yet to return — Silver Lake had come to a sort of standstill, a dark pall falling over camp that had nothing to do with the weather. People moved about like shadows, going through their daily rituals and routines, but lacking the color they once imbued.

Maria and Betsey stood huddled together behind the serving line, shoulders hunched, mouths drawn into tight lines as they scooped eggs from a pan. "Willow." Maria forced a smile even as her eyes glistened with unshed tears. "Haven't seen you much lately — how are you?"

"Um, okay, I guess," I stammered, shrugging weakly.

Handing me a plate of eggs, Maria clasped her hand around mine and squeezed. "He'll be back," she whispered hoarsely. "They'll all be back."

"Yes, they will," Betsey said firmly. "Any day now."

I stared at the plate of eggs in my hand, wondering what Logan might be eating out there. Wondering if he was eating at all. Wondering if he was even...

"I, um, I need to go." The words had barely squeezed from my too-tight throat before I was halfway across the dining hall, shoving my plate of eggs at a passing person. Outside, I broke into a run, running as fast as I could in the direction of Doc's, bursting inside the cabin, breathing hard. Doc glanced up from her book with a start, a medical tome that was nearly as thick as it was wide and raised a finger to her lips, pointing to where EJ was sprawled across several waiting room chairs, his mouth hanging open, a steady stream of drool dripping from his bottom lip all the way to the floor. And then to Joe—seated on the floor outside of Britta's room, his eyes were closed, his head pressed back against the wall, his loud snores rattling both him and the gun balanced precariously in his lap.

"What's with the gun?" I asked once I'd caught my breath.

Closing her book, Doc came to stand beside me, hands on her hips as she looked over Joe. "We had some concerned folks stop by last night worried about the possibility of Britta being infected and the infection spreading through camp. Of course, I alleviated their concerns but Joe wasn't satisfied—he's got it stuck in his thick skull that someone might try and do something to Britta." Doc shook her head. "As if anyone here would ever hurt her."

"How is she?" I asked. "Any change?"

"Nothing yet, honey," Doc replied, rubbing my back. "You remember what I said—sometimes the mind needs to sort itself out before the body can follow." Pausing, Doc glanced at a still sleeping EJ. "You know I had to pry the IV from him last night before he passed out from blood loss. I've never seen someone so eager to donate blood before."

"I bet he'd donate his foot, too," I muttered, "if Britta asked him for it."

"He sure would," Doc said, still shaking her head. "Lovesick fool."

"I heard that," EJ said, yawning. Sitting up, he wiped the drool from his mouth. "So, what's the word, Willow — any news?"

"No," I said tightly. "Nothing."

EJ smiled weakly. "No news is good news, right?"

"Not sure that rule applies to the end of the world," Joe muttered, his eyes still closed.

"Why the hell not?" EJ snapped.

One eye cracked open. "Think about it, you fucking moron."

"I heard there're eggs for breakfast today," Doc quickly interjected. "If you want some, you'll need to hurry."

At the mention of eggs, both men sat up a little straighter, though neither seemed overly eager to leave.

"Oh, would you two stop this petty horseshit!" Doc sent the toe of her sneaker into Joe's thigh before marching across the room and grabbing hold of EJ's arm, yanking him from his chair. "Up and at 'em boys," she said tersely, dragging EJ toward the door. "It doesn't do Britta any good to have the two of you fighting over who gets to guard her doorway."

While Doc wrangled both men from the cabin, I leaned my head against Britta's door, hearing muffled noises coming from within. Slowly turning the knob, I found Ella seated at Britta's bedside, her forehead pressed to the bed railing, clinging to it with both hands.

"It's your fault, you know," she was whispering. "I never would have slept with him if it hadn't been for *you* getting yourself hurt. So now you need to wake the fuck up and stop me from making even more bad decisions."

Britta remained still and silent on the bed, her eyes closed, her skin shining with a light sheen of sweat.

"Jordy," Ella groaned softly. "I can't believe I had sex with… *Jordy.*"

Brows raised, I pushed the door the rest of the way open. "You had sex with Jordy?"

Ella's head jerked up, her bloodshot eyes narrowing. "Don't you judge me, Willow," she snarled, sniffling. "Don't you dare judge me with your *harem of brothers.*"

My eyes went wide. Marching up to Ella, I glared down at her. "You know you don't always have to be such a hateful bitch, right? Especially now…" Despite my anger, my voice broke. Spinning around, I inhaled deeply, trying hard not to cry.

Clearing her throat, Ella shifted noisily. "So, I'm guessing Logan isn't back yet?"

I gave a brisk shake of my head.

"Yeah, that sucks." Ella's harsh tone softened slightly. "How bad are you freaking out right now?"

"Really bad," I admitted quietly, turning to face her. "Really fucking bad."

"Yeah." Ella looked away, an apologetic look flashing across her usually frigid expression. "Well, just so you know, you dodged a bullet with Jordy." Making a face, Ella pushed out of her chair and crossed the room. Pausing at the doorway, she said, "*He likes to cuddle.*"

As the door closed behind her, I stared for a moment, shaking my head.

"So you've clearly had a more eventful morning than I did," I said to Britta as I took the seat at her bedside. "Ella and Jordy, huh? Care to spill all the dirty details?"

"On second thought," I continued, wrinkling my nose. "I don't think I really want to know…"

"Not much news on my end—they're still not back. Oh, but *Betsey* thinks they'll be back any day now…" I trailed off with a scoff. "Only it's been a week—a fucking week. What could have happened out there…" I trailed off again as an unwanted image arose—Logan and Lucas side by side, their blue eyes leeched of color, their skin shredded into ribbons of rot. Mauled by the very same horde, brothers in both life and death.

Gasping through my next breath, I squeezed my eyes shut, picturing Logan alive and well instead. In my vision, I reached for him, running my fingertips over the slant of his cheekbones, and across the harsh line of his mouth. I dipped my hands into his hair, unbound and wild with waves, before returning to explore more of his face. As I smoothed the pads of my thumbs over his heavy brows, he stared back at me, his ocean-blue eyes burning straight through. Up on my tiptoes, I was leaning forward to kiss him when Britta's hand suddenly twitched in mine.

I bolted upright, my eyes flying open. It wasn't the first time she'd twitched; however, it was the first time she'd twitched in a way that didn't feel reflexive in nature, but very much deliberate.

"Britta," I breathed, shaking her hand. "Can you hear me? Britta? Squeeze me if you can hear me."

Britta's dry lips parted, a wheezy groan rattling from her chest and I dropped her hand, my heart thudding in my chest. My gaze darted up and down her body, looking over her too-pale, sweat-slickened skin. *Please be alive*, I chanted silently. *Please be alive.*

"Britta," I squeaked, terror squeezing my throat. "Britta?"

Her eyes opened—bright blue and fixed on me.

"Britta!" I cried, clasping my hands over my mouth. "Oh my god, Britta!"

There was a loud clatter beyond the door. Swinging open, the door crashed into the wall as Joe and EJ shoved against each other, plates of eggs tumbling to the ground as they raced to Britta's bedside.

"Brit," Joe gasped, his shotgun still in hand. "You awake, girl?"

"Britta." EJ staggered to a stop beside Joe. "Are you... *you*?"

Another groan rattled as she attempted clearing her throat; her fingers wiggled in her binds, reaching for me. Clasping her hand between both of mine, I began to laugh even as tears poured down my cheeks.

Britta blinked sluggishly between the three of us, pausing on Joe. "What's the... gun for... Joey?" she asked hoarsely and with immense effort. "You gonna shoot... little ol'... me?"

Joe's slack-jawed expression morphed into a stunned smile. "Not you," he rasped. "Just... everybody else."

"You're tellin' me that Ella—the Ice Queen of the East, got her groove on with *Jordy*?"

Britta was propped up in bed, a marked improvement after only two days awake, while I finished brushing out the tangles in her hair. Her amputated limb was freshly bandaged and held up in a sling that EJ had fashioned from the ceiling, and her pain was being managed by both the meds dripping slowly through her IV, and the cup of hot tea at her bedside, made from willow bark and calamus root.

"That's what she said." Pulling the chair over near the bed,

I sat down with a sigh. I was bone tired and yet unable to sleep more than a few minutes at a time, always waking with my heart hammering frantically against my ribs, hoping that this time would be the time I'd awake to find Logan had returned only to realize over and over again that I was still alone.

Britta chuckled. "That's a match made in hell, if I ever heard one. You wanna put bets on who kills who?"

"No way," I muttered. "We both know if anyone's killing anyone—it's going to be Ella killing Jordy. Apparently, he likes to *cuddle*."

"Ya never know," Britta mused. "Could be that cuddly kangaroo has a dark side we don't know about. Wouldn't put it past our little Hella-Ella to make a good man go bad. "

When I didn't respond, Britta's hand appeared over the bed railing, her fingers wiggling. "Did I lose ya again, sugar—you awake over there?"

Straightening in my seat, I met Britta's drugged gaze over the top of the railing and tried to smile.

"Nah—hell no. Mm-mm. Now, I may be higher than a giraffe's ass right now, but I can still spot insincerity a mile away. Don't be pullin' happy faces for my benefit. You wanna cry, sugar, you go ahead and cry."

My smile slipping, I gripped my hands in my lap, twisting them. "I don't want to cry," I bit out softly. "I'm sick of crying. I'm sick of feeling sick. I just... I just... *need to know what happened*."

"I know that feeling—Lord knows I do." Fumbling through the bedrail, Britta grasped my clasped hands. "Not knowin' is the worst feelin' in this whole... *cursed* world." Britta's voice broke and her hand disappeared from mine.

"Alright, that's enough of that." The soft slap of Doc's voice across the floor broke up the palpable silence that settled over the room. "That's enough of that. Now, I know things might seem bleak, but that doesn't mean we have to dwell on them. Britta — you need your rest more than anything right now. Willow — honey, you need a happy distraction. How about you come with me for the day — I've got some foraging to do — I'm out of astragalus and sambucus and a whole host of other things. Britta — if you need anything, Joe's right outside the door."

"He got his gun on him?" Britta sniffled.

"Got it right here!" Joe called from the other room.

"Yeah? Which one you got today?" Quirking half a smile, Britta sent me a teary-eyed wink. "The big one?"

There was a pause before Joe appeared in the doorway, lips twisted into a devilish smile. Reaching overhead, he gripped the top of the doorframe, causing the muscles in his arms to noticeably swell. "You wanna see it?" he drawled.

"Jesus, Mary, and Joseph," Doc said, whisking me out of the chair and shooing me toward the door. "That is definitely enough of *that*. Joe, you and your gun better get back in your seat — Britta needs her rest!"

THIRTY ONE

WILLOW

We'd left camp on foot, traveling east of Silver Lake, headed to a creek that split through the thickening forest, where uprooted trees folded over the winding water like clasping hands, and wildflowers and weeds grew in abundance. It had been an uneventful journey, without a single Creeper sighting and very little conversation.

"See this?" Doc rose from her knees, where she'd been hidden almost entirely among waist-high foliage. In her hand, she held out a small green and purple plant, its dangling undergrowth still covered in wet earth. "You'll have to look for them—they like to hide. And be careful when you're digging them up—it's the roots I need."

"Got it," I said, as Doc ducked back into the grass.

Following along the water's edge, I dug through the soft soil, pulling up the plants and placing them in the burlap sack slung over my shoulder. To try and keep my mind from wandering down a dark path fraught with foreboding, I made a concerted effort to work diligently, even humming along with rhythmic sounds of water rushing over rocks each time my anxiety began to rise.

Bugs buzzing in my ears, salamanders slithered out from under rocks and toads jumped quickly out of sight as I dug around, disrupting their hiding places. Before long, the forest had dimmed considerably. My bag was bursting with green and purple plants, each with their roots intact.

"Time to go." Doc emerged from the tall grass, holding up the limp body of a white rabbit. "Found us a snack, too."

It wasn't anything I hadn't seen before—in fact, I'd arguably seen far worse things than a dead rabbit. Even so, sorrow struck me fast and hard and I found myself sinking to the ground in tears.

"Willow?" Doc dropped beside me, pulling me into a hug. "Oh, Willow—talk to me, honey."

"I can't do this," I sputtered over her shoulder, glaring at the peaceful sight of the creek beyond. "The only reason I survived losing my parents was because of Luke, and the only reason I survived losing Luke was because of Logan. I can't survive losing Logan, too. I can't do it… I can't…" I trailed off, gasping, my tears falling faster. "I've got nothing left."

"Alright, alright, slow down. Take a breath for me—that's it. Now take another—there you go." Pulling away, she placed her hands on my cheeks. "Now you listen to me—you might think the only reason you're here right now is because of those boys but let me tell you what I think—I think *you all* survived as long as you did because you had each other.

"You were a family, Willow, and families hold one another up, each of us in different ways—no one way being more or less important than the other.

"And now you've got an even bigger family. You're not alone in this pain. We are all here with you, each of us holding one another up. And whatever happens next, if they don't come home again, I promise you, we will keep holding one another up."

If they don't come home again. My ragged breaths stopped short as sharp pain sliced through my chest. My hand flew to my heart, as if it might beat its last beat if I didn't hold tightly to it.

"Hey, now," Doc soothed. "I didn't say I'm throwing in the towel just yet, did I? Leisel and Xavi and Logan—those are some of the strongest people I've ever encountered. Let's give it a few more days before we really start to worry, alright? Come on—up we go. One foot in front of the other. There you go."

Tucking me to her side, Doc steered me away from the creek. "Now let's get ourselves home before nightfall."

"They're back!" a woman shouted down from the guard tower, pounding on its wooden ledge. "Open up, they're back."

"You see anything out there?" a second voice called down.

"Just dinner, I'm afraid," Doc replied, holding up the rabbit by its ears. "I'll share, if you cook."

"Doc, you've got yourself a deal."

As the gate slid open and Doc paused to speak with guards in the tower, I continued on, with plans to change clothes and then hurry back to Britta. I was halfway home when I saw EJ running down the path; doing a double take when he spotted me, making a hard swerve in my direction.

"Willow!" he shouted, waving his arms around. "Willow! It's Leisel—she radioed! She's on the radio!"

"Radioed?" I stammered. "Where?"

"Their cabin," EJ said, beckoning me to follow him. "It's in their cabin."

The run from one side of camp to the other was little more than a blur. I burst into Joshua and Leisel's cabin, tripping over the threshold into a scene inside that was nothing short of chaotic. The room was overly full of people, with too many voices talking at once—though I only had eyes for one. Seated behind the desk piled high with radio equipment, was Maria. With tears streaking down her cheeks, she clutched a radio mouthpiece between trembling hands.

The many voices mixed and melded together. My heart began to pound, its fitful rhythm ringing loudly in my ears. "What happened?" I asked hoarsely. No one answered; no one even looked at me. "*What happened?*" I screamed. "*What the fuck happened?*"

The cabin fell silent, all eyes on me. Joshua, who'd been pointing to a large map on the wall, hurried through the crowd. "Willow," he said gravely, his solemn expression as serious as ever, his eyes shining with tears.

My vision wavered and narrowed until Joshua was all I could see—every line, every unruly hair, each and every pore. "He's gone?" I gasped through air that felt too thin.

"No-*no*," Joshua rushed to say. "Willow, no. He's alive—they're *all* alive."

"What?" A wave of relief washed over me, so strong it caused my knees to buckle. "He's alive?" I rasped, grasping for the wall. "Logan's alive?"

Maria pushed through the throng of people, grinning through

her tears. Pulling me into a crushing hug, she cried, "They're safe. My Jimmy, your Logan, Xavi, Lei—they're all safe in Everdeen."

What followed was a celebration amid a whirlwind of information—Leisel's team had managed to locate Xavi's team, trapped only a handful of miles up the highway from where we'd lost Davey. Together, both teams managed to finish turning the second horde away from Silver Lake. Though, try as they might, they couldn't turn the original horde from its current path—a road that would take them straight to Everdeen if they were to continue on unobstructed. Making a split-second decision, Leisel decided to head to the lesser camp and alert them of the approaching danger.

There was talk of evacuating Everdeen, of possibly helping to fortify their gates, and a dozen other strategies that I'd already forgotten by the time I'd slipped into bed for the night.

All I cared about, all I could focus on, was the grainy sound of Logan's voice coming through the radio, telling me he was coming home.

THIRTY TWO

WILLOW

"Would you stop your dang fidgetin' — you're more worked up than a long-tailed cat in a roomful of rockin' chairs." Britta eyed me over a mug of steaming Calamus root tea.

"They were supposed to be home yesterday," I said irritably, pacing the length of the small room. "Joshua said it could take them up to four days to return. Which means if they're not back today then—"

"It don't mean nothin'," she interrupted. "Time works differently out there, you know that. Hiccups happen ya can't account for. Take my dang foot, for example." Britta gestured to her bandaged stump with a frown. "Ain't exactly how I saw myself endin' up, but here we are. Gotta account for them hiccups."

"I love you, Britta," I said, grabbing the foot of her bed. "But I don't understand you. If I'd lost my foot..." I trailed off, shaking my head. Truthfully, I had no idea how I'd react to losing a limb in a world like this one—a world where you relied on your physical prowess more than anything else.

"Aw, shoot, there ain't nothin' to me, sugar. I'm just a girl wantin' to make the most of what I got left. And speakin' of makin' the most of shit—do ya really wanna be lookin' like *that* when Logan rolls in here? If that were my man comin' home, I think I'd want to be lookin' my best."

Glancing down at my dirt and sweat-stained work clothes, looking over my soil encrusted fingernails, I groaned. "Shit," I muttered, wiping my hands on my jeans, merely smearing the dirt around. "*Shit.*"

"Go get fancy," she said, pointing at the door. "Go spit shine that gorgeous face of yers. Go now, 'fore he gets here!"

I'd just finished with my hair when I heard it—the unmistakable sounds of celebration rising up through camp. Heart leaping into my throat, I gave myself one last look over in the bathroom mirror. My hair, after having been wound in a tight knot all day, now hung in long loose curls around my shoulders, and I was wearing the top Logan liked; the black button-down with a bow at the collar. I took a steadying breath and then I was bursting outside, leaving the cabin door swinging behind me and flying across the grass. I wasn't the only one running, though I couldn't tell who I was running alongside; I had a single-minded focus: to reach the gate, and Logan, as quickly as possible.

The gate was open, vehicles pulled in single file as I reached the wall. I slowed to a stop, frantically searching the faces inside each vehicle as they pulled past me.

"Maria!" Jim shouted from the open window of a truck. Jumping from the moving vehicle, he tackled his fast-approaching wife, crushing her to him and spinning her through the air.

Behind Jim's truck, a fortified SUV was rolling to a stop, all four doors flinging open. Logan emerged from the passenger seat, looking dirty and disheveled, wearing a backpack slung over his shoulder.

My lips split into a smile even as tears filled my eyes. Breaking into a run, I shouted his name. Logan spun in my direction, going still at the sight of me, his hands falling limply to his sides—as listless as the lifeless expression on his face. Confused, I began to slow, my gaze moving to the man exiting the seat behind Logan.

Tall and slim, the man was cleanly shaven, with short blond hair cropped close to his head. I didn't recognize him, and yet... I absolutely knew him.

I staggered to a stop, my hand moving to my mouth, heart sputtering in my chest.

"Willbraham!" His face split into a wide, familiar smile. And then he was running, reaching me quickly and lifting me straight off my feet. As he spun me around, his scent engulfed me, strange and unfamiliar and yet... the most familiar thing in the world.

"*Luke,*" I gasped, gripping him tightly as we continued to spin. "*You're... alive.*"

"It's insane—this is so crazy insane!" Lucas was shouting between bursts of happy laughter. "I thought you were both dead.

You know, I went back to the farmhouse looking for you. And then I searched the ravine and I found all your stuff at the bottom and I thought… I thought I'd lost you both."

The three of us were alone in our cabin—Logan sitting at the table, me on my bed, while Lucas paced the space in between, talking animatedly. I hadn't said much, while Lucas couldn't seem to stop. At the gate, his excitement had rapidly drawn the attention of everyone in camp, and as the three of us quickly became Silver Lake's focal point, Leisel had suggested we move our reunion to our cabin.

"I broke my arm when I fell off that cliff. See?" Lucas bent down on one knee before me, pulling up his shirt sleeve, revealing a mass of pink and white scar tissue. I reached out to touch him, changing my mind at the last second and clasping my hands back in my lap.

"I twisted my ankle pretty bad, too," he continued, tugging down his shirt sleeve. "I almost didn't make it inside that car before they got me. I was lucky, you know? They'd been down there so long I think they were half petrified. If they'd been Runners, they definitely would have got me.

"I don't know what happened after that. I think I passed out and when I woke up, it was dark and the Creepers were gone and it took me forever to find a way out of there. And I was so out of it and disoriented, and I got so turned around…" Lucas trailed off. "Anyway, Logan told me you were sick, too. Like really, really sick and that the doctor here saved your life."

At the mention of Logan, I looked to the table; our gazes crashed together, each of us quickly glancing away.

"Willow, come on—you gotta say something." Lucas's hands grasped my thighs. "Talk to me! Tell me how you are!"

I swallowed and tried to speak. "I, um, I'm sorry," I whispered, wringing my hands. "I guess I'm just confused. Have you been at Everdeen this entire time?"

Lucas shook his head. "Just these last two months. After I crawled out of the ravine, I'm not sure how many days passed before this guy found me—his name's Anthony, only everyone calls him Ant. He fixed me up as best he could, but it was weeks before I was good on my feet again. After that, we ended up staying at the farmhouse for a little while—that's when I found your gear at the bottom of the ravine and I thought... well, you already know what I thought."

I merely blinked at him, speechless. Lucas had been at the... *farmhouse*? All this time... all that pain... and all we'd needed to do was wait for him to return to us? The revelation was agonizing, as was the realization that if Logan and I hadn't left the farmhouse that *we* would have never happened. My eyes cut to Logan again, finding his head hanging low, his gaze on his feet.

"Once we ran out of supplies at the house, Ant took me to Everdeen. He's from there, you know? He'd been there for a few years until he'd lost his friend in this freak accident and decided to head out on his own for a while. Crazy how things work out, right?" Lucas let out a low whistle. "If Ant hadn't lost his friend—if he hadn't been out there and found me when he did—I wouldn't be here right now."

"Crazy," I repeated dumbly.

"So crazy," Lucas agreed, squeezing my thighs again. "I still can't believe you're here. Both of you. *And living together.*" Chuckling, Lucas glanced around the room. "How the hell are you both still standing? I figured you would have ripped each other to shreds by now."

My cheeks flamed hot. Lucas had no idea just how badly we'd

shredded one another. Or how often. And on how many surfaces inside this cabin.

"Yeah, well, we haven't had to see that much of each other. We work long hours." Logan spoke for the first time, staring across the cabin with a flat, hard look in his eyes. I watched him briefly, willing him to look at me, desperate to know what he was thinking.

"That's right, you have a job. Logan said you work in the gardens—and you've been scavenging—tell me about it. Tell me about everything!"

Rubbing my hand over my forehead, I shook my head. "I don't even know where to begin," I said softly. "I don't know what to say or what to—"

Lucas pulled me off the bed and to my feet, wrapping his arms around me. "You don't have to say anything," he murmured, dropping his face in my hair. My cheek pressed against Lucas's chest, I could see Logan out of the corner of my eye, his eyes on me, his flat expression giving nothing away.

"Aw, Will," Lucas whispered, squeezing me tighter. "You have no idea how much I missed you."

My mouth floundered and my eyes filled. "Me too," I whispered hoarsely, my eyes still locked with Logan's. "I thought... I thought I'd lost you forever."

THIRTY THREE

LOGAN

Both body and mind balked at the events unfolding before me — Willow and Lucas reunited, in each other's arms once again.

Jesus Christ. No matter how much I'd prepared myself for this exact moment over the last few days, nothing could have truly prepared me for how I would feel watching it play out in real time.

It was excruciating. It was enough to send someone straight into madness. To make someone do something they'd definitely regret. It was enough to make me wonder if I might understand my father, *and what he'd done,* far better than ever before. Because the thought of losing Willow to my brother had turned my mind to a very dark place.

"I still can't believe it," Lucas said, pressing a kiss to the top of

Willow's head, and another to her forehead. "We're all alive. We're all together again."

Crazy was the least of it. Sheer fucking insanity better described the events over the last week and a half. From the moment we'd arrived at Everdeen, straight through till now, I'd been existing inside some sort of hellish psychosis — trapped somewhere between the joy of finding my brother alive... and wishing he would have stayed dead.

"And look at this place — curtains and carpets. Paintings on the wall." Lucas gestured to the wall of paintings Willow had salvaged. "It's so homey. Who decorated? You, Willow?"

As they continued to embrace, I was tracking his hands — one hand was ruffling through her hair while the other toyed with the fraying pocket on the back of her jeans. A wave of heat rose in my throat. *Mine* — the lone word pounded through me like a battering ram, despite knowing better. Willow wasn't mine; she never had been. Willow had always belonged to Lucas, and vice versa.

Even knowing that, I still wanted to break his fingers. *Every. Single. Fucking. One.*

I shot out of my seat, stalking toward the door. I had to get out of there, away from them, before I imploded. "I'm hungry," I bit out. "I'm going to grab something from the dining hall."

"Wait up," Lucas said. "Why don't we all go? I'm starving — Willow, you hungry?"

Willow, who'd untangled herself from Lucas, was glancing awkwardly between us. "I guess so," she mumbled.

"Great," I muttered miserably. "Let's all go."

All eyes were on us as we entered the dining hall, the din of noise dropping as everyone turned in their seats to stare.

Lucas was oblivious; he was still reeling from seeing Willow again and marveling over all the make-do machinery in camp. Meanwhile, all the unwanted attention had caused Willow to pale. Her steps unsteady, she looked as if she might pass out at any second. I fought the urge to grab her—I'd been fighting that urge since the moment I'd seen her. To grab her and kiss her and tell her how fucking sorry I was for leaving her—a decision I'd regretted since finding Lucas alive.

"You'll have to forgive everyone, Lucas," Leisel announced, standing from her seat. "We're not usually so rude."

"Please, join us," she continued, gesturing to the empty seats at her table. "And let me formally welcome you to Silver Lake. I know that I speak for everyone here when I say that we're so happy you've been reunited with Logan and Willow. I know I'd give anything to find someone I loved alive and well, *as would anyone else here*." Sending a pointed look around the room, curious expressions instantly shifted to somber nods of agreement and individual conversations quickly resumed.

"This place is great," Lucas said around a mouthful of food—a vegetable stew that I hadn't touched. "Ant told me there was another camp but he never mentioned how good you guys have it. Everdeen is still using outhouses." Shoveling another spoonful of stew into his mouth, he said. "And after what that horde did…"

Our group had reached Everdeen with more than enough time to help evacuate the small community; however, we weren't able to prevent the dead from trampling through it, leaving a considerable amount of damage in their wake.

"Of course, we'll be helping in whatever way we can," Joshua murmured. "I've already spoken to Marcus—we'll be sending our next trading party with as many supplies as we can spare—free of charge."

"That's awesome," Lucas said, nodding. "Maybe I'll go back and help—you could come, Willow. And meet everyone."

Willow and I glanced up at the same time. The thought of her leaving... the thought that I might never see her again... I felt instantly sick.

"Oh, um, yeah. That would be... great." Willow resumed poking at her stew, not actually eating any of it. I found myself scrutinizing her, noting the weight she'd lost since I'd left.

"You should eat something," I growled softly.

Willow's eyes widened in my direction before blinking back to her plate. "I'm just not very hungry," she mumbled.

"You're not eating, *again*," I accused, just a little too loudly, and a little too angrily, drawing the attention of everyone in earshot. Again Willow's eyes shot to mine, wide and full of accusation, and I cursed inwardly, biting down on the inside of my lip. I hadn't meant to scold her.

"I think she looks great," Lucas said, smiling at Willow. "And I'm glad to see some things never change." Looking to Leisel, he chuckled. "They're always fighting, right? I can't even remember a time when they didn't."

To her credit, Leisel's expression gave nothing away. Smiling and nodding, she said, "They've definitely had their share of disagreements."

"I can't even imagine what it was like without me to play referee. These two fight about everything—they literally invent stuff to fight about!" Laughing heartily, Lucas grabbed hold of one of Willow's hands, threading his fingers through hers and tucking their joined hands in his lap while I fought back a surge of envy and rage so potent I was temporarily breathless.

Uncomfortable laughter tittered around the table; even Willow was forcing a smile. I couldn't seem to do anything but sit frozen in my seat and try not to throw my plate of food across the room.

Still smiling, Leisel placed her hand on Joshua's arm. "Did I hear you mention that it might rain tonight—maybe Logan could help you hang the tarps over the unfinished cabins?"

I stared at Leisel, stone-faced. There wasn't a single person at this table that thought it might rain tonight. Most people hadn't survived this long without forming an up close and personal relationship with Mother Nature.

Joshua coughed into his hand. "You know what, I think that's a good idea—Logan, would you mind giving me a hand?"

"Happy to," I bit out. Leaving my untouched food, I was out of my seat and across the room before Joshua had even stood. Outside, I didn't bother waiting for him, seeing as there wasn't actually any rain to be concerned about. Forgoing the path, I cut straight through the grass center of camp, headed toward the water.

Marching myself across the rocky beach and onto the boat dock, I folded my arm across my chest and peered into the water beyond, watching it ripple softly toward the shore, gently rocking the docked boats in time with the waves… leaving me wondering how long it would be before Lucas was gently rocking inside of Willow.

Violent, ugly things welled up inside me; slapping the palms of my hands over my eyes, I spun away from the water with an angry growl.

"Hey, watch it!"

Dropping my hands, I found Ella stumbling backward over the dock. Holding her flask in hand, there was wet splashed over the front of her shirt.

"Sorry," I muttered, backing away.

"Oh, it's *you*," she slurred. "I guess I can forgive *you*, what with your brother coming back from the dead and taking his girlfriend back an' all." She let out a nasty laugh. "I mean, I'm assuming they're back together, right—that's what that big, ridiculous scene at the gate was all about? And that's why you're out here pouting?"

I went still, scowling at her. "Do you ever think about not speaking, and maybe shutting the fuck up for once?"

"Nope," she said, shrugging as she staggered. "Hey—you want some?" She shook her flask at me. "You look like you need it."

I stared at the flask, swallowing hard. At this point, what did it matter? What else did I have to lose? I'd already lost the only good thing I'd ever had—the only person who'd ever made me feel... somewhat normal.

"You know what—*fuck it*." Snatching the flask from her hand, I brought it to my mouth. As the liquor burned a hot path down my throat, leaving me sputtering and coughing. Ella started to laugh. "Aw, Logan's a lightweight," she mocked in a singsong voice.

Glaring at her, I proceeded to down the remaining liquid, breathing fire through my next several breaths. It hit me quickly—a warm rush down the center of me that left me wanting more. I shook the empty flask. "Where's the rest?"

Ella's lips split into an impish smile as her fingers beckoned me. "Follow me."

"He's my... brother," I muttered. "Of course I love him."

Seated around a small metal folding table inside Ella's cabin, Ell and I passed a half empty bottle of scotch between us.

"But you love Willow more, right?" Slumping forward, Ella drunkenly wagged her finger at me. "It'ssss okay, you can tell me. I will not tell a single, solitary person."

I tried to glare at her, managing only more or less a blurry-eyed squint. "I'm not telling... you... jack... fucking... shit."

"I knew these guys who were like brothers," she said, grabbing hold of the bottle and slouching back in her seat. "Oliver and Anthony..." Taking a swig of scotch, she continued. "Oli and Ant..." She took another swig. "I loved Oli and Ant loved me and everything got... messy. Hey, that rhymed." Snorting, Ella continued to drink until scotch was dribbling down her chin.

"Ant?" I frowned at her. "Ant... from Everdeen?" I'd spoken to Lucas's new friend only long enough to thank him for helping my brother. We'd been otherwise occupied evacuating their camp after that.

"That'ssss him," Ella said, again pointing her finger at me. "Dark eyes, dark hair, kinda looks like a bargain-basement Jason Momoa. You should stay away from him—he's a bad guy."

"Huh." I leaned back in my chair, gazing up at the ceiling, feeling warm and numb and without a care in the world. No wonder my father loved to drink—a couple of swigs and you could forget how to feel.

Feeling a weight drop down over my legs, I startled upright. Ella was straddling my lap, pressing the bottle to my lips. "Drink up," she laughed, pouring aimlessly and spilling it down the front of my shirt. "Oopsy-daisy."

Grabbing the bottle from her, I leaned my head back, taking a long swallow while Ella began wriggling on top of me. "Stop," I growled, grabbing her hip and holding her still.

"Why?" She giggled, grinding herself over my growing

erection. "There's no more girlfriend to worry about, right? And you obviously like it."

I did like it... sort of. In my warm, numbed state of existence, it certainly felt good. Only, the more aroused my body grew, the more my thoughts turned to Willow. Willow and... *Lucas*. Cursing, I resumed drinking until Ella snatched the bottle away and began guzzling what was left. Coughing through her laughter, she sent the empty bottle rolling across the table. "And that's the last of the good stuff." She turned back to me. "Now where were we?"

Bleary-eyed and feeling sluggish, I blinked at her as her mouth came crashing against mine, kissing me with cold, thin lips that felt nothing like Willow's. She continued to rock over my lap as her hands slipped beneath my shirt.

"Mmmm," she moaned. "You're as hard as you look."

Batting her hands away, I turned from her mouth. "Get off me," I muttered.

Still laughing, Ella kissed me again, this time reaching for my belt.

"Get the fuck off!" I shouted, a sliver of clarity sending me shoving to my feet. Ella hit the floor hard, sprawling backward in a laughing heap while I staggered forward, clutching at furniture.

Blindly pushing past her door, I broke into a run, zigzagging drunkenly through the moonlit camp. Sickness swelling in my gut, I sagged against the nearest tree, collapsing at the base of it, heaving until I'd emptied my stomach onto the grass.

Leaning back against the tree, I dragged a shaking hand across my mouth and squinted out across the spinning landscape. Whereas earlier, I'd felt warm and numb—now I only felt desolate. Desolate and desperate to see Willow. To know what she was doing right this second.

Pushing myself up off the ground, I stumbled off in the direction of home. Passing one of the water pumps, I filled my hands and took long gulps to clear the taste of vomit from my mouth before taking off, stumbling once again. Reaching the cabin, I staggered noisily through the door.

The small lamp between bunk beds glowed in the darkness, highlighting the cozy scene on Willow's bed—Lucas sprawled on his back with Willow nestled against his side. Seeing them like this—cuddled together as if nothing had changed, as if Willow and I had never happened—felt ten times worse than I'd thought it would. Yet another blow to my already battered soul.

While I stood there swaying in the center of the cabin, wishing it was me in bed beside her, Willow's eyes opened. Lifting her head up, her mouth began to move, her lips forming silent words I couldn't make out. Frowning, I shook my head, creeping closer until the floor creaked loudly beneath my feet. I went still as Lucas shifted in his sleep, tightening his grip around Willow and pulling her closer to him.

Pulling her farther from me.

Everything went black—as black as the dark, terrible part of me that wished Lucas had stayed dead.

I ran from them, from the cabin and from the violent feelings churning within me. I didn't have a clue where I was going; I only knew that I needed to put as much space as possible between me and my brother, and the woman we both loved.

THIRTY FOUR

WILLOW

Sitting up in bed, I scrubbed the sleep from my eyes, gazing across the room at Logan's empty bed, the cyclone in my belly picking up speed and doubling in size.

He'd staggered in here in the middle of the night, reeking of booze and looking several shades of miserable, running out before I'd had a chance to explain myself. I knew what it looked like—Lucas and I snuggled in bed together. Yet, we'd only spent the evening talking—catching each other up on our last several months apart… minus one very important detail on my part.

Careful not to disturb Lucas, I climbed quietly out of bed and tiptoed across the room. Pulling one of Logan's flannels from his top bunk, I slipped into it, wrapping it tightly around me and burying my nose in the collar. As his scent engulfed me, and I continued staring at his neatly made bed, wave after wave of crippling guilt and worry continued to wash over me.

"'Morning," Lucas whispered against my ear. Shrieking, I spun around, shrieking again as he lifted me straight off my feet and planted a kiss on my lips. I froze against his mouth, quickly turning away as his tongue touched mine.

The cabin door swung open, crashing into the wall. Logan stood on the threshold, his clothes covered in mud, dark circles ringing his eyes. Taking in the sight of Lucas and me clutching one another, his nostrils flared.

"Bro," Lucas said, setting me down. "Where were you last night?"

Logan, his stormy gaze meeting mine for only one brief, horrible second, headed to his dresser. Stripping out of his mud-streaked shirt, he tossed it away. "I had stuff to do."

Lucas chuckled. "You had *stuff* to do? That's code for a girl, right?"

Pulling on a clean shirt, Logan muttered, "There's no girl."

"Is it the girl with short brown hair?" Lucas teased.

"There's no fucking girl," Logan growled, shoving past Lucas. The bathroom door slammed shut behind him.

Lucas looked at me, grinning. "There's definitely a girl, right? Why else would he be out all night?"

I only stared and shrugged, my stomach still swirling with dread. I couldn't even dream up a lie like that. Just thinking about Logan with someone else, my entire body vehemently rejected the very notion.

"Come on, bro." Lucas knocked lightly on the bathroom door. "Tell me who it is. It's the blonde, right? It's gotta be the blonde."

The door flew open; Logan, his jaw locked and ticcing, glared at Lucas. "I said, there's no fucking girl. So would you please shut the fuck up about it?"

The smile slipped from Lucas's face. "It was just a *joke*," he spat, his tone rising with anger. Straightening, he stepped closer to Logan, bringing them nose to nose, his light, chiseled features shrouded in dark discontent, his body simmering with rage. "*So why the fuck are you getting so bent out of shape?*"

Logan looked just as startled as I felt. Lucas didn't curse, and he definitely didn't stand up to his big brother. For several seconds, I could only stare dumbly at the two men until Logan's stunned expression shifted into a sneer.

"All grown up now, huh?" Logan bit out.

Lucas responded with a lift of his chin and a squaring of his shoulders.

"Hey," I said, shoving between them, grabbing hold of Lucas's hand. "Remember how I wanted to introduce you to Britta today? We should get going before I have to be at work."

As I pulled Lucas from the cabin, he continued to glare over his shoulder. "Did you see him?" he demanded. "I thought he was going to fucking hit me."

No, I thought you were going to hit him, I wanted to say. Instead, I muttered, "He was a mess after you... disappeared. He was really angry at me. At the world. I think he's still angry at... everything." It wasn't exactly a lie; although it could hardly be considered the truth, either. Not the whole truth, anyway.

Lucas remained tense, his expression tight. Looking up at him, I couldn't help but feel that the differences in my childhood friend went far deeper than a haircut and a shave and a couple of curse words. Who he'd been when he'd dropped out of sight many months ago wasn't the same person that reemerged.

We had all changed, though, hadn't we? In the blink of an eye our trio had become a duo, and in Lucas's case, he'd been forced to forge an entirely new way of living. It only made sense that he would change alongside his circumstances, and I certainly had no right to hold those changes against him—especially not after I'd developed such intense feelings for Logan in his absence.

But, I wondered dismally, *where did all these changes leave us?*

"Lucas," Britta drawled. "So it's true? The dead boyfriend returns—and here I thought Doc was just yankin' my chain."

Britta, who lay in her hospital bed flipping through an old magazine, looked Lucas over with a grin. Each day she looked better than the last; in terms of healing, she still had a long road ahead of her, but her color had returned, as had the mischievous glint in her eye.

"Not quite so dead after all," Lucas replied dryly. "Britta, right? Willow told me all about you."

Britta looked at me, her brows peaked. "Did she now? A good an' glowin' review, I hope?"

"Five stars," Lucas replied with a chuckle, some of the earlier tension easing from his expression.

"Only five? Did she mention I used to have two feet? Maybe you can tack on an extra star for all my troubles?" Britta made a face at me. "You didn't bring me any breakfast, did ya now? What's a girl gotta do *to get some grub around here*!" Britta shouted the last half of her sentence toward the door.

"I swear to all that is holy and good in this world, Britta, you are the worst patient I have ever had!" Even from two rooms away, Doc's irritation rang through loud and clear.

"You're driving her insane, aren't you?" Shaking my head, I turned to leave. "I'll go grab you something."

"No, wait." Lucas stayed me with his hand on my arm. "I'll go. I need to get the lay of the land if I'm going to live here, right? You stay with your friend."

"Are ya sure, sugar?" Britta purred, smiling coyly, and my gaze shot to hers, narrowing.

"Yeah, it's no problem," Lucas said, bending down to give my forehead a quick kiss. "See you in a few."

Britta and I lapsed into silence, merely staring at one another until Lucas's footsteps had faded, and the telltale click of the cabin door echoed, signaling his departure.

"Lord Almighty, Willow!" Britta gaped at me. "Two good lookin' brothers — both of 'em hotter than a two-dollar pistol! How much hot can there be in one family? Couldn't ya have left one for the rest of us, ya goddang greedy little man hog?"

"Britta!" My laughter was sharp and abrupt as I clutched my stomach — laughter that quickly tapered into a sob. Sitting down hard in the chair beside the bed, I buried my face in my hands. "Oh my god, what am I going to do? Britta, I don't know what the fuck to do."

"Oh-no, nu-uh. No way, Jose. There'll be no more cryin' at my bedside, sugar. If anyone's gonna be gettin' misty-eyed, it's gonna be the woman without the foot. Definitely not the woman with two hot brothers and all her limbs."

My hands dropped from my face. "Did you really just say that to me?" I demanded. "I don't have two of anything — I don't even want two of anything! None of this was what I wanted!"

Britta tilted her head to one side, studying me. "So what do ya want? Or, better yet, *who* do ya want... an', more importantly, can I have the other one?"

"Britta."

"Alright, alright, I'll stop now. Time to be serious."

"Thank you."

A moment of silence passed before Britta cleared her throat and said, "But, seriously—sharin' is carin'. Throw a girl a bone! Get it? A bone! Ya know, 'cause I'm missin' a few?"

I made a concerted effort to avoid being alone with Lucas for the rest of the day, worried that he might try to kiss me again—a task that was easy enough when there was no shortage of work to be done in camp.

We spent the first half of the morning at the store, helping Stuart sort through several boxes of books that had been recently scavenged from the Elkin's Point library. The remainder of our morning was spent in the gardens, helping Cassie with the fall harvest, who was grateful to have Lucas's help after Ella showed up for work several hours late and ended up falling asleep under an apple tree.

"I'm going to be speaking to Leisel about her," Cassie muttered, stepping over Ella's legs. "Poor thing is going to drink herself to death one of these days."

By late afternoon, Cassie was shooing us from the potato beds, urging us to take showers before dinner. I showed Lucas to the bathhouse, introducing him to Jordy, and giving him a brief overview of the shower system.

"You're not gonna join me?" Lucas asked, the corner of his mouth quirking into a shy smile. My heart began to hammer—this was my Lucas, the sweet and gentle boy I'd grown up with. And even as I ached for Logan… I found myself recalling how much I'd loved this side of Lucas.

A nervous smile trembled on my lips. "The water is really cold—you'll see. I'm going to go home and get cleaned up—I'll meet you at the dining hall, okay?"

Without waiting for his reply, I hurried from the building, feeling awful. Whatever this was—whatever we were doing—it couldn't continue. I couldn't live like this; I couldn't keep another secret from Lucas, especially not one as monumental as this. If the three of us were going to move forward, Logan and I would have to come clean.

But first, I needed to summon the courage to do so.

Dinner was brief and quiet. Logan remained noticeably absent while Lucas and I sat alone, and I avoided looking directly at the others in the dining hall, afraid of what I might find reflected in their gazes. With every breath, I felt the fist of condemnation beating on my chest. I didn't need to see it on the faces of my friends as well.

"It's getting cold," Lucas murmured, sliding his hand into mine. I gazed up at the dark sky, the days growing shorter as winter crept closer, and shivered inside my hoodie.

"Hopefully Logan will stay gone tonight," Lucas continued, tugging me closer. "And we can warm each other up without having to deal with *his shit*." Lucas's tone grew progressively sharper. "You'd think he'd be happy to see me, but he's been a dick the whole time."

"He is happy to see you, he's just… Logan," I replied helplessly. "You know how he is."

"Yeah," Lucas bit out. "And he's even worse than he was before. And since when do you defend *Logan*?"

"Since when do you curse?" I snapped suddenly. "And why are you so angry?"

We both stopped in the middle of the path, looking at one another. I stared into the eyes I'd stared into a million times before, yet not really recognizing them anymore.

"I'm sorry," I hurried to say. "I don't know why I said that."

"No, I'm sorry," Lucas said. "Losing you guys really fucked me up. And I don't know—I think seeing this place, seeing your house—I guess it kinda feels like you guys moved on without me."

Tears pricked my eyes. "Luke, we thought... *we thought you were dead.*"

"I know. Fuck, I know." Lucas scrubbed his hands down the sides of his face, sighing hard. "Look, forget it. It doesn't matter. It is what it is, right?" He stepped closer, one of his hands coming to rest on my hip while the other cupped my face. "By the way, have I told you how amazing you look? Civilization really suits you, Willowby."

"Shut up, Lucky Charms," I mumbled, turning away.

Not to be dissuaded, Lucas cupped my face with both hands and bent his head to mine. I went stiff at first and then attempted relaxing into the kiss—into Lucas. Moving my lips over his, I attempted channeling the feelings I felt for him, searching for what we had once had, only... those feelings felt far away now. Breaking the kiss, I turned away, swallowing back tears.

"Willow," Lucas growled. "Why won't you kiss me?"

I covered my mouth, stifling the sob that threatened. *Because I'm in love with your brother.*

"Are you going to say something?" Lucas demanded. "Or are you just going to stand there looking like you're going to cry?

Goddammit." His fists clenched. "What the fuck is wrong with everyone? I'm back from the dead but everyone's acting like it's a fucking funeral!"

With a disgusted shake of his head, Lucas took off down the path, leaving me staring after him, still trying not to cry.

That evening, long after Lucas had gone to bed, I sat awake, staring across the dark room, my fingertips trembling fretfully across the tabletop.

Lucas and I had spoken very little after returning to the cabin. The growing silence between us made worse by our close quarters. Our once effortless camaraderie and easygoing banter had become painfully strained and downright uncomfortable. And I felt physically sick over it.

Sick over Lucas, worried about Logan, unable to sit and stare at Logan's empty bed for another agonizing second, I jumped to my feet. With one last look at Lucas's sleeping form, I slipped quietly into the night.

Camp was silent, the ground cool and hard beneath my bare feet. Looping around dark, quiet cabins, and finding no sign of Logan, I checked the construction site next, hoping to discover him hiding out in one of the unfinished buildings, only to find them all empty.

Approaching the main gate, I called up to the guard tower, finding Xavier and Joshua playing cards within. Neither had seen Logan, though they assured me he hadn't left camp.

Circling back through the cabins, the lake was the last place I looked. As I tiptoed down the weathered, water-worn dock, the boards creaking softly beneath my feet, a figure emerged from behind the boathouse. Shoulders slumped, hands shoved into his pockets, Logan froze when he saw me.

We stood there staring at one another, me wishing desperately to touch him. I swallowed. If things had gone differently, if he'd come home without Lucas, we'd have gone straight to bed. And after, picking back up where we'd left off, bickering and arguing. I was even aching for that — to be fighting with him again.

"You've lost weight," Logan eventually said, his tone flat and lacking his usual gruff condemnation, reminiscent of the cold, detached way he used to speak to me. Speaking in a way that made me want to grab him and shake him and demand that he stop avoiding and ignoring me, treating me as if the months we'd shared together hadn't happened. As if *we* hadn't happened.

"I tried to eat," I stammered. Everything that I'd wanted to say to him since the day he'd left had fled in the face of his indifference. Indifference I was dying to scrub from his infuriating face and replace it with the hungry look I'd come to crave — the look he wore when he was buried deep inside of me and it *still wasn't enough*. Part of me thought that he must have realized this — that he absolutely must sense the desperation bubbling within me, ready to erupt like molten lava and burn us both to dust — because how could he not? How could he not see how my lips trembled, the way my fingers twitched, the way my body bowed toward his?

I took a deep breath and tried again. "I tried to eat, but I was so worried about you. And Britta wouldn't wake up, and... Logan, why didn't you warn me about Luke?"

His gaze flicked away. "I should have said something on the radio," he muttered. "I wanted to, but Luke wanted to surprise you and I couldn't... I couldn't—" Logan abruptly cut off, his jaw locked, his nostrils flaring as he tried to compose himself. And there it was—a breathtakingly beautiful flash of anguish across his formidable features and the green light I needed to propel me the remaining distance between us, to send my hands flying to his face and my body crushing against his.

I kissed him carelessly, biting his lips, dragging my teeth down his tongue. Logan growled, a deep guttural rumbling in his chest that echoed in my own, sending shivers up my spine.

"I need you," I demanded, roughly pulling at his shirt. The buttons popped free, the worn flannel ripping beneath my hands. And then I was tearing at his bare skin, digging my nails into his hard, muscular body. The feel of him, the smell of him, the taste of his skin on my tongue leaving me begging for more.

My back slammed into the boathouse wall, my breath leaving me in a hard rush. Logan unzipped my hoodie, freeing my breasts and tore down my jeans, tossing them away. Then we were kissing again, our mouths fused with heavy, heated breaths, while Logan fought to free himself from the last shred of clothing between us.

My back still flush with the wall, I wound my legs around his hips. Our naked chests pressed together, the hot pulse of him was heavy between my thighs, pushing at my entrance.

"*Logan.*"

He slammed inside of me. My eyes locked with his, my muscles tensing as breathless, incoherent demands burst past my lips. Harder and faster, he moved until my head rocked loudly against the wall, and my back dragged painfully across the broken wood.

He continued to batter my body with his, each jarring thrust sending me hurtling further into euphoria, soon turning my tense muscles to little more than jelly, until it was all I could do just to hold on to him. My head lolled back, my fluttering gaze blinking languidly to where the moon hung low over the lake, looking fat and full and so beautifully close to bursting—a mirror image of how I was feeling.

My body tensed, my pleasure building. Burying my face in his neck, I let out a muffled cry. I was still whimpering, still flooded with the aftershock of sensation as his thrusts continued to pick up speed, until finally, with a teeth-clenching groan, he slumped against me.

Still breathing hard, Logan slowly lowered me to my feet. I clung to his neck, gazing up at him through hooded eyes. My legs shook, my arms trembled. We kissed slowly, his hands dropping to my hips, his fingertips biting possessively.

The dock creaked loudly. Jerking, Logan and I faced the walkway. Illuminated by the light of the full moon, Lucas stood at the rise, his wide eyes glowing white. "Holy shit," he rasped, backing slowly away. *"Holy fucking shit."*

"Luke." His name slipped from my lips and his eyes locked with mine, hurt and anger flashing across his frozen features. Then he turned, breaking into a run.

"Luke," I cried out, shoving Logan back even as he tried to hold me. Clutching my hoodie closed, I grabbed my discarded jeans and took off down the dock. "Luke, wait!"

THIRTY FIVE

LOGAN

I could hear Lucas yelling halfway across camp, the raging cadence of his shouts causing me to pick up my pace. All over, lights were turning on inside cabins and residents were sticking their heads out their doors to better hear the commotion.

"What the fuck, Willow! *What the fuck!* You and Logan? Really?"

"Please!" Willow sounded frantic and close to tears. "Please, just listen!"

"Listen? I don't need to listen to you—*I fucking saw you!*"

There was a crash followed by a shriek as I was bursting through the door. Willow and Lucas stood on opposite ends of the room— Willow, with tears streaming down her face, Lucas, his face red from fury. The small lamp that had sat on the dresser lay shattered on the floor.

"Perfect," Lucas growled in my direction. "Now you can both explain to me what it was that *I fucking saw*." His hands were curled into fists, his body tight and straining. He didn't look like my little brother anymore. Without the scruffy beard and long hair, with his easygoing expression replaced with one of barely restrained violence, unease fluttered through me. I knew that face; I'd grown up fearing it.

"Luke, please understand," Willow cried. "We thought you were dead!"

"That's your excuse—you thought I was dead so you fucked my brother?"

"It's not an excuse—it's the truth! We thought you were gone and we... we..."

"It was me," I interrupted. "I started it—it was my fault."

Lucas slapped his hands against his face, a flash of astonishment mixing with fury. "What the fuck—what the fuck, Logan! You hate her! *You fucking hate her!*"

"I don't hate her," I gritted out. "I've never hated her."

Lucas choked over angry laughter, rife with disbelief. "Is this a joke? This is a joke, right? You're trying to tell me that I haven't spent half my life stopping you two from killing each other? So what *was* I doing then—stopping you from fucking each other?"

"Luke!" Willow screamed. "Please stop—*please just listen*!"

Lucas swung himself in Willow's direction, snarling, poised as if he might charge her. I went still, ready to dart across the room and tackle him if he as much as flinched in her direction.

"You hated him! And you hated her! And the second I'm gone, you're all over each other?"

"No, it wasn't like that!"

"What was it like then? Have you been doing this behind my

back the whole time? Was it all a fucking act?" His chest heaving, Lucas grabbed at his short hair, pulling frantically at it.

Willow stepped forward, her hands raised in supplication. "Please just listen. It wasn't like that—I promise you it wasn't like that." Her voice cracked; her eyes filled with fresh tears. "Nothing was an act. *Nothing.*"

Bitter laughter bubbled past Lucas's lips. "You used to say how unlucky we were—that, out of all the people in the world, we'd gotten stuck with Logan." He laughed again, shaking his head in disbelief.

"And *you.*" Lucas pinned me with a vicious glare, even as he continued to laugh. "Do you remember how many times you'd told me to leave Willow behind? Saying I was better off without her?"

Shame flooded me; I couldn't even look at Willow. "Luke," I growled. "Listen to me—"

Lucas's eyes flashed, his expression sharpening. "Don't tell me what to do—you don't get to tell me what to do ever again!"

"I'm not telling you what to do," I continued through my teeth. "I'm just asking you to hear me out. Can you give me that? You're my brother and I—"

"You what?" Lucas laughed coldly. "*You love me?*"

"Yeah," I ground out. "I fucking do."

Lucas only stared at me, a dark and sinister smile overtaking his face, a look that had me clenching my fists in response.

"How many times, Logan?" he demanded, his tone as cold as his expression.

I stared at him hard. "How many times... *what?*"

"*How many times did you listen to me and Willow fucking, and wish it was you?*"

"Luke!" Willow shouted. "What the fuck—*stop it!*"

"Did you watch us, too?" Lucas taunted. "Of course you did—

you were always staring at her. You were always pissed at her, but you were always staring at her. I should have known—*holy shit,* I should have realized."

Lucas stepped toward me, his hate-filled eyes boring holes through mine. "All those years of me having something you didn't—that killed you. You couldn't let that stand, could you? Not *Lucky fucking Logan,* the guy who always gets everything he wants. You had to take the only thing that was ever mine."

Guilt and anger swarmed me like warring hornets. All these years, I'd kept us safe, clothed and fed, too. And I'd never asked for a damn thing in return. I'd never even wanted anything for myself. At least, not until now.

"Don't call me that," I growled. *"Don't fucking call me that."*

"Oh-no." Lucas laughed bitterly. "Lucky Logan doesn't like his nickname anymore?"

"How the fuck was I lucky?" I exploded. "When I had to deal with Dad's inability to finish a fucking job? When I had to stop him from slapping Mom around? When I had to clean up after him when he passed out drunk? When I had to go to school with black eyes and bruised ribs and play it off like it was no big deal?" I paused and took a breath.

"Or how about when I had to pick up all the pieces after Dad… *blew everything to fucking hell?"*

It was early evening, though the sky looked the same as it had since morning, the same as it had every day for the last few months—varying shades of gray, not a shred of sunlight to be found. The same went for the bed-and-breakfast itself; without electricity, the only source of light was from the fireplaces—a dull substitute inside these dingy, gaping rooms.

Standing in the entryway of the sitting room, I rubbed my gloved hands together in a vain attempt at keeping warm. The smell of burned plastic clung to the cold room, much like the way the stench of vomit clings to a carpet—bitter and unforgiving. One story up, Willow's mother was having another coughing fit that echoed through the hallways and down the winding staircases. If I listened hard enough, I knew I'd hear the pitter-patter of Willow's feet as she rushed to and fro, tending to her mother's needs. Lucas, I assumed, was with her.

My mother, along with Mrs. Gleason—a soft-spoken elderly woman—sat side by side on the couch, each of them clutching a steaming mug of coffee, Mrs. Gleason muttering beneath her breath. She was always praying these days; as if the power of prayer would get us through the winter. As if the power of prayer could accomplish anything at all.

Just a few yards away, Mackenzie and her mother stood huddled by the fireplace, talking among themselves. Every so often, Mackenzie would glance in my direction, her pretty, pert features furrowing. She was always frowning at me these days; whatever her problem was, I found I didn't care. The merciless reality of our situation had made not just mine and Mackenzie's, but all the relationships inside the small bed-and-breakfast, dysfunctional at best. Freezing cold temperatures and not enough food seemed to bring out the worst in people.

As for the rest of our obligatory companions, two impromptu search parties had departed early that morning: one group seeking food while the other searched for medical supplies.

What they thought they'd find, I didn't know. Willow's mother had been sick since early fall, and we'd exhausted every option available and yet her health continued to decline. At first, it was thought that she might have a lingering case of pneumonia, although lately I'd heard the term "lung cancer" bandied about. Not that an exact diagnosis mattered at this point; in this world, a world where doctors were suddenly in short supply, I assumed either illness would kill her.

The front door opened; three men blew in alongside a frigid breeze. Willow's father—the first to enter—tracked snow across the room as he came to stand by the fireplace. Gripping the brick overhang, he stared into the flames until his shivering had subsided. The utterly dejected look on his face told me everything I needed to know—the search for medicine had been a failure.

"Find any food?" Mackenzie's mother asked, as her husband joined her at the fireplace. The man shook his head solemnly, snow falling from where it clung to his thick eyebrows and beard.

"I'm going to check on my girls," Willow's father muttered. Still wearing his heavy winter gear, he padded slowly across the room, tracking water in his wake. From the couch, my mother watched him ascend the stairs, a look of pity pinching her features.

"She's not going to last the winter," Mrs. Gleason whispered to her coffee.

"Neither are we," Mr. Hart added miserably. "There's nothing left here—we've got to move on." The former art teacher at the local middle school had twisted his ankle early on and still had yet to get full mobility back. Doing nothing was making him bitter.

"Be quiet!" My mother hushed, gesturing at the staircase. "Don't let the kids hear you talk like that."

Lucas and Willow, shoulder to shoulder, were traipsing noisily down the stairs. At sixteen years old, they could hardly be considered kids, yet everyone continued to treat them as such.

"Come sit down, Luke. Willow, you too — sit down right here where it's warm." My mother got to her feet, gesturing for them to take her place on the couch. "I think I'll head upstairs and lie down. The coffee hasn't helped at all." Tucking her blanket over Lucas and Willow's laps, she disappeared quietly up the stairs.

Eventually, the door opened again, another cold blast of air whipping through the house as the second search party tumbled inside, my father at the helm. "We got lucky at the Five & Dime out in Friendship." Jeffrey Gleason, Mrs. Gleason's adult grandson, set down a heavy-looking pack. "Lots of canned goods — enough for everyone."

Excitement *spread through the group as everyone gathered to view the findings, while my father backed away from the others. Rummaging through his knapsack, he produced a half-empty bottle, its black and red label revealing its contents as vodka. Still dressed in heavy winter wear, he unscrewed the cap and took several healthy swigs before replacing the cap. As his stormy gaze raked the room, I took a quick step back, falling just out of sight.*

"Where's my wife?" he demanded.

No one answered him — everyone was busy sorting through the pilfered goods that now lay scattered across the floor. Scowling, my father stormed up behind Lucas, gripping the back of his neck, dragging him away from the others. "Did you hear me, boy? I said — where's your mother?"

Willow stood up abruptly, watching with a worried expression. Meanwhile, Lucas had gone still.

"Hey, idiot — I asked you where your mother is." He shook Lucas roughly. "All them goddamn holes in your face must be causin' your brains to fall out."

The others began to scatter. Throwing sympathetic glances in Lucas's direction, some hurried toward the stairs, while others made their way to the kitchen. No one wanted to be around my father – especially when he was drinking.

"I-I don't know, sir," Lucas stammered.

He released Lucas with a shove, sending him scrambling to where Willow waited for him. Clasping hands, they backed away slowly.

"Logan!" he shouted, between more swigs of vodka. "Where the fuck you at, boy? You better get your ass over here 'fore I – "

With a heavy breath, I stepped inside the room. Our eyes met – his narrowed into slits, mine carefully blank.

"Creepy little shit," he snarled. "You're gonna get yourself shot, you hear me? You keep sneakin' up on people, you're gonna wind up on the wrong end of a gun."

"Yes, sir," I replied coolly. There was no talking to him, no engaging with him, and definitely no arguing with him. Whatever he said, no matter how ridiculous, no matter how ignorant, I simply agreed.

"Where's your mother?" he continued. "She sleepin' again – off takin' goddamn naps while I'm out huntin' down food for us all?"

"I don't know, sir."

"I don't know – I don't know," he mimicked, the scent of alcohol on his breath washing over me and making me nauseous. "Neither of you know nothin', huh? Two shit-for-brains for kids – how'd I get so fuckin' lucky?"

"I'll go look for her," I offered, moving toward the stairs.

"You'll stay fuckin' put!" he thundered, knocking me back with a fist to my chest. "I'll go get her – she's my goddamn wife." Shoving his bottle at me, he started shedding his winter gear.

"Clean this shit up," he demanded, waving at the pile of wet clothing. Snatching his bottle back, he turned to the stairs.

One, two, three…

As his heavy steps ascended the old staircase, I began counting silently – knowing the fighting would start before I'd reach ten. It always started before ten.

Four, five, six...

And once the fighting began, it would be my responsibility to end it. No one else was going to willingly pry my father off my mother, and, in turn, get the shit kicked out of them for daring to interfere.

Seven, eight, nine...

"Logan?" Lucas whispered.

The sound of a door slamming echoed throughout the house. Heavy footsteps pounded the halls above us. Another door slammed, followed by muffled shouts.

"Do you think we should go up – " Willow began, her words cut off by the blast of a gun. Frightened, frantic screaming followed. Another gunshot, and more screaming, and then the screaming abruptly stopped.

Lucas and Willow's gazes swung in my direction, wide-eyed and full of fear; I was already in motion, charging up the stairs. Mrs. Gleason, helped along by her grandson, nearly crashed into me as they hurried past me, their expressions stricken.

I paused at the top of the staircase; a hint of sulfur hung in the air, along with the acrid scent of burning. There was a muffled thump in the distance, growing louder as I raced toward the noise. Turning into the last room on the left, I stopped dead.

I saw the gun first – my father's large caliber handgun, lying unattended in the center of the room. Mere inches from the gun was Willow's dad, sprawled across the floor, his wide, unblinking eyes staring straight through me. There was a hole in the center of his forehead and another in his cheek, thin trails of blood dripping from each.

Across the room, my father was straddling my mother, his considerable weight dwarfing her small frame. His large hands were wrapped around her neck, shaking her violently, bashing her head into the floor, a pool of *red growing beneath her.*

"Cheating... whore..." he ground out. "Goddamn... whore..."

I charged him. Barreling into his side, I sent us crashing across the room. We rolled wildly, him grabbing at my face, me hooking my fist into his rib cage, each of us struggling to gain the upper hand.

His jagged fingernails scored my cheek, and as I flinched away, he gripped my throat. My air supply abruptly cut off, he flipped us, smashing my head into the floor, all the while squeezing my throat tighter. Everything went blurry and then black. I couldn't breathe, I couldn't see, and then —

A series of explosions punched through my quickly clouding thoughts. Pop-pop-pop — one after the other, their shrill echoes rang painfully between my ears. The grip on my neck loosened, the weight on my middle fell away; my hands went for my neck as I began to sputter and cough, gasping for air.

Blinking through blurry eyes, I found Willow standing over me. Frozen in place, her arms were outstretched, my father's gun trembling in her grip, a trail of smoke rising from the barrel. Behind her, Lucas stood in the doorway, gripping the doorframe as if he might fall.

And behind me was my father.

He lay on his side, his eyes wide and bulging, blood dribbling past his lips and down his chin. Gripping his chest with one hand, he took one last wheezing breath before falling still.

"And here we are again," Lucas seethed, nostrils flaring. "Like mother, like son, right?"

At the mention of our mother, my entire body revolted with rage. None of us knew what my father had walked in on. We could surmise all we wanted—maybe they'd been having an affair, or maybe they'd been friends, merely seeking comfort in each other. We would never know the truth—they'd taken that knowledge to the grave.

"And who are you in this supposed scenario, Luke?" I shouted, my voice cracking alongside the casket of memories being unearthed. "Are you *Dad*?"

"Do you want me to be? That's what you need, huh—me to be the bad guy so you can justify what you've been doing?" Lucas's angry gaze flicked to Willow. "*What you've both been doing.*"

Willow's breath shuddered from her lungs. "I'm sorry," she gasped through her tears. "I'm so, so sorry."

"Oh, you're going to cry now?" Lucas sneered. "You were my girlfriend, *my best friend*, and then the second I'm gone, you're fucking my brother—*and now you're gonna cry.*"

"You were right about her, Logan," he snarled in my direction. "She is a stupid bitch and *I do deserve better.*"

Once I'd recovered from the shock of hearing Lucas—good, kind, softhearted Lucas—speaking to Willow the same way our piece-of-shit father had spoken to our mother, I jumped between them. "Don't you dare," I growled at Lucas. "Don't you fucking dare. You come at me all you want, but if you come at her—"

"You'll what?" Lucas shouted, slamming his hands into my chest, shoving me back. I blinked in surprise, shocked by his strength. "You'll leave me for dead and start fucking my girlfriend? *Oh, wait a minute...*"

Gripping his shirt collar, I yanked him to me. "That's not what fucking happened!"

"*Fuck you!*" Lucas spat, his fist slamming into my gut. I folded over, the air whistling from my lungs in a hard rush. I recovered fast, shooting upright, tackling him, trying to wrestle him to the ground. As we fought for control, we crashed around the room, knocking into furniture and nearly knocking over Willow. Lucas had grown stronger during our time apart, leaving us more evenly matched than we'd ever been.

While I struggled to subdue him, Lucas sent another heavy fist to my middle. Groaning, I staggered backward, Lucas rushing me before I could right myself, ramming his elbow into my ribs and sending me slamming into the wall. I watched in what felt like slow motion as his hand barreled toward my face. My head hit the wood, pain erupting in my cheek and jaw. Dazed, with warm blood pooling in my mouth, Lucas gripped my shirt, yanking me to him.

"Stop it!" Willow screamed. "Lucas, no!"

I saw glimpses of Willow as she rushed around Lucas, grabbing at his arms in a vain attempt to pull him off me. With a frustrated shout, Lucas released me and spun away, shoving Willow in the chest and sending her flying across the room. Arms pinwheeling, she tripped backward over the seat of a chair, falling into the table beyond; the hard thump of her head hitting wood echoing throughout the room.

For a moment, I could only stare in horror, a thousand similar memories paving the way to my rage. And then I was roaring at the top of my lungs, charging Lucas, tackling him to the floor. Scrambling over top of him, I grabbed his collar and sent my fist into his face.

"Don't touch her!" I thundered. "Don't you ever fucking touch her!"

"*Logan.*" Willow was on her knees, her hand pressed to her forehead, blood running down the side of her face. "I'm okay. Please... *both of you...* stop."

Lucas was motionless beneath me. Staring up at me, his eyes wide, his skin pale, he began to tremble. "I didn't—I wouldn't," he mumbled, stumbling over his words. His eyes filled with tears just as the cabin door flew open, Joshua and Joe bursting inside.

"Jesus Christ." Joe kneeled beside Willow. "You alright?"

"I'm fine," she rasped. "Just make them stop... please."

Joshua's eyes met mine, dropping to where I still held Lucas in my grip. Releasing him, I staggered back, crashing against the wall. Lucas pushed himself up, his hand rubbing his jaw.

"Joe, get her out of here." Joshua jerked his thumb toward the door. "I'll deal with these two."

I wanted to argue with him. I wanted to go to Willow and take her in my arms and see for myself that she was alright. But I couldn't seem to move, let alone speak; frozen in place, I could only stare at the remnants of the colossal mess I'd made.

THIRTY SEVEN

WILLOW

"What the heck happened?" Doc exclaimed. Having thrown open her front door, she stood in the entrance in her pajamas, squinting into the darkness.

"She's bleedin' pretty good," Joe said, relinquishing his supportive hold on my arm as Doc ushered me inside, seating me beneath a flickering overhead light. Taking my face in hand, she peered closely at my forehead.

"You're going to need a stitch," she muttered. "Joe, go grab a towel and press it to the wound—I'll grab my sewing kit."

"I'm fine," I told them, even as my head throbbed.

"I'm fine," I whispered, even as Doc's needle pinched my skin.

"I'm fine," I whimpered, tears slipping free as I crawled into bed beside Britta.

"Hush now, sugar. Just close them eyes. Your mess'll still be here come mornin'."

Sleep came in short fitful bursts, ebbing and flowing alongside the swell of sickness that refused to leave me. Each time I closed my eyes, all I could see was Lucas standing at the edge of the dock, pain and betrayal flashing across his face. And every time I opened them, all I could think of was Logan and the haunted look in his eyes as Joe led me, bleeding, from the cabin.

I'd done that—I'd destroyed what little was left of their family.

I left Britta's bed just before sunrise, the morning twilight not yet visible on the horizon. The grass shimmering with dew, splashed with heavy fog, I flew through camp like a wraith, my bare feet barely skimming the ground. I didn't know who or what awaited me at the cabin, I only knew that this was my mess, and I had to be there, too.

"Willow." Lucas stood from the table as I blew through the door, his eyes bloodshot, his chin swollen and mottled with purple and blue. The thud of Logan's fist crashing against his face echoed and I flinched, shoving the memory away.

"How's your head?" he asked, touching his own.

I reached for the two sutures at my hairline, flinching as my fingertips grazed them. "It's... fine," I said, my words sticking in my throat. "How's your... face?"

"Fine," he said.

A beat of silence passed, during which Lucas dropped his gaze and began to fumble with his hands. "I'm so sorry," he whispered. "I never would have... I mean, it was an accident. I swear it."

My hand flew to my mouth, as if I might hold back the sob that threatened. "I know that. *I know you*. I know you'd never hurt anyone, least of all me."

But even as I said it, the words felt wrong. The old Lucas, yes—he wouldn't have been capable of hurting someone. This new version—I wasn't quite so sure about.

"Willow." Lucas rounded the table, though he didn't approach me. "What do you think about maybe coming to Everdeen with me? I mean, it's not as nice as this place, but it could be a fresh start for us."

A fresh start. The same two words Logan had said to me many months ago. I shook my head, my tears spilling over. Oh god, my heart was breaking. It was literally splitting in two, their names etched upon each piece. Lucas. *Logan.* The boy I'd loved. *The man I loved.*

"Last night you said that you and Logan happened because you thought I was dead; well, I'm not dead, am I? I'm right here. We can fix this, Willow. I know we can. We'll go back to the way things were—me and you against the world, right?" His voice contorted as his eyes implored me.

A single breath left me in a painful puff. His plea was a punch to my already aching chest. "Luke, I don't think we can."

"No, *I know we can.* You were grieving and Logan took advantage of you. This is on him. *We* can work through it."

"Luke, no, that's not what happened. He didn't take advantage of me. He wouldn't do that."

Lucas's lips thinned, his jaw clenching. "Holy shit," he ground out. "*You're fucking defending him, again.*" As his voice rose along with his temper, I took a step back, nearly tripping over the shoes stacked against the wall. Blinking down at them, my breath froze in my chest.

They were all mine.

My gaze swung across the room, pausing on the empty space

beneath Logan's bed.

The emergency backpack was gone.

Darting across the room, I yanked Logan's dresser drawers open, one by one.

Empty.

"Luke." I pressed the back of my trembling hand to my mouth. "Where's Logan?"

Lucas only stared at me, his stare growing more intense the angrier he grew, until he was red-faced and visibly shaking. I stared back, my breath coming in rapid pants, as if my lungs were attempting to keep time with my furiously beating heart.

"*Lucas!*" I practically screamed his name. "Where is he?"

"Why do you care where he is?" Lucas roared. "Why does it fucking matter?"

He already knew why — I could see it in his eyes and the twist of his mouth — but he still needed to hear me say it, no matter how painful the admission was going to be. For the both of us.

"Because *I love him.*" Though softly spoken, my admission was pained and poignant, akin to the scratch of a nail across a chalkboard, the cry of an injured cat, and the squeal of a poorly played violin, and sounded every bit as bitter as it tasted leaving my lips.

But it was true.

The girl I'd been had loved Lucas with her whole heart. We'd shared a million unforgettable moments. He'd been my safe space, my happy place, and my shelter in a storm when I'd needed someone to hold me close and calm those riotous feelings inside me. But that was then and this was now, and I wasn't the same person anymore. The woman I was didn't want to feel safe or comfortable. I didn't want to subdue my passion. I wanted every heart-pounding, stomach-dipping, half-crazed moment and every intense, exhausting, all-consuming second.

And I wanted each one of those seconds with Logan.

Lucas's eyes blinked closed. My soft words as effective as if I'd screamed them. His face contorted, a thousand different expressions flickering before he settled on a slow-growing sneer. "Logan's gone," he spat. "He left last night. *Hours ago.*"

He was only confirming what I already knew, even so, I felt my stomach sink straight to my knees. He'd left hours ago. Which meant, depending on how fast he was going, he could be miles away by now.

Cursing, I dropped to the floor, pulling out an old military field pack that had belonged to Davey from beneath my bed. I didn't have much in it, I'd only just started putting together an emergency pack, but I was hoping I wouldn't need much—only a few days' worth of supplies.

"What are you doing?" Lucas snarled as I was stuffing clothing inside the bag. "Are you actually going after him? Do you really think you'll find him? He's had hours of walking time and you're... *you.*"

Ignoring the slight in favor of pulling a pair of socks on, I turned my attention to lacing my boots up.

"You couldn't even find me." Lucas laughed bitterly. "And I was right below your fucking feet."

I snapped upright, pinning Lucas with an equally cold glare as the one he was leveling at me. Even glaring at him, my eyes began to fill. "*Days,*" I said, my voice thick with emotion. "We searched for you for days and we would have never stopped if I hadn't gotten sick."

"But you never went back out, did you? After you'd found this place and you were better, neither of you went looking for me again. You didn't want to find me, did you?" More horrible laughter rang through the cabin.

I couldn't speak. There were a thousand things I wanted to say to him, to make him understand, but I already knew he wouldn't hear me. So what was left? Lucas was entitled to his anger, even if he was wrong. Tears rolling down my cheeks, I shouldered my pack and turned to the door.

"Willow," he bit out suddenly. "If you walk out of here — if you go after *him* — you're never going to see me again."

I froze with my hand on the doorknob.

Lucas. *Logan.*

My tears fell faster.

Lucas. *Logan.*

Closing my eyes, I took a deep, shuddering breath and when I opened them again, I opened the door.

"Goodbye, Luke."

THIRTY EIGHT

WILLOW

Standing in the center of Main Street, with the post office to my left, the shattered storefront of Carole's Café to my right, I stared up at the town's barricade looming ahead. I'd spent the entire morning and most of the afternoon searching through Elkin's Point and its surrounding neighborhoods, without any sign of Logan. It was time to cross the barricade and reenter a world I was no longer accustomed to. A world I'd never traveled alone before.

Shifting the pack on my back, heavy and cumbersome, I groaned. My body was no longer used to the weight and the old familiar aches between my shoulder blades had already begun to flare.

"A vehicle would have been nice," I muttered out loud, for at least the hundredth time. Only there'd been hardly any fuel left in the reserves and I would've had to wait at least another forty-eight hours before there would have been enough for a full tank. Knowing how fast Logan moved, I knew I didn't have that kind of time. I'd have to set out on foot.

Pulling a map from my pack, a crudely rendered drawing Joshua had jotted down for me before I'd left, I gazed over each route out of town, wondering which Logan might have taken. On one hand, I thought he might want to travel through the once populated neighborhoods, possibly in search of supplies. On the other hand, I thought he might avoid those areas altogether, seeing as his emergency pack had been well stocked and most necessary supplies nearby would have been long ago scavenged.

Stuffing my map away, I climbed over the barricade, landing on the other side with a grunt, the noise drawing the attention of a nearby Creeper camouflaged between two trees. It lumbered forward at surprising speed, and I hurried to pull my knife from my belt. Meeting it head-on, I ducked its hands and emerged behind it, slamming the blade into the base of its skull. As it folded to the ground in a graceless heap, I turned in a circle, searching for more.

Check your surroundings, Logan would have said. *Creepers usually travel in packs – make sure there aren't any others.*

Sure enough, another Creeper appeared through the trees, closely followed by a third. I jogged backward, unbuckling my pack as I went. Shrugging out of it, I bent down to pull a second blade from my boot and exploded forward, dodging its hands while I circled it, sinking one of my blades into its temple. As it ceased moving and folded to the ground, I found my blade stuck in its skull. Without the time to pry it out, I jumped back from the body just in time for the second Creeper to lunge. Tripping over its dead companion, it made a wild grasp for my leg, snagging its spindly fingers on my boot laces.

Cursing, I kicked, smashing the tip of my boot straight into its snapping maw, dislodging whatever teeth it had left. Still clinging to my boot, I kicked again, this time shattering its nose. Free from its grasp, I stepped on its back, holding it still with my weight and brought my arm down like a battering ram, jamming my second blade through skin, blood and bone, and straight into its brain. The Creeper twitched several times, and then it was still.

Relieved to find myself finally alone, I pulled my blade from where it remained wedged inside a Creeper skull, wiped both blades clean on the grass and sheathed them in their holsters. With one last glance down the road that would lead me through the surrounding towns, I grabbed my pack and turned to the highway, heading in the direction I hoped would lead me to Logan.

As the sun began its descent and the sky faded into a collage of blues and yellows, I stopped searching for Logan and started seeking a place to spend the night. Having not come across anything for the last several hours, I already knew I'd be forced to wait out the darkness at the next structure I came across, no matter its condition.

It was nearly dark when a small, dilapidated house finally arose on the horizon, with a small cemetery off to the side. I wound my way through the crumbling gravestones, each of them boasting lives lived and died before the end of the world, before making my way up the gravel drive.

The front door of the house hung on one hinge, swinging unsteadily with the breeze. Toeing it the rest of the way open, I slid through the gap, holding my breath as I listened for any sounds that might be coming from within.

Hearing nothing, I moved down a short hall, finding myself inside a living room, its dusty, decrepit contents looking as if they'd been fashioned in the 1940s. Numerous pictures lined the walls and mantle; wiping the dust from the frames, I found the story of a couple, beginning with an old black and white photograph of two young people, ending with the colorful portrait of a family that had long since tripled in size.

Staring at the evidence of a life well lived, I found myself wondering what my own family might look like someday. What mine and Logan's family might grow to become.

If I found him.

Biting down on my bottom lip, I spun away from the photographs and resumed my search through the house. Once I was satisfied that I was alone, I wedged the front door closed, reinforcing it with a heavy piano bench, and began setting up camp for the night. Before long, I was working by moonlight.

On my own, in the dark of night, small things began to feel monumental. Something as simple as a bathroom break felt more dangerous than ever before. The same went for sleeping—without someone standing guard, every whistle of the wind and every creak of the house sounded like a possible threat. Even the simple fact that there was no one to talk to was messing with my head. I was all alone with my thoughts and completely at the mercy of this world.

Burrowing deep in my sleeping bag—another hand-me-down from Davey—I closed my eyes and I began reciting my favorite story, meticulously reciting each line, right up until Alice was due to return home, back to the life she'd always known. Instead, she chose to stay in Wonderland, not alone though, but with the Mad Hatter.

They argued incessantly. The Mad Hatter was almost always *mad*; he was stoic and stubborn, and didn't seem to understand Alice and her weird, wild ways, often finding fault with her for reasons Alice couldn't fathom. He would call her selfish and silly, and yet, in the very same breath, he would demand she eat cake, telling her she needed to grow big and strong to survive this crazy world.

That was the thing about Hatter; beneath his thorny exterior lay a bed of roses... if you knew where to look. And Alice knew just where to look. In fact, Alice had found that she quite liked his thorns as well, and maybe the Hatter had begun to like Alice's weird, wild ways a little bit, too.

But the Hatter was also foolish, always thinking he knew better than Alice... thinking he knew her heart.

He'd practically thrust her back into her old life, into her old world, and run off, thinking that Alice could somehow forget their mad times together, as if his maddening ways hadn't changed her forever.

Alice scoffed. There was only one place she belonged now.

"I'm going to find you," I whispered, just before drifting off to sleep. "... and then I'm going to punch you."

Two days had passed since leaving Silver Lake—two days spent walking aimlessly, searching fruitlessly, while an ever-growing coil of nerves continued tightening inside me.

As the sun began to set on the third day, I found myself wandering a desolate stretch of highway, nothing but crumbling pavement bracketed by thick, imposing groves of trees as far as the eye could see. My solitary steps echoed; cold chills ran up and down my arms.

Each day was more bitter and drearier than the last. Staring up at the sunless sky, it didn't yet smell like snow, yet the air had a distinct cold and wet quality, meaning winter was just around the corner.

It was only going to get colder; how much longer could I continue to wander?

Without any sign of Logan, without even knowing the direction he was traveling, I was beginning to think that it might be time to head home — back to Silver Lake — if only to load up with more supplies and, this time, hopefully make use of one of the vehicles at my disposal.

Winters in the wild had always been the most difficult and dreaded season; it was unfathomable how we'd survived so many. This winter had been the first I hadn't feared; in fact, living comfortably in Silver Lake almost had me anticipating the colder months. Shorter workdays and longer nights, a fire burning in the stove and me tucked safely away in the warm crevice of Logan's arm.

Now though, the thought of spending the winter without Logan was almost as unfathomable as having to spend it in the wild.

One more day, I decided, picking up my pace. One more day of searching and then I would turn around.

Already feeling the bitter sting of defeat, my thoughts slipped into gloomy silence. Shoulders slumped, feet shuffling, I nearly missed the sign on the side of the road.

Stumbling to a stop, I blinked up at the haphazardly hanging piece of metal, partially covered in overgrowth, and read it aloud. "Road not in use."

"Look, Willa-Pedia." Laughing, Lucas nudged my side, pointing at

the sign. "This road isn't in use."

It was the end of the world; we hadn't seen another person in well over a year. I couldn't even remember the last time we'd slept in an actual bed or used a working bathroom — there was no such thing as a grocery store or a restaurant, and sometimes we went weeks with little more than roots to eat.

Road not in use? Please, the whole goddamn world wasn't in use.

Laughing, I spread my arms wide, turning in a circle as we walked. "I mean, it's pretty busy out here — what's everyone gonna do now?"

"Turn around and head home, duh." Lucas cupped his hands around his mouth. "Okay, everyone — you're gonna need to back it up! This road is not in use! Did you hear me — this road is not in use!"

"Not even a little bit in use?" I asked, between chuckles. "Not even a teeny, tiny bit?"

"Nope. Not even on your tiptoes."

"Not even if I hop?" I asked, hopping from foot to foot.

"Nope, sorry, not even then."

"What if I — "

"Stop fucking around, you two — you're falling behind!" Logan, who was at least a dozen yards ahead now, stopped to glare at us.

Exchanging looks, Lucas and I resumed walking, though we continued on, whispering and nudging one another, and stifling our laughter behind our hands.

I cleared my throat. "Umm, Logan?" I asked.

He didn't turn around. "What?"

"This road... it's, um... it's not in use."

As Lucas and I erupted into laughter, Logan swung around, his eyes narrowed, his mouth tightly pinched. His glare was always the most prominent in the declining daylight — the summer glow highlighting the deep crevices of his frown.

"Are you fucking kidding me right now, Willow?"

"Yes, Logan," I sneered. "I am fucking kidding you right now – that's the point."

As we continued staring at one another, me refusing to back down, Logan's angry gaze turned downright homicidal.

"It's my fault," Lucas said quickly, jumping between us. "We were just messing around."

Running his hands over his hair, Logan's glare veered off in the distance. "We need to set up camp, get a fire going, boil water, and – I don't know about you – but I'm fucking starving, so excuse me if I don't give a shit about some stupid sign –" Logan abruptly cut off, his gaze narrowing. Together, Lucas and I turned to find the peak of a rooftop just barely visible over the treetops.

"There's a house over there," Logan said. "Get your weapons ready."

I spun around, spying the top of the farmhouse poking above the tree line, and broke into a run, barreling through dense thickets, my pack hammering against my back as I shot into the surrounding forest, not slowing until I'd breached the property line.

Up the gravel driveway, thick with weeds, and over a disintegrating walkway, more mud than stone, the house was still and silent, looking every bit as imposing and as overbearing as I remembered it, even in its neglected, run-down state – the crumbling brickwork, the missing windows and thick cobwebs that clung to their gaping remnants.

Pushing through the partially open door, both lock and knob now missing, I crept quietly down the hall. Fingertips tracing the pattern of the torn wallpaper, I listened to the hazy echo of Lucas and I laughing, until I found myself stopped outside the office door, my hand hovering just over the knob.

Everything had changed here.

Everything.

The door creaked slowly open and I stepped inside, freezing mid-step.

Logan was sitting beneath the bay window, his knees bent, his head buried in his hands. At my sharp intake of air, Logan's head jerked up, his red-rimmed eyes rounding with surprise. Though pulled back, his hair was messy, sticking up in every direction, while smears of dirt and dark bruising colored both his cheeks and forehead.

"Willow," he stammered, hastily swiping at his eyes with the heels of his palms. "What the fuck—how did you get here? Is Luke—" Pausing, he shook his head as if to clear it. "I mean, where's Luke?"

Unbuckling my pack, I let it clatter to the floor. Crossing the room, I dropped down beside Logan and quickly took his hand in mine, clutching it to my chest. A shiver swept through me, followed by a sigh of relief so great tears pricked my eyes. "Luke doesn't want anything to do with us," I whispered.

"Us?" he asked, blinking at our joined hands.

"Us."

Logan's hand squeezed mine. "You came after me," he said, his voice hoarse. Raw. It matched how he looked. "On your own... Jesus Christ, Willow, I would have never left if I'd thought you do something so fucking stupid."

"Me?" I looked up at him with half a scowl. "You realize you're the one who left first?" Still scowling, I pulled my hand from his. "Besides, I realized something important."

Logan recaptured my hand and threaded his fingers through mine once more, gripping it twice as tightly. "Tell me what you realized."

Sighing, I slumped against him, resting my head on his shoulder. "Just that I never thanked you for saving my life."

Snorting, Logan bent his head to mine. "Which time?"

A slow-growing smile split my scowl. "All of them. Every stupid time."

Laughing, Logan pulled me into his lap and pressed his mouth to mine. I clutched him tightly, burying my hands in his hair and deepened our embrace, stroking his tongue with mine. Eventually our kisses slowed and fell away. Forehead to forehead, his hands on my hips, Logan shuddered through his next breath.

"Willow... " he trailed off and swallowed. "I never thanked you for saving my life either."

I pulled back, our gazes colliding, both of our eyes filling with tears. Memories flooded me—some good, some sad, and some downright horrific. But for the first time, I didn't shove them away and bury them beneath a mountain of guilt and regret.

For the first time, I simply let them come.

And then, one by one, I let them go.

EPILOGUE

WILLOW

One Year Later…

"They're back—they're back from Everdeen!" Béla ran excitedly around us, making circles in the snow, before taking off toward the gate.

We were each fresh from work—Britta, who'd spent the day on the lake, fishing, Ella, who'd been busy harvesting parsnips and winter cabbage in the garden, and me, who'd divided my day between both the garden and the store.

While Ella and I shivered inside our many winter layers, Britta was surprisingly fine in much less, her easy gait unhampered by her prosthetic limb—a slim, lightweight contraption with a hinged ankle. It had been Joe who'd found her a new foot; traveling far and wide, he'd spent months bringing back every prosthetic he'd come across until Britta had found one that suited her.

Waving my friends in the direction of the dining hall, I said, "You guys go ahead—I'll meet you later."

"You sent another letter, didn't you?" Ella shouted after me, her exasperation clear. "Willow, you need to let it go!"

"Aw, leave her alone, ya bitter bitch," Britta replied. "If writin' letters make her feel better, what's the harm in it?"

"The harm is, that she's miserable every time he doesn't write back and then I have to suffer through listening to her whine about it."

"How 'bout you try mindin' your own dang business for once?"

"It's a free fucking country," Ella snapped back.

"Is it?" Britta chuckled. "You forget about the wall, sugar?"

As their bickering faded off into the distance, I wondered if Ella might be right. This would be Silver Lake's third trip to Everdeen since Lucas had returned there, and each time a trading party departed, I'd made sure to send a letter along. He'd yet to send a reply.

Finding Joshua at the garage, busy unloading one of the trucks, I hurried to help, grabbing a heavy wooden crate and setting it on top of a growing pile of traded goods—both handmade and scavenged. Glancing at me, Joshua flashed a small, sympathetic smile and my hope deflated like a punctured balloon.

"Did he at least read it?" I asked. The first letter I'd sent had been tossed in a fire, and the second shredded and left in pieces.

"Can't say for certain. But he did put it in his pocket."

A glimmer of hope shone through the shroud—maybe Lucas would read it this time—maybe there was a chance that we could heal from this.

"How's he doing?" I asked. "Does he seem… okay?"

"He's looking healthy and strong, if that's what you're asking,"

Joshua said. "But if it's his mood you're after, I'd say he's a lot like his big brother—you know, he keeps mostly to himself and is ornery as hell for no good reason."

While Joshua headed back to the truck, my heart plummeted to my feet. Hearing that Lucas's infinite sweetness and gentle charm had yet to return, and knowing that I was to blame for it, was yet another bitter pill to swallow in a world where bitter pills were already a dime a dozen.

After helping unload the rest of the Everdeen haul, I headed for home. As I walked, the wind picked up speed, its blustery chill sending shivers through my heavy layers. I ran the rest of the way home, flinging open the door to the cabin—a recent upgrade from its flimsy predecessor—and wrestling it closed. I slumped against it, grateful for the warmth of the nearby fire.

Standing in our kitchen, a cordoned-off section of our living room, our table now boasted four chairs, along with a mini-fridge and a hotplate. The larger portion of the room held two mismatched couches and a hand-carved coffee table made by Logan. An old stereo system sat on top of the coffee table, softly crooning a song I didn't recognize—courtesy of the dozens of CDs we'd scavenged when we'd found the stereo.

"Hey." Logan stood in the threshold of our bedroom—the most notable add-on to our home. Built off the bathroom, the bathroom had ended up twice its previous size and now boasted the luxury of having two entrance doors. Logan, however, didn't see it as a luxury—Logan saw it as being both *defendable and escapable.*

"Cold?" he asked.

Shivering, I only nodded.

Pulling my scarf free, Logan set it aside and kissed me. Layer by layer, he removed my winter wear, until I was left in only my sweatshirt and jeans. Hooking his fingers into my belt loops, Logan hauled me up against him.

"Warmer?" he growled, kissing me again.

"Mmhmm," I mumbled against his mouth. "Except for my feet."

We both looked down to where the melted snow from my boots had made a good-sized puddle around our feet.

Breaking apart, Logan bent to clean the mess while I headed for the bedroom. "Did you see that the trading party is back?" I called over my shoulder.

There was a lengthy pause before Logan appeared in the bedroom doorway, his expression grim. "Did he write back this time?"

"No."

Another pause stretched between us. "Are you okay?" he asked.

Dragging in a heavy breath, my hands fell limply at my sides. "I don't know."

"You know you've got to stop beating yourself up over this, right? Luke's safe in Everdeen—he's got friends there, too. What else do you want from him?"

I gave a small shrug. "I don't know. I mean, I know things will never be the same, but I just thought that someday we might be—"

"Pen pals?" Logan bit out, brow cocked. "Friends in different area codes?"

Mouth snapping shut, I spun away from Logan and stormed across our room—the newest addition still smelling faintly of fresh pine. Our bed sat centrally, pushed up against the far wall and piled high with a vast array of colorful pillows and comforters. Logan had long ago disassembled the bunk beds, reconfiguring their metal framework into one, much larger bed frame, enabling a queen-size mattress to fit sideways over two twin box springs.

Identical nightstands hand carved by Logan hugged either

side of the bed, with mismatching lamps set upon each. Nearby, a second wood-burning stove had been installed, its freshly stoked fire burning brightly from within its iron confines. Our dressers still sat side by side, mine with its drawers open and clothing hanging out, while Logan's drawers were closed and every item inside neatly folded.

As I rummaged angrily through my dresser, Logan moved into the room. "I'm sorry. I didn't mean that. It's just—*fuck, Willow, you know how I feel about this shit.*"

Ignoring him, I chose a fuzzy blue sweater and a pair of fleece-lined leggings from my ever-growing collection of clothing and began to change. *Of course* I knew how Logan felt about Lucas—he preferred not to discuss his estranged brother. Or even think about him, if he could help it. He felt that constantly worrying over something you had no control over was the same as picking at a scab—all it did was hurt.

How very fucking zen of him.

"It's fine," I snapped.

"It's not fine—I shouldn't have said that. *Jesus, Willow, are you gonna pick that up or just leave it on the floor?*"

"I'm going to leave it there."

As I moved to step around him, Logan caught my hand. "Look," he said, sighing. "If it makes you feel better, then keep writing the letters. We'll give Luke until spring to answer—if he hasn't responded by then... maybe... maybe we should make a trip to Everdeen."

I glanced up sharply. "You'd really go? You're not just saying that to make me feel better?"

"Since when do I ever say anything just to make you feel better? Besides, he's my brother—I want to fix this. I just don't know how.

I thought he needed time — these things take time, right?"

"How would I know? This is literally the one and only time this has ever happened to me." Jerking my hand from his hold, I stormed into the living room, spluttering, "Splitting up families and coming between brothers is just another Monday for Willow, right Logan?"

"For fuck's sake, Willow — that's not what I meant."

"*For fuck's sake, Willow,*" I mimicked, flopping down on one of the couches. Logan followed me out, stalking closely behind me throughout the cabin, and taking the seat directly beside me. Scowling, I scooted away. "Get your own couch."

Logan hefted himself closer, bringing our bodies flush once again. "If this is how our night's gonna go, I say we skip dinner at the dining hall — we've got food here, and no one else needs to be subjected to your moody ass."

"Whatever," I muttered, crossing my arms over my chest. "I know what you're really doing — *you always want to stay in.*"

"Because I always want you all to myself."

I had zero intention of heading back out into the cold tonight, zero intention of even leaving this couch. Even so, I replied, "Good for you. Maybe I want to see my friends."

"You see your friends every day."

"I see you every day, too."

"Only after work."

"And all night long. And in the morning. And sometimes on break."

"Which is your favorite?" he asked, a sly smile creeping across his expression. "In the morning, all night long, or during break?"

I eyed him stonily, even as I felt myself softening. "You tell me," I said. "*Since you know everything.*"

"Morning," he replied, sounding positively pleased with himself. "It's definitely morning." Dropping his mouth to my ear, he rumbled softly, "When you're half asleep and pushing your ass up against me and making that *fucking noise*. I love that noise, Willow. I love your ass, too."

Breath hitching, I shoved him away, ready to wipe the self-satisfied look off his face, only to find that he didn't appear smug at all. In fact, his eyes were dark and burning, the look on his face undeniably hungry. And every nerve in my body fired up in response.

"Goddamn you," I hissed as I climbed into his lap, gripping fistfuls of his shirt. "You're lucky I love you."

I kissed him ruthlessly, pouring all my angry, antagonistic energy into loving him instead of fighting with him. He met me thrust for thrust, lick for lick, each of us sparring with our lips and tongues until we were both breathing hard and wanting more.

"Maybe *you're* lucky I love *you*." With a flick of his wrists, Logan had me sprawled on my back along the length of the couch, legs spread. Pouncing on top of me, he dropped his hips between my thighs and his mouth to my neck, biting down with a growl.

I dragged one hand up his back while the other clutched a handful of his hair, using it to tear his teeth from my neck, forcing his furious kisses back to my mouth.

It was always like this with Logan, and I already knew it always would be—fighting and fucking, making up and making love, day in and day out until we were both wrung dry and left still somehow wanting more.

We were oil and water, fire and ice, *the sun and the goddamn moon*—almost never visible at the same time and orbiting hundreds of thousands of miles apart and yet, inexplicably bound together.

And maybe we didn't always work and maybe our complicated story wouldn't always make sense to everyone...

But much like the Mad Hatter instilled in Alice *that she was under no obligation to make sense —*

—neither were we.

The End

ABOUT THE AUTHORS

Fantastical realm dweller Madeline Sheehan is the author of the bestselling Undeniable Series. A Social Distortion enthusiast, and fan of anything deemed socially inappropriate. Madeline was homegrown in Buffalo New York where she can still be found engaging in food fights and video game marathons with her husband and son.

For a complete list of works by Madeline Sheehan, please visit madelinesheehan.com
Find Madeline on Facebook, Twitter, Instagram, and more!

Claire C. Riley is a USA Today and international bestselling author.
Eclectic writer of all things romance, she enjoys hiking, movie marathons and old school board games with her family.
Claire lives in the United Kingdom with her 3 daughters, husband and naughty rescue beagle.

She is represented by Lane Heymont of the Tobias Literary Agency, and can be found on Facebook, Instagram and more!

For a full list of her works, head over to Amazon.

*Gryffindor * Targaryen * Zombie Slayer *

Made in United States
Orlando, FL
25 August 2023